Book 1 was shortlisted ... ucer
Award 2022; a Finalist i...
Quarter-Finalist in Th...

From the award-winning author of the Historical Fiction series *The Troubadours Quartet* and the *Natural Forces* eco-fantasy trilogy

Praise for *The Ring Breaker*

'Absolutely brilliant. A tour-de-force of storytelling, Viking lore, and the rugged landscape of Orkney.' Deborah Swift, *Italian Renaissance* series

'A skilfully written, beautifully researched coming-of-age story set in Viking Orkney.' Lexie Conyngham, *the Orkneyinga Murders* series

'An immersive coming of age tale set in Viking Age Orkney filled with court intrigue, sea voyages, and a society where two belief systems battle. The historic details are accurate but lightly woven into the story which takes real skill. As a fan of Viking history and folk tales I loved the feeling of being in their world, listening along to stories of the deadly whirlpool or watching them training and feasting in the Jarl's court.' Grace Tierney, *Words the Vikings Gave Us*

'The Odyssey kind of epic, yet softer and kinder on the mind, and quicker-paced, but without losing its glorious intensity and genius.' Jessica Bell *Can You Make The Title Bigga*

'A stirring coming-of-age tale forged in love, inheritance and adventure - in 'The Ring Breaker' Jean Gill skilfully brings the poetry and magic of the Viking world to life.' Emily Brand, *The Fall of the House of Byron*

'The way Gill has crafted the mysterious historical evidence into a coherent story gives the reader an unforgettable world, harsh and startling, but tinged with magic.' Jessica Knauss, *Our Lady's Troubadour*

'If you're a fan of the Viking Age, the television shows Vikings *and* Valhalla, *or the excellent works of authors Kristian Giles and Peter Gibbons, the world of* The Ring Breaker *will feel familiar. (In this novel) all of a reader's senses are stirred by rich details of the medieval experience. But what makes for the best Viking tales? The adventures, of course, found in this novel too.'* Lisa J. Yarde

'Ms Gill blends fact, fiction and legend to create believable characters who straddle the real and mystical world in a truly enthralling story.' Annie Whitehead, *To Be a Queen*

'To read Jean Gill's historical novels is not so much to see into history, but to live it and breathe it with a feeling of utter authenticity.' Paul Trembling, *Local Poet*

'The captivating story of a young man's search for his true voice, and struggle with forbidden love. A vivid picture of the harsh beauty of Viking life. I will happily follow Jean Gill to whatever time and place she chooses to lead me next!' Melodie Winawer, *Anticipation*

'Reads from start to finish like a saga straight from a skald's mouth.' B.A. Morton, *The Favour Bank*

'All the hallmarks of a Jean Gill novel - political intrigue, action and adventure, and a love story fraught with difficulties!' Jane Davis, *Small Eden*

'If you're a lover of Viking history this book will tick all the boxes. A great read.' Kath Middleton

'Reading the sea voyages made me almost sea-sick... a deeply, deeply researched authentic story with well-developed characters. (The author's) core theme of intertwining human and nature is present in a spiritual and visceral level.' Alison Morton, *Roma Nova* series

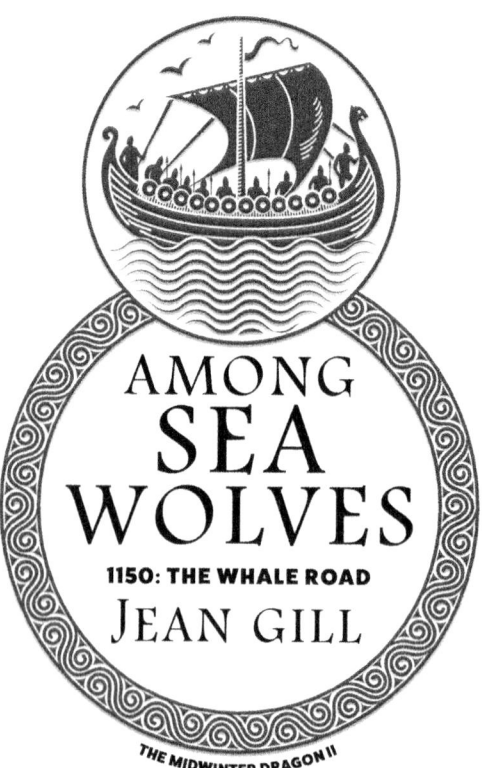

AMONG SEA WOLVES

1150: THE WHALE ROAD

JEAN GILL

THE MIDWINTER DRAGON II

© Jean Gill 2023
The 13th Sign
ISBN 9791096459476
All rights reserved

Cover design by Jessica Bell

Jean Gill's Publications

Novels
The Midwinter Dragon - HISTORICAL FICTION
Book 1 The Ring Breaker *(The 13th Sign)* 2022

Natural Forces - FANTASY
Book 3 The World Beyond the Walls *(The 13th Sign)* 2021
Book 2 Arrows Tipped with Honey *(The 13th Sign)* 2020
Book 1 Queen of the Warrior Bees *(The 13th Sign)* 2019

The Troubadours Quartet - HISTORICAL FICTION
Book 5 Nici's Christmas Tale: A Troubadours Short Story *(The 13th Sign)* 2018
Book 4 Song Hereafter *(The 13th Sign)* 2017
Book 3 Plaint for Provence *(The 13th Sign)* 2015
Book 2 Bladesong *(The 13th Sign)* 2015
Book 1 Song at Dawn *(The 13th Sign)* 2015

Love Heals - SECOND CHANCE LOVE
Book 2 More Than One Kind *(The 13th Sign)* 2016
Book 1 No Bed of Roses *(The 13th Sign)* 2016

Looking for Normal - TEEN FICTION
Book 1 Left Out *(The 13th Sign)* 2017
Book 2 Fortune Kookie *(The 13th Sign)* 2017

Non-fiction
MEMOIR / TRAVEL
How White is My Valley *(The 13th Sign 2021)* *EXCLUSIVE to Jean Gill's Special Readers Group*
How Blue is my Valley *(The 13th Sign)* 2016
A Small Cheese in Provence *(The 13th Sign)* 2016

WW2 MILITARY MEMOIR
Faithful through Hard Times *(The 13th Sign)* 2018
4.5 Years – war memoir by David Taylor *(The 13th Sign)* 2017

Short Stories and Poetry
One Sixth of a Gill *(The 13th Sign)* 2014
From Bedtime On *(The 13th Sign)* 2018 (2nd edition)
With Double Blade *(The 13th Sign)* 2018 (2nd edition)

Translation (from French)
The Last Love of Edith Piaf – Christie Laume *(Archipel)* 2014
A Pup in Your Life – Michel Hasbrouck 2008
Gentle Dog Training – Michel Hasbrouck *(Souvenir Press)* 2008

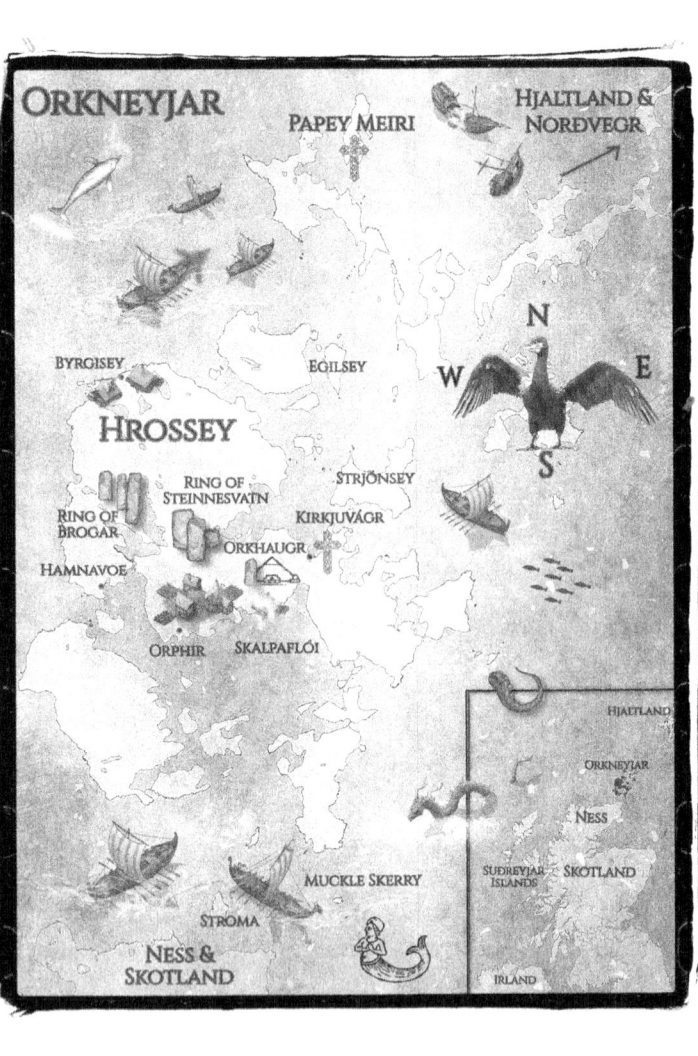

PLACE NAMES

In the 12th Century, Orkney was an earldom (jarldom) ruled by two jarls, and part of the kingdom of Norway, as was Shetland/ Hjaltland. The Jarls of Orkney also ruled Caithness / Ness, the north-eastern tip of what we now call Scotland. I have mainly used Norse names for places in the novel and aimed for consistency within the world of *The Midwinter Dragon*.

The old letter ð, pronounced 'th', is often represented by a letter 'd' in modern spellings, so the god known to us as Odin was Óðinn in old Norse, pronounced Othin. The modern choices made are not consistent and the most common representation of Norðymbralanda seems to be Nordymbralanda, although we spell and pronounce the modern name, Northumberland. Faced with an impossible task, I made choices in spelling place and character names that I thought gave an authentic feel. Here are the place-names I used, with their modern equivalent.

Norðvegr/ Norway
Biörgvin – Bergen

Orkneyjar/ Orkney
Brogar – Brodgar
Byrgisey – Birsay
Egilsey – Egilsay
Gareksey – Gairsay
Hamnavoe – Stromness
Heraðvatn – Loch of Harray
Hrolfsay – Roussay
Hrossey – Mainland
Kirkjuvágr – Kirkwall
Orkhaugr – Maeshowe
Papey Meiri – Papa Westray

Pentlandsfjord – Pentland Firth
Sandvik – Sandwick
Scalpeid – Scapa
Skalpaflói – Scapa Flow
Skarabolstadr – Scrabster
Steinnesvatn – Loch of Stenness
Strjónsey – Stronsay
Vestrey – Westray

Suðreyjar/ Hebrides, Southern Isles, Isle of Man
(sometimes the kingdom of Man and the Isles, sometimes directly ruled by Orkney or Norway)
Hjaltland/ Shetland
Skio/ Skye

Ness/ Caithness
Lambaburg – Bucholie Castle
Vik – Wick

Albion/ England
Nordymbraland – Northumberland
Dunholm – Durham
Jorvik –York
The Holy Land
Jórsalaheim – Jerusalem

Ireland / Írland
Mikligard/Constantinople/ Istanbul
Novgorod / Russia
Snaeland/ the Old Country/ Iceland
Hispania/ Iberia/ al-Andalus – Spain
Sicilia – Sicily (a kingdom at this time)
Miðjarðarhaf/ the Mediterranean Sea

MAIN HISTORICAL CHARACTERS IN 'THE MIDWINTER DRAGON' SERIES BK 1 AND BK 2

The Norse naming convention, still used today, usually creates a girl's second name from her mother's first name e.g. Ingeborg Asleifsdottir and a boy's second name comes from his father's first name e.g. Kali Kolsson. One exception is when the mother or father is dead and the child takes the survivor's name e.g. Sweyn's father was murdered and he is famous as Sweyn Asleifsson, Asleif being his mother.

- Al-Idrisi – Sicilian Muslim map-maker
- Bishop William – Jerusalem-farer, Bishop of Orkney, later nicknamed 'the Old'.
- Botolf – Icelandic skald living in Orkney
- Eindridi – Jerusalem-farer, Norwegian noble who inspired Rognvald to go on pilgrimage to Jerusalem
- Eleanor/ Aliénor of Aquitaine – Queen of France, then Queen of England
- Emperor of Byzantium – Manuel Komnenos
- Erling 'Wry-neck' – (Crick-neck) Jerusalem-farer, who earned his nickname in a skirmish during the pilgrim voyage
- Ermengarda – ruler of Narbonne in her own right
- Frakork Maddansdottir – 'the witch', alleged murderer, Sweyn's enemy, grandmother to Thorbjorn and Olvir Rosta (see family tree)
- Gunni/ Gunnr Asleifsson – brother to Sweyn and Ingeborg (Inge), exiled for living 'in sin' with Jarl Harald's widowed mother
- Hlif (Hlifolfsdottir) – one 12th century runic message in Maeshowe is signed 'Hlif (female name), Rognvald's housekeeper'

- Hlifolf – the cook who killed Jarl Magnus (later Saint Magnus) on Jarl Hakon's orders
- Holbodi – Lord of Tiree, who sheltered Sweyn during one of his periods of exile
- Jón Fót / Jón Fót (leg/foot) Pétrsson (Jón Halt-foot) – Jerusalem-farer, married to Rognvald's sister and wounded in the leg/foot by Rognvald in the years they were enemies.
- Ingeborg – Rognvald's daughter
- Ingeborg (Inge) Asleifsdottir – Sweyn's sister, married to Thorbjorn Klerk, then to Thorfinn (Finn) Bessasson as mentioned in *the Orkneyinga Saga*
- Jarl Erlend – claimant to Orkney, son of Jarl Harald Smooth-tongue
- Jarl Hakon of Orkney – predecessor to Jarl Rognvald, co-ruler with Jarl Magnus, whom he had killed
- Jarl Harald of Orkney – Harald Maddadson, foster-son to Thorbjorn and Jarl Rognvald (see family tree)
- Jarl Paul of Orkney – successor to Jarl Hakon, 'disappeared' by Sweyn and replaced by Rognvald
- Jarl Rognvald of Orkney (ex Kali Kolsson)
- King of Norway – Haraldr Gilli (king from 1135-1136).
- King of Norway – Three of Gilli's sons co-ruled as kings of Norway until 1155
- King David of Scotland – died in (1150-1153?)
- King Malcolm of Scotland – ruled from (1150-1153?) Took the throne at age (9-11?)
- King of Sicily – Roger II
- Kol – Norwegian father of Jarl Rognvald, first builder of St Magnus Cathedral
- Macabru – Occitan troubadour
- Margaret Hakonsdottir – mother of Jarl Harald, with her first husband Maddan (Earl of Caithness), then lived 'in sin' with Sweyn's brother, Gunnr.
- Olvir 'the Brawler' Rosta – Sweyn's enemy, grandson to Frakork

- Raimon Berenguer IV – 'El Sant', Count of Barcelona and Prince of Aragon (by marriage to Queen Petronilla)
- Roaldsson (Cup-bearer) –Jerusalem-farer, Rognvald's cup-bearer
- Rognvald's wife – one of Rognvald's poems mourns his lady but she is never identified
- Saint (ex-Jarl of Orkney) Magnus – Rognvald's maternal uncle, murdered on Jarl Hakon's orders
- Sweyn Asleifsson – sea-rover extraordinaire
- Thorbjorn Klerk – guardian to the young Jarl Harald, clerk and advisor to Jarl Rognvald
- Thorfinn (Finn) Bessasson – Lord of Stronsay, Inge's husband
- Other Jerusalem-farers – The leaders: Magnus, the son of Hávard, Gunni's son; Thorgeir Skotakoll, Oddi the little, Thorberg Svarti, Armód the skald, Thorkel Krókauga, Grímkell of Flettuness, and Bjarni his son; Aslák and Guttorm.
- The Maeshowe rune-carvers – Hlif, Eyolfr Kolbeinssor, Vemundr, Ottar, Ogmundr, Arnfior, Oframr Sigurdsarsonr, Hermundr 'hard', Arnfithr 'food', Helgi.

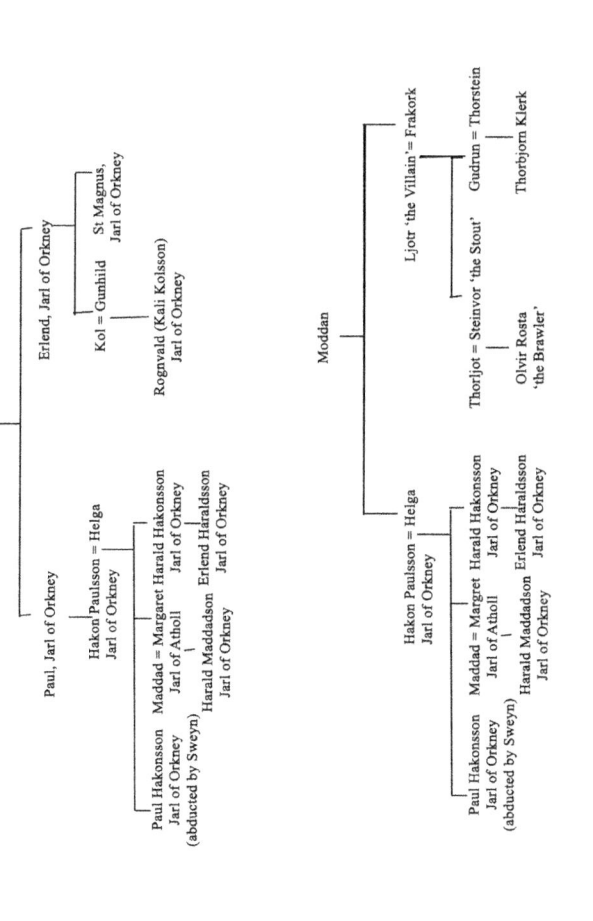

MAIN FICTIONAL CHARACTERS

- Skarfr (Cormorant) Kristinsson – orphaned ward and apprentice to the skald (poet) Botolf
- Hlif – (developed from one Maeshowe inscription) orphaned and cursed, daughter of St Magnus' murderer, Hlifolf, ward and housekeeper to Jarl Rognvald
- Brigid – woman kidnapped from Ireland, working with Fergus in Botolf's longhouse in Orkney, caring for Skarfr
- Fergus – man kidnapped from Ireland, working with Brigid in Botolf's longhouse in Orkney, caring for Skarfr
- Mouthy – old sea rover
- Coal-Pilot and all the other pilots
- Arn – Jarl Rognvald's cook and steward

Fictional minor characters in *The Midwinter Dragon* series but main characters in *The Troubadours* series

- Dragonetz los Pros 'the brave' – commander and troubadour to Queen Eleanor of Aquitaine
- Estela de Matin – troubadour at the court of Narbonne

For Mathilda,
who wants to go sailing

CHAPTER 1

SKARFR

A man needs wisdom
if he plans to wander widely;
life is easier at home.

The Wanderer's Hávamál

For the fifth morning since they'd left home, the sea fret the Orkneymen called haar shrouded the dragon ship in grey wisps, rolling towards the invisible coast. Blown by the easterly winds that prevailed on this coast, the haar complicated mornings, gliding like an army of ghosts from the open sea towards the land.

If the white army was thickest on his left, then Skarfr reasoned that the shore must be on his right, and they were sailing southwards, on course for the friendly harbour of Grimsby. With such seafaring knowledge, Skarfr fought against his instinctive panic at sailing blind. And he trusted his captain.

He licked the salt from his chapped upper lip in a futile battle against the sea spray as the ship carved a path though the choppy grey waves of the Norð Sea. He ran his finger along the greased cloak stowed below the rowing bench and transferred the rancid grease onto his lips to prevent cracking. As he'd been shown by that ever-practical woman, Hlif, before she sneaked a lightly oiled kiss.

The only woman on the ship, Hlif was now lying on her back between rowing benches. She was also the only person small enough to fit neatly in the sleeping spaces of legroom between the thwarts, apart from the ship's young horn blower. Although lying down, she was not sleeping.

Ghostly in trails of mist that revealed her face and then covered it, like clouds unveiling the moon, Hlif was looking upwards, her white face screwed up in concentration.

'Well?' asked Rognvald, ship's captain, Jarl of Orkneyjar and Hlif's self-appointed guardian.

The plaintive note of a horn sounded from the prow, a regular warning of the ship's presence. The horn blower blew the long note used in hunting for 'Stag at bay', translating at sea to 'Ship ahoy'. Wrecking reefs would pay no heed to the horn, but it would save them from crashing into another vessel. Fourteen horns echoed, each in their turn, indicating the positions of the other ships in the company, behind the *Sun-chaser*.

Skarfr noticed the upward tilt of Jarl Rognvald's mouth and guessed why his lord was so cheerful. Rognvald's company of ships was following *his* lead despite the haar and despite the arrogance of their guide Eindridi, one of the other captains, forced by the weather to defer to Rognvald's competence.

'I can feel the swelling waves moving from my left calf to my right shoulder,' declared Hlif, 'and some choppy ones in the same direction.'

Skarfr interpreted the information for Rognvald and the navigator. 'The swell matches the haar so we're heading slightly out to sea. Sou'-sou'-east?' he queried, applying his recent understanding of navigation.

Rognvald grunted and muttered to himself. 'Choppy waves mean we're not far from the coast. Best keep the sail to a single reef till we can see again.'

From the moment the Jarl had discovered his ward's sensitivity to the direction of the swell, he'd asked her to check it twice daily, early and late, so their pilot could check the ship's course.

'Aye, slow and steady. Hold this course,' agreed the pilot. 'Take us out until there's only swell. And with any luck, we'll be out of the sea fret all the quicker further from land. Another hour or so and we'll see again.'

'Praise the gods,' said Hlif. 'Another hour on my back checking every roll and dip will be quite enough for me.'

There was a snigger from some unfortunate seaman.

'I know that's you, Bandy-legs,' Hlif said, 'and you'll regret that thought when we break our fast and your share is smaller than it might have been.'

'Wasn't me, Hlif, honest,' the accused replied, with the speed of habit.

Skarfr controlled his equally habitual instinct to punch anyone who insulted Hlif. He hated this pretence that she was no more to him than his liege lord's ward. He hated that their handfasting was secret. But what else could they have done?

Like an otherworldly echo of the horns, a plaintive cry came out of the white blanket obscuring the midships. Not just once but repeated, an eerie sound that lodged in a man's guts and twisted. And it was prowling the ship, nearing the stern and the woman lying vulnerable on the deck.

'Christ Jesus! That cursed cat!' swore the pilot and crossed himself, as a furred monster emerged from the mist. Black as an imp save for a white moustache, as if he'd brushed against the mist and some had stuck, the cat homed in on Hlif. He headbutted his mistress before snuggling under her waterproof cape, complaining loudly.

'He's just hungry,' Hlif translated, as the reverberations of a purring cat replaced the wailing.

'Then he mun work for it like the rest of us, till we're out of this fret. We're all hungry,' observed the pilot sourly.

He wasn't the only one who hid his fear of the cat under rough jokes about skinning methods and fur hats but nobody on board ship would disobey Rognvald's orders or risk Hlif's anger by harming the beast. And even if the cat's fur were not marred by a warrior's fight history, black was little prized. Reluctantly the ship's crew agreed that the ugly, one-eyed cat was worth more alive than dead.

By the time Rognvald had realised his ship carried a stowaway, home was far behind and his threat of drowning the brute met with an impassioned argument from his housekeeper regarding rodent control, provisions and providence.

'He has *one eye*,' Hlif had pointed out with heavy emphasis.

Christian pilgrims they might be but not even Rognvald could ignore this resemblance to Óðinn. And all knew what punishments had been dealt out by the One-eyed Wanderer when he'd sought hospitality among men and been turned from the door.

During the debate over his future, the cat licked his paws and washed himself thoroughly. When Rognvald qualified his grudging assent with 'But he'd better catch some rats,' the cat bestowed a contemptuous green one-eyed stare on the Jarl and settled in. Although Hlif called him One-eye, an indirect reference to his celestial protector, the crew had other names for him.

Cat and pilot had taken an instant dislike to each other from the moment Rognvald had picked up the local navigator at the Tyne port of Newcastle on the previous day. The pilot knew his own worth and was accustomed to telling others what to do. The same could be said of the cat but the pilot felt his skills as a navigator counted for more than rat-catching ability.

He knew this journey even in darkness as black as the coal he usually carried on such trips. He would pilot them as far as Grimsby, then negotiate a cargo and ship back up the coast to Newcastle. Maybe the captains would find another man to pilot the next stretch of the journey or maybe not. The further south they sailed, the less they'd be bothered by haar and the more Rognvald could use his own men's skills. After all, his fellow-captain Eindridi had sailed this course before, travelled all the way to Jórsalaheim.

Eindridi had inspired Rognvald to make the pilgrimage but would never accept his leadership, whatever the King of Norðvegr's decree. From the ostentatious ornaments on his ship to the patronising advice he offered, Eindridi attempted to take the wind from Rognvald's sails at every opportunity. Rognvald's response was to call on Eindridi's knowledge of the route only when he had to, between gritted teeth.

'Take the steerbord, Skarfr, and tell Coal-pilot of any changes Hlif senses,' said Rognvald. From this moment on, the pilot was named more personally than merely Pilot, as was usual. 'I'll let the men on all the ships know we're fine.' He picked his way forward, yelling encouragement. The words were lost in the mist but the tone was true. Even the horn sang out with more confidence.

We're here. We're doing fine. You're doing fine. Follow me.

His hand steady on the steerboard to the right behind him on the stern of the ship, Skarfr watched the rise and fall of Hlif's supine body, wrapped in her oiled bedsack. He tried not to think along the same lines as Bandy-legs.

In the eerie white of otherworld, he waited for a change in the wave pattern, and words for a poem came to him.

Wave-walkers, soul-stealers, wraith-robbers

This time, the scream that interrupted Skarfr's thoughts was no cat's.

CHAPTER 2

FERGUS, ORKNEYJAR

Fergus was crouching, milking the cow in the far pasture, his thoughts drifting, fluffy as sunny-day clouds, while his hands deftly coaxed a warm stream into the pail. Creamy yellow, rich and buttery. Brigid would be happy and their newly-built dairy would fill with cheeses.

This year's calf was tied to a post beside her mother, impatient for her turn to suckle. Fergus couldn't decide whether he would keep the little beauty or sell her and invest in more sheep. If she were like her mother when she grew up, the calf would be a treasure. If she was well cared for. Rauðka, named after her russet coat, was the proof that a farmer reaped what he sowed, with beasts as with barley.

Having taken his share, a full pail, Fergus unloosed the calf, which immediately latched on to a teat. Rauðka lowed and let down more milk, generous as always.

Pail to the dairy, then water from the well. Fergus listed his last chores for the day, but he could not prevent a niggling worry from surfacing again.

The letter should have reached his master, Skarfr, if the ships hadn't sailed yet. With any luck, Skarfr would have read the words of atonement from the man who'd blighted his childhood and repented on his deathbed. Skarfr's long sea voyage would be blessed with that knowledge and he could forget the past. Or even forgive. Only in his twenties, he was too young to carry such a weight of blood debts, whether for himself or his friend, Hlif.

With all of this in mind, Fergus had granted the old man's last wishes, in Christian manner, despite the cruelty he and Brigid had also suffered when Botolf was their master. But when he handed the letter to the messenger and showed the name on the outside of the parchment, confirming that Skarfr was the recipient, the man had taken his word for that and not even checked.

When it was too late to allay his fears, Fergus began to worry. In unchristian manner, he kept wondering whether such a spiteful master had truly repented, even at the end. Botolf knew Fergus could not read. What if the letter contained something quite different? What if those had not been the letters of Skarfr's name? If only the messenger had looked, had read the name aloud and confirmed it. If only Fergus had not been too proud to ask what the writing said.

Still, he shouldered the pail. *No point crying over spilt milk.*

That's when he smelled it. The wrongness reached his nose first. Then his fluffy clouds darkened to smoky-grey, to smoke itself, acrid and horribly familiar from the time when Vikings had torched his village in Írland.

He dropped the pail. Scanning his surroundings for the source of the smoke, he hardly noticed the precious liquid creaming the spring grass before trickling down long blades to disappear.

Even as he prayed it be not so, he could see birds scattering above a plume of smoke in the direction of the longhouse, where Brigid was cooking their evening meal and waiting for him to bring the milk home. Such luxury they lived in now. The smoke darkened the sky, billowing up from the longhouse as the fire took hold. Greedy for air, the first flames blazed high.

Fergus stumbled into a run as he tried to understand what his senses told him.

How could this be a Viking raid when they now lived in Orkneyjar, not Írland, and their master *was* a Viking? Brigid had surely been careless, dried a shirt too close to the hearth-fire or some such accident. Terrible but not as much as the thing he feared.

Brigid, pulsed his heart as he ran. *Brigid*. He could picture her as a girl, tied up by the raiders, her blue eyes warning him as she lied. Her prattle of his nobility, and of a ransom, had won him a place beside her on the enemy ship. As a woman, she'd taken him to bed in this cold longhouse where they slaved on a foreign shore. As his wife, she'd shared in the joy of running the homestead for their young master, now he'd come of age. *Brigid.*

He was halfway across the first field, cursing his fancy for milking outdoors. If he'd brought the cow to the byre, he'd have been at hand, in time to put the fire out. Now he could see the thatched roof flaming skywards in an evil puppet-play, as if straw figures burned alive above their home.

Then he heard men shouting, laughing, as they do to encourage each other in acts of violence.

And Brigid screamed.

His fears were not wrong. His legs pumped faster and blood pounded in his ears so loud he almost missed the words that came in a desperate shout, words in Írish, cut off by a grunt of pain.

'Remember *Drom Reagh!* Go to the lady across the water. RUN!'

He stopped in his tracks, understanding but rebellious. *Drom Reagh* was their home settlement in Írland, a reminder that they'd survived worse, that she'd saved him.

But that was why he couldn't leave her to *them*. He would die protecting her.

Exactly so. And her last words had been protecting him*. So* he *wouldn't die.*

He turned to run away from the longhouse as fast as he'd run towards it, but he was still in two minds. He hesitated.

What use will you be to her if she lives and you're dead?

But what use is my life if she's dead?

Above the crackle of flames, he heard a man hurl orders while horses whinnied in fear. Then curses and shouts headed his way, along with thudding hoofbeats.

Brigid had given away that there was someone else nearby. Did they already know that Fergus lived there with her? Was this attack aimed specifically at them, not just a random raid? Something in Brigid's words was important but he had no time to think. There was no time to do more than follow her last instruction so run he did.

He ran back past Rauðka and her calf, shouted at them, waved his arms around, praying they too would run away. Whether his crazed behaviour had its effect or the whiff of smoke spooked them, he couldn't tell, but they galloped off. For once, Fergus hoped they'd escape as far as possible.

'May God and the Dagda protect us all,' he murmured, without any real hope that any gods of Írland were looking out for his kin or kine this day.

In the open landscape of Orkneyjar, his only hope of hiding was in buildings or boats. He could not expect his neighbours to shelter a thrall against the men on horseback. He could see the nearest longhouse, an impossible distance away. Between him and the house was an outbuilding, little more than a shed but it would do. They had not seen him yet.

CHAPTER 3

FERGUS, ORKNEYJAR

His heart bursting, Fergus made one last effort and reached the mud walls. He ducked behind the building, walked to the other corner, then dropped to all fours to head south to the shore, where his own boat was beached. His quarter-turn in direction would throw the raiders off the scent if they carried straight on towards the neighbour's longhouse, as would seem natural.

They were close now, approaching the outbuilding. Only tall grasses were between him and his pursuers. They must surely smell the sweat that stuck his shirt to his body as he crawled stealthily towards his only hope of escape.

The horses drew up and Fergus held still, his cramped muscles protesting.

'Leave him go,' said a rough voice in Norn, the local version of the Vikings' language and one in which Fergus was fluent after years living here. 'The lord said to avoid being seen and nobody will believe a thrall's ravings.'

'Not in the time between him speaking and us stilling his tongue,' said another, then laughed.

'The lord's happy with the one he's got. Let's go before his mood changes again.'

Clicking their tongues, they urged their horses back the way they'd come.

Fergus dropped onto his belly in the grass, shaking, unable to move.

The lord? Who had done this?

The one he'd got? Brigid was alive? Taken once more by a raider?

An ant changed course in front of him, crawled up a vertical green blade without slowing down. It crossed the bridge offered by broken cow parsley. Then went down another blade of grass and out of sight, the Fergus-shaped obstacle bypassed and forgotten. If only he could avoid danger so easily.

The bellow of a terrified cow seared his eardrums. Had the riders taken out their frustration on Rauðka? The thought hardened something in Fergus. After all he and Brigid had been through, this should not be how their story ended.

He dragged himself to his feet, heedless of whether he might be seen. The raiders had gone.

Their message, however, was visible for miles. Local men were running crossing the fields, the word 'Fire!' on their lips. All farmers were neighbours when it came to fighting a common enemy that could race across the windswept grassland faster than raiders, to destroy their harvest and kill their livestock,

'Here man, take this.' The words were in Norn but the accent was as foreign as his own.

Fergus started at the voice, at the waterskin held out for him to drink from. A kindness that came from a different world, one where his home had not been burned to the ground.

The speaker was a thrall like himself, a burly low-browed man, slow of speech and slow to anger, nicknamed Ox. Fergus knew him from the baths, didn't know if Ox had any other name.

His master was behind him, showing no interest in another man's thrall when there was an emergency threatening his own homestead.

'Get going, Ox. If that fire spreads, we're all in trouble.' Ox's master didn't wait but ran off himself towards the burning longhouse.

Fergus grabbed the big man's arm, told him urgently, 'My cow and calf, they were spooked by the fire. If you find them,' *alive, please God,* 'keep them till my master returns.'

Ox nodded and left him.

In a daze, Fergus saw men rushing towards him from the other houses in the settlement as word reached the scattered inhabitants. They ignored him and ran past, carrying their spades and buckets, to dig trenches and throw water, to stifle and quench the fiery threat to their own properties.

The house was a lost cause but Fergus was too numb to care. Even so, he had to know what *they* had done, to see for himself – and to see if there was a corpse in the ashes.

He trudged heavily back across the pastureland of which he'd been so proud. He passed the ropes he used to tie up the cow and calf, still dangling from the tethering posts, ominous as nooses. No sign of Rauðka. He prayed that was good news and forced his unwilling legs onwards to the site where his home used to stand.

To the flames, his home was just fuel; it had been reduced to ashes in the time it took a man to milk a cow. The wind had done its part too and was still whirling sparks and black specks. Around the charred earth men made a chain, passing buckets from the well to wherever sparks flared up anew. Choking, swearing, they pulled their tunics up over their mouths and noses, but they had the spread under control.

The ashes were too hot to walk over but he could see that nothing of value remained. He would have to report to his master one day, when he returned from his long sea voyage, so he itemised the damage as best he could.

Gone:
One longhouse with all contents.
One cow and calf. No corpses, so maybe they had run from the smoke.
One stable. No corpse, so they must have stolen the pony.
One female thrall. No corpse, so they must have stolen her too.

There was still hope for Rauðka and her calf. So a god had heard his prayers, he told himself, which meant there was still hope for Brigid.

Remaining:
One stone byre.
One spade leaning against the byre.
12 sheep, grazing.
Two cookpots and the metal chain which hung the pot above the hearth.
One male thrall, simmering with fear and anger.

Something glinted on the ground and he stooped to pick it up. One thing of value did remain: Brigid's silver ring with a blue stone in it, that he'd bought her from the market, when he'd been richly paid for his services to a lady. Sapphire, the jewel-seller had told him, and maybe it was. She'd have put it on when she finished her chores, with some daft fancy of looking pretty for him. She always looked pretty to him, although he knew her face was careworn and her body lumpen with years and overwork. The stone matched her eyes, blue, sparkling, as Írish as his true home. He slipped the ring on his little finger.

She'd stopped him spending all the coins in the pouch and, true enough, they didn't need to, now they were guardians of the homestead in their master's absence. Skarfr had meant to formally register their freedom with the Thing, their local council, but he hadn't had the time and Fergus hadn't thought it mattered. Maybe it didn't. But now Brigid was missing, maybe it did.

Fergus had listened to Brigid, as he always did, and he'd buried his pouch of money. Not so near the longhouse as to be found by raiders – was that a premonition or caution born from experience? But not so far that others would think it their own land and accidentally come across it.

He walked away from the house to the nearest remaining grass, lay on his back and shut his eyes. But he could not stop seeing. If men spoke to him, he did not reply and they soon gave up. For hours he lay there, until there was silence.

Then he stood up, filled the waterskin Ox had left him, picked up the spade and walked to the place marked by a pattern of stones that looked natural to anyone but the man who'd laid them in that pattern. He moved the stones and dug up his pouch. A pleasing, jangling weight in his hand. He slipped Brigid's ring into the pouch for safe-keeping, until he could place it back on her finger.

The clink of coin had made him so happy once, imagining what this money could do to make Brigid's life better. He had earned it too, rowing at night across the dangerous waters of the Pentlandsfjord to save a lady's life. His master had said her husband would kill her if they did not take her to safety on the mainland and so the two of them had rowed the small faering with only the Lady Inge herself to steer them.

The lady across the water.

He knew what was being asked of him. Brigid wanted him to go to Inge, to Ness on the mainland. The lady would shelter him because of what he'd done for her.

But there was more than that. Fergus ran the day's events through his memory again, the raiders' words. *Their lord.* Not wanting to be seen.

And there it was, clear as day. Someone bearing a grudge had torched the longhouse. Inge's husband must have found out what they'd done.

Someone had told Thorbjorn Klerk *who* had helped his wife escape. Thorbjorn Klerk, who was the godfather of Orkneyjar's Jarl Harald and the real power on these islands while Fergus' master and *his* lord, Jarl Rognvald, were away at sea. No wonder Brigid wanted Fergus to leave the islands.

But why now? Who could have told Thorbjorn? Had one of Inge's servants noticed and betrayed them? If so, they'd have spoken out at the time, years ago, and claimed a reward. Why would Thorbjorn take revenge now?

Fergus tried to recall the sequence of events. His master Skarfr had arrived in a hurry at the longhouse, with Hlif, the woman who'd come with him before, and with Inge, her friend. Brigid had fed them all before the two men left to row across the sea with Inge, leaving Hlif to recover overnight and put up with the vicious tongue of the old man, Botolf.

Fergus checked himself. *Botolf.* What if that feckin' letter had been no act of repentance but a last act of spite from the old man, the hearth-worm? Botolf, who had been Skarfr's guardian and teacher for five years, and as harsh a master to his ward as he'd been to the two thralls, until twelve-year-old Skarfr escaped to become pot-boy at the Jarl's court. Once he came of age, he had allowed Botolf to stay on in the house, out of pity. Then when Botolf died, Fergus had buried his body with due rites, also out of pity.

And he had carried out his last wishes regarding a letter, left with Fergus to be delivered after Botolf's death. Fergus had believed it was for Skarfr and honest. True enough, no good deed went unpunished!

Bile rose as Fergus realised what the name must have been, the one he did not know how to read. The messenger must have read the name, assumed Fergus was mistaken and had delivered the letter betraying Skarfr directly to Thorbjorn. Fergus had indeed carried out an old man's last wishes – for revenge, not for atonement.

His stomach heaved. This day's events were his fault. And however many years Skarfr spent sailing on his pilgrimage to Jórsalaheim, Thorbjorn would be waiting for him when he returned. There would be a reckoning because of the mistake he, Fergus, had made. Because he couldn't feckin' read.

Only two people would understand. One of them was in Thorbjorn's hands. The other knew intimately what the unthroned ruler of Orkneyjar was capable of. Fergus made his way to the beach, to catch the tide. He must once more battle the Pentlandsfjord in a rowboat to reach the lady across the water, Inge Asleifsdottir. He had nothing to lose and if he drowned in the attempt this time, so be it. He would rather die than give up on Brigid.

CHAPTER 4

SKARFR

Value a ship for its speed
a shield for its protection,
a sword for its sharpness,
and a woman for her kiss.

The Wanderer's Hávamál

After the scream came a splash, and a silence that was not absence of noise. The creak of wood and whoosh of the wind still marked the ship's slow course, with one reefed sail. But no human voices could be heard. Men were listening, and straining to see what was out there in this sea of clouds.

During a lull, when the sail flapped and the ship stalled briefly, something knocked against the ship, an insistent 'Let me in' rat-a-tat on wood. The men nearest the noise cursed or prayed.

'It's one of Eindridi's men, Captain. They called him Fire-starter. He's dead!' yelled Black-hammer, a swarthy veteran of many raids and no pilgrimages.

'Drowned?' Rognvald's tone held a question that should not have been needed.

'No.' Black-hammer's answer confirmed what the scream had suggested. 'The water's red around him. There's a chest wound. He was stuck with a blade.'

'Push him away from the ship,' ordered Rognvald, his face grim. 'We can do nothing for him now but pray. May the lord have mercy on his soul.'

Under his breath, he added, 'For I shall have none on whoever did this.'

In glimpses through the swirling mist, Skarf could see two shipmates using an oar to push the corpse away from the side of the ship, swearing as it returned each time to gently knock, knock against the wooden barrier.

Let me in, brothers.

Finally, after the men used two oars to push the corpse away from the ship, it found its own course, bobbed along like a fishing-float and disappeared from sight.

'Turn against the current,' Rognvald told him, ordering the ship further out to sea and away from whatever remained of Fire-starter. The pilot made no objection.

Skarfr's arm muscles tensed as the steerboard fought the slight turn and his dragon tattoo rolled like a swelling wave, sending the dragon's strength through him in fire and smoke.

Smoke, he thought, and suddenly the otherworldly whiteness was no threat but an element in which he could find his way, trust the dragon in himself. The veil between worlds was but dragon breath.

'It's clearing.' Hlif staggered a little as she stood up beside him and Rognvald lurched back to join them. Visibility had indeed improved but the future was still dark and their course dangerous.

'I'll get you some food before you set the watch,' Hlif told the Jarl and she scrambled up to the storage section midship, where she kept the company's stock of dried fish, bread and ale. As housekeeper, she was in charge of provisions and rations. Between mealtimes, she curled up between the thwarts and kept out of the way. Whenever the ships pulled up onto the sands, Hlif was queen, organising scavenging forays and cookfires, storing leftovers for the next day's voyage. On the occasions the company reached a port, she seized the opportunity to trade and to restock.

She'd worked hard over the years to win respect from Rognvald's people despite her father's infamy, but not all of the ship's company considered her an asset. Beside Skarfr in the stern, Jón Halt-foot watched Hlif with disapproval. Married to Rognvald's sister in Norðvegr, Jón bestowed opinions like largesse on less fortunate companions. However, the Jarl tolerated and trusted Jón, so his crew did likewise – and marvelled at the unlikely relationship.

Jón's halting gait came from a wound given to him by his brother-in-law, back in the times when they were related only by a long feud and a violent clash. Had they really resolved their dispute with a marriage? The alliance had been a gesture of truce, apparently accepted by both. Jón's loyalty over the years since could not be disputed, so maybe miracles did happen. Skarfr could only hope that, when they reached Jórsalaheim, Rognvald would show the same magnanimity to him as he had to Jón.

'This is no place for a woman,' Jón complained to Rognvald. 'How she talked you into it I'll never know. Thank the lord she's ill-favoured and past marrying age or you'd be dead of exhaustion fending off would-be suitors.'

'She knows marriage is forbidden her,' said Rognvald. 'As do my men. And she's a good housekeeper.'

Skarfr watched Hlif totter past the ropes and stanchions and brace herself against the motion of the heaving deck to bring them food. She opened the cloth wrapping and offered the bannocks and fish to Rognvald first. The Jarl took his share and washed it down with a swig of ale from the skin she'd passed to him.

Struggling to hold his peace, Skarfr sipped some water from the leather bottle that he, like the others, kept in his pack. His throat was as salt-dried as his lips. Ensuring fresh water was replenished was another of Hlif's responsibilities and they were lucky to have her on board. He silently rebuked Jón. Did the man think Hlif was deaf?

Apparently so, as Jón mitigated his harsh judgement. 'And at least she's sensible. Despite wearing that *thing*. It doesn't behove a pilgrim. And Bishop William has made his opinions clear.'

Luckily, the bishop was at the other end of the ship, no doubt taking the Lord's name in vain every time he spotted One-eye. His antipathy to the cat rivalled Coal-pilot's and Skarfr didn't blame either of them.

Still holding her food parcel, Hlif's hand moved protectively to the wand attached to her practical belt, where it jostled with weights, scissors and other tools of her trade as housekeeper. With its iron tip and ash stem, the wand could be as useful a weapon as a dagger but its true protective value lay in making men wonder what otherworld powers she could call upon. Her sharp tongue completed her armoury.

Tiny, indomitable, she ignored the aspersions cast on her appearance and shouted over the wind and creaking planks. 'If your great-granny hadn't sailed on a longship, you'd not have been born, Jón Petersson! Nor would Grimsby be a friendly port, if Norðwomen hadn't settled there.'

She held out the open cloth and added, 'If you know a man who can trade, store and ration provisions better than I can, drop me off at Grimsby Port and I'll take up employment with someone who appreciates my skills.'

Jón took his portion of food, spitting bits of bread as he muttered, 'Worse claws than her cursed cat. I'd pity her husband if she *was* allowed to marry. She's her father's daughter.'

Rognvald passed the ale-skin to Skarfr without comment, at the same time as Hlif offered him food. Hlif, the cursed daughter of the man who'd killed Saint Magnus. She'd worked so hard to gain respect from those who feared her and yet still her father's crime tainted her.

'Thank you,' Skarfr told her, his eyes saying more. They could only steal moments together when they beached the ship. On board, there could be nothing more than covert glances, or an accidental brush of hands; undercurrents as dangerous as those of the Norð Sea.

She grunted acknowledgement but kept her attention on Rognvald.

'One more day,' said the pilot. 'Then we'll be in Grimsby.'

'You'll like Grimsby,' Rognvald told his ward. 'Good trading.'

Then he asked Skarfr, 'Have I told you about the time I got into a drinking competition with a Norðvegr man in a Grimsby tavern?'

Skarfr smiled. He'd heard the story before but he didn't mind. Repetition helped him commit it to memory, shape it into part of the saga that would one day be Rognvald's memorial.

The Jarl went on, 'We drank, bragged and spouted poetry like all young men and he confided he was the king's son, born on the left side. I thought this a great joke and we parted good friends.'

'When Gilli – for that was his name – became King of Norðvegr, you could have knocked me down with a feather. But all he said was true. He was King Bare-legs' bastard and stayed as true a friend to me as any a man I've met.'

Something in Rognvald's tone alerted Skarfr to the change, a wistfulness. Sure enough, his lord's furrowed face showed how many hours he'd been guiding the ship.

'My lord,' said Skarfr softly. 'If I take this watch while you sleep, you'll be ready for the entry to harbour.'

'You'll wake me if I'm needed?' The question was acceptance. Rognvald needed sleep.

'Aye.'

'Keep up the horn till it's clear,' Rognvald yelled, and the message was passed on from the stern through the midship and as far as the horn blower, who answered with the customary long note.

Skarfr imagined him at the prow, puffing mist and mournful notes, a replacement figurehead for the carved dragon that had been unscrewed and stowed during what should be a peaceful passage.

Fourteen horns echoed the first. Fifteen ships and their captains, in harmony – while the fog lasted.

'Hlif,' Rognvald commanded. 'You get some sleep too.'

Skarfr sighed inwardly. He'd hoped to talk to Hlif without worrying as to what they might let slip.

It would be a very long voyage.

One more day. Then another. And it had just begun.

CHAPTER 5

SKARFR

*Where the beaches are small
it's a small sea that washes them –
and so it is with little minds.*

The Wanderer's Hávamál

What a luxury to pull the ship up to a wooden jetty in a calm haven rather than drop anchor off an unknown shore or run her up a beach at the whim of wind and tide. The port of Grimsby was on the south side of a wide river mouth, which was silting up enough to make wooden walkways a necessity rather than a bonus.

Such an arrival called for verse and of the many skalds Rognvald had welcomed on pilgrimage, it was Armód who rose to the occasion. Although no warrior, Armód could wield words effectively and was a foil to Rognvald's wit and to Skarfr's mastery of the skald's craft. The friendly rivalry Rognvald encouraged by his example and his contests inspired all the skalds to new heights and Grimsby honours went to Armód, whose lines were repeated and passed on from man to man.

Such rousing verse lifted even Skarfr's spirits, which were still too troubled by the memory of Fire-starter's corpse in its shroud of fog to contribute his own lines in celebration of their voyage. Armód's poem exaggerated somewhat the size of the waves but what good story did not grow in the telling? Also, he had reminded them all what adventures they were living, unlike those who'd stayed behind to endure endless meetings of the Thing in council.

Up the white-capped mountains
we climbed to reach the Hvera's mouth.
Our oak masts bent like reeds till
the low land calmed the waves
with long sand fingers.
Our eyes are blind with salt-spray
while the stay-at-home youths
plod hearth-ward from the Thing-meet.

Jón Halt-foot threw the rope to the man ashore, who tied up the *Sun-chaser* to one of the mooring posts. The slap of water and clunk of wood against wood told of fourteen other ships finding berths where they could, between the merchant ships and fishing boats. A ferry had just set off for the north bank, leaving a tempting space but Eindridi's *Crest-cleaver* was turned back by gesticulating dock-hands. The place was reserved.

Gulls and other seabirds complained of the disturbance, swooping down in search of titbits. A cormorant quit her perch on the furthest wooden post and flew low enough past the *Sun-chaser* for Skarfr to see her blink green eyes at him. Until that moment of reconnection with his cormorant, he had not known he felt adrift, so far from the only home he'd known.

He knew that a man could not claim respect from others if he had not seen the marvels of the wide world, but he had not expected to feel this backwash of home-longing that hit him sometimes. He fought it by telling himself the sagas of adventures lived by past heroes and by imagining those yet to come. If his cormorant travelled with him, all would be well.

With the ease of years as an apprentice, and an unleashed imagination, he shaped the words that would tell of this voyage. Of the ship and of the cormorant.

Foam-flyer, sea-skimmer, depth-dipper.

Hlif gave him a knowing smile as he helped her off the ship, as if she'd heard his thoughts, not just seen the cormorant.

All knew the tale of how Skarfr was given his name, meaning 'cormorant': the strangeness of his second birth, when the seabird added an abandoned baby to her brood, and his human mother found him in a nest. But only Hlif knew that the connection bridged the worlds of men and gods.

When the cormorant spoke, Skarfr listened. And if all she said was, 'I'm here,' then Skarfr was on the right path. He felt buoyant once more as he jumped out of the ship after his liege lord.

However, the Jarl's mood had changed in the opposite direction. Skarfr sensed Rognvald's coiled anger as they waited on the wooden walkway at Grimsby harbour for the other ships to be tied up.

Hlif stood quietly beside her guardian. She had metamorphosed into a demure maiden, her hair neatly hidden under a brown scarf. Drawing her cloak tighter, she studied the planks underfoot as if to memorise the grain patterns in each one. Sure signs that human storm clouds were on the horizon.

Jón Halt-foot also joined Rognvald on the jetty, watching the other captains organise their men as the ships bobbed gently. As if he too sensed the atmosphere, he tempered his words more carefully than usual.

'You could wait until Bishop William is with us, for support?' he suggested.

'I need no support,' growled Rognvald.

The first captain to jump ashore was Eindridi, his face aglow as he greeted the Jarl. 'You must have thought we'd be stuck in that hell-fog forever – and so we would have been – but the gods heard my prayers. Let's go and celebrate!'

The Jarl's stillness should have forewarned him, but Eindridi was either unobservant or rash. He bestowed a radiant smile on his leader.

'One of your men floated past my ship, dead. How did that happen?' Rognvald's tone was calm but his fists were clenched.

Eindridi looked puzzled at the Jarl's slow-wittedness and raised his voice. 'As I said, I made an offering to the gods and it's just as well someone took action. I'm sorry if your men were spooked.' The sneering tone made the accusation clear: Rognvald was incompetent and his men were weak-stomached.

Eindridi shrugged and conceded, 'He should have been disposed of more efficiently.' His eyes gleamed. 'I can make an example of the crewman who threw the body overboard and my men can demonstrate how an offering should be consigned to the sea. Is that what you want?'

'No more men are to be wasted,' Rognvald snapped. 'And I doubt Bishop William will look kindly on your *offering*.'

Bishop William's opinions could only be inferred as he was among those left on watch aboard ship, based on the assumption that he would be able to control the crew, his appetites and the ship's cat, better than less pious mortals.

Showing no sign of deflation, Eindridi said, 'Tell him we sacrificed to the Christian God like that man in the bible – and Fire-starter's death was more useful than his life, so not a waste at all. He was nothing but trouble and won't be missed.' He shrugged again. 'The gods accepted the sacrifice and the fog cleared.'

He turned to the men pouring onto the jetty, and yelled, 'Here we are – Grimsby! So let's make the most of meat, ale and beds that don't buck like a horse with a saddle bur.'

'I wouldn't mind a buck in bed,' said one joker and Eindridi threw his head back in a teeth-baring show of laughter. Men from the other ships crowded behind him as he confronted the small group formed by Rognvald, Skarfr, Hlif and a handful of the Jarl's crew. The majority of the *Sun-chaser's* shore party was heading into town, an advance warning of the sea-rovers' arrival.

Eindridi swaggered towards Rognvald, as if he would walk through him unless the Jarl moved aside.

Before the two leaders could physically clash, Skarfr moved between them, hand on his dagger hilt, his head reeling from words thrown like a torch on thatch, a lethal mix of blasphemy and arrogance.

Four heartbeats measured time, then Eindridi laughed and stepped back. 'Call off your dog, Rognvald. I was going to suggest we drink together, and I can tell you tales of Jórsalaheim and Mikligard to whet your appetite.'

The two leaders were attracting attention from their men, who must have sensed the tension even if they couldn't hear the conversation.

Brushing past Skarfr, Rognvald gave Eindridi a hearty clap on the back and grasped his arm in a friendly way. For the benefit of the growing audience of men around them, he raised his voice. 'I remember your tales well. You convinced me that a pilgrimage was a saga in the making and I thought you a true follower of the White Christ. You inspired me to lead this expedition.'

The grip on Eindridi's arm tightened. Rognvald whispered, 'And by God, you will not dishonour it. You will sacrifice no more men, to the gods or to your own vanity. You can't help your ignorance but you will not spill blood because the sea makes fog. Do you spill blood to make sure the wolf chases the sun across the sky each morning? No, because you know this is nature's way, not caused by your prayers. We are not savages. We are pilgrims! Do I make myself clear?'

Skarfr readied himself for the coming fight. This moment had been inevitable since Eindridi defied the orders of the King of Norðvegr and ordered a new boat to rival Rognvald's in splendour, from the gilt weathervane on the prow to the carved serpent's tail on the stern. Not that Jón Halt-foot believed any ship could outdo Rognvald's *Sun-chaser* – he'd built it. And he was fingering his axe as if he'd like to chip corners off Eindridi, the moment Rognvald released the offender.

The only way Eindridi could free himself from that vice-like grip would be in open wrestling or by drawing his dagger – awkward with his left hand. Either movement would be an act of treason which he would have to follow through to the death.

CHAPTER 6

SKARFR

The watchful guest,
when he arrives for a meal,
should keep his mouth shut.

The Wanderer's Hávamál

Rognvald was slightly shorter than the other man, but the more experienced in battle, in leadership – in everything except pilgrimage to Jórsalaheim or service in Mikligard. He did not give way, nor did he offer provocation.

After a pause that seemed endless, Eindridi gave a forced smile, said loudly, 'As you say, my lord. These are the joys of us travelling together.'

Rognvald expelled a slow deep breath and the moment passed. 'I swear I can smell the stew from here. And with no rationing from some tight-fisted woman!' He winked at his ward.

'It's just as well somebody rations you all.' Hlif tried to match her guardian's jocular tone, but Skarfr recognised the frown-line and the tremble in her chin that betrayed the strain of witnessing the leaders' clash.

Uneasy laughter marked the change in mood and, leaving a skeleton crew guarding each ship, the pilgrims descended on Grimsby, to the profit of all those residents who provided physical sustenance for hundreds of hungry, randy men.

Rognvald, his captains and a cadre of his chosen men were welcomed like long-lost sons in one of Grimsby's biggest houses. Although the incessant drizzle through the hole in the turf roof made the fire smoke, the hearth was convivial. Better to be a little watery-eyed in a warm hall, which smelled of damp wool and drying sweat, than to be drenched outdoors – again.

Skarfr stowed his pack on the shelf behind one of the long benches where he hoped to sleep that night. Then he sat down near enough the Jarl to protect him should the need arise, but modestly apart from the small group formed by host and captains.

Their host was introduced as Hugh Neville, one of the town's leaders, known as 'burgesses'. He sported a long-skirted red tunic over yellow stockings, garb expensive in cloth but garish and lacking all manliness, to Skarfr's eye. Would he grow more accustomed to strange habits, as he travelled?

Although Frankish in name and ways, Neville seemed at ease speaking in the local version of Anglish, which could be understood by all the Norðmen. The Danelaw past of the town was evident in its architecture, its people and its trade links; he seemed proud of this history. He waxed lyrical about the river route from Grimsby to Jorvik and Rognvald had to politely decline the invitation to join in his host's merchant ventures in that direction. Undeterred, Neville extolled the skills of the town's craftsmen, with more success, as Rognvald promised to send his housekeeper on a trading expedition the very next day.

The housekeeper in question missed this disposition of her time as she had disappeared behind a curtain with the ladies of the household. If she were lucky, they'd take her to the baths, Skarfr thought with envy. He wondered what day it was and whether the local custom was bathing on the sixth day, Laugarday, as at home.

Laugarday was also the day of Loki, the trickster god, and Skarfr felt he'd had enough malicious turns of fate for one day. Maybe he could wait a day or two for a bath.

He watched the people important to him, reading their humours, watching for any threat to their safety. Rognvald was in animated conversation with Neville about mutual friends and old adventures. Even Eindridi seemed more interested in scoring points as to who was most widely travelled – a contest he always won. Skarfr wondered idly whether Rognvald had started up such a conversation expressly to show Eindridi to advantage and smooth the man's ruffled feathers. But he was too tired to analyse politics and his thoughts drifted, bathed in warmth. Skarfr relaxed his guard enough to close his heavy eyelids. Just for a moment.

He jerked awake to a friendly elbow in his ribs and raucous laughter from his fellows, who shoved in beside him on the bench, full of their activities in town that afternoon. Whether fish-hooks were a better purchase than an hour with the fishwoman herself was loudly debated but all agreed that Grimsby was a fine place, even in the rain.

'I've slept all afternoon?' Skarfr shook his head to clear it of the fug of sleep and smoke.

'Seems that way,' said Cup-bearer Roaldsson cheerfully. He was one of the captains, a rotund Orkneyman whose red face suggested he'd taken every opportunity to fill his own cups as well as others' in Rognvald's hall.

One glance reassured Skarfr that the Jarl was safe. He realised that the hall was now full of men who'd presumably passed the afternoon elsewhere, and there were women interspersed among the guests at the top table. In the buzz of conversation, which reached him in snatches, were the silvery notes of a voice that always reached his heart before his ears.

'If you wish, Sire,' Hlif told Rognvald; the two of them rose.

The Jarl exchanged words with his host and was given assent, with an airy wave towards a curtained chamber behind the table, beside the one from which the women were still emerging.

'I'd like some privacy with my ward before the meal.' Rognvald's mysterious leave-taking floated across all the other conversations. What madness had taken him now?

Skarfr could see Eindridi's eyes glitter as he leaned towards Rognvald, caught his arm and made the Jarl pause.

On his feet in a heartbeat, Skarfr struggled to get past his companions to reach Rognvald. As he forced his way to the high table, he reached for his dagger but then remembered all weapons had been left at the entrance, as was only polite. At least Eindridi bore no arms either. Nor did he seem intent on harm although there was something jibing in his tone as he spoke.

'As you said to me earlier, Sire, what *would* Bishop William think of that?'

Was it Skarfr's imagination or did Rognvald's face pale and his jovial expression harden?

'First we need to *reach* Jórsalaheim,' Rognvald replied, '*then* be worthy of it.'

'Exactly my thoughts,' said Eindridi, nodding and beaming. Rognvald's riposte had lost its sting. 'So we do understand each other.'

Hlif was silent, one hand resting calmly on the arm Rognvald offered. But Skarfr's attention was drawn to her other hand, clutching at the pouch on her belt where she kept her wooden rune-dice. Then he understood. The Christian Jarl was giving in to a need he despised. He'd asked Hlif to read the runes for him.

'Skarfr.' The Jarl summoned him and Skarfr quietly followed the couple behind the curtain.

Simply furnished, with a large bed, a kist, and two tapestries on the wall, these were no doubt the sleeping quarters of the burgess of Grimsby but Rognvald wasted no time on niceties. As if it were his own bed, he took his ease on it, gesturing to the kist then lying back on one elbow.

'You can roll them there,' he told Hlif, as curtly as if she were the one forcing him to this reading rather than the reverse.

Without haste, Hlif detached her leather pouch and placed it on the wooden top of the clothes chest.

'Why now, Sire?' she asked.

Skarfr might have been invisible for all the attention paid to him as he stood with his back to the curtain, silent. But he knew why Rognvald wanted him there. As witness, as skald, as the one who would collect the stories of this voyage and shape them for the future in Rognvald's saga. Skarfr was not the only skald travelling with the Jarl, but he was the only one who'd been dragon-touched and so the Jarl had chosen him, acclaimed him as the best of skalds. A public honour and a private scourge, but the pain was none of Rognvald's doing. Skarfr would do everything he could to live up to his liege's trust. Except give up Hlif.

The Jarl had dropped his jolly façade now the three of them had privacy, a rare luxury for him too on this voyage.

'It has begun badly.' Rognvald hesitated. 'So many ill omens. I want to know if the old gods are against this voyage to the White Christ's holy place. Is Eindridi right to placate them in the old way? Ask them what they want of me for safe passage.'

He fingered the pathfinder brooch fastening his cloak and traced the rune-like emblems that formed dark shadows in the glistening gold surround. 'If they want me to turn back, I will not pit the old gods against the White Christ. I will turn back.'

Rognvald shut his eyes. Skarfr realised how exhausted their leader was. How old was he? Nearer fifty than forty? The grey was winning in his grizzled hair and furrowed face, as if days of constant rain in the open sea had leached all colour from the once flamboyant jarl.

Hlif began her prayer to Óðinn, the rune-bringer and poet, the One-eyed wanderer. As her sing-song spell took her into the trance state of her visions, the hairs on the back of Skarfr's neck rose and he was afraid, not for himself but for her. He knew what she paid to walk between worlds and how she struggled to draw the veil after opening it. But however much it hurt to watch her in such a state, his duty was to stand still and watch, keeping one curtain closed as another one lifted. She would not thank him for interrupting, nor would his jarl.

Her grey eyes focused far away, Hlif tipped the wooden rune-dice into her hand, gathering up the few that spilled onto the table without looking at them. Her hands were so small she needed two hands to hold all twenty-two runes.

Rognvald now sat straight on the bed, in respect and supplication, his hands clasped, his back rigid as a ship-mast.

Hlif paused with the runes in her palms, chanted Rognvald's questions and cast the dice onto the tabletop formed by the lid of the kist. Only one face of each dice displayed a graven letter. She collected those which had fallen blank side up, careful not to displace those with runes visible. These, she studied, chewing her bottom lip, sighing.

'Well?' prompted Rognvald, just when Skarfr thought his own patience would give out.

She shook her head. 'You know how a reading works. I can tell you what I see but only you can interpret what this means. And both of us could be wrong.'

'Tell me,' he ordered.

She pointed to the rune that had fallen nearest to Rognvald, the letter Skarfr knew as the sound 'a'.

Then she named it. 'Ansuz, Óðinn's rune, has fallen beside the 'r', raido, for riding, also for ruling, as a leader rides his people…'

She chewed on a finger, contemplating the runes, and carried on, 'Maybe not on horses but riding wooden steeds across the sea-fields…'

Rognvald nodded, listening intently. 'Yes, riding could refer to our voyage and I must sometimes ride our company hard. But Óðinn is with us. May he inspire deeds worthy of our skalds' verses. This is good, I think.'

Hlif gave no judgement but moved on to the next wooden die, in whatever order the spirit guided her to choose them. She named the letters still on the table in turn, making an association with each written character and its relationship to another. Then she let Rognvald interpret further and apply the reading to his own questions.

She lingered over the sound 'f', the fuhu. 'This tells of gold and golden deeds, but the stories tell us that such brightness is one face of the coin with avarice on the other: dangers without and dangers within as a man chases the wealth of property or the wealth of reputation. All must be earned, and payment is always taken.'

Rognvald interrogated her sharply. 'Here is glory and the treasure we seek but with a warning. Will there be honour for all?'

Hlif shook her head. 'I cannot say.' She studied the two runes beside the fuhu and sighed. 'Warnings again, that emphasise the dual nature of gold. The brighter gold shines, the more tarnished appear some of those closest to him.'

Skarfr shuffled his feet, only too aware of the failings of two of those closest to Rognvald now in this very room.

'Eindridi,' said Rognvald. 'I need to make him look good or his spiteful nature will wreck our venture.'

Finally, Hlif reached the last of the nine runes revealed and intoned, 'The 'n', the naudiz, need which cannot be denied. Frost will always freeze those who are naked.'

Her voice growing faint, she murmured, 'Payment is always taken,' then sank to her knees. She would have dropped further if Skarfr hadn't caught her and laid her gently on the bed, curled up like a cat beside the Jarl.

Rognvald swept the rune-dice up in one hand, dropped them into the bag and drew the string tight, staring into the future.

'My death is no weight to carry but other men's deaths are a heavy burden.' He seemed to grow in stature, once more the confident leader who'd battled to win his inheritance in Orkneyjar. 'A burden I am better suited to carry than a man like Eindridi.'

He repeated Hlif's last words. 'Need cannot be denied. We need to succeed in this pilgrimage so our names are forever honoured among men, and we need the blessing that awaits in the Holy City to make sure of our place in heaven. It is true and right that payment is always taken.' He chewed his lip, then nodded, decision taken. 'Yes, old gods or the White Christ, Ragnarok or Judgement Day, we must live our best lives and be judged accordingly. Is it not so, Skarfr? You have needs too.'

The direct question and even more direct gaze hit Skarfr like a mailed fist, as unexpected as it was on target. Luckily, no answer seemed to be expected, or he would have confessed his treacherous love for Hlif in the wave of guilt that flooded him. No, he was not prepared for judgement by man or any gods. Nor was his honour untainted. What could he do to put things right, to live his best life?

'I trust you both and we will say no more of this. Come,' his liege told him. 'Let's sup and make merry. Hlif, join us when you are recovered. You have my thanks.' There was fondness underlying the gruff words, which only made Skarfr feel worse.

He elbowed his way into a place at table, having lost his earlier one nearer the Jarl and Hugh Neville. After noting that Hlif had reappeared and all seemed calm at the top table, Skarfr relaxed enough to listen to the conversation around him. Hunger ensured that he supped well but making merry was not on the menu.

He did, however, find distraction in the pilot's stories of navigating waves and whirlpools, caverns and kraken. Now that his journey with Rognvald's company was over, Coal-pilot boasted of heroic feats, secure in the knowledge he would not be asked for a demonstration. While he spoke, he toyed with a leather pouch as a man does when he is protecting something precious.

More rune-stones, guessed Skarfr, surprised that a man should bear these tokens of a seer's skills. Coal-pilot had not drawn attention to this pouch during their voyage together and, now Skarfr came to think of it, the pouch must have been hidden until now. He was not the only person at the table to notice Coal-pilot's prized possession. Two of Eindridi's men who'd introduced themselves as Matt-hair and Horse-snipper seemed fixated on the object.

'Something interesting in there?' asked Matt-hair, nodding

towards Coal-pilot's belt, where the pouch hung in plain view, between a lead plumb weight and a miniature plywood sundial.

'No, nothing,' replied Coal-pilot. 'Just a little thing I made to get me back to Newcastle. It would be no use to anybody else.' But the speed with which he squirrelled it away inside his tunic suggested otherwise.

Tactfully, Skarfr drew the men's attention away from Coal-pilot to something happening at the top table. Hugh Neville had stood up, was in deep conversation with one of his men, gesticulating with enthusiasm, and Rognvald was nodding in approval. The scene was a familiar one at the stage in an evening when all had eaten well and drunk better.

'Entertainment at last!' Skarfr observed, feigning enthusiasm. He found the local speech difficult to understand and the prospect of a lengthy tale was daunting. However, professional curiosity was aroused once the Grimsby bard took to the floor, waved an arm for quiet and introduced the lay of Havelok the Dane with suitable dramatic gestures.

This was clearly a familiar and well-loved tale in Grimsby. Every time the storyteller mentioned the hero Grim, the locals cheered and stamped their feet, right from the start when a poor fisherman was commanded by the King of Danmǫrk to drown little Prince Havelok, so he would never be a rival for the throne. Of course, he did no such thing. A radiant light coming from the mouth of the sleeping prince gave Grim a clear sign that he must save this extraordinary boy and off they sailed to England – where another evil king held sway.

The bard switched between a bright heroic voice for Grim and Havelok and a villain's sepulchral tones for the evil kings, who were duly booed. Well-timed pauses allowed for enough audience participation to keep everyone awake and invested in the twisty plot. The reward was a happy ending for Havelok as King of England, married to the true heir, now Queen.

Caught up in the storytelling, Skarfr's thoughts were all about Grim. He was hoping for another tale and was disappointed when the bard returned to his table, laden with gifts. In courtesy, Rognvald did not call on his skalds to follow and thereby diminish the story's impact. The last lines of Havelok's saga lingered in the hall and in Skarfr's mind. For the people of Grimsby, the hero was not the king. The saga bore Havelok's name but their town bore Grim's. Could a man in a saga steal listeners' hearts even if he were not the hero?

CHAPTER 7

SKARFR

*A woman's beauty
often strikes harder
on a wise man than a fool.*

The Wanderer's Hávamál

The blessed relief of sleep when stretched out on a straw pallet was a pleasure postponed for Skarfr. He listened to the grunts and snores of his sated comrades and watched through half-closed eyes as their lumpy shapes rolled under blankets, tossing as if still at sea. With Rognvald asleep in the centre of the company and two sound men on watch, only one person mattered.

Grim's story sang itself again in his mind. The founder of Grimsby had been cheered throughout and yet who was he? An ordinary fisherman with an ordinary family, who'd cared for somebody else's child. Hlif would say that it was Grim's wife who'd been the real hero in that family. Or maybe both of them had been mere instruments in fulfilment of Havelok's heroic fate.

Havelok had a king's blood and a high destiny. He was the one who mattered and Grim was nothing, a nobody. He and his wife never even knew that their kindness had led to such momentous events. They died before Havelok gained the throne, their deaths as ordinary as their lives.

What if a man wanted to be Havelok and could only be Grim? wondered Skarfr. He'd been told by his mother that he was special, that the cormorant prophesied he would make sagas. And so he did – as a skald. But he was not the hero of his sagas. Rognvald was.

When the curtain finally stirred, moved by an invisible hand, and a silent figure tiptoed out, negotiating the sleeping men like a will-o'-the-wisp, Skarfr's wait was over. He let a few minutes pass before following Hlif out of the door and into the pale moonlight.

She said nothing, just nodded and started to walk away from their shelter. He understood. Any of the sleepers might feel nature's call and catch them together.

When she vanished into the shadows behind a ramshackle structure that no doubt housed a sleeping family, he followed and would have bumped into her if not stopped by the hand she held out, palm pressed against his chest. He caught it in his own and kissed it, then pulled her into his arms. Her head lay against his heart and they stood silent for a moment.

They had so little time and Skarfr could feel it counting down in each heartbeat. *One moment less, one moment less.*

He shook off the paralysis caused by too much to do and say in too little time, and spoke, as did Hlif.

'We must tell Rognvald,' he said.

'We can't meet up like this,' she said simultaneously. 'It's too dangerous.'

She gave a self-conscious laugh. 'You first,' she told him.

He didn't know what more needed to be said so repeated, 'We must tell Rognvald.' *Grim*, he thought. *Grim did his duty even if it's Havelok's story.*

The silence told him that Hlif did indeed want further explanation. He swallowed and said, 'I didn't know there was a King of England named Havelok.'

Hlif said, 'There wasn't. There was no Havelok.'

'But...I don't understand. Grim? Why is the town named after him?'

A sigh. 'I have no idea, Skarfr. Just as I have no idea what that has to do with us telling Rognvald. Or why we're wasting precious time. Much as I would love to discuss the Lay of Havelok with you, can we leave it for another time.'

'How am I supposed to know the difference between a story that's true and a story that's not?'

'Ask me,' said Hlif.

He laughed, aware she was teasing him. He still felt stupid but it stung less if Hlif was entertained rather than contemptuous. 'I do know how stories are made. I just thought... it sounded so convincing...' He pulled himself together. *One moment less. One moment less.* And he was wasting time.

'It's not right,' he said. 'Hiding that we're together. Rognvald is my liege lord and I want to ask him for his blessing, in a proper manner.'

There was no longer laughter in her voice when she replied. 'Rognvald *is* your liege lord. You know he has forbidden me to marry. And made his decree public. He even told you personally not to think of me, didn't he?'

She was guessing but she'd hit the mark. 'Yes,' he confessed.

'And do you think he's changed his mind? That he'll think how lovely it is for his ward and his skald to marry and produce a bevy of cursed children? That he won't wonder what we've been up to behind his back? That he won't put you on another ship or choose to leave you behind in exile? That he'll ever trust me again? That I won't lose my work as well as my chance of marriage?'

'But,' countered Skarfr stubbornly, 'why do you think he'll change his mind in Jórsalaheim?'

'Because I will pray in the holiest place there, and the saints will lift my curse, and they'll show Rognvald a sign. I know it! *Then* I can ask him for his blessing on our marriage. If I ask, he will know that you have been loyal to him.'

'But I haven't.' Skarfr's voice broke.

Unflinching, Hlif told him, 'You are loyal in all the ways that are his due. What is between us is not his to command. That's why he mustn't suspect, so we can make all right once we reach Jórsalaheim. This is our fate and we have sealed it many times, like this—' Her tone softened and she stood on tiptoes to kiss him.

Fate. He could no more have spurned her kiss than food if he were starving; she ripped apart his noble intentions with her mouth and hands.

It came to him that he could continue kissing her, part her legs as easily as he parted her lips... He broke off suddenly, remembering another man, another woman, against a wall. And the woman's *I won't cry* face.

Hlif's hand touched his arm gently. 'It's all right, Skarfr. I understand your needs – and mine. You are not like *him.*' Her contempt for the man they'd left behind in Orkney showed. Neither of them would forget that Thorbjorn thought nothing of forcing a woman. '*That* has nothing to do with us or how we are. I miss you too, how we could be if we were alone together.'

'I can't do this, Hlif. Seeing each other every day, so close but unable to touch. I shall go crazy.'

'I feel the same.' Her hand dropped from his arm and he didn't dare reach out to her again. The proximity was too much. He stepped back, further away, turning to go back to the hall before he lost control.

'I know what we can do,' she murmured in a low voice. 'If you are brave enough.'

'Anything!' His answer was instant but was he sure? Was he brave enough? A premonition chilled his skin, raised the hairs on the back of his neck.

'We can meet in the dream world,' she told him, as if the dream world was a house on a street. Maybe to her, it was as ordinary as that. 'Do you remember the ancient tomb and the dragon?'

How could he forget? Back home in Orkneyjar on a snowy winter's night. Scrambling through a hole in the roof of the burial chamber they'd called Orkhaugr, and down the scree of stones into the shelter that was even more perilous than the blizzard outside.

Rognvald and his men carving rune messages into those outraged walls, rousing some creature from the deep past that only Skarfr saw. The dragon.

While Hlif watched through her seer's eyes, Skarfr was tested and proved true. The proof was carved into the wall of the chamber and twinned on Skarfr's arm in his tattoo. A reminder of the Midsummer Solstice when he found his voice as a skald. A reminder that nothing would mute him ever again and fear would never be his master.

So why was he afraid at the thought of returning to that place, even in his mind? Of meeting Hlif in the dream world?

Payment is always taken.

He shivered. 'I don't like you using your powers. There will be a price to pay.'

He heard a shrug in her voice. 'Then I will pay it. When the Jarl calls on my skills to read runes, I must obey, and he never asks how it makes me feel.'

There was no bitterness in her voice and Skarfr understood. Her role as a wise woman was as important to her as being a warrior was to him. If Rognvald commanded him to make a last stand against impossible odds, he would obey his leader's decision, not feel hurt that the man did not value his life. A man's own death was nothing. But Hlif's death would break him. That was what he most feared. That she would walk between worlds and never come back to him. How hard it was to accept that a woman cared about honour too, not just her man's but her own. That she had as much right to take risks as he did.

'It hurts too much,' he said. 'You taunting the gods in this way. I am afraid for you.'

'Don't be. I am not a little girl anymore, afraid of the ghosts. I walk with them and learn. And I would rather use my gifts to be with you than to predict what our shipmates will quarrel about next!'

One moment less. One moment less. And he was wasting time on an argument he was bound to lose. He always did. Not because he was too weak but because his love for Hlif was too strong. Never for a moment did it cross his mind that what she offered him was impossible. If she said they could be together in the dream world, then so they would be.

He looked around him, seeking a sign to convince her that this was madness, or seeking a sign for his own reassurance but there was only a slice of moon and a dog barking. No dragon, no cormorant, no pathfinder runes pointing the way.

He held out a little longer. 'No!' What would she have to do to make such a thing possible? 'We will anger the gods even thinking of using the way between worlds in such a manner.'

'I think the gods will understand.' Hlif's voice was cool and distant. 'After all, they know the fates we have borne since childhood.'

'And the fates to come. We must be careful.' Skarfr's voice held a plea but for what, he no longer knew. He just knew something scared him and not on his own behalf.

'Exactly,' said Hlif. 'We must be careful. This way we can be together without Rognvald knowing.'

She took his silence for assent.

'Picture that place as you shut your eyes before sleep and I will find you there, in the dream world, where we can be free.'

'It shall be so,' Skarfr agreed, doom-ridden.

'We'd better go back,' she said, without moving.

He was glad she found it hard to leave him, even more so when she confessed, 'I thought Havelok was real. It was Rognvald who told me he wasn't. I liked Grim.'

'You'll pay for that, you hussy!' he told her, laughing, feeling as if the burden he carried was lighter.

'Only if you catch me,' she teased.

Then she left him, an airy sprite floating along the empty street, as if they were still two children on an Orkneyjar beach, bonded for life.

He hung back to let Hlif go into the hall well before him, and then worried that he'd taken so long she might be asleep, and he'd missed whatever strange ritual would bring them together.

Slipping quietly into the hall, he found his place among his sleeping companions and lay down, tucked under his cloak, head on his pack. He closed his eyes, taking himself back to the cold stone interior of the ancient tomb, the snow coming through the hole in the roof and whitening the rock scree he'd just clambered down. He laid his hand on the dragon he'd carved on the wall, traced the cormorant embedded in its body like a sword.

Skarfr.

Her voice thrummed like a lute string made from his gut and when he turned she was there, summoned by love.

'*Elskan min*, sweetheart.'

His words drew her the last three steps across the chamber floor and they melded into one. She was as real as freckled skin and fiery hair. Nobody watched them. The dragon on his arm rippled approval as Skarfr stopped worrying about how fast moments passed.

Make them precious, breathed the dragon.

CHAPTER 8

SKARFR

*Wealth is like
the twinkling of an eye –
no friend could be more faithless.*

The Wanderer's Hávamál

Skarfr awoke with a start, adjusted to the reality of men stirring and performing their morning ablutions all around him. They combed their hair and beards after a perfunctory face wash, using hands dipped in the buckets provided. Cursing himself for being last to use the greying water, Skarfr cast surreptitious glances at his fellows. Surely his night activities must have disturbed every man sleeping in the hall. He remembered crying Hlif's name, which would be more than enough to condemn him without all the other memories that made him feel refreshed, despite the dirty water.

Nobody showed any sign that he'd behaved oddly during the night although Cup-bearer Roaldsson did ask, 'What's put a smile on your face so early in the morning?'

'A night lying stretched out,' replied Skarfr with the easy bonhomie of seafarers on shore.

'A day haggling over dried fish and barrels of ale will wipe it off,' commented Jón Halt-foot.

Skarfr tried to look as if his spirits were dampened at the thought of accompanying their provisions mistress on her rounds but the prospect of legitimate time with Hlif, on Rognvald's orders, filled him with joy. He would not find it hard to treat her with mere camaraderie after the night they had enjoyed, and he would only have to pass the daylight hours in honest toil before having Hlif to himself again. His previous fears of what she might pay for walking between worlds had vanished like haar in the joy of finding somewhere they could be alone. The dream world belonged to them now.

Morning brought a sense of purpose to the company, with only one day in which to overhaul the ships and to make the most of the benefits of being on land, whether meat stew or women. Those unlucky enough to be switching places with the crew guarding the ships mostly had hangovers severe enough to prove they'd doubly profited from their time on shore.

Their Jarl did not, however, show signs either of a hangover or of enthusiasm for the delights of Grimsby. Unusually surly, he did not break the morning fast, pausing at table only to speak to Eindridi and Jón, as Skarfr trailed behind him, ignoring his own hunger pangs.

After a curt greeting, Rognvald said, 'I'm not needed if you're there checking the ships over, Eindridi.'

A little smile played about Eindridi's lips as he replied, 'No, Jarl Rognvald. If I'm there, you're not needed,' but the words sounded innocent enough and Rognvald ignored any insolent intent.

'Good,' said the Jarl. 'Jón, keep an eye on the men in the town and make sure no hotheads cause trouble. There's a purse here that you can use judiciously, if need be, to smooth any ruffled feathers.' He handed over the purse, a small leather scrip with a drawstring, not unlike Hlif's bag of runes or the pouch Coal-pilot had hidden.

Rognvald declared, 'I shall go alone to the abbey and talk with the black friars, seek their blessing for our pilgrimage.' So, after the rune reading the day before, today was to be Christian confession day. The usual see-saw of guilt and repentance, neither affecting Rognvald's compulsion to consult the runes.

Eindridi was right: Bishop William would disapprove of the rune-readings and give Rognvald a hard time. But no doubt the black friars would be more tolerant if well enough motivated. The Jarl would not have given Jón his only purse, thought Skarfr cynically.

Whatever the confusion in Rognvald's soul, there was none in his orders. 'Skarfr, go with Hlif to buy provisions for the journey. You'll need handcarts and men to take the goods to the ships. Just do as Hlif tells you to – she knows her work.'

Skarfr's heart lifted but he tried not to show too much enthusiasm for his assignment. Rognvald must not know that he'd given his skald the prospect of a thoroughly enjoyable day.

His sense of well-being lasted all the way through loading barrels of dried fish and ale onto handcarts and sending them to the ships but it did fade during a long debate between Hlif and a cobbler over some job she wanted done straightaway, using an offcut of leather. As far as Skarfr could work out, she would only pay the asking price for a pair of boots if the cobbler did this other job free and the craftsman was most unhappy with the proposal.

'It will take me hours,' he said. 'How am I to feed my wife and family if my orders for other customers are delayed because I'm working for you?'

Hlif beamed at him. 'Why didn't you say so in the first place, dear man? Then I shall pay you in dried fish and your wife will love you for all the better.'

This was not at all the outcome for which the cobbler had angled but he succumbed to Hlif's logic. Skarfr wasn't thrilled either as he had to get the fish out of the barrel and weigh the required amount in a new receptacle. At least the process was speeded up once Hlif verified the accuracy of the cobbler's small weights, using those attached to her belt, and permitted the use of the bigger ones on his scales.

Impatient now, Skarfr watched the cobbler fashioning a long

strip of leather, like a thin belt but at least twice the length of even Jón's girth. Following Hlif's instructions, he used a gimlet to make holes, then attached a buckle at the end where the holes were, which made no sense at all. When he'd finished stitching the little buckle in place, the cobbler said, 'There. All done'

'Perfect, thank you,' Hlif told him. 'And it took you less time than you spent arguing about the price.'

His mouth set, the cobbler gave Hlif the boots and the belt-thing.

She told Skarfr, 'I'm finished now.' He heaved a sigh of relief. No more worrying that she'd haggle her way into a fight; finally they could return to their temporary accommodation, going slowly so as to make the most of the time.

'You're not usually as…' he searched for a word that wouldn't come back to bite him.

'Unyielding?' she suggested and he nodded gratefully. 'They don't know me here; I won't be back and they hope to cheat a little country girl with a foreign accent.'

'Well, you taught them to think again.' Skarfr thought he was probably safe saying so, but he was never sure when she wanted him to admire her independent spirit and when she wanted him to be protective.

'I did, didn't I.' The streets which had been empty the night before were now bustling. The fishy smell suggested that the catch of the day had made it up from the harbour to various households in the town. Grimsby residents were either about their usual work or waylaying the visiting pilgrims, endeavouring to sell them everything from pies to pikestaffs.

Skarfr was tempted by the pikestaffs but Hlif was charging ahead, intent on getting back to their lodging.

'Mind where you're going!' Skarfr pushed back against a man jostling him and he maintained a safe space around Hlif, who paid no more attention to the throng than she did to the crew on the dragon ship.

Just men being men, she would say.

'What is the leather thing?' he asked, no longer able to contain his curiosity, even though he knew she was likely to make him guess or tease him with outrageous fancies.

As she did. 'A leash for One-eye,' she said.

'No, seriously. What is it?'

'A leash for One-eye,' she replied with a hint of impatience.

He sighed. He would never be able to distinguish between truth and fiction. The leather thing was, unbelievably, a leash for One-eye.

Whether Bishop William would hate the cat more, or less, if One-eye were tethered, was yet to be seen. It was unlikely to make the beast better-tempered and he would still stalk the ship with a piratical swagger when on rat-duty. With a cat's unerring instinct for targeting the person who most detested him, One-eye would rub up against the bishop, shedding hair and making him sneeze. Then the cat would freeze, back arched, hissing and giving every indication there was an undead rat on the bishop's thigh. One-eye would swipe the enemy with unsheathed claws unless Hlif was in time to avoid bloodshed (the bishop's blood). If his mistress scooped him up, One-eye became a purring, cuddly toy, to the annoyance of every man on the ship. But she would hear no criticism of her cat.

'Not for on the ship,' proceeded Hlif blithely, 'but for trips ashore.'

Appalled, Skarfr opened his mouth to voice his objections but was distracted by a scuffle, a blockage in the movement of the crowd that made him draw his dagger and shove his way through to the source of the problem.

A man trying to do the reverse smacked straight into him and dropped the object he was carrying. Skarfr recognised Matt-Hair, who was now bending to pick up a leather drawstring bag.

He reached for it, twisting to get under Skarfr's outstretched arm but Skarfr was quicker, scooping up the pouch and concealing it in one deft motion as he smacked Matt-Hair in the face with the other arm. All those sessions training with Thorbjorn in glima wrestling had hardened muscles, quickened reactions and made winning moves instinctive.

Skarfr whirled, tripped the man as he tried to flee, kneed him in the back and pinned him against the mud path, chopping Matt-hair's arm with his hand. The dagger flew out of reach as Matt-hair's arm jerked instinctively.

Thank you, Thorbjorn, thought Skarfr, maintaining his hold.

A circle had formed around the scene: at its centre were Skarfr and Matt-hair, and Hlif leaning over a body. Skarfr already knew who lay there.

'Is he alive?' he asked Hlif, keeping full pressure on the man under his knee.

'No,' she answered, her voice wavering. 'He's been knifed in the back.' She lowered her voice so only he could hear her. 'He said, "Skarfr owns it now. He will use it well." Whatever that means.'

Skarfr could feel the lumpy shape of the pouch under his shirt but there was no time to solve mysteries. He kept up the pressure on the man he'd pinned and yelled, 'This man's a thief and a murderer!'

'Why don't you just kill him? If you're not man enough, there's plenty who are!' someone jeered.

A woman's voice added, 'Shipmates, they are. Thick as all thieves are. There was two of them did it, so this is just a bit of play-acting to get off without paying for what he done.'

'Who cares?' said another. 'One foreigner kills another, what's it to us?'

'Your lord and mine uphold the law,' roared Skarfr. 'And this is no shipmate of mine! He's broken the peace and a good man is dead, a man from—' where was he from? '—Newcastle. A regular here and a good man. He deserves justice and so does his family. Give me some rope and I'll take this bastard to your lord and mine for judgement. You can follow me to see it done.'

Someone threw a piece of rope to Skarfr, who bound Matt-hair's hands behind his back. The evidence of the crime lay still and bloody in the street. Skarfr could hardly leave him there, but he couldn't carry a corpse *and* haul this criminal along the street. He didn't trust anyone else with the live man but the dead was beyond harm.

'You,' he ordered a lanky youth, who was staring open-mouthed at the day's excitement. 'Get the dead man into that handcart and follow me.' Two of the lad's friends eagerly grabbed the body. Hlif winced as they manhandled it into the cart. The strange procession passed the guards at the entrance, and carried on into Neville's hall.

Rognvald and Neville jumped to their feet, and Skarfr pushed Matt-Hair to his knees in front of them.

'My lord, this man murdered Coal-pilot. Half the people in this hall witnessed it and I bring him to you for judgement.'

Which lord he was speaking to was not clear but Rognvald answered first. 'The tide is good; the ships need no repair, so we leave on the morning tide. This man will not leave with us.'

Neville nodded grimly. 'I'll send word to the Reeve. He administers justice here – or approves it after the fact. The man will get what he deserves.'

'And so will Coal-pilot's family,' said Rognvald heavily, removing a silver arm-ring and breaking it. He handed over two pieces to Neville. 'Please send this to them and tell them he was a good man who served us well.'

The burgess nodded again. 'Ships come each week from Coal-pilot's home town. It shall be done.'

He ordered, 'Take Coal-pilot and bury him with respect.' Then he strode over to Matt-Hair and punched him in the face, making Skarfr stagger as his prisoner reeled and the rope took the strain. 'And take this piece of shit to the hanging tree so the crows can start their work. May his name be forgotten. He had no honour.'

Skarfr had to be reminded to let go of the rope so the guards could take Matt-Hair. He'd been holding it so tightly, his hand was rubbed raw and red. The blood rushed back, stinging and prickling.

Why had he not mentioned the robbery and the bag that was tucked inside his cloak? He needed to see Rognvald alone as something about this murder troubled him, beyond the waste of life.

CHAPTER 9

SKARFR

*The ignorant man
does not know how little he knows.*

The Wanderer's Hávamál

Although Skarfr had been as keen to discover the land pleasures of Grimsby as any of the crew, he was not sorry to leave. He patted his chest frequently to check Coal-pilot's leather scrip was still hidden below his shirt on the leather thong he'd tied to it but he dared not investigate the contents with so many greedy eyes around him. He knew it was not coins. Through the leather, he could feel a chunky object, too big to be a jewel – unless it was one to be set into a crown. Too small to be a part of a weapon, like a hilt or crosspiece. The leather blunted any guess at texture. He must bide his time and then catch Rognvald alone, to share what he knew and confide his misgivings.

Easier said than done with fifteen ships rocking in the harbour, ready to sail, and fourteen captains gathered around Rognvald, awaiting orders. Or enduring orders, as the case might be.

Hlif was already on board the *Sun-chaser*, presumably wasting her attention on that ugly rodent-bane, if Bishop William hadn't dispatched the creature while they were ashore. Luckily, all her barrels and provisions were on board the ships, so that was one less task to distract Skarfr from Rognvald's briefing.

'There aren't many harbours like this where we know we can tie up fifteen ships and find a welcome for three hundred men,' the Jarl was saying.

'We can *make* ourselves welcome,' yelled one joker, who'd clearly enjoyed himself the day before, to judge by the comments that followed.

Rognvald raised his voice and the men quietened. 'We are strongest as a fleet but if we splinter into two or three groups for overnight shelter and forage, there is no harm in that. I will sound the horn each day and hove to if I can, until I see the rest of you before setting sail again. Cup-bearer and Norð-Erling, you stay with me, whatever happens.'

The two captains nodded.

The Jarl had chosen well: Cup-bearer and Norð-Erling, a Norwegian nobleman, were both loyal and experienced.

'Eindridi and Magnus Havardsson, you can split the twelve ships as you and the captains choose, if need be.'

Magnus, a trustworthy Orkneyman, nodded. Before he could speak, Eindridi rattled off five captains' names and the division was made. Eindridi's selection also showed discernment. Men loyal and experienced – but not necessarily to Rognvald.

The Jarl seemed to ignore the sour droop to Magnus's mouth but Skarfr was certain Eindridi's arrogance had been noted. Again.

'Wind and wave might separate us, in which case every captain must do what is best for his ship and crew. Eindridi and some of his men are the only ones who've made this journey before and if I've understood him correctly, our only sure place of a welcome for fifteen ships is Narbonne so if we *are* separated, we meet there.'

Skarfr caught fleeting expressions cloud Eindridi's gaze – surprise and irritation at Rognvald stealing his thunder as the fount of all navigational wisdom. Then the captain responded to Rognvald's glance with a curt nod of confirmation.

The Jarl went on briskly, 'So it makes sense to have a man on my ship who knows the journey, and one on Bishop William's too, as well as what pilots we can pick up on the way.'

The atmosphere changed, tension in the air. This was something unexpected. And unwanted, judging by the clouds gathering once more on Eindridi's face.

Of course. He 'and some of his men' knew the route. Rognvald intended to poach Eindridi's crew. The captain would never accept such a public insult. However veiled in courtesy, the implication was that he couldn't be trusted.

Skarfr watched Eindridi's hands, shifting his weight, preparing to launch himself. One move towards his sword or dagger and Skarfr would floor him. A headbutt in the guts should suffice; the man had it coming.

'My men are used to my ways.' Eindridi had come to the same conclusions as Skarfr. 'They would be a liability on any other ship.' *Meaning: don't take my men. I'm warning you.*

Watch his hands, Skarfr reminded himself. He'd learned this lesson sparring with Thorbjorn, who used his gift for amusing chatter or shocking insult to advantage when distracting an opponent at the crucial moment. Thorbjorn himself had analysed every tactic he used against his young protégé, made Skarfr turn every weapon against the wielder. Until Skarfr *was* the weapon, a warrior forged by a master-craftsman.

Eindridi was no Thorbjorn. He mistook high self-esteem for worthiness and Rognvald played on that.

'I would never take your men,' Rognvald assured his captain, 'I merely want to borrow two, in exchange for two of my own. I am over-endowed with skalds while you have none to bruit your fame abroad when we return.'

Skarfr stiffened. Surely, Rognvald would not banish him to Eindridi's company on such an adventure. Not when there were others less gifted as skalds or as bodyguards. Not when Rognvald had expressly tasked Skarfr with the telling of his saga, one day, when the story was complete? How could Skarfr tell such a story if he was not at his lord's side, riding the seas with him?

He calmed his breathing, named the other skalds who could be the pawns in this exchange. The obvious choices were Armód, whose song before Grimsby was much repeated; Oddi the Little, or Sigmund Ongul.

'Skarfr will sail with Eindridi,' announced Rognvald, and the rest of his words turned to a screech-owl's hunting call, unintelligible and doom-ridden.

He knows, thought Skarfr. *He's punishing me for Hlif.*

The urge to confess, to throw himself on Rognvald's mercy, ask for Hilf's hand, promise *any* service, was so strong he would have thrown himself to his knees but before he could do so the Jarl clasped his arm.

Breath warm on Skarfr's ear, Rognvald whispered, 'I trust only you. Be my eyes and ears on that ship.'

A reprieve. *He doesn't know.*

'You'll find my man true in word and deed,' Rognvald told Eindridi, who could hardly object to being offered the Jarl's finest warrior, regardless of his skaldic talents. Skarfr wasn't convinced that 'true in word' was what Eindridi hoped for in a man and he knew how far short of such a glowing endorsement he fell as regards deeds. If Rognvald only knew…

But he didn't. Shame warred with relief and Skarfr could only comply with his orders. He shouldered his backpack and followed Eindridi. He hadn't taken in the name of the crewman taking his place with Rognvald until he saw Horse-snipper leaving the *Crest-cleaver*.

Now it was too late to warn the Jarl and he must hope to find time with Rognvald in some foreign harbour, soon.

※

Grey churning seas made no distinction between one captain and another, nor between one sailor and his replacement. From necessity, Skarfr and Eindridi worked together, at first in sullen resignation, and then with reluctant respect as each gained the measure of the other's seamanship.

The ships were all organised the same way, divided into six sections with about eight men in each. The men's duties matched their placement on board. Skarfr had always worked aft, beside the captain. When younger, he'd attended to braces and sheets, the ropes attached to the wooden yard spar and the corners at the bottom of the sail. Pulling on these would change the angle of the sail. He could still lend a hand on this duty if needed, just as he could row if required – all the men could. But he'd become invaluable relieving the pilot or the captain on the steerboard, a task that required both strength and navigation skills.

The day was also divided into six sections: watch and sleep alternating three times a day, whether sun or stars were in the sky. Eindridi chose to keep Skarfr beside him for his steerboard skills. Inevitably, voyaging together bridged their antipathy.

An unexpected boon was gaining that knowledge of the journey which had proved a bone of contention between Eindridi and the Jarl from the very start. The *Crest-cleaver's* captain pointed out the chalk cliffs that marked their crossing from Angland to the Frankish coast, their course south-west.

Then he set the sail to catch the east wind and the fickle tide. Fourteen longships did likewise, their full sails and common goal lifting Skarfr's spirits.

'You thought the Pentlandsfjord was dangerous,' Eindridi told Skarfr, brushing wind-whipped hair out of his eyes. 'This channel between the English and Frankish lands has double high waters, so if you get the tide right and have the wind with you, the ship will fly. Get it wrong and you'll be driven backwards. Then there's the cross-currents and eddies. The sea can froth to a frenzy. This is where the sea-gods race their white horses, as fast as lightning, collecting ships for their stone palaces underwater.'

When Eindridi told his travel tales, Skarfr could see the *Crest-cleaver* as a wreck on the seabed, with shoals of small fish darting through the oar-holes. If they successfully navigated these forbidding waters, Eindridi made clear that it was entirely thanks to the expertise of the most travelled member of the expedition. The fourteen ships which followed his lead should be suitably grateful.

Despite Skarfr's mistrust of Eindridi's much-vaunted experience, his sense of adventure grew ever stronger as he listened to the captain. He discovered new lands in his imagination and wondered about the people who lived there. People whose forebears had lived there for hundreds of years while his own world stretched no further than the Jarl's *Bu* at Orphir.

They sailed west, then south, still hugging the Frankish coast. Bishop William could speak the foreign tongue, having studied at the University of Paris; he almost rivalled Eindridi in his new status as expert. But he lacked the latter's flamboyance and merely used his skill to find pilots.

This took time because the locals tended to head for the hills when they saw the square sails, but if the other ships hung back and the bishop went ashore with a small party on the landing boat, he sometimes got close enough to speak with the villagers.

Eventually he found two pilots, who spoke traders' Norse and a variety of other languages. Rognvald claimed one for himself and placed the other with Eindridi, who protested against the unnecessary addition to his crew. He knew his way well enough, and his sword spoke all the languages needed en route.

Despite Eindridi's objections, *the Crest-cleaver* gained Pilot, a wiry man whose deep brown eyes were always fixed on a distant horizon and whose wrinkled, golden skin spoke of southern origins and long journeys in all weathers. Eindridi varied his own watch so that sometimes Skarfr had Pilot for company and sometimes the captain, learning more about both of them.

'Good wine and fine foods to be had here but they'll eat your hand off for our wool, raw or dyed,' Eindridi commented on the local trades as they hugged the Frankish coast. But he and his crew were not traders and at the sight of their sleek drakkars, the small fishing boats sped for home.

'Gone to tell their wives to set the tables for us,' joked Mouthy, a seaman so ancient his gummy mouth was innocent of even one blackened tooth. He'd told Skarfr he planned to see Jórsalaheim before he died. He might see his dream come true, but it seemed unlikely he'd make it back home, and Eindridi must know that. Truly, all men had many sides to them.

And whatever Rognvald expected Skarfr to report on Eindridi, he could only speak true. That the captain spoke no ill of the Jarl, ran a tight ship and knew where he was going. That Eindridi's arrogance, which Skarfr had condemned, seemed less heinous, the more he realised it was built on a foundation of knowledge and experience, not just on a grand scale but in small practical details.

Were it not for Eindridi, the men's skin would have fried to a crisp with their first taste of southern sun. He told them to make a clay paste on shore and to smear it on their faces and any parts of their bodies exposed while on watch. When resting, they used their oiled cloaks as shade tents.

Sensitive-skinned and ever observant, Hlif was quick to take Skarfr's hint about this behaviour, when they managed a few words on a beach-stop. Soon, all the ships had a pot of clay aboard, which could be scooped out with a damp hand to gain skin protection. Hlif still covered most of her face with a swathe of linen improvised from a wimple, but she too used clay where needed, on the backs of her neck and hands.

When the captain had talked of his first, successful journey to Jórsalaheim, Skarfr had not realised the scope of the adventure. Rognvald himself had been inspired by Eindridi's tales. Was Eindridi so wrong to see himself as the obvious choice of leader, unfairly passed over for someone who merely outranked him? Skarfr began to wonder as fair winds allowed the kind of talk men shared at sea.

CHAPTER 10

SKARFR

*In every hand hidden by a cloak
I expect to see a weapon.*

The Wanderer's Hávamál

Despite fair weather and inhabitants who weren't hostile unless provoked, the Frankish coast was not without dangers. The fact that many were invisible, made them all the more dangerous. The local name for the sea was in itself a warning; Bishop William knew it in Latin as the *Mare Tenebrarum* and translated it as the Sea of Shadows.

Two men died crossing a narrow channel of shallow seawater from a sandy beach to a settlement the other side, hoping to bring back provisions. They were sober and careful. They took a few steps, pointed to the level of the water on their legs – barely up to their calves. They waved cheerfully, took a few more steps, then screamed as they dropped down, as if over a shelf. A churn of water took their footing and dragged them down, in front of their horrified shipmates who did not dare attempt a rescue.

Even Rognvald, for all his strength and experience as a swimmer, watched and did nothing. He gave his sombre judgement. 'We will only lose more men to this monster.'

When the tide receded completely, they understood what made the monster. The sea had retreated but a channel of water remained. Cautiously, Skarfr walked to its edge and threw a pebble in. As he expected, it plummeted, deep and out of sight, even though the water was clearer here now the tide was out. Skarfr knelt, scooped a handful of the water and tasted it, prepared to spit out the salty liquid.

It was freshwater. He filled his waterskin and returned to the camp.

'It's a river mouth,' he told Rognvald.

The Jarl looked grim. 'When the sea tide meets the river's current, no man stands a chance. And the river runs deep, hidden through the core of the seawater.'

'It could have been any of us,' Jón said.

Rognvald broke the silence. 'Fill your waterskins now, while you can see the river. And be careful!'

There was no banter as men obeyed.

As long as they stayed on their beach, they were safe. All of the ships were checked over and minor repairs conducted, replacing nails and a rope.

When the tide turned again, Skarfr looked at the short walk across the shallow seawater to the settlement. He thought about the death running through the middle, lurking. Once you knew it was there, you could never again see the village as close. Or as friendly.

On one occasion, the *Sun-chaser* needed a sail patched, a simple matter of sewing the sides of a tiny rip together to stop it worsening. Eindridi recommended to Rognvald that he head for the coast straightaway, while the rest of the company anchored at sea and waited.

'No!' The *Crest-cleaver*'s pilot yelled across to the Jarl. 'They call that the 'Death Coast' because of the rocks as you approach the shore. Sail on further!'

'He is mistaken,' Eindridi said, with a face like thunder.

Is he? wondered Skarfr. And if Pilot was right, had Eindridi known of the coast's reputation and sent Rognvald there anyway?

Skarfr only saw Hlif on shore and their dreamwalks were rare. Neither knew which watch the other was on and sometimes Skarfr was too tired to conjure up their trysting place before he fell asleep. She looked wan and he worried about her.

He overheard Rognvald asking her if she felt better, and his heart flipped to think she might be ill.

Her eyes flicked to Skarfr as she answered. 'I'm fine. It was just the rebound of the swell when we anchored off the coast. That always makes me seasick.'

'I told you this voyage was no place for a woman,' muttered Jón Halt-foot.

The next time Skarfr saw Hlif, she was smiling and herself again, giving Jón as good as she got, if he started carping.

In between such dramas, there was time for Eindridi to tell the tales that had made Rognvald dream of this expedition in the first place.

'Jórsalaheim is worth visiting, with miracles daily for those who can afford the intervention of the crooks who serve themselves by serving the saints,' Eindridi told him. 'And you can buy a pilgrim's badge to take home.'

'What's on the badge?' asked Skarfr.

Eindridi laughed. 'Whatever you want,' he said. 'The Virgin and Child, a palm leaf, a cross – or any saint you choose. Say what you want and if it's not for sale already, it'll be metal-worked within a day, and you'll be told it's an ancient relic.'

Skarfr's anticipation of visiting the holy city took a dent from this cynical description, but Eindridi's tales were not all disappointing.

'Wait until you see Mikligard, city of cities, as big as the whole realm of Orkneyjar, one city as rich as all of the Frankish lands. With as much gold in the lowliest home as there is peat in Orkneyjar. And an emperor whose palace is filled with singing birds and women veiled only in perfume. Whose realm stretches over vast deserts and motionless seas.'

When Eindridi spoke of Mikligard, Skarfr could *see* the golden city and his heart leaped at the prospect of walking paved streets, of bathing in the streams of hot water that ran through the palaces. He was less entranced at the idea of eating with some tool known as a fork, which seemed likely only to complicate the natural pleasure of eating. But when he heard about the Varangian Guard, Skarfr understood how small Orkneyjar – and its jarls – must seem to Eindridi.

'The emperor, Manuel Komnenos, asked me to join the Varangian Guard,' Eindridi said, pride in his voice. Yet for once, there was nothing of the braggart in his words, no embroidery.

'You've trained with the King's Hird in Norðvegr, Skarfr. Imagine an elite troop like that but an army a hundred times bigger and better, the personal guard of an emperor, the only men he trusts.'

Skarfr remembered his summer with the Hird, honing his skills as a warrior, learning strategies for fighting at sea, for battle on horseback, for protecting a king. How could there be a fighting force better than the Hird? And yet Eindridi was not a man to give praise lightly.

'And why does he trust them?' the captain continued. 'Because every man is a foreigner, loyal only to the emperor, not to any of the warring families that play Mikligard politics with poison and partisans. And which foreigners does the emperor recruit? Norðmen! Because we are the best warriors in the world.'

'You served with the Varangian Guard.' Skarfr couldn't help his awe showing.

'I did.'

'Why did you leave them? The same emperor is there now, isn't he? Will he welcome you, if you left his guard, when he values loyalty so much?' There was so much Skarfr wanted to know.

Eindridi's tone chilled, as the sea loses sparkle when clouds hide the sun. 'You ask too many questions. You will see Mikligard for yourself, after Jórsalaheim, which is your Jarl's goal.' The sneer was back. Perhaps Skarfr shouldn't have mentioned loyalty.

Unlike his tales of Mikligard, Eindridi's descriptions of Jórsalaheim did not inspire enthusiasm. This was not the same place he'd shown Rognvald in his stories. It was as if Eindridi wanted to spoil Skarfr's innocent anticipation. 'There are more pilgrims than residents, and more services to pilgrims than a man could pay for in a year a-viking. And a widowed trollop for a queen, who – unbelievably! – pretends she can rule without a man's authority.

'Not a court worth visiting. No hospitality for Norðmen from such an ignorant collection of many-hued races. The holiest place in Christendom has the unholiest men – and woman – in power. Unlike Mikligard, where the very windows, walls and tessellated floors shine with jewelled saints in gilded haloes.'

So much for Hlif's hopes of redemption in a Jórsalaheim shrine and of Rognvald's blessing on their marriage. Neither she nor Skarfr could donate jewels or precious books as offerings. Such riches were well beyond their means.

He was conscious of Coal-pilot's pouch, now become a familiar accessory. He had not dared take the object out and examine it, with so many sea-rovers around him at all times. Nor did he want to explain to Eindridi how he'd come by it. There was still the matter of Eindridi's man being Coal-pilot's killer, of the conversation at table when Coal-pilot let the pouch be seen.

When taking his rest between the thwarts, Skarfr had slipped his hand into the pouch and tried to make out what he had gained in such a bloody manner. His fingers traced the sides of a block, with six sides, he thought. Too lightweight for gold and rougher-edged. Like the coal he'd seen in Grimsby in weight but not in shape. This was squarer, more even-sided, a bit like a huge die. And this block left no traces of black on his hand when he withdrew it from the pouch.

It was too big for a raw jewel, unless it was one that would start a war, but it had something of the jewel about it. Something hewn. Maybe a stone blessed by a saint – or a rune-stone with a witch's spell laid on it. Maybe this would be an offering suitable for a saint and Hlif would have her wish.

Which saint? he wondered. Would the other saints be offended by her choosing one and lay a different curse upon her? What price would be taken? He must talk to Hlif about Pilot's legacy.

But he never did. When he closed his eyes, he would conjure up the ancient tomb, the place where they could be together in dreams. Sometimes he would find her there and know sweet release and new poems, which came back to the waking world with him.

But he never remembered when dream-walking to pose questions about Coal-pilot's purse.

On rare occasions, the fifteen ships found a beach broad enough to accommodate them all and men caught up with gossip from their hours apart. Hlif took an inventory of their plunder and foraging, shared out provisions for store and to cook on the fires she'd organised. She was everyone's housekeeper and nobody's woman.

She didn't even glance at Skarfr as she went about her duties, allocating jobs with her usual efficiency, her status reinforced by the implicit otherworldly threat of her yowling companion. The goddess Freyja's cats pulled her chariot: Hlif's stalked beside her on his leather leash.

Nobody truly believed Hlif was a völva, a seer wielding Freyja's magic, but nobody wanted to put it to the proof. Not with the essential catness of One-eye challenging all that was normal by padding beside his mistress, tail whipping in disdain. There was no doubting who'd get the best portion of freshly fried fish when it was available, fairness without favour applying only to humans.

Skarfr felt a stir of something very like jealousy. Of a cat! But he knew Hlif could not acknowledge him in public. He could not arch his back and rub his side against her legs in such ecstasy he nearly fell over. He could not drape his body around her neck like a scarf, nor hang on one shoulder as if it were a branch of the tree Yggdrasil that linked the worlds of men and gods.

She didn't even serve him personally but passed food along the line to him, as if he were nobody special to her.

Nevertheless, he took his share of the fish and bread, and ate it with the pleasure hunger gives. Not bannocks, he noted. Some fresh, lighter bread, found by the men in a scavenging hunt among some fishermen's cottages, which had been abandoned in a hurry not unconnected with the appearance of fifteen square sails.

Fine food, Eindridi had said. Skarfr took a swig from the leather bottle being passed around. *And good wine.*

He arranged his pack as a lumpy pillow, drew his cloak around him and savoured the pleasure of stretching out his long limbs. Of moving without the worry that he'd rock the ship or blacken a shipmate's eye by accident. No need to be careful, except with Hlif.

He sighed, closed his eyes, pictured stone walls, a slide of rock from the broken roof onto the earthen floor. Light from the tunnel entrance painting a shadow on the floor. A shadow that shimmered into wild red hair, laughing sea-grey eyes and a mouth that said, 'Skarfr,' before meeting his lips.

All his resentment disappeared, as did all thought of whatever it was he wanted to ask her. Only the moment mattered. *Together.*

Days passed, sailing in fair winds or foul, sunshine or rain. Nights were spent on shore, when possible, either as a whole fleet or as groups of ships. If the shores were too rocky for landing or the waves too rough, they dropped anchor and took what rest they could in the cramped quarters between thwarts, under the rough tents made by their oiled cloths. The fragrant combination of bilge-water, soil buckets and farts perfumed such nights.

As they continued southwards, the coast was no longer Frankish but Saracen territory, and more nights were spent at anchor than risked on shore. When the company rounded the southern-most headland and changed course eastward, there was a growing sense of exhilaration as the fleet headed for friendly territory.

Trusting Pilot that the narrow straits would indeed lead to the next great stretch of open sea, they sailed past barren land masses and between two bare-rocked land pillars that looked like petrified troll twins, split by Thórr's hammer, still reaching out in the vain effort to touch.

Weeks had turned to months and all was smooth sailing on a sea that was still recognisably grey and boisterous, although it had a different name. No longer the Sea of Shadows but the Miðjarðarhaf, the sea in the middle of the world. As they sailed east, hugging the coast to larboard, they reached the mouth of a wide river on the southern Hispanic coast. What the difference between Frankish and Hispanic was, or which Hispanic territories were occupied by Moors, Skarfr could not divine, despite lectures on the subject from Pilot, whose Norse had improved greatly from their discussions. In exchange, Skarfr gained a smattering of Pilot's languages, and he was fascinated by the tools and tricks of navigation.

The shadow of the sun on Pilot's little wooden board could be read easily and, combined with the tell of the ribbon on the mast, gave them the wind direction. Skarfr was already familiar with the way steerboard and sail worked together, so he picked up quickly on Pilot's contributions, especially his knowledge of this coastline.

Eindridi made it clear he needed no input but Pilot quietly made his readings, observed the shape of the coast and let the captain know they might safely pull in overnight to that particular sheltered cove, or that they should give a wide berth to that rocky island. Though he feigned deafness, Eindridi often followed these suggestions, making it clear by his attitude that his actions were entirely his idea.

As they talked, Skarfr found out as much about Pilot's background as about navigation. He was happy to be called Pilot and needed no other name. He had grown up in Narbonne, taken to the life at sea and had made a living voyaging around this coast since he was seven. The prospect of going back to Narbonne had attracted him to sail on the *Crest-cleaver* even though he knew he would be bored within a month and seeking another ship, another voyage of discovery.

In his turn, Skarfr described his home: wide grey skies and deep lochs, the wind knifing across the fields, cold seas crashing against the cliffs.

Whether either man could picture the other's homeland, or whether he merely envisioned a version of a place he already knew, a bond grew between the two of them.

All of which might help them when Eindridi abandoned them at the mouth of that same wide river on the Hispanic coast.

CHAPTER 11

INGE, NESS

Inge was brusque with her steward. She was trying on her wedding gown and had neither time nor inclination to consider the supplications of some delirious man who'd washed up on the Skottish shore and been brought to her family's stronghold in Ness.

'He insisted Lady Inge would want to hear his news and he will speak to nobody else,' repeated the steward, who must have been impressed by the man's perseverance to come in person on such an errand.

'I heard you the first time,' snapped Inge. 'There are a hundred such men who think they can reach my brothers through me. Or rather reach my brothers' money. Give him food, water and a place to recover, then tell him alms are given weekly at the gate. If I show personal interest in any of these people, I'll have a thousand laying siege to me the next day.'

'And where shall I put him, my lady? There are guests everywhere for the ceremony.'

'How should I know!' She waved an airy hand, observing the fall of the fine wool sleeve with the movement, the way the gold thread in the braided border caught the light. 'The stables or the woodshed – or wherever! He'll be happy with whatever shelter he gets.'

Was she being too harsh? A bride-to-be should show charity. She relented a little. 'I know you'll do your best and it won't do any harm to show this man some kindness. Treat him as if he might be Óðinn the wanderer travelling in disguise and testing our hospitality,' she instructed.

His expression showed scepticism at the possibility.

When her wrist and slim hands sketched her impatience, the steward bowed acquiescence and withdrew. Before he'd even lifted the curtain that separated Inge's quarters from the communal area, she'd forgotten him. Her hands arranged a double row of beads between the gold brooches pinning her overdress. The exquisitely painted blush-hued glass spheres, interspersed with carved bone, were a bridal gift from her husband-to-be but her thoughts were not about him. Against her will, she kept thinking of her first marriage.

Thorbjorn Klerk. Strong and muscular as his two namesakes, god and bear. Dark, dangerous and moody. Seductive when he chose to be. He had not so chosen for their first private encounter, outside the Jarl's hall, at night, against a wall.

Her maid's warning came too late and the over-wrought string broke, spinning beads around the stone flags.

'Freyja's tits!' swore Inge.

The maid hid her blushes as the two women picked up beads and put them on a scarf laid out on Inge's bed. Each rosy bead bore a unique design overlaid in azure and gold, the perfect colours to bring out the blue in Inge's eyes, the pale sunshine of her hair and her milky complexion.

'Thirty-six!' declared Inge at last as she picked up the last one, which had rolled under the curtain. A number she was fast approaching in years, she thought bitterly. She'd been so young when she married for the first time. Was it really eleven years ago?

She added bead number thirty-six to the precious pile, knotted the scarf into a makeshift knapsack and told the maid, 'Take them to Alfhild and ask her to string them urgently. Wait for them. I need them back today as I must wear the beads tomorrow.'

The maid needed no more instruction. Everyone knew Alfhild, the weaver, who also did repair jobs such as bead-stringing. But her tight lips said this was an ill omen as she made her escape through the heavy blue curtain.

Inge hoped no beads were cracked. Everything would be fine as long as they looked all right. That was what mattered at a wedding.

She knew she'd looked beautiful the first time. The Christian ceremony in Orphir's round kirk had taken place on Frigg's Day under Orkneyjar's wide skies, clear blue for the occasion. The best of old Norðmen's traditions combined with the new ones of the White Christ, under the auspices of Jarl Rognvald himself, who was overjoyed at this alliance between Inge's family and his advisor, Thorbjorn Klerk.

Orkneyjar's most powerful men had been there, one of whom she'd married. Another had been her swaggering, sea-roving brother Sweyn, to further whose political aims she'd agreed to the marriage.

She could almost hate her brother at times for his ignorance of a woman's life. His swerving loyalties left his sister drowning in his wake while he sailed new waters. His charmed instinct for enriching himself and surviving every drama did not extend to those closest to him..

Yet she loved him too. How she wished she could defy jarls and kings as he did, laugh off exile and pop up again as an ally to the very men he'd robbed.

For a woman, such a life was impossible. Worse still, as Sweyn's sister, she reaped his whirlwind.

Thorbjorn, she thought again and shivered. Years ago, when she'd escaped him, she'd vowed never to marry again, so what was she doing here, preparing for her wedding the next day?

At first, she'd revelled in the comparative freedom of her family's estate in Ness, Orkneyjar's territory on the mainland, far enough from the island to feel safe from Thorbjorn.

While Sweyn was away at sea, or causing mischief for King David in neighbouring Skotland, or back on their Orkneyjar island of Gareksey, she'd enjoyed taking his place as lord. Especially as she knew she was far better at land management and accounts than her brother, whose response to his bondsmen's complaints usually came in the form of fire, axe, and bloody examples. His approach did indeed reduce the number of complaints but it did not make the land more productive, nor did it increase revenues.

At regular intervals, Sweyn would return to Ness and, in a few days, destroy all Inge had achieved. He and his men would descend like a plague of locusts on their own settlements just as they did on the shores of Írland, leaving empty barns and villagers doomed to starvation.

Inge was not naive enough to challenge him over his cruelty but even her tactful suggestion that he should take only the tithe that was due and leave the villagers thriving so they could produce more the next year, fell on deaf ears.

He laughed at her softness, told her, 'The strong take and the weak give up.' He was a raider to his marrow, like their father, who had died in his Ness longhouse, burned alive in a feud with neighbours.

And Inge was once more merely Sweyn's sister, her voice silenced. However much she'd hated Thorbjorn, her marriage had made her the most influential woman in Jarl Rognvald's hall, filling the empty place of the Jarl's dying wife. Inge had used that influence with a woman's guile. Like a gadfly, she'd pricked her husband to action with stinging words, belittling him so cleverly that onlookers were never sure whether it was intentional.

A substitute mother to the young Jarl Harald, she'd shaped the malleable child like a sapling, so he grew away from Rognvald's grey practicality and towards Sweyn's golden light.

How she missed being at court, shaping events. Instead of a haven, Lambaburg keep had become a cage. She was tired of being 'Sweyn's sister'. She prayed to all the gods that she could endure him during the marriage festivities, which of course he'd insisted on attending, presumably so he could lord it over the feasting.

She considered her options. She could cross the sea and join her mother Asleif on their Orkneyjar island of Gareksey, living in female harmony along with Sweyn's wife and young children.

That dream vanished into sea fog. Gareksey meant daily

complaints about Sweyn from both mother and wife. She could hear them carping. Sweyn rarely visited, he did not love them, he did not treat his wife as he should. He'd fathered two children on her and cared nothing for them until they should grow old enough to go raiding with their father and abandon their mother. Sweyn's wife was an Írish princess, widowed by his hand, so she'd demanded marriage in compensation. His protection had been the worst bargain she'd ever made. As she never tired of pointing out.

Much as Sweyn annoyed Inge, such interminable complaints wearied her, however true they might be and she thought of his wife as *Bleating-booty* . Both her mother and Bleating-booty thought of nobody but Sweyn and his absence weighed on them more than his presence.

Even Inge's younger brother, Gunnr, found the constant reproaches of the women too much and stayed at his own house on Gareksey, well out of earshot. However, he'd destroyed whatever peace he'd known there when he installed his own woman, whose name was known throughout Orkneyjar for all the wrong reasons.

Inge could not decide whether she was more shocked or fascinated by Gunnr's choice, a woman even older than she was, willing to live out of wedlock with a man more than ten years her junior. A woman who also happened to be mother to Orkneyjar's young Jarl. When the Jarl's father died, Margaret Hakonsdottir proved to be a very merry widow indeed and Gunnr was still infatuated with the woman he'd taken home to Gareksey. His mother and sister-in-law were *not* infatuated with Margaret and the small island witnessed volcanic disputes over her scandalous behaviour.

Gunnr had no doubt jumped at the chance of escaping to 'do his duty at his sister's wedding' on the mainland, and Inge would have to put up with both her colourful sea-rover brothers until she was mistress of her own fate, in other words – married. No, the family estate on Gareksey was not an option for Inge and marriage was the only way to escape the tedium of Lambaburg.

But was Finn the right man? He was not the only man willing to brave Inge's reputation as a barren shrew. A reputation she did not refute.

Was she making another mistake? Just because Finn Bessasson was red-blond with freckles, not dark and brooding, did not make him trustworthy. Nor did his lack of ambition.

No, what had won Inge over was his devoted attention to her, starved as she had always been of any interest in her for her own sake, rather than the reflected glory – or resentment – due to Sweyn's sister.

People talked of a man paying his attentions to a woman, but she'd experienced only a brief period of compliments followed by complaisance, mutual sniping or outright cruelty. She'd never known or seen quiet devotion before. Except perhaps from a boy once, who'd grown into a kind man: Skarfr.

Yes, Finn had reminded her of Skarfr, although in looks they were chalk and cheese. Skarfr's black hair and lean muscle spoke of Írish thrall ancestry whereas Finn was all Orkneyman, sunshine hair and skin, bulky as a bear. Finn was also a fresh start, a man who listened to her and responded with his own thoughts, in few words but practical ones. A man who found out what she liked, whether the colour blue or tabby cats. Who learned what mattered to her, whether that was weaving or an investigation of farmers' complaints against her brother's taxes. If he thought she cared about something, he always showed an intelligent interest.

And she'd bedded him, so as not to make *that* mistake a second time. He'd proved equally attentive to her body, surprising her into experiments her old self would have considered wanton. But a divorced woman did not need to consider either the loss of reputation or her brother's opinion. Let brother Sweyn sail his own ship and take his hand off her steerboard!

When she'd said yes to Finn's carefully worded proposal, he'd even voiced his concern over living on his home island of Strjónsey, wondering whether an Orkneyjar island would bring her too close to difficult memories. What he meant was that the entire world knew Thorbjorn had divorced her, so she might prefer to stay further away from those who'd rake over old ashes.

He was safer not knowing the truth, so she didn't enlighten him. If Thorbjorn had preserved his reputation at the cost of hers, he was less likely to do either of them harm.

'Inge?' Finn's voice, low and tender, waiting permission to come through the curtain.

'You can come in,' she told him.

A woman shouldn't be thinking of her previous husband the day before her wedding, but fears are born of experience and she needed to face them. She was moving back to the islands and could not avoid Thorbjorn. He wouldn't hurt her if he were sober: too risky for his reputation now they were divorced. But if they met on a dark night after he'd been drinking, only one of them would return home. She swore it on the name of Freyja's magical torc, Brísingamen.

She shook those thoughts aside as she greeted Finn with a kiss, which he returned gently, carefully.

He held her at arm's length, his clear gaze searching her face. 'Are you sure?' he asked.

Had her kiss tasted of doubts? She met his eyes. 'What woman would hesitate?' she said, smiling as she took his arm to go through the curtain into public view.

CHAPTER 12

INGE, NESS

Inge should not have worried about her own patience snapping but rather about the impact of ale and bad news in heating her brothers' blood. Not that it took much.

As weddings go, the ceremony was unremarkable, as might be expected of a second marriage between worldly-wise adults. Formalities were observed. Once more Inge was married on Friggsday, from respect to the goddess, and blessed by a priest of the White Christ while her hands were bound together with a man's.

But this was a small chapel inland, not the round kirk of Orphir where the wind whipped your hair and smashed waves against the rocks nearby. This was not a ceremony where your heart was black with hatred for the man you were marrying.

'Inge,' whispered Finn, hesitant, reading her face, guessing who she was with but knowing nothing of what it had been like. And she could never tell him.

'Finn,' she replied, her voice firm, loud enough for all present to hear.

'You are *my* wife from this day on, in the eyes of God and man,' he declared, as was the ritual. The priest nodded his approval and turned to Inge.

Was there a challenge in the emphasis on 'my'? Men were so

possessive. 'I am your wife from this day on, in the eyes of God and man,' she echoed, in front of enough witnesses to make it as formal as any man could wish.

This time, there had been no dowry, no one-upmanship between Sweyn and the husband over which of them was the wealthier and the more generous. Practical matters had been resolved quickly and Inge need have no fear that she would lose the dowry she'd reclaimed when she'd left Thorbjorn. Finn had offered all he possessed as bride-price and she knew he meant it, although she'd accepted only a fraction. In case things went sour.

Crashing waves were for the young, for a foolish, romantic Inge who'd died on the eve of her betrothal. This marriage would be peaceful and practical, and if there was disappointment in Finn's eyes this day, she would make it up to him in ways that would last longer than a night's passion.

Light drizzle doused the spirits of even the most determined merrymakers as the procession trudged back along the track from the chapel to the great hall in the tower, where the customary ribaldry fizzled out for lack of a bride who blushed. Inge's expression of contempt as she surveyed the gathering was the final dampener.

Her new husband was no more fun: he declared to those badgering him that he had no need to bury his sword in a beam to prove he wasn't impotent. Instead, he offered his arm to his lady wife and led her to the top table, where they sat down. The other important guests joined them and that was it. As exciting as peat-stacking.

The side tables filled with Asleifsson bondsmen and their women, and with men-at-arms loyal to Finn, Sweyn or Gunnr, their weapons hung behind them on the walls.

The moment all were seated, table boys rushed in from the kitchens with pitchers and trays heaped with bloody meat, steaming hot, carrying the scent of roast boar to every hungry diner's nostrils. The boys distributed bread trenchers and cups. While all unsheathed knives and speared meat onto their trenchers, Sweyn stood up to make a speech.

'My sister,' began Sweyn, holding out his horn to a boy with a pitcher. No cup for him. Inge remembered his drinking challenge with Thorbjorn during her betrothal feast, remembered the glittering eyes of her husband-to-be as he humiliated the girl who was only Sweyn's sister to him.

She gritted her teeth, prayed to Frigg that Finn was proof against any pissing contest her brother might start.

With desperate jollity, men called for ale, hoping there would yet be some entertainment at this most miserable of weddings.

'My sister is Inge Asleifsdottir,' Sweyn went on, 'and in my name you should show her due reverence.' He threw the words out at the hall, a challenge, and narrowed his eyes at Finn for good measure, just in case the message had not been received. 'Pay your respect in the name of the Jarl-maker, the man who can make or break the lords of Orkneyjar, the man who—'

At that point, the heavy wooden door flew open. Those nearest the entrance were treated to a gust of wind and a flurry of rain as three men rushed in, battling to close the door behind them.

Men jumped to their feet, reached for axes and spears, but the intruders threw themselves to their knees before the top table and their first words showed they had no ill intentions. Or at least, not to those gathered in the hall.

'My lord Sweyn, my lord Gunnr.' They made greeting as if the brothers were well known to them.

Interrupted in full flow, Sweyn was struck dumb so it was Gunnr who addressed the men.

'I know you, men of Gareksey. Stand and speak freely.'

As they rose to their feet, the three men exchanged nervous looks and a shove in the back selected their spokesperson, a pock-faced beanpole of a man.

'We were sent by your lady mother,' he began, the words increasing pace as if he wanted rid of the whole unpleasant history. 'To tell you that Jarl Harald has exiled you from Orkneyjar.'

CHAPTER 13

INGE, NESS

'What do you mean, *exiled?*' shouted Gunnr, hurling a cup full of ale across the table. 'Is the Jarl touched by the gods? I've done nothing against him but live peacefully on Gareksey, loyal to him. Even more loyal to him since– There's some mistake. It's something *you've* done, isn't it!' He turned to his brother and poked him aggressively in the chest.

In retaliation, Sweyn pushed Gunnr backwards. 'I've done nothing new.'

Inge could think of many reasons Harald might exile Sweyn, and he would be the second jarl to do so. Her older brother did not wait for trouble to find him. He charged into the thick of it, joyful in action. *Jarl-maker indeed!* She wondered what political pot he was stirring now, while Rognvald was absent.

Without giving Gunnr time to reflect on what 'nothing new' might mean, Sweyn ordered, 'Explain yourself, man.'

With shaking voice, Beanpole told Gunnr, 'The Jarl's message said you've ruined his mother's reputation and must be kept away from her.'

Sweyn gave a belly laugh that probably expressed what most in the hall were thinking.

Gunnr erupted. 'That boy on a man's throne dares to exile me because I'm fucking his mother! Who's not complained once!'

'Calm yourself, man. This is not the time or place, not on Inge's wedding day.' Sweyn laid a warning hand on his brother's arm but Gunnr shook him off.

'You're not the one exiled, though why not, the gods only know!'

Inge recognised the signs of hurt pride looking for an outlet and sighed inwardly.

Margaret, Maddan's widow, was as much trouble as Sweyn. She had barely buried her husband before Gunnr had caught her fancy. Now *there* was a lady who didn't agonise over second marriages or consequences. She'd taken what she wanted and Gunnr would pay the price while she grew bored and big with child on Gareksey.

'I won't be able to see her.' Gunnr's face had turned from red to white as he understood what his sentence would mean.

'It's not *seeing* her you'll miss,' guffawed Sweyn, slapping his brother on the back as if it were all a huge joke.

Inge winced.

'The whore can wait,' declared Sweyn cheerfully. 'Come with me to Írland. There's booty for all of us. Let Harald make more enemies while we play elsewhere. Then when we go back to Gareksey, you'll be forgiven and can make him some half-brothers.'

There was sense if not tact in Sweyn's words, far more than he'd have shown if he were concerned in such a slight to *his* honour, but Inge shut her eyes. She knew what was coming.

Gunnr prodded Sweyn's richly embroidered tunic hard in the chest with each word. 'Don't. Call. Her. A. Whore.'

Sweyn smacked away the offending hand and stepped back, equally red-faced and indignant. 'Everyone calls her a whore. Because so she is! Are you going to fight them all?'

Gunnr's first punch was easily ducked and Sweyn swiftly landed one of his own. Then the hall erupted into ale-fuelled fistfights, whether because men were taking sides in the brothers' quarrel or because they were settling old scores of their own.

When Inge opened her eyes, her brothers were rolling on the earthen floor, not close enough to the central hearth fire to do themselves any damage. They had long practice at thumping each other without doing too much damage, so she wasn't worried. With any luck, that would also be true of all the other guests.

Finn was still sitting beside her, supping ale thoughtfully, observing the fracas. He caught her eye, raised an eyebrow and looked towards the stairs that led to their private quarters, where they would spend the night..

Inge smiled, nodded and discreetly extricated herself from the bench and the hall, unnoticed. Within minutes, Finn joined her, and took her in his arms.

'Wife,' he said. 'My wife.'

Was there a question in his eyes? She held his gaze firmly. She was not a duckling to have been imprinted forever by that first experience.

'Husband,' she told him. 'My husband.' In the flickering rushlight, his shadow against the curtain looked like a bear, arms raised to crush her, but she was not afraid.

She took off her beads first, placed them carefully on the kist beside the bed, then added their clothes, folding each item, taking her time. She first removed his best tunic, noting the soft blue wool and silver thread in the embroidery, then her matching overdress. The ritual was gentle, pleasing, as was what followed.

Thanks to her brothers and their contagious brawling, whatever noises she might make in pleasure would not be heard. She would be as wanton as Margaret Hakonsdottir.

༺❀༻

The next morning, Inge threw on enough clothes for decency, then slipped through the curtain and down the spiralling stairs to the scene of the previous evening's celebration.

Flushed and still sleepy, she regarded the chaos. Every surface was a makeshift bed: benches, tables and the floor. Those who'd been sober enough had found their packs and lay on bedrolls, under their cloaks. Others lay pillowed on the men with whom they'd probably been fighting before exhaustion claimed them.

Inge dug a leather-clad toe into one such pair, reeking of stale beer and male sweat. The mass grunted and shifted into two distinct and dishevelled blond giants. Her brothers were alive and no doubt proud of themselves.

She left them to recover what sense they might still possess and resumed her progress through the hall. Women lay together in a more decorous group, crowded together against a protective wall with their packs in an outer defence-work, strategically placed to trip up any drunken brawler who lost his way.

The damp atmosphere had swollen the wooden bar across the door so she had to loosen it in a sawing motion but the key turned smoothly. Her reward was a morning that glistened and shimmered.

Mist plumed up from the chopping-block and the pile of logs beside it as dawn gilded the sky. The rain had stopped and slanting rays of pale light made diamonds of the raindrops hanging from leafy branches. The trees that fringed the settlement sparkled and danced in the breeze. Such a day was a gift to the new bride, and she thanked the god Dellingr, the shining one, for opening the gates and letting the sun through.

A few paces took her to the kitchen buildings, which were already a hive of activity and needed no direction. The steward was well experienced in Sweyn's notion of a celebration, and a small army of pot-boys was ready with sweet-smelling rushes, buckets and scrubbing brushes to reclaim the hall as a place for eating.

The second team of boys was organising pitchers of watered wine to chase away the ale headaches, to be served with dried fish and bannocks for those whose stomachs were strong enough.

Inge made her satisfaction clear and commandeered a servant to take two portions of the best provender up to Finn in their chamber. The hall held no attractions and the bedchamber held many, so she would leave her brothers to clean up the mess they'd made. With any luck, they'd have gone off to Írland before she came back downstairs. If not, she and Finn would take their own ship as soon as possible.

'My lady,' the steward called after her. 'Before you leave for Orkneyjar, don't forget…'

The rest of his words were lost in the general hullabaloo of the kitchen and Inge was already on her way out of the door, anticipating renewed pleasures. The steward had spoken to her recently about some matter, before the wedding, she vaguely remembered, but too much had happened since for her to bring it to mind.

No matter. He was an honest, conscientious man and would undoubtedly deal with whatever it was more effectively than she would. Maybe she could poach him from Sweyn to manage Finn's estate in Strjónsey.

CHAPTER 14

INGE, STRJÓNSEY, ORKNEYJAR

Standing beside her two kists of clothes, Inge watched the island that was to be her home loom larger. The familiar Orkneyjar coast of wrack-rimmed beaches and wave-sculpted cliffs was unfamiliar in its detail. So often she'd sailed these waters, between the family homes in Mainland Ness or the isle of Gareksey, or to the Jarl's court in Orphir. But she'd never been to the isle of Strjónsey, Finn's domain.

'What are you thinking, my lady?' asked Finn, never taking his eyes off the sail and the direction of ribbon on the mast. He was as much a sailor as she was, as they all were.

'The sea on which we travel,' she told him. 'We try to plough our own furrow but some are lost in the troughs.' Her eldest brother had been claimed by Aegir, the sea god, on his way to the Jarl's Yule feast, two days after her father was burned alive in their Ness longhouse. Since then, they'd occupied the old stone tower in Ness. Stone did not catch fire.

Nobody was a stronger warrior than her father. Nobody was a stronger sailor than the brother who'd died. The Norns mocked people's strengths and struck where they were vulnerable. And everyone was vulnerable.

'Does it make you fearful at sea?' asked Finn gently. 'Knowing how your brother died?'

Grey ripples lapped at the sides of the boat like whales testing and tasting before devouring the whole meal.

'I was on Gareksey with my mother when we got the news. I must have been sixteen. My other brothers were away.'

She gave a bitter laugh. 'Away at sea, of course. My mother made a terrible sound, like a hare torn by an eagle, then she sat down, rigid as stone. I started to cry, screaming at the gods' cruelty and she slapped me across the face.

'She grabbed my hand and marched me down to the beach where our small rowing-boat was moored. I shouted and fought, said I wouldn't get in, that she wanted me to drown too but she merely gripped my hand tighter and bundled me into the boat. I sat on the bench, shaking, too frightened to move.'

She glanced at Finn. She could tell he was listening from the stillness of his face but he kept his eyes on the sail.

She swallowed and sought the right words. 'A mother gains her son's strength after he dies, for long enough to do what must be done. Grieving can wait. My mother ran the boat down to the sea with me in it, then jumped in and told me to row. I thought she meant us both to die.

'When we were in deep waters, like this,' Inge gestured to the expanse of grey on which they sailed, 'she stowed the oars and talked to me while we drifted. She said, "Imagine you are in a battle and the Norns have woven your death today. What should you do?"

'I had heard her ask my brother Valthiof – the one who drowned – this very same question and I knew the answer, so I told her, "I cannot change my fate but I can fight and die with honour." She nodded and then asked, "You are in a battle but the Norns have not woven your death today. What should you do?"

'"Fight with all my strength and live with honour," I replied.

'Again, she nodded. "Life is a battle we did not choose. But we can choose how we live. We have a hard loss to bear but it is not the fault of Aegir in the sea or Thórr in the sky, and we are not craven fools to shout at either. We do not need to speak of this again."'

Inge glanced again at Finn and smiled a challenge. 'I am not afraid of the sea.'

'I truly believe there's nothing you are afraid of,' he told her. She wished she could decant the admiration in his eyes and stopper it in a bottle to sniff when she lacked courage.

Some land feature caught his attention. 'There,' he yelled to his men. 'Reef the sail and man the oars. We're turning for home.'

Unobserved, her smile faded. If only there were nothing – or rather no-one – she feared. And her monster was now within easy rowing distance.

CHAPTER 15

FERGUS, NESS

Fergus sipped the water he was offered, his head clear for the first time in however long he'd been sweating on this straw pallet. With clarity came pain more intense than the stabbing pangs of fever. *Brigid.*

He grabbed the hand holding the bottle towards him.

'Steady on, man!' complained the unlikely saviour, an ostler probably, to judge by his smell of leather and horses.

Unless it was Fergus' surroundings that smelled of the stable? Still gripping the young man's hand, he raised himself on one elbow, looked around in the dim daylight slipping through a distant entrance.

Yes, stable, he thought, having spent enough nights sleeping in a cow byre to smell the difference.

'Lady Inge! I have to get word to her.'

The stable hand laughed, a gritty sound without humour. 'Then you mun go to Orkneyjar for she's wed Finn Bessasson and gone to be lady of Strjónsey.'

He rubbed his wrist as Fergus' hand dropped back onto the rough bed. 'There's work here if you want it.' He rubbed his wrist again for emphasis. 'Now you're well enough.'

And he stepped back hastily as Fergus rose to his feet, lumbering but determined.

Fergus had no time for niceties. 'My thanks for your care but I must go. Where are my things?'

Lowered eyes and a shifty look. 'I'll fetch them.'

What was left of them, no doubt.

His heart sank when the man returned with Fergus' pack. His noticeably light pack. But what could he say? He'd have died without the care he'd been given.

'Master Steward said if you was to come through the fever, you should see him afore ye go. He kept some of your things for you. Some you'd want to take with ye, so he said.'

Fergus' spirits lifted. Maybe there was hope. Of reclaiming his coins. And of finding his wife. Brigid was indomitable. She'd talked her way to safety during a Viking raid. Surely to God, she'd talk her way out of whatever Thorbjorn had planned.

He had to believe she was alive and that he'd find her. Wincing as his weakened muscles took his weight, he made his way towards the daylight.

First, he'd see the steward. Then he'd get passage back to Orkneyjar on whatever ship would carry him.

CHAPTER 16

SKARFR

*A torch is lit by another
and burns till it's burned out;
a fire is kindled by another fire.*

The Wanderer's *Hávamál*

It had started innocently enough with Skarfr asking Pilot questions about the route around the cape known in Almería as the Cape of Venus or Cape Agatus, distinguished by ash-grey volcanic peaks, and then northwards to Narbonne. They were speaking in the Hispanic language and, with hindsight, Skarfr realised that this must have annoyed Eindridi beyond his usual resentment at having a pilot foisted on him. He might guess what they were talking about but he could not impose his own greater knowledge on the conversation in a language he barely knew. His pretence of taking no interest must have been just that – a pretence.

Somewhere among the detail of inlets and hostile occupants, Pilot mentioned a river known to traders for the wealth of its settlements. A river so long that a ship could travel ninety days from the sea mouth and not reach the narrows which dropped from its mountain source. A river called the Ebro. One daring foray inland would make them all rich.

As Skarfr explained to Eindridi, 'Pilot says he knows of traders who do this all the time. The river is wide and fast, so the return would be speedy. And the voyage upriver would not tax our oarsmen on such a wide channel. We would see Christian territory so rich, men use gold coins as if they are toothpicks.' His heart raced, 'And we would be the first Norsemen to go this way.' *What stories they would add to the saga!*

As Eindridi's face darkened, Skarfr rushed on. 'We are approaching a port, not on the river of gold, but Pilot says it's somewhere suitable to bide until Rognvald catches up and we can consult him. We should drop the sail now to enter the estuary and we can keep watch for the other ships, sound the horn when they come near.'

Suddenly registering the captain's reaction, Skarfr added tactfully, 'Of course, the Jarl may prefer to stick to the planned route, even when he hears about the river.' Unable to give up his hopes for such an adventure, he added stubbornly. 'At least he'll have had the choice.'

Eindridi erupted, red-faced and wild-eyed. 'You talk in gibberish with this foreigner who listens to travellers' tales and, all of a sudden, you're the expert? You know more than I do, more than the great Sigurd who travelled this way before us?

'Well then, you can tell your Jarl of your wonderful plan in person. Tell him from me that if he has any sense, he'll catch us up along the coast. If he's as stupid as you think he is, we might meet in Narbonne but I won't wait more than a month for him.'

He shouted, 'Reef the sail!' and the men in charge of the rigging hastily set to work on the ropes.

'Thank you,' Skarfr said, thinking Eindridi was going to head for port, hold back and consult Rognvald. He could understand that his conversations with Pilot had seemed furtive to one who did not speak the language and he wanted to explain. 'Pilot and I,' he began, 'were only plotting—'

'You think I don't know that?' screamed Eindridi.

'—courses for the journey,' finished Skarfr lamely but his words were lost in the volley of instructions Eindridi shouted at his crew – and at anyone within earshot. Slack-sailed, the other five longships waited for the *Crest-cleaver* to move again, so their captains could follow. Small fishing boats bobbed close enough to hear the arguments on board and then pulled away.

Only Mouthy risked speaking to Eindridi. 'Captain, they were talking pilot-talk. The boy meant no harm, just wanted to learn and ask questions. Like you did when you were his age.'

Skarfr did not take kindly to being called 'boy,' but he supposed that, for someone of Mouthy's age, Eindridi too was a boy.

Eindridi's rage burned hotter. 'Plotting,' he said, 'and that's the truth of it. I want no spies and plotters on my ship. Nor old men who've lost their wits along with their teeth. You can thank the gods I'm not in a mood for sacrifices today – I'd rather make good speed on the *right course* – but get off my ship before I change my mind, all three of you.'

He hailed the nearest small boat, 'You there! These three men—' He pointed at the miscreants, '—want to go ashore.'

He pointed at the harbour settlement nestling at the mouth of a river wide enough to be the subject of the dispute. His hand gestures and shouting made the fishermen curious enough to come alongside.

Burning at the unfairness of Eindridi's actions, Skarfr became even more determined to lay the matter before Rognvald. He *would* go ashore and quit the *Crest-cleaver* and its obnoxious captain.

Instead of disputing the punishment, Skarfr called out to the puzzled fishermen and made clear what was required, waving one of the precious silver bits given to him by the Jarl. Its glint was mirrored in the fishermen's eyes and the deal was done.

Muttering, 'I can get work anywhere,' Pilot clambered over the side into the fishing boat.

Skarfr shouldered his pack and jumped in. When the boat steadied, he held out his hand towards Mouthy.

'No.' The old seaman no longer looked weathered and

experienced, but frail, as he looked over the shields on the bulwarks to the small, bobbing boat, then back at the magnificent ship.

He faced up to Eindridi. 'I've served you since you were a boy,' he told him. 'You promised me Jórsalaheim and a warrior's death, whenever the Norns should choose. Not this shame.'

The captain gave the old sailor a shove that nearly felled him. 'Things change. I thought you could still be useful but Fire-starter crossed me at the wrong moment, so I offered him to the gods instead of you. That's all you're good for – offering to the gods. You've spoken against me once too often. Get in that boat or join Fire-starter in the deep. Either way, we save on rations.' He shrugged and turned his attention back to his ship.

He adjusted the steerboard to catch the wind again. 'Let's go!' he yelled. 'Oars in – now! Out – now!'

The rhythm he set was picked up by the oarmaster and the ship was already pulling away when Skarfr shouted, '*Now*, Mouthy!'

The old man scrambled over the side to dangle there for a dangerous moment before Skarfr caught him and pulled him to safety. He collapsed in a heap on the ship's bottom, beside a net full of crabs.

'First time I've been grateful for a dose of crabs,' he joked, his voice shaking.

'There will be plenty more on shore,' Skarfr reassured him. 'Just use your natural charm.'

Mouthy's answering toothless grin wavered and the castaways were silent as the fishermen pulled efficiently for the harbour, negotiating the gaps between trader ships and rowing boats.

This was indeed a significant port and, for all his outrage, Skarfr's spirits were rising. When the green-eyed cormorant flew overhead and grunted her greeting at him, he knew he'd plotted the right course. He watched her heading for the other waterfowl, which were diving deep and surfacing with silver in their beaks. A fisherman's nightmare, but for him, a blessing on his choices.

However, being right was not in itself the solution to all the castaways' problems. Skarfr needed to alert Rognvald to their abandonment and there was only one way he could think of doing so. Only one person was so close to him in spirit that she would understand such a message. He could not wait until nightfall or Rognvald would sail past the river mouth, none the wiser.

In silent communion, Skarfr summoned the cormorant and told her. 'Tell Hlif to come to me, to bring the ships.'

The cormorant dipped a wing, altered her own course and circled past her fellows, out to sea.

'What do we do now?' asked Mouthy.

'I can ask around, see if a ship's short of a pilot?' The only one of the three who would be guaranteed a welcome here, Pilot's tone showed none of the fear Mouthy was battling against. Old age was a burden Pilot and Skarfr did not carry – yet.

'No,' Skarfr told him, the cormorant's assurance filling him and the dragon rippling on his arm. He wanted to crush Eindridi with his bare hands. In his frustration he punched a sack beside him on the docks. *That* was for treating Mouthy like a moth-eaten bedsack.

For a moment he let the battle rage sing in his blood, then he sighed. He was a better man than Eindridi and so was his jarl, who was on the way.

'No. We wait,' he told his crew of two. 'You are *our* Pilot. Mouthy, you're one of my crew now. What do you say to trying the river route and proving Eindridi a coward and a fool?'

CHAPTER 17

SKARFR

*If you spend time wandering
by land or by sea,
bring plentiful provisions.*

The Wanderer's Hávamál

Skarfr had seated himself on a small barrel, which was waiting on the dockside, either for loading or for taking. A man who stank of fish opened his mouth to object to Skarfr's choice of seat, but a glare made him realise it wasn't his barrel and he wasn't looking for trouble. Skarfr toyed with his dagger and was left in peace to wait with his two companions. He knew how to look like trouble. He'd been well taught.

There were richer goods than fish all around him. Men loaded bales of fabric onto handcarts, displaying samples to buyers who wanted first pick, too impatient to wait for the goods to reach a marketplace.

Skin-breaker, blood-bather, wolf-tooth, he thought, absent-mindedly sheathing his dagger as a black shape winged its way from open sea towards the harbour, silhouetted against the sun in the west.

Velvet, silk, damask, linen. Sales talk. Perhaps this *was* the marketplace.

'Crk, crk,' grunted the cormorant in her strange porcine voice, circling over Skarfr's head. *She's coming.*

Then she flew off to join the group of black divers in the deep water, where she'd been heading before Skarfr summoned her. They were still fishing, undeterred by the shouting and stones lobbed by their human competitors. Too far from the shore for the stones to reach them, they avoided the little boats in a graceful display of plunge-and-surface, leaving the bewildered fishermen looking to one side of their boat while their black enemies appeared far on the other side. The cormorants flexed their gullets, swallowed the silver wrigglers, then dived again before the fishermen could hit them.

Skarfr was not afraid for the cormorant. Nor for himself. The feeling of being just where he was supposed to be thrummed in his blood so strongly that he was startled by his fellows' exclamations. Had they not known Rognvald would bring his ships to this haven?

Never had the striped sails been such a welcome sight. The sun glinted on the gold carvings and the ships rode the waves like the sea destriers they were.

The fishermen did not shout at the newcomers or throw stones. They rowed their boats to safety as fast they could, avoiding the wakes of the newcomers' ships and whatever dangers came with them. Other men scurried about the wooden jetties to give a wide berth to the incoming ships. Skarfr strode to meet the *Sun-chaser*, followed by Pilot and Mouthy.

He caught the rope thrown to him and had barely tied it to the mooring post when Rognvald jumped out beside him.

'Where's Eindridi? I can't see his ships.' The Jarl was scanning the harbour as if six drakkars would suddenly appear amidst the rowboats and trading vessels.

'Gone,' said Mouthy dourly and Rognvald's face darkened.

There was no point varnishing the truth. 'Pilot suggested a detour up a river famous among traders, called the Ebro, where no Norðmen have ever been. I said we should put the idea to you.

Eindridi would hear none of it and is set on the course he knows, the course Sigurd took, and Mouthy—' Skarfr looked at old man's toothless grin, remembered Eindridi's callous words and suddenly felt that varnishing the truth was not such a bad idea. '—Mouthy agreed with me that it was only right to consult you as our leader. Eindridi took that badly and cast us off.'

As the other ships were made fast, crew members came ashore, heading towards Rognvald. Skarfr's words swept through them like a brush fire.

Jón Halt-foot's greeting turned to curses. 'You could have died here! A leader who abandons his men has no honour.'

'I think Eindridi saw them as *my* men,' observed Rognvald. 'Therein lies the problem. You have seen it now, Skarfr? Seen Eindridi for what he is?'

So Skarfr had not been placed with Eindridi for Rognvald's sake but for his own, to grow in the study of men. Once more, he had underestimated his jarl. The habitual sting of guilt pricked him.

'Yes,' he said. No more was needed. Eindridi was not a man of honour.

'And Jón is right,' Rognvald went on. 'If Hlif hadn't insisted that we reprovision here, regardless of how far ahead Eindridi might be, we would have sailed past and you would have rotted in this place.'

Pilot shrugged, 'I won't rot. If you don't want me, I'll find a captain who does.'

Skarfr told him, 'Let the Jarl judge. He is not Eindridi. Let me tell him about the river route.'

Once Skarfr had finished his impassioned plea for an inland adventure, Rognvald looked thoughtful rather than fired up and of course went straight to the heart of the difficulty. Or rather difficulties. And those only the ones known in advance to a pilot who'd never travelled the route himself.

Fingering his beard, Rognvald summed up. 'So, we navigate this river upstream, tiring our oarsmen. We then stop at random settlements and steal their treasure, relying on the same tired men to deal with any resistance. On the return, the current is fast and with us, and all is plain sailing on the broadest, most beautiful river ever seen, with trees overhanging the banks and gold coin dripping from the branches. Or of course, the inhabitants have sent warning of our passage and we sail back into fully prepared warfare.'

Men laughed, Skarfr flushed, and Pilot looked indignant. He might not have understood all the words, but he certainly sensed the scepticism. 'No gold coins on trees,' he protested. 'You can trade, not steal! And you could leave the trading stops for the return journey. This route has been taken many times.'

'But never by you,' said the Jarl quietly. 'I can understand why Eindridi wouldn't listen to you. He follows a course he knows, one travelled before him. Skarfr, why in the name of all the gods do you think this is a good idea?'

Skarfr did not think it was a good idea. He *knew* it was. But how did you share a bone-deep conviction with another man? He'd already put all the enthusiasm he felt into his explanation of the choice. He looked over Rognvald's shoulder towards the river and saw that the cormorants had left off their fishing and were poised like ship figureheads on wooden mooring posts.

As he searched for words to sway the Jarl, and wondered whether he *should* try to sway the Jarl, the cormorants took flight as one, circled and arrowed out of sight up the river. All but one.

She remained on her post, near enough for Skarfr to see the deliberate turn of her head towards him, a flash of green eyes. She flapped her wings, held them out to dry them and then turned, flapping towards the river, away from the sea. She croaked at him, *Make sagas!* then flew after the others, upriver. *Upriver*. It was a sign.

Rognvald turned to see what had attracted Skarfr's attention and the irritation in his eyes showed he'd noted the cormorant. He knew the significance for his vassal, but he shook his head in exasperation.

'It would be sensible to follow Eindridi,' Skarfr agreed, 'and to follow in the footsteps of Sigurd. But you are a leader, not a follower, and you are making a *new* saga, not retelling an old one!

'I do not know what adventures this River Ebro holds – and we never will if we aren't bold enough to find out. If Pilot says other ships make this journey, then I say we do it. The worst that can happen is that we find nothing of interest, and we return to take the sea route. Then we will know more about this region, which will be useful to those who come after us. How do we create the future if we only do what has always been done?'

Rognvald gave an ambivalent snort. 'The worst that can happen is Eindridi crowing about us wasting time.' Then he laughed. 'Let's do it! And it will be fast downstream to come back!'

He glanced at Skarfr's companions. 'Pilot will earn his keep, and will either be able to say he has sailed this route or go home tail between legs and warn others. If we come back with nothing, you're dismissed.'

His gaze lingered on the old sailor, whose mouth twitched in a nervous, gummy smile. 'We'll need all the experience we can get. Make yourself small and useful, Mouthy. How many years did you sail with Eindridi?'

The smile set hard. 'Twenty, Sire.'

Rognvald looked into the distance, out to sea, as if he watched the *Crest-cleaver* sail away, leaving three men behind. Then he turned his attention to his new crew member.

'And what is your opinion about this change of route?'

Mouthy didn't hesitate. 'I don't have one, Sire. I'm no captain and I'll go where you tell me.' A more diplomatic man would have left it at that. 'Might well be that my lord Eindridi has the right of it and Skarfr is all young hothead and no sense.'

'What?' Skarfr exploded, while the Jarl's mouth twitched upwards.

Mouthy ignored the interruption and persisted stubbornly. 'But what I said and I still says is that you had the right to hear Pilot and Skarfr and throw the dice. And that you have. And nobody's calling you young hothead, so let's get on with it, I say.'

As if he suddenly remembered that he had no opinion on the matter, he added, 'That's only what I think, not worth a mildewed bannock.'

Another pause and he added, 'My lord,' to be on the safe side.

Rognvald stroked his grizzled beard. 'No,' he agreed, 'nobody is calling me young hothead, so let's get on with it. Skarfr, go cool your head by sorting out provisions with Hlif.'

His liege's evident amusement, and the prospect of time with Hlif, lessened Skarfr's irritation at being seen as a callow youth. Being seen as such by Mouthy was something he could laugh off, but not when the insult came from Eindridi. That was *not* easy to stomach. There were several scores to settle with that arrogant noble, and not just on his Jarl's behalf.

Decision made, Rognvald turned to more pressing matters. 'Hlif,' he yelled, 'if you want provisions, you'd better get a move on. We'll have three more men with us and if I hear one complaint, your cat goes overboard.'

CHAPTER 18

SKARFR

> Be most wary about drinking,
> about other men's women
> and about a third thing:
> about men and their temptation to steal.
>
> The Wanderer's Hávamál

Like wary puppies, the local residents at first kept their distance, ready to flee, then gradually the bolder ones approached the Orkneymen, gesturing and pointing at fish or sacks, offering trade.

Hlif interrupted the heated discussion between the two pilots over the proposed course change, with a peremptory demand that one of them interpret for her, to speed up transactions. Skarfr's pilot (as he now thought of the man cast off Eindridi's ship with him) accepted the role and the other pilot disappeared.

Even with Pilot's help, the provisioning would take until evening, so the nine ships were clearly destined to spend the night moored at the port. Skarfr learned that this place was called Almería and had been under Genoese rule for the last three years. Previously, when Eindridi sailed this route, the Saracens held sway, as in most of the

Hispanic southlands. No wonder he wanted to pass by quickly. But he hadn't hesitated to abandon three of his men in what he thought was hostile territory.

While Hlif was haggling over a barrel of fish with Pilot as intermediary, Skarfr was struck by a sudden thought and interrupted them. What if the cormorant meant *this* river?

'What if we go up *this* river?' he asked Pilot. 'Ask these men if there's anywhere worth going to up-river.'

The man shook his head. 'Not by river and not for men of your faith.'

Skarfr knew enough vocabulary to jump in. 'What do you mean?'

Holding up three fingers, the tradesman said, 'In three days' walk, you would reach the citadel of the red hill, the Muslims' biggest stronghold.' He made a slicing motion with his hand, at the level of Skarfr's neck and somewhat lower. 'You would see treasures and you would lose your own.' He wheezed out what was meant to be laughter, his shoulders shaking and tears in his eyes.

'I don't think we want to go to any Muslim stronghold,' said Hlif firmly. 'And we do want a barrel of fish. Pilot, remind him that's my last offer or we'll go elsewhere.'

Before complying, Pilot asked the merchant for his opinion of the great river further north, the Ebro, and of the city Tortosa, which guarded its entry.

'Tortosa, yes, you will like Tortosa.' This time the man's smile seemed genuine rather than mocking. 'Genoese in Tortosa. Good for trade. Like Almería.'

'So, we're going to Tortosa,' Hlif summarised. 'Barrel of fish?' she reminded Pilot.

Reluctantly, Skarfr conceded that Almería's river was of no interest and that a mountain trek to some stronghold manned by a Moorish army crossed the line from heroic to downright stupid. How impregnable a Moorish stronghold could be was well illustrated by the walled citadel towering above them.

High above the port was the Alcazaba, its multiple towers and crenellated walls evidence of the earlier Moorish inhabitants. Within its walls, the populace of an entire town could shelter. Skarfr could only admire the ingenuity of the Genoese and their Christian allies in taking the fortress for themselves.

When he told the Jarl what he'd learned of the town, he half-hoped for a visit to the stronghold on high. But Rognvald had no intention of making himself known to the rulers. Already conscious of 'wasting time,' he gave orders that the company sleep on board the ships or outdoors on the rocky shore. As tides made little difference to this sea, they could leave at dawn, causing as little fuss as possible before then.

A broad interpretation of 'fuss' gave tacit permission for sorties in shifts, around the harbour-front, where men could barter for the goods on offer. Fortunately, the pilots had smoothed the way and passed back the message that the locals were hospitable, happy to provide food and drink. Fortunately for the residents, that is. Rognvald and his men always appreciated hospitality when it was given – and they took it anyway when it wasn't. Even without Eindridi and his followers, two hundred and fifty Orkneymen made a formidable force, not to mention one woman and one cat. They could all bite.

The choice between rocks and a hard place found Skarfr and Rognvald lying awake together, between the thwarts, with empty spaces around them, while half the men took their chances with all the bedding they could muster between their bodies and the ridges of scree and rock slabs. The balmy evening made the open air a pleasure, apart from the whining insects with stings that made the prick of Orkneyjar midges seem like tiny kisses.

As he shifted position to avoid a dint in his hip, Skarfr once more envied Hlif her slight stature. Either she or the cat was already purring in deep sleep.

'Anchovies,' she murmured. 'So salty. Watch water rations.' Her words tailed off into an incoherent mutter.

'It's not an easy thing, provisioning ships in strange lands,' observed Rognvald, his disembodied voice intended only for Skarfr's ears. 'She is excited about new foods to try but worries about their impact on our guts. No doubt she'll spend her dreams worrying about whether drinking river water will do more harm than good to our insides.'

As if Skarfr needed Hlif's thoughts to be explained to *him*, who knew every soar and dive of her imagination as well as he knew those of her supple body. But Rognvald was right about her dreams. There was little chance of joining Hlif in the dreamworld when she was so far ahead of him, and he would only sleep in fits and starts.

Other than the recumbent form of Hlif, nobody was within earshot of Skarfr and the Jarl for the first time since they'd left Grimsby.

Rognvald's voice wafted again through the darkness and this time his words startled Skarfr into opening his eyes. It was not so dark after all. The moon had risen and silvered all in its path, from those shields still hanging on the bulwarks to the faces of sleeping men. The golden ornamentation glittered, turning the ship into a dwarf-crafted wonder that might fly through the stars or dive under the sea.

'Do you want to tell me something?' Rognvald repeated.

'Yes,' Skarfr replied. 'In Grimsby, when Coal-pilot was murdered, I was there.' He fingered the pouch, felt the hard angles of its contents through the leather.

Rognvald stopped his restless shifting, the focus of his listening tangible, like One-eye's stare before he pounced.

Skarfr continued. 'There were two men who set on Pilot, not just Matt-hair. I'd seen them before, at table in the hall. They took unusual interest in a pouch that Pilot let show by accident, then hid again.' He moistened his lips. 'I was too late to save him when they attacked in the street—'

'You brought a murderer to account, risked your own neck for an outsider. And I have not been appreciative.' The Jarl's tone was reflective.

Rognvald must think Skarf was bragging in hopes of reward. He rushed on, 'I don't need appreciation.' That was worse, sounded petulant, as if he didn't realise how generous Rognvald had been to him. He forged onward, hoping to clarify.

'I knocked the other man as he fled and he dropped the object he'd taken. I grabbed Matt-hair and the rest you know, except that Pilot spoke to Hlif before he died, said I should keep his treasure.'

Rognvald sat up suddenly, his eyes wide. 'You have it?'

'Here.' Skarfr passed the pouch over to Rognvald, who dipped in a hand and brought out the cloudy stone.

'But I don't know what it is,' Skarfr admitted. 'Nor why a man was murdered for it, so I've kept it hidden, as Pilot did, until I could show you without others seeing.'

A ray of moonlight caught the stone, bumping against some unseen flaw and coming out at a different angle, like a broken arrow.

'I don't know how its magic works,' admitted Rognvald, 'but I know what it is. I have heard of such treasures but have never seen one. It must be the crystal called a sunstone. Some pilots can use these to find the sun when the sky is clouded.'

Skarfr turned the sunstone in his hand, puzzling over the broken arrow of light and the black spot marked on one facet.

'Then why didn't Pilot use it in the fog? And if nobody else knows how to use it, why steal it and kill him?'

He put the mysterious object back in its pouch and the rays of moonlight resumed their straight course.

'Who was the other man?' asked Rognvald.

'Horse-snipper,' replied Skarfr.

'Also Eindridi's man.' The Jarl's tone held no accusation but Skarfr answered what was unspoken.

'All lords have untrustworthy men.'

'But?'

'But,' Skarfr hesitated, reluctant to be the one to actually say the words. 'But Eindridi is an untrustworthy lord.'

Rognvald did not deny it. 'Why would he want this sunstone? It might well be worth a house or a horse, or a full suit of armour and weapons, but Eindridi is wealthy. He has no need to sell such a thing.'

'You say they are rare and he is voyaging so he could not buy one.

And a pilot would never part with one.' Skarfr turned the question around in his head, the way he'd turned the sunstone to find the right angle for a true course. 'To be one up on you,' he told Rognvald. 'He always wants to shine brighter. And with this,' he waved the pouch even though Rognvald had his eyes shut and saw nothing, 'he could navigate in cloudy weather when you were lost.'

'Yes.' Rognvald was almost smug. 'I told you that you would learn from being on Eindridi's ship and you did. Now you have the sunstone and I have you. Show Pilot and ask if he can teach you how to use it.'

'Which pilot?' asked Skarfr.

'Yours. I've sent the other one on his way. He'll find a ship easily enough. If I kept both, they would only bicker and I don't need two. I want yours on my ship now as this river expedition is his idea.'

Skarfr was sorry Pilot was among those sleeping on the rock or he'd have interrogated him that instant. But it would have to wait till morning and he was actually feeling sleepy now.

'If you'd told me all this before we decided on some mad course upriver, I'd have chosen the sea route, with the sunstone to speed us.'

Skarfr opened his mouth to say they could use it on the river and then shut it again as he realised. Rivers flow one way. Even a green navigator like Skarfr could tell upriver from downriver and know the banks when he saw them.

Unless the river was so broad there were islands in the middle, he thought, his sense of adventure overcoming his feeling of foolishness. Sagas would be made on this river. He knew it.

And he was not sorry to lose Eindridi for however many weeks the journey to Narbonne took. Losing him permanently would draw no tears.

In his dreams, Skarfr captained a silver dragon-ship up a moonlit river past trees bending under the weight of the anchovies they bore.

CHAPTER 19

SKARFR

*You will never
get a reward for dealing with
a bad man.*

The Wanderer's Hávamál

Urgent squawking and the rush of air below wings woke Skarfr, who had slept with the lightness that comes from unburdening. His hands reached automatically for the precious, dangerous pouch as he watched the cormorant loop upwards and straighten, heading out to sea. The sun was well above the horizon, which was already broken up by the outlines of fishing boats.

Rognvald was nowhere to be seen but Skarfr could hear the Jarl's voice, rallying the men on shore. The horn rang out its imperative. In the time it took Hlif to shake out her hair and braid it, then unstopper the water barrel and fill her leather bottle, the ship's crew were on board once more. With their captain.

Watered, and their stomachs settled with dried bread and anchovies, the men unshipped their oars and waited for the signal. Eight ships' captains passed on a wave of raised arms, each to the next, to show they were ready. Rognvald responded with an order sent from stern to bow, where Horn-blower raised his instrument and gave two blasts.

A seaman slipped the mooring rope and fifteen pairs of oars dipped. The *Sun-chaser* slid across the still water of the harbour out onto the gently rocking sea, followed by eight shadows. The ribbon on the mast lifted, fluttered north. Skarfr and Pilot exchanged glances and there was a smile on the Jarl's face. A fair sou'-westerly wind.

Skarfr watched the sail fill, felt the change in the ship's energy, from man-power to gods-driven. The difference between making your fate and flying with destiny.

The yellow and blue stripes on the square banner proclaimed their pride in who they were. A sail made of sunshine and sky.

Wind-bellied, high-hoisted, weather-woven.

Hlif would tell him how many women had worked on the weave and how much wool had been spun to make their sail over the winter, but the numbers never took away from the magic of ploughing a sea furrow.

A black bird flew ahead of them, before heading back to shore, to her own kind. The Jarl's golden cloak brooch glinted in the sun, its rune-like arrows showing many paths. Pilot glanced from shore to sun, to the streaming wind-tell and the rippling sea. Many paths but only one true course; each man navigated his life as best he could.

'Three years ago, that place was Saracen, hostile to us,' Skarfr mused aloud.

'Then Eindridi was wise to sail past, not knowing that had changed,' said Rognvald.

'Pilot knew of the changes. And Eindridi didn't listen!' Skarfr's sense of injustice was still raw. He didn't add that if Eindridi had not known of the change of ruler, he'd cold-bloodedly abandoned three men to Saracen enemies. Rognvald would have worked that out for himself.

'Sagas are not written by men who only follow in others' footsteps, even if they are heroes' footsteps,' Rognvald quoted

Skarfr's own argument for trying the river diversion. 'On the other hand, foolhardiness is not courage.'

Skarfr wasn't sure whether to take the comment as praise or rebuke, or both. In an effort to be diplomatic, he thought he was agreeing when he said, 'Valhalla is for warriors, not idiots.'

'Heaven,' corrected Rognvald gently. 'Heaven is for the godly – and for pilgrims like us. You heard how Almería was taken by men of faith, blessed by the Pope, and that the heathens must kneel to the Christ, who will rule in this world and the next.'

A swirl of his cloak in the breeze covered the pathfinder brooch.

Each man navigates his own life as best he can, thought Skarfr once more, saying nothing. Nine days' sailing to reach the mouth of the great River Ebro, the gateway to honour and riches. Nine days spent sailing like this would be joy. The wind a caress against his bare neck, the waves a dance and tease of turquoise and blue. A course so easy to maintain that his hold on the steerboard was relaxed, a mere safety precaution.

'First watch.' Rognvald sent the message along the ship and, reluctantly, men who'd slept all night obeyed. They needed no rest yet, but the rota must be obeyed. They would appreciate whatever repose they managed during the routine quarter of the sun when they were on watch, and there would surely be nights sleeping on board before they reached the city of Tortosa. Such nights were always restless and a man must doze when he could.

'I'll take first watch,' the Jarl told Skarfr, who could only accept, although he knew he had the easier task. There was no courtesy in turning down a gift, be it silver links from an arm ring or a thoughtful turn of duty.

He glanced towards Hlif, who immediately looked out to sea, avoiding his gaze. One-eye had more luck, and attracted her attention with a piteous mew, then snaked around her ankles, rubbing and purring. She laughed, murmured soft words and slipped him some dried anchovies. Then stroked him as he rumbled ever louder.

As if he sensed Skarfr watching, the cat turned his head,

narrowed his one green eye and let his face flatten to whiskered smugness.

Damned cat!

Skarfr looked away first as a battle of wills with a cat was evidently ridiculous. Totally ridiculous.

He pulled the pouch out from under his shirt and took out the faceted stone. 'Pilot,' he said. 'How does this work?'

The man dropped the steerboard. 'Mother of God and all the saints,' he swore softly as he crossed himself. 'Where in the name of Jesus did you get that?'

The intensity with which none of the crew looked towards them, told Skarfr that every man on the ship now knew of his treasure, and he no longer cared. He was no longer a boy whose precious bones and pipe had been strewn on a beach by Sweyn's men in mockery. Let any man try to steal what was his! He glanced at Hlif, now curled up on the deck.

'The pilot before you gave it to me.' Skarfr let the light catch and deflect as it passed through the sunstone.

Pilot had regained his composure along with the steerboard and his scepticism was cutting. 'No living pilot parts with his sunstone.'

'Just so.' Skarfr hesitated, wondering how much to share. But if he expected this man to share the secrets of his trade, he must be open himself. 'He was killed for this, and I was there, too late to save him. He bequeathed it to me in his last words. My Lord Rognvald has told me what it is, but we know nothing of how to release its magic.'

'Here, take the steerboard and give me that.' Pilot swapped the wooden handle for the sunstone, his eyes glinting and hands grabbing in a way that made Skarfr want to hide the crystal back in the safe darkness of the pouch.

But the proverbial cat could never be put back in the bag and, besides, he wanted to learn what this thing was, that had come his way. A raucous noise overhead gave him encouragement and he didn't even look up to confirm that dark wings kept him company. He knew this course was true.

'Don't worry.' Pilot's eyes softened. They sparkled with sunlight not avarice. 'There is knowledge I can give you but the right to this stone is yours and I pity any man who steals it. He would not die well.'

'The would-be thief did not die well,' agreed Skarfr. But what about the other one, Horse-snipper? And if Eindridi was behind their attempt, what fate awaited him?

Not for the first time, he wondered about the gods' notion of justice. What was their purpose in demanding his father's self-sacrifice, and his mother's grief-death? What was their purpose in passing the saint-killer's curse on to his daughter, Hlif? He must untangle such thoughts before composing the saga Rognvald expected 'one day' but for now, all he needed to know of the future was how to find the sun through clouds.

Pilot was turning the crystal, inspecting the facets, holding it out at arm's length and squinting through it. He pointed out the black spot etched onto it.

'I can't show you while Sol is blazing in the sky but when she's hidden, you will be able to try this.' Pilot bowed his head in prayer. 'When glorious Sol is veiled, may the wily wolf Sköll catch her chariot, to show an unworthy pilot which course to steer. Let Skarfr the Navigator see the wolf chase Sol.'

He nodded to Skarfr, who repeated the prayer, rather liking the sound of 'Skarfr the Navigator.'

Then Pilot held the sunstone out, towards the sky but away from the burning sun, the facet with the black spot on it furthest from him. He closed one eye and peered through the stone.

'Grace be to God,' he declared, his face beatific. Presumably, Sol was more tolerant of her rival than the White Christ's God seemed to be of His, judging by the bible stories Skarfr had heard.

'I can *see* wily Sköll chasing Sol.' His hand shook with excitement at whatever he saw through the sunstone.

'Let me try!'

Pilot took the steerboard and Skarfr seized the sunstone, expecting to see the leaping wolf, fangs and lolling tongue. Instead, he saw two black spots. Swallowing his disappointment, he considered this.

Two.

He brought the sunstone close to him so he could see what had marked a second spot beside the first, although he had no idea when this could have happened as the stone had not been out of his sight. Maybe it had rubbed against some charcoal or black dye in the pouch.

Or maybe Pilot had worked some sleight of hand and marked a second spot, misdirecting his attention with the prayer. The thought he'd been tricked gave him a sour taste.

But when he turned the stone so he could inspect the facet with the black spot, there was still only one. He turned it away from him and looked through it. Two black spots. He remembered the moon ray like a broken arrow and puzzled over this.

Pilot watched him and smiled. 'Now look through again and move your arm nearer to the sun. Just a little.'

Skarfr did as he was bid, and one spot neared the other. Whether the wolf speeded up or the sun grew weary, he could not tell but in the little world of the sunstone, Sköll caught up with Sol. He moved his hand faster with the wolf, heading towards the sun.

'Careful!' Pilot dashed Skarfr's hand down and they both fumbled to catch the stone before it disappeared into the bilges.

Shocked, Skarfr closed his fist around it while Pilot shook his head at the rashness of youth.

'You'll go blind! Sol is not kind to a man who looks on her naked radiance with his own two eyes, never mind through such a tool. Never use this to look at the sun!'

Chastened but still curious, Skarfr asked, 'But I still don't know how to find the sun behind clouds.'

'When you look through the stone and find the part of the sky where the wily wolf catches the sun, there she shall be.'

For the first time in his life, Skarfr wished for clouds, so he could try out his legacy. Hlif was not the only one wielding an object of power.

CHAPTER 20

SKARFR

*I know a ninth spell
if the need arises
for me to save a ship upon the sea.*

The Wanderer's Hávamál

'I am glad you are learning the use of the sunstone but you will be of no use to me blind.' Rognvald's dry comment as he took his turn on watch was a reminder that not all who lay down were asleep and that clinkered planks had ears. Perhaps it was as well that Hlif had taken the same watch as the Jarl.

For the first time, Skarfr wondered what words came to this world from the dreams he and Hlif shared beyond the veil. Certainly not 'anchovies'. He hid his flushed neck against the damp boards and tried to get comfortable, too hot for any covering. The breeze sang a lullaby, and the gentle rocking of the sea floated his worries away. The goddess Rán was a tender mother, the ship a crib on her waters, rocking a man to sleep.

Wave-wafted, crest-cradled, sleep-shushed...

A slap of salt water across his face woke Skarfr seconds before Rognvald shouted his name. Both had the same effect.

Had he slept until night? A wall of black clouds billowed and sped across the sky behind and to the left of the ship, coming from the west, as if chased by an entire pack of wolves. No longer motherly, Rán was enraged, rising up against Thórr in a host of frothing white caps. One broke against the side of the ship, and drenched Skarfr, who staggered as he rose to his feet.

'Storm coming,' Rognvald told him curtly, as men were roused from sleep to join their fellows on full alert, ready to row or reel in rope, whatever their captain judged best.

Skarfr was not the only man aboard who'd seen death's threshold during a shipwreck and the mood was sombre. He glanced towards Hlif, who sat where she usually slept, between the oarsmen on their benches. White-faced, she huddled in her oiled cloak, clutching at something she sheltered beneath it. The something stirred but did not show its one green eye.

The air was thick with rain that did not fall, a threat increased by the rumble of thunder.

'It comes,' said Pilot, who'd taken the steerboard while Skarfr slept. 'We'll be dashed against rocks if we head for shore so we must run before it. At least it's not pushing us too far off course.'

Rognvald grunted agreement, ordered the sail reefed down to its smallest surface, while the oarsmen at the front of the steerboard side rowed and turned the prow. Pilot moved the wooden handle to shift the stern to the left, and the *Sun-chaser* circled enough to the right, away from the wind, for the waves to slap her stern. Then the oars were stowed and the ship flew before the breakers, even with its small sail.

The pressure was on the steersman to hold the *Sun-chaser* steady, despite buffets from wind and wave, as they dived into a valley of water and surged up again. Although they no longer risked being swamped and rolled from the side, riding the peaks and troughs induced a different kind of terror.

Skarfr made the mistake of looking towards the prow just as the ship balanced on a crest, then dived down the other side. Heart in mouth, he turned his attention back to the rope that was his responsibility, the one attached to the bottom corner of the sail. *Steady as she goes. Please gods, may we keep surging up again.*

His shipmates in the stern did likewise, pulling or loosening braces and sheets to trim the sail. And praying. Amidships, the crew were roping barrels and packs, tying down and tightening anything mobile. And bailing water.

Rognvald never took his eye off the sail. He exuded the same crackling fire as the storm, about to burst into action.

'Do you remember Hjaltland?' he yelled, as if they were sitting around a campfire, not shouting over a wind that howled for blood, while thunder crashed and lightning forked.

'You saved me from drowning,' Skarfr shouted back. He tried to match the Jarl's tone as water smacked his face like icy spears, from above and below.

Rognvald shrugged. 'I'm a good swimmer. But I meant the fun we had afterwards. And how we laughed at the idea of the gods dressing up in Hawknose's oiled hat and all the other clothes that had gone to the bottom of the sea.'

Although his heart pounded, and his mind told him these would be his last moments, Skarfr laughed and recited loudly,

'Our clothes are seeded in the ship's field
of wide waves and will be seen again
only on the white sea-horses
we left such splendid gifts.'

'Yes,' said Rognvald. 'That was a good time.' He too laughed.

Remembering their survival of the shipwreck and the good cheer afterwards, Skarfr's spirits lifted in the joy of combat. The laughter passed along the ship like orders from its captain.

What tales they would tell of this fight against the elements. Let each man be prepared for Valhalla or Heaven, for they would earn it whether victorious or dead, as brave pilgrims.

Not just the men. Hlif raised her head and smiled at him. A blessing and a promise, whatever happened.

Then she stood up, unsteady but determined, leaving her cloak in a misshapen heap at her feet. A flash of lightning seared her silhouette onto each man's eyeballs.

Her arms were outstretched, the iron-tipped wand raised in challenge, a völva casting a spell, her hair and gown whipping around her. Some of the words she shouted were loud in the eerie quiet between wild gusts of wind and some were stolen by the next onslaught. Enough could be heard to enable men to guess the rest.

'The gods challenge the brave to make sagas worth hearing. You are worthy!' She stood there a moment, völva and Valkyrie. Then the ship reared and the effect was spoiled a little by her sudden subsidence onto her bottom on the deck, and a pained yowl. Not from Hlif.

Practical as ever, Hlif now settled back onto the deck, under her cloak, and kept out of the way. But her words had added to Rognvald's in changing the mood. As if in battle someone had yelled, 'Shield wall!'

The loudest thunderclap yet made speech impossible. Immediately, the lightning struck, Thórr's hammer Mjölnir struck fire in the war between sky and sea, with nine ships caught in the middle.

Skarfr spared a thought for the other ships, considered briefly – hoped! – that Eindridi might be facing the same storm further around the coast, then the black clouds opened again, and hurled rain-spears and ice-balls the size of bannocks, down on the ship. Never had Skarfr been pelted with frozen water in this way in summer! The waves reared up in defiance of the sky's assault, and battle was joined.

'Loosen the sail completely,' yelled Rognvald. 'We need to slow down!'

His words whirled away on the wind, but the crew was well trained and the men midship were already paying out ropes.

The ship had veered around in the confusion of the sea and was taking the force of the storm against its side once more, waves charging like battering rams and breaking over the bulwarks, threatening to swamp the vessel.

'We have to turn it back,' the Jarl told Pilot, who was struggling to hold the steerboard against the force of waves and wind. 'But keep to larboard side. The storm's path is steerboard side and we have to let it pass us.'

Pilot nodded grimly, then yelled, 'Skarfr!' as the steerboard bucked from his grip.

Skarfr threw his rope to Jón, and grabbed for the swinging steerboard handle, which slammed against his forearm as another wave hit. The tendons in his arm tensed, a rock against the breakers. He called on the dragon, summoning every ounce of strength.

The ship heeled so badly that the steerboard was completely out of the water; the wind played with the ship as if it were a toy. The loose sail flapped like a monstrous bird caught in a net, then fell slack. The lack of resistance brought the ship upright again, then Rognvald hurled instructions to haul the sail in and tighten the ropes, to use the wind to help Skarfr.

Oarsmen could do nothing in such a turbulent sea and the force of the storm itself was their best tool, if they could control it without capsizing. The steerboard bucked like an unbroken stallion but Skarfr fought it inch by inch, and gradually returned to the position they needed, running prow first into the waves. He held it there, following a course that veered at a slight angle to the left, taking them slowly out of the path of the storm.

He could see calm patches of water now, as could Rognvald. Working sail and steerboard together, they tacked their way out of the diminishing storm.

The thunder growled defiance in the distance then the skies were silent as the last black cloud scudded east, revealing the full glory of the sun, blazing as if the storm had never happened.

Skarfr cursed. He'd completely forgotten about the sunstone and had missed his chance to use it.

'Tighten the rigging,' yelled Rognvald. Within seconds, the sail was taut and the ship could once more tack north.

The men looked dazed at the sudden restoration of normality and their movements were as slow as if they'd wakened from a dream that held them in another world.

Hlif hauled herself upright, still white-faced but defiant. She pointed the iron tip of her wand at the skies, shouted, 'We are Thórr's warriors, forged in his fire, and Rán's warriors, reborn from the storm-waves. Beat the shields and let the gods know who we are!'

The battle fervour still upon them, those men who could reach the shields that still hung on the ship – by a miracle and strong ropes – drummed on them with an oar. Those who couldn't reach shields whacked their hands or axe-heads against whatever made a noise; bucket or barrel, leather or wood. To add to the racket, each man yelled his name along with whatever victory chants came to mind. Most settled for reciting their entire ancestry at top volume.

The celebration was taken up from ship to ship. Two, three, four... Skarfr counted their fleet and reached nine. All were safe. But they would need to bale out all the storm water they'd taken on board and only when they beached and inspected the ships from hull to mast-top would they know how much damage had been done. The *Sun-chaser* had lost no men but not all its ropes had held.

'My anchovies!' mourned Hlif, watching the barrel as it bobbed far out of reach, already attracting some interest from creatures in the bubbling sea. A steel-grey triangular fin circled the barrel, then another.

The ordeal was not over. *Sharks.*

Something surged upwards and a smile like the mouth of hell opened, splintered the cooper's careful bands. Within moments, the barrel was dragged below the surface. Only the froth above hinted at the thrashing below.

Had he imagined that maw, shaped like a hammer-head? Was Thórr taking payment for rescue from the storm? Skarfr touched his amulet and shivered, knowing how close they'd come to being in the barrel's situation. Wind and current were already taking the ship away from the disturbed water and he put thoughts of jagged death behind him, concentrating on what Pilot was telling Rognvald about their course.

Then a sudden exclamation from Hlif caught his attention.

Pain?

She stumbled, stepped to one side awkwardly in the small space available and Skarfr glimpsed a pool of red where she'd been standing, a trail dripping to where Hlif now stood, reaching for the soil bucket. There was a long moment before his mind made sense of what his eyes told him. In that time Hlif squatted over the bucket, dropped her skirts over it for privacy and attended to nature's call.

Unlike the rest of the crew Skarfr did not politely look away as usual. This was *not* as usual. When he saw the bloody rag thrown into the bucket, then Hlif hurling all the contents overboard, he understood.

'Don't!' he shouted but he was too late.

In a sea full of grey, triangular fins, Hlif had unwittingly baited the water around the ship with blood.

Hlif sank once more onto the ship's deck, a huddle of misery, but Skarfr had no time to wonder why her face was so wet, even though the rain had stopped.

The sea frothed with giant predators in feeding frenzy, randomly bumping and rocking the ship with their hammer heads. Skarfr had not imagined Thórr's mark on these creatures. The sharks' movements were unpredictable, so the measures taken against the storm were no longer useful. Water splashed in from random directions and men were bailing as fast as they could.

The only way they could avoid capsizing was to get away from the grey monsters as quickly as they could.

'Row! Unfurl the sail!' The Jarl's commands were obeyed but not fast enough.

Skarfr hung onto the steerboard, sinews straining as unseen teeth clamped on the wood below the water, then released the tasteless morsel. How much damage had been done, he had no idea.

With what seemed painful slowness, the sail unfurled, caught the wind and the *Sun-chaser* started to move more quickly.

As did the sharks, following the ship.

Skarfr saw the trail of blood to the figure hunched on the deck and he understood. Drops of blood were leaking through the bilges to the sea below, attracting the enemy. They had no chance against the growing numbers of sharks.

The sunny sky and light breeze mocked him, as if the gods' battle had never taken place and this whirl of jagged death had been their intention all along. Thórr's jest.

'Crrk! Crrk!'

He looked up. Unbelievably, a dark shape arrowed over the ship, flew to a calm patch of water and dived. She re-appeared some distance from her entry into the sea, waving her silver trophy as she flew up and away. The cheek of the cormorant, sneaking her own prey amid such dangers!

What was she telling him? he wondered.

What if…?

He would only find out if he tried.

'Pilot, take the steerboard,' Skarfr ordered. 'Mouthy, help him. It's heavy work.'

Rognvald turned a sombre face towards him, questioning, but there was no time to explain.

Skarfr stumbled forwards, rummaged through the store of weapons and untied three long spears. They couldn't afford to lose more than that, so he gave terse instructions to Sigmund Fish-hook, a man who excelled in target practice and, as his name suggested, in fishing. Then Skarfr took up a position on the other side of the ship, with his two spears. Timing was everything.

The ship rocked as an unseen giant hit the side.

'Fuck! I missed,' yelled Fish-hook.

Skarfr's heart sank. It was too difficult.

Then, 'One coming your way!' the other man yelled and Skarfr prayed to Njǫrðr for his aid in the sea-hunt.

A fin rose above the surface, just below Skarfr. He wouldn't have a better chance.

He leaned out and threw.

The spear stuck.

Was it deep enough to draw blood? Skarfr held his breath.

The wounded shark sped away, a double wake behind it as the water streamed down both sides of its sleek body. Trailing behind it was a wavering line of reddened water.

Gods be thanked.

'Hold your course,' shouted Rognvald, guiding the ship on its trajectory a quarter turn away from the gathering of sharks. Fins and giant shadows showed their passing, called by the imperative of their nature. Blood. Even that of their own kind.

Skarfr's own blood sang a victory song, insisted on more action, a different imperative. He attached one end of a rope to the second spear, and the other end he looped around a shield as an impromptu winch.

As the last sharks passed below, he struck again. Once more, the spear hit its target, but this time the shark could not flee. When it felt the constraint of the rope, it dived.

Whooping as the rope paid out, men rushed to join Skarfr and haul in their catch. The shark put up less fight than the steerboard in the storm and knives completed the work begun by the spear.

'Dinner,' grinned Skarfr, as the crew admired the shining monster sliming the deck. The huge hammer head was no longer Thórr's anger but merely a wonder of the voyage, to be turned into food and tales around a camp-fire.

The poem began to take shape in his mind.

Thórr wielded dread Mjölnir,
struck with sky-flash and cloud-crash,
pounded with blunt-nosed sea-hammers.
True to her course, the Sun-chaser
ran before the wind—

Skarfr pictured Hlif, huddled and forlorn, and the heroic tale faltered. What price had been taken?

'Dinner waits until we're safely ashore,' Rognvald told them. 'This ship stinks enough without fish guts in the bilges and we've baited the waters enough.'

Horns were sounding from the other ships, a roll call and a sign. They were on a westward course, heading for the coast. As if the gods had ended the trials for the day, a sandy bay hove into view and the Jarl gave instructions to follow the rest of the fleet.

Pilot took what was left of the steerboard and the ship limped into shelter, lower in the water than was ideal but without a single lost crew member. And only one mysteriously wounded.

Skarfr finally had time to attend to Hlif, and none of her worries about revealing their secret would stop him.

She was still in that hunched position and barely lifted her head when he crouched beside her and whispered, 'Are you all right? Are you hurt somewhere?'

She raised a tear-streaked face. 'Everywhere,' she replied in a broken voice.

She never cried.

'I don't understand,' he said.

'I lost the baby. He was two months old.' Her voice was a dead thing, so quiet he thought he'd mis-heard. 'And I will never have another one. The gods have spoken. Tell them I have a fever and need a healer.'

She dropped her head back into her arms, hiding her face.

Skarfr had no idea what to say to her, so he spoke to Rognvald instead, using the words she'd given him.

'My lord, Hlif is ill and needs a healer.'

'We'll see what – and who – we can find when we land.' Rognvald's tone had regained its authority but Skarfr was not reassured.

His heart resumed its panicky thumping. Two months old. How could Hlif be with child? They had never talked of such a thing. Two months with child. He counted the months since they had lain together.

It could not be. Unless from their dream walking. His heart thumped worse. A baby from dream walking. How could that be?

Because the gods do as they will, across worlds.

And now there was no baby. Hlif had thrown it to the sharks.

CHAPTER 21

SKARFR

You'll rarely see memorials or graves
standing near the road
that were raised for men without sons.

The Wanderer's Hávamál

Hlif had not spoken another word. Not when Rognvald sent Pilot with men to explore behind the beach. Not when they returned with news of a settlement. Not when Skarfr carried her to the village, her arms around his neck, light as a dead bird. Pilot and Mouthy accompanied him in silence.

The sight of Hlif spoke more convincingly than Pilot's words and silver, and a woman was sent for. Dark-skinned, beady-eyed and wrapped in swathes of black cloth, the healer beckoned Skarfr into a stone house, shutting the door quickly behind him to keep the heat out. He laid his burden on the bed, where Hlif turned to face the wall.

Skarfr had learned enough to understand the healer's Hispanic and her gestures were clear enough.

'Women only. Women things. Leave your wife with me,' she said as she shooed him out.

He left.

Wife, he thought. *Better if they believe that.* He ignored the strange hiccup in his heart's rhythm at the word *wife*.

Pilot and Mouthy stood looking hopeful by a cookfire, above which a large pot released the irresistible scent of chicken stewing. To their disappointment, they were ignored.

'She has a fever,' Skarfr told them, 'but she's being looked after. Go back and let the Jarl know. I'll stay here until she's well enough to continue the voyage and then I'll bring her back with me. These people will do me no harm.'

If the men observed any sign on Skarfr's face of the turmoil in his gut, far beyond what Rognvald's skald should feel about the illness of the ship's housekeeper, they made no comment. They were only too happy to return to their fellows, where there was a better chance of being fed. But what one man knew on a ship, all knew, and Skarfr felt heavy with the extra burden of secrecy at such a dark time. All he could do now was wait.

As a break from his self-imposed guard duty outside the healer's hut, Skarfr went for a walk, taking his bleak mood with him. Villagers gave him a wide berth as if he were a skerry against which wild waves rebounded, threatening to sink their ships.

He kept walking until he found a clearing among the stunted trees between village and beach and sat down on a tree stump. His view of the next line of trees awaiting the axe made little impact on him as he looked only inward.

He ached for Hlif and didn't know what words would comfort her for her loss, for *their* loss. Hers was of body and blood. She'd had time to think about motherhood, whereas he hadn't. She should never have had to face those thoughts alone, brave lass that she was, but how could he berate her now for keeping this to herself?

He'd become a father and lost his child in the same breath, before he'd ever thought of having children. Alone, in silence, he asked himself, *What do I feel?* And the question that he knew must be on Hlif's mind and that he must touch as carefully as a sharpened blade when he spoke to her. *How do I feel about never having children?* The answer could cut them both.

Men were supposed to want descendants, heirs, name-bearers with noble lineage. He imagined such offspring, created from his seed, their names and their lineage.

For him to be a father, there would have to be a child, a Skarfrsson or Hlifsdottir. Hlif had said 'he,' but she might have been wrong. Maybe she was also wrong about never having children. A woman's natural fears rather than gods-given knowledge. But try as he might, he could not picture this being, this child, nor could he name the might-have-been.

Skarfrsson or Hlifsdottir. He rolled the formal words on his tongue to see how they tasted, seeking sadness in this vanished future. Instead, he found strangeness. Like when he dreamwalked with Hlif, except that in this new world they were not in the ancient tomb but in their longhouse and children played around them.

He had never known his father except through his mother's memories of him. What could he learn from a man so impoverished he'd thought it kindness to offer his sickly baby to the sea? A man who'd obeyed his Jarl and offered his life to pay his liege's blood debt, and to make his family rich? A man whose widow grieved herself to death within a year.

Kindness killed. Loyalty killed. Love killed. These were the lessons left by Skarfr's father.

For the first time, he thought of the other men who'd marked his life and asked himself what kind of fathers they were. As examples of what he might have been – or might yet be.

The father replacement provided by the Thing Council: his talented, brutal foster-father Botolf, who had taught him a skald's craft but prevented him expressing himself. Botolf, who'd ended his days as a spiteful hearth-worm, relying on the generosity of the foster-son he'd beaten daily.

Skarfr shook his head. He might teach his son skaldcraft but not that way. And he would not grow old. He would seek death with honour. He would rather die like his true father and find his place in Óðinn's hall than shiver by his son's fire, a shadow of a man.

What kind of father was Sweyn Asleifsson, who lived like a saga hero, a-viking twice a year and home enough to dazzle those he left behind at the first opportunity? Skarfr *had* been dazzled as a boy, had wanted to sail with Sweyn to World's End. When he'd first seen Sweyn, leaping ashore from his dragon ship, Skarfr had thought him a god, sun gilding his blond hair, immortal and unstoppable. Sweyn had laughed off exile, done as he pleased and taught more than one jarl to say 'Sweyn is Sweyn' rather than demand obedience that would never come.

His sons must idolise such a father, want to be like him, treasure every one of the few moments he spent with them. But what if they disappointed their father as they grew to manhood? (And what son would not disappoint such a father?)

Skarfr remembered screwing up all his courage to ask Sweyn to take him as a crew member. Yes, he'd been just an unskilled boy but boys could be useful on a ship, agile enough to climb a mast and play the horn. He could have done both. Sweyn had not even considered the idea. Instead, he had made sport for his crew of the pathetic youngster, of his meagre belongings and of his hopes.

No, Skarfr would not want to be a Sweynsson. Skarfr might never be dazzling but he saw no honour in hitting an easy target. A *drengr*, a true warrior, would not mock a boy.

Sweyn's dark equal, Thorbjorn, had also turned his sharp wit against the lad Skarfr had been. And Skarfr had to admit that his mind had grown tougher from the storm of words he'd suffered, just as his muscles had been strengthened by wrestling with Thorbjorn in their friend-days. Was there a need to temper children, judge the forging of them so the fire was not so hot as to shatter them but hot enough to make their mettle true? Would he, Skarfr be able to make that judgement?

He shied away from acknowledging the feelings he'd had for Thorbjorn. Only with Hlif had he found anything like that closeness. Thorbjorn had been both the father and brother Skarfr had never known. In their friend-days, he'd learned sailing and scrivening, philosophy and fighting. Somewhere on a monkish bookshelf was the bible page Skarfr could see with his eyes shut, the page illuminated by Thorbjorn in his role as clerk. The cormorant flying. A priceless gift to Skarfr and yet given with the same insouciance with which Thorbjorn dropped his project for the next young man – or woman – to capture his restless imagination.

Thorbjorn had many facets but not all of them glittered. Skarfr had watched him take Inge against her will, forgiven him for it, and then judged him for it again, when Inge's life was threatened. He had rescued Inge and even made plaint against Thorbjorn to Rognvald for an assault on Hlif. Neither assault nor plaint came to anything and from this distance, Skarfr wondered now whether that was for the best. Was a man's ill treatment of women to condemn his every good quality? Skarfr had believed so but Rognvald had not.

And Thorbjorn had so many good qualities – not just good but exceptional qualities. What kind of father would he have been? He longed for children and if he'd offered them what he gave Skarfr in the friend-days, surely that was everything a child could wish in a father. What he'd tried to give Harald too, although the child-jarl was less fertile ground.

Still, Harald had loved his foster-father, despite Inge's efforts to turn the boy against him. Inge was not blame-free in the mutual wounding of their marital combat. And she had never provided him with an heir, a revenge in which she revelled.

Maybe the father Thorbjorn might have been, was one Skarfr could be. While treating women with respect, of course.

When he had seen Hlif rebuff Thorbjorn's assault on her, Skarfr had wanted to murder him. But now? He had seen many men's ill treatment of women. Why condemn only Thorbjorn?

Was the real reason because that mercurial, intelligent, fascinating man had dropped Skarfr for a new interest? Just as he would drop one mistress for another. Surely a man should be appreciated for his good qualities, whatever his bad? Like in the accounts books that Thorbjorn and Hlif had explained to him, with summings-up on both pages. What total Thorbjorn deserved at the bottom of the page, Skarfr could no longer say, but he knew Rognvald valued his advisor. Just as he accepted that Sweyn was Sweyn, and tried to prevent the two warriors killing each other.

And what was Rognvald himself like as a father? He'd been kind, given sage advice when Skarfr was merely a pot-boy. He'd let Skarfr learn by watching his godson Harald's lessons on leadership and responsibility – and religion. Always a bit dry, a bit pious, a bit – boring – compared with Harald's other guardian, Thorbjorn. Always the Jarl.

Yet there had been glimpses of some bolder spirit like the blue in a kingfisher darting across a stream. Fired up by danger or challenge, Rognvald could out-swim, out-smart and out-versify the best in his entourage.

When he was old, Skarfr might want to be such a father but not yet. Thank the gods, he did not have the fate of nations sitting on his shoulders, to vie with his duty to a child. With a start, Skarfr remembered that Rognvald did have one child from his own seed, the motherless baby brought up with family in Ness. She must be twelve now, ready for betrothal. And her knowledge of her father came only from his winter sojourns on the mainland. A visitor.

Was that good fatherhood? Skarfr turned the question different ways to find an answer, as the sunstone found the sun.

He had no doubt that Rognvald had acted as he thought best for his daughter, whatever pain he might have felt from the absence. Just as he had laid on his ward the doom of never marrying, a doom that pained her as a curse – and pained Skarfr too. Hlif did not think Rognvald a good father, though she served him as housekeeper with unswerving respect. How complicated people were.

'What the?!' Skarfr swore as a stabbing pain in his head and a jabber of squawked insults roused him from thoughts that circled like an *Ouroboros* serpent, mouth endlessly chasing tail.

The cormorant sat on a branch opposite him, head cocked on one side, waiting.

He did not move.

Her rant became hysterical and she flapped her wings, ready to attack him again. She clacked her beak to make her intention plain.

His head cleared and he understood.

'Crrrrk,' she admonished him. *Stupid son, thinking of fathers while the mother bleeds. Go to her.*

She flew at him, pecking, driving him away from wherever her nestlings hid and suddenly he knew what to say to Hlif.

CHAPTER 22

SKARFR

*That wise girl
was my flesh and my heart,
though I could not call her my own.*

The Wanderer's Hávamál

Skarfr had to use the word *wife* a lot to barge past the healer and into her house, where Hlif was being tended. Now he sat on a wooden stool beside the bed, studying the back turned to him. Such a fragile wall in its sea-stained dun linen that smelled metallic, but a wall nevertheless.

The strap of Hlif's over-dress seemed too broad for the narrow shoulder beneath it and flapped like a sail with no wind. The other strap was pinned beneath her on the bed. Despite her ailment – if that was the right word – and the sweltering heat, she was still wearing all her usual clothes. Her skirt was pulled carefully around her ankles but her bare feet peeped out, naked and vulnerable. The same feet he'd seen dancing in the waves when they were children on an Orkneyjar beach.

Not the same feet. Not dancing.

Skarfr swallowed. Should he touch her or not? This was uncharted water and he might steer them both against the rocks. If they weren't already wrecked.

He reached out, gently placed a palm on the square edge of the pinafore dress, his fingers splayed out on the linen beneath. One layer of fabric between his hand and the freckle-laced skin he loved to stroke. He kept his hand still and she did not move, which he took as encouragement.

Talking to your loved one's back is never easy but Skarfr had to try.

'You don't have to say a word if you don't want to,' he began, 'but I'm here and I'll stay unless you ask me to go.'

He paused. No response.

'You can tell me anything. How you feel, what happened... this *thing* happened to both of us. You are not alone.'

The back shifted a little.

'A *drengr* only feels his wounds when the battle is over. Then there is pain and he weeps for those he's lost. You are the strongest *drengr* I know and,' Skarfr felt a tremor in his words, a catch in his throat, 'and our weeping is payment for the journey of our child to the otherworld.' Then he choked, beyond speaking as a sob rose, dragging at his guts like a dagger.

Slowly, Hlif turned towards him, dry-eyed and angry.

'It was nothing,' she said. 'Just blood in a bucket. Women things.'

He recoiled at her callous words, then he understood how deep the pain must be. In the wild, wounded animals attacked.

He edged onto the bed beside her, stroked her cheek, her hair, her slim shoulders that carried too heavy a weight.

'It was something,' he contradicted her quietly, a lump in his throat. 'Something... someone you carried alone, our new path with —' he swallowed again. How could this be so hard? 'Our new path with a child made pictures in your mind. Pictures of the years ahead. Him learning to walk, to talk, to fight – or her, learning to spin cloth for sails.'

She rubbed impatiently at her face, as if one of his tears had dropped there. But she listened.

'We will remember,' he whispered. 'The gods have taken a sacrifice we did not want to make, and we must accept that. But we can mourn.'

'That's not what women do. We pretend it never happened. We do not speak of it. Men don't want us to speak of it.' Her words were harsh, but her body softened a little, her eyes closed and her hand crept towards his body.

He enclosed her hand in his own. 'This man wants you to speak,' he said.

'The sea took our baby,' she murmured, 'but Aegir will offer something in return, and it will be your choice whether to accept such a difficult gift.'

Her words made little sense and he was uncertain whether they came from delirium or prophecy.

Wife. The rightness of the word pulsed in his body and found its way to his lips.

'Wife,' he said, as she nestled against him. 'I shall tell Rognvald the truth. No more secrets.'

'No! We must wait until Jórsalaheim.'

Whether the seer spoke or the woman, he could not argue with her at such a time and merely stroked her back, assent implicit in the gesture.

How had she become so thin without him noticing? Surely, she should have put on weight these last two months. Had the voyage been so hard for her? When men bled, they boasted. When women bled, they were ashamed, told to be ashamed by the priests of the White Christ. How they hid the monthly curse of Eve, Skarfr had no idea. Yet another curse that Hlif bore with quiet courage.

Her face sheltering against his chest, she murmured, 'I did not know an emptiness could be so vast.'

They lay in silence, holding each other, until the door creaked open and the healer interrupted them, bustling and over-bright.

They jerked apart, as if caught in some guilty act, as the woman was quick to observe.

'It's too soon for making another babe but at least you know it works.' Her coarse joke made Skarfr wince but it was well meant. And to another woman, another couple, it might have brought comfort. He squeezed Hlif's hand, trying to send the message that his concern was all for her and he had no need of an heir.

'Out with you,' the healer told him. 'She needs five days in bed and then she can sail with you.'

'Four,' said Hlif weakly, her eyes daring him to disagree.

Skarfr managed a smile for her. 'No point,' he said. 'Rognvald needs five days to repair the ships. Those sharks made a few dents and the deck needs swabbing down. It's covered in slime and stinks of dead fish. You'll only get asked to join in the scrubbing if you come back sooner.'

'I'm very tempted,' she said, the shadow of a spark returning. 'But you've convinced me to take five days. Maybe I'll be appreciated more when I go back.'

'Jón Halt-foot will be saying every day how much he misses you,' Skarfr joked. He'd settle for the shadow of a spark, and hope for more, in time.

'Go mend ships,' she told him. 'And when you come back for me, you can recite the saga of Skarfr the Shark-fisher.'

'Skarfr the Shark-spearer,' he corrected her. But he knew that when he declaimed the saga of Rognvald, in some future when the Jarl was no more, there would be no mention of sharks. Some stories were too private to tell and, for him, the true hero of this one would always be Hlif.

The scene that met Skarfr when he returned to the beach was one of frenzied activity. Rognvald's men had been busy. One ship was upturned and a man was hammering new planks onto a damaged section. The *Sun-chaser's* carpenter was fitting the repaired steerboard. As Skarfr had predicted, decks were being thoroughly scrubbed and bilges emptied.

Large chunks of shark meat were grilling on a rack above a cookfire but there was no room for the whole shark. The rest was in strips, drying in the sun on driftwood rafts, attracting flies and a persistent one-eyed cat, which were shooed off with curses and flapping arms. Flies and cat were equally undeterred.

When those working on repairs declared that they were running out of raw material, Pilot and five men were sent back to the village to trade for anything suitable and also for whatever food provisions they could get.

They returned a few hours later pushing three handcarts heaped with wool scraps, wooden planks and poles, bread, rounds of cheese and a dead goat covered in flies. They also brought good news.

Skarfr had been making new rigging to replace ropes frayed in the storm, but he left his work to join Rognvald and see what new resources they'd gained.

'Your wife is doing fine,' were Pilot's jovial first words, clearly addressed to Skarfr, and the men sniggered. Apart from Rognvald.

The sky whirled around Skarfr for a long moment.

'The villagers mistook what they saw,' he explained to Rognvald. 'And I thought it best to leave that impression, so they'd show Hlif every courtesy.' *Especially given what was wrong with her.*

He faked a grin. 'I don't suppose I'll ever hear the end of it.' For extra authenticity, he added, 'And Hlif will give me an earful for the deception.'

Pilot laughed. 'I wouldn't want to be in your shoes. She'll be back in four days, they said. Right as rain.'

'What did the villagers see, Skarfr,' asked Rognvald, his gaze loosening Skarfr's bowels, 'that gave them the wrong impression?'

The best liars spoke truth as much as they could and evaded when they couldn't. 'Me carrying a sick woman, seeking their healer.' Skarfr met the sharpness of those brown eyes with his own honest gaze, a clash like two swords meeting.

'Fever, you said,' Rognvald stated.

Skarfr allowed himself to look down, embarrassed. 'The healer was a woman. I did not pry further.'

What normal man *would* pry further? Not Rognvald, who said, 'Someone needs to do Hlif's work until she's back. Skarfr, ask the other captains what stores of dried food they have, then share it out across the whole company. Get the water barrels emptied so the men can refill them from the stream. Mouthy can show them where the stream is. And remind the men to fill their own waterskins too.'

Rognvald marched off to check how repairs were going on the *Sea-Chaser's* steerboard and Skarfr added a few instructions of his own, thinking that Hlif would have approved.

'Oddi, get that stinking goat skinned, gutted and spitted. The sooner it's roasted, the less chance of us eating more maggots than meat.

'Jón, can you take the wool to the men re-caulking the stern of the *Destiny*. They have plenty of tallow to mix with it.

'The rest of you, take the planks to Carpenter. He'll tell you where they're needed, and any spares can go on board the *Sun-chaser*.'

The men worked in stints, like their shifts when sailing, alternately sweating under the dazzling sun and sheltering under tents made with the same oilcloth covers they used on board to protect them from rain and cold. Already, rain and cold were difficult to imagine in the blinding light and heat reflected by the sand.

Cup-bearer Roaldsson had rigged up a makeshift spit, passing a spear through the goat and, despite grumbling from the blacksmith, setting up two inverted pairs of tongs to form the uprights. The rotation was achieved by prodding the meat with another spear and at the stage morsels started falling into the fire below, the meat was judged to be cooked and work ended for the day.

Over morsels of goat, shark and cheese, wrapped in bread that was no stale trencher to use as a plate but actually moist and edible, the tale of the storm grew into a saga. The circling sharks were the size of Jörmungandr, the worm that circled the world. When Skarfr called on Njǫrðr for help, the god joined him and lent his strength to spear the monsters while Hlif, Rognvald's völva, tamed the storm with her spells, undaunted.

As they wove their story from its individual threads, it became apparent that the whole company had been 'undaunted'. Each man related his own act of courage in the face of the raging elements. If they mentioned their fear, it was to highlight their bravery. And who was to say they were wrong?

Skarfr listened and ate his fill, gave the story of the Shark-spearer when he was asked for it, and accepted the applause graciously, even played the buffoon. This was what Hlif expected of him, a different kind of courage.

As his stomach settled and the sun dipped low, Skarfr sat on a foreign shore and watched the strange sea called the Miðjarðarhaf. The sea in the middle of the world. So calm today that mere ripples tickled the beach and the tide line barely moved all day. A vast emptiness.

'Shall we swim?' Rognvald asked him and his gesture included the whole company.

It was so like the Jarl to issue a disguised challenge, knowing full well that every man there saw grey monsters lurking below the placid surface. That every man there feared the appearance of triangular fins. As did Rognvald himself, which was of course the reason for the invitation.

'Yes!' Skarfr accepted the challenge, threw off all his clothes bar his braes and ran into the water after Rognvald, who was already swimming out of his depth.

The sea was warm and buoyant, a caress soothing Skarfr's aches, cleansing him of the day's grime. A giant bath. He ducked his face, opened his eyes underwater and saw ghosts twisting and turning, pursuing their silvery prey. His stomach clenched and released. The shapes moved like seabirds, diving underwater and soaring up, breaking the surface to rise into the sky. Creatures at home in water and air. Cormorants? Or a trick of the shimmering light in the aquamarine depths?

He pulled his face up to breathe, revelling in the lightness and strength of his body as the ocean cradled him, and struck out towards Rognvald. Whether the Jarl held back or whether Skarfr was now the stronger swimmer, they were soon swimming abreast. For men hardened in the freezing seas and even colder lochs of Orkneyjar, swimming in warm water, without effort, was a novelty; Skarfr was disappointed when Rognvald turned and headed back for shore, but he kept him company.

Emboldened by their temporary equality, just two men swimming, Skarfr turned his head so his voice carried and asked, 'Do you fear nothing?'

'I fear dishonour.' The disembodied reply was too predictable.

But after a few strokes the Jarl spoke again. 'No, I can avoid dishonour, so need not fear it.'

Skarfr waited, feeling that something important might be said while sky and water turned golden, as their arms powered forward in the same rhythm.

'Betrayal,' said Rognvald. 'I fear betrayal.'

Then he dipped his face into the water and increased his pace, turning the last stretch into a race. When they emerged onto the sandy beach, there was much laughter and back-slapping. Allusions to Rognvald's swimming fame were gracefully accepted, wineskins were found, and the day ended in the camaraderie that the Jarl created so easily. The bigger the hardships, the deeper Rognvald drew on his skills for uniting his men.

Yet he feared betrayal. And he had told Skarfr this.

Sleep should have been impossible but fatigue has its own imperative and, with his last waking thoughts, Skarfr sought Hlif in the ancient tomb.

He found himself in the right place but not inside the ancient tomb. He was outside, the grassy mound in front of him, bathed in blood-red light. Perhaps it was the Summer Solstice. He'd lost all track of holy days or even months while they'd been voyaging.

Months. Something had happened today that meant losing track of months was important, but he couldn't remember what. He had to see Hlif. She would tell him. He did remember that there was an entrance, a passageway, so he walked towards the dark hole, stepped from light into darkness and was blasted by flames, his ears deafened by roaring.

Burning, roasting alive, he could only stumble backwards out of the passage and fall to the ground, his skin hanging in black tatters.

'No!' roared the dragon. 'She does not want you!'

He curled around the pain, trying to protect something that might still be alive, but he didn't know what.

His burned mouth would not work but he knew the dragon heard his thoughts and he fired his confusion at it. *You're part of me. You can't keep me out!*

Another blast of flames blew towards him through the passageway.

A monstrous growl told him, 'I *am* part of you. So, who do you think is keeping you out, dreamwalker?'

Skarfr refused to play with riddles, and he was determined to get into the tomb, find Hlif. There was a hole on top of the knoll, a rock-slide into the chamber. He found himself looking down into it, driving snow around him.

Not the Summer Solstice then.

He would slip down into the tomb, fight the dragon again.

He sat down, ready to slide down and just as he realised the rocks were teeth, one green eye opened and watched him slide down into its open maw, into fire and darkness, into the dragon. Where the poem he would never speak aloud shaped words from pain. Through unshed tears, he could see his child playing on the sea-bed among the *Nykrs*, the water-spirits who sometimes took on human form.

Dream-born,
My hearth-fire would have welcomed you
and my heart-fire warmed your blood that
bled instead to redden shark-teeth
in the killing-field of stormy seas.
The fish-shifters played gut-strings,
sang you too soon from your first home

claimed you for a Nykr.
Rán caught you in her net and
she will see your first steps,
hear your first words,
watch you swim wild and fast
in the waves of Otherworld.
I will not.

CHAPTER 23

INGE, STRJÓNSEY, ORKNEYJAR

Inge had felt at home in Finn's well-maintained longhouse from the moment she hung up the patterned wool curtain to partition their bedroom from the hall, where guests would sit at tables around the central fire pit. The sheltering porch entrance in front of the door was bigger than that of her previous Orkneyjar longhouse; a cosy little room in its own right.

Don't compare, she reminded herself. *Love the island you're on.* And there was much to love about Strjónsey. The very name of the island meant 'profit' and the herds of cattle on rich grassland made the source of that profit obvious.

Inge stood in the open entrance looking at the view of white sands and restless sea beyond the grassy slope that led to low buildings, dots in the distance growing larger and more solid nearby. Dwellings and workshops; church, smithy and tannery; kitchens and smokehouses. Everything needed for a comfortable life could be found on the island and in less than two weeks it had become *her* island.

The house was south-facing, protected from the spiteful winds that prevailed, and the porch was agreeably warm in the afternoon sun. She and Finn had neither dog nor goat to make its home in the porch so the space was wasted. The thought niggled at her until a startling idea formed.

She had set up her loom out of sight, behind another curtain, in a space where she could find peace and privacy. As had been her habit when peace and privacy were her defence in the daily acts of war that defined her first marriage. A sanctuary as dark as her thoughts, lit only by one rushlight that she guarded as if it were her soul, touching it to a new one just before extinction.

Don't compare.

In a bold fit of optimism, she went into the gloom of her tiny chamber, dismantled her loom and set it up again in the porch, where the colours of the wool glowed in the daylight. She attached her grandmother's weights to bundles of warp threads, their familiarity calming her as she drew the shuttle back and forth.

Once she'd settled into the routine, she could glance up at the view, see the blacksmith in his leather apron rushing out of the forge to dip something into a barrel that flamed. Or a woman with a wicker basket, empty as she walked down through the village, and full of turnips when she returned.

Sometimes people would glance her way, perhaps wondering at the strangeness of their new neighbour sitting in an open doorway, weaving her bright threads.

She could feel the smile she wore, as new as her clothes. A little stiff but growing more comfortable each day.

Her gaze flitted to clouds and breakers far out at sea as the fabric grew, row by row, until a figure coming up from the beach path caught her attention. Hair red-gold in the sun, lumbering in gait and solid as his longhouse. Well-made.

She finished the row and sat still, fighting the urge to rush into the dark curtained space she could rightfully call her own, the new smile trembling a little.

Finn ran the last yards to their house, words tumbling out as he reached her.

'That's what was missing from this house!' he told her, a smile in his eyes. 'My beautiful woman lighting me home.'

He stood awkwardly, the loom between them. Then he touched the fabric as if it was delicate lace.

'So fine,' he said, stroking the wool.

His eyes met hers, dark with the sun behind them, dark with more than shadow.

He reached across the loom and stroked her cheek. 'So fine,' he repeated. 'So fine.'

Her smile steadied.

Later, much later, Inge presided at Finn's table, where the guests were newly come from Hrossey, so keen to share their news that they dropped hints and winks throughout the meal. But they were discreet and controlled enough to wait till the pot-boys had left before they served the real meat.

Weasel, a small, sharp-faced man in a red tunic, glanced at Inge, before saying pointedly to Finn, 'Lady Inge looks tired. Perhaps she'd like to withdraw.'

Inge flushed and half-rose from the bench, unwilling to place her husband in an awkward position among men who were strangers to her and could do him harm.

But Finn's hand on her arm told her to stay and she sat down again.

'My wife's counsel will be the better for hearing what you have to say directly from your own mouths rather than at second hand from mine. You need not worry that she will speak out of turn.'

Weasel frowned but accepted Finn's offer of more ale and came straight to the point. 'Jarl Harald has been taken by the King of Norðvegr.'

'It's true,' confirmed his companion News-nose, with scarcely hidden relish. 'The King's ship lay to, off Thorsa and plucked the young Jarl easy as a nut in May, then off they sailed, who knows where.'

'But why?' Finn expressed Inge's own puzzlement. 'What does the

King want from his own vassal? Orkneyjar already belongs to Norðvegr, even if the King leaves the two jarls to rule over us. Surely Harald's not challenged the King?

Weasel shrugged. 'All we know is that Harold's sent word to Thorbjorn for ransom to be paid so he can be released.'

Inge suppressed a shudder at a name she must harden herself to hearing.

'And meanwhile the 'advisor' Thorbjorn Klerk rules Orkneyjar.' Weasel's tone dripped sarcasm.

The men laughed. 'No change there.'

'Jarl Rognvald should never have left Orkneyjar in the hands of a youngster as sole Jarl. Even with Thorbjorn as advisor – and to give the man his due,' he looked an apology at Inge, 'he is experienced and educated. But, as the saying goes, *One jarl rules for himself but two jarls must heed their people.*'

'If only we *had* our two jarls,' Finn mused aloud. 'But with Jarl Rognvald gone for a pilgrim, we have only half a ruler.'

'The years will be long till he returns,' agreed Weasel.

'If he returns,' pointed out News-nose.

Inge couldn't hold back any longer. 'This tale of kidnapping shows Harald's weakness. There's another man who will take his chance. A man who won't wait to see whether Rognvald returns or not before claiming his right to be jarl.'

Weasel and News-nose looked at Inge as if one of the giblets left on a platter had spoken.

Finn merely nodded and named the man. 'Erlend.'

Rallying, Weasel nodded and said, 'Ay, true enough. Word is that Erlend shouts loud enough in Skotland that he should be jarl but I don't think he'll have the islanders' support.'

Finn observed, 'But you tell me Harald's not here. And the more he behaves like a sullen boy, the more people will look elsewhere for leadership.'

'And what do you think Harald will do, the moment he's released?' asked Inge.

'Move against Erlend?' Weasel hazarded a guess.

What further thoughts they might have on the actions of their betters would never be known as they were interrupted by a pot-boy, who rushed in and addressed Inge, stammering.

'My lady, sorry to disturb you but the man says he's come from Ness, just missed you there, and it's urgent.'

'I'm sure it can wait.' Inge was curt. She would speak to the steward about training his boys better.

Red-faced but dogged, the boy persevered. 'He said you would want to know. To tell you his name is Fergus and he's Skarfr's man and he brings you private news.'

Her heart clenched, then relaxed. Her friend Skarfr was far away at sea and, like the pot-boy, his man Fergus was overreacting. No doubt there was some problem with the farm that could easily resolved.

She gave an apologetic smile, said, 'I expect my brothers have been causing trouble again. Excuse me please.'

But a sense of foreboding tensed her guts, and she knew from Finn's fleeting glance of concern, that he was not fooled.

CHAPTER 24

THORBJORN, HORSEY, OKNEYJAR

Thorbjorn dipped his quill in the inkwell and shook it once over the blotting rag, which was already splotched black. He reflected a moment, then carefully wrote the date and amount in the ledger open on the lectern in front of him. The date matched the day he noted it down but he had no intention of releasing such a large sum so quickly for such a ridiculous purpose.

Three gold marks. Or eighty pennies in smaller coin. A hefty sum indeed to throw away on a boy's stupidity, but insultingly small as ransom for the Jarl of Orkneyjar. If Harald were horseflesh valued at eighty pennies, he'd be no more than a sturdy packhorse. Perhaps King Gillisson of Norðvegr was correct in his valuation of the young Jarl but what in the name of the White Christ did he *really* want?

He was making some point with regard to the money, so easily gained, and there was surely some political goal here, if Thorbjorn could only see it. Maybe Harald's report on the encounter would shed more light on the King's motives but Thorbjorn was in no hurry to get his foster-son back home, to be a drain on his attention. Managing the young Jarl's erratic humours wasted time better spent on managing the jarldom itself.

No, Harald could stew for a few weeks, safer in the hold of King Gillisson's ship than in Orkneyjar, where his enemies would not be bought off by three gold marks. Enemies that now included the entire Asleifsson family, may the gods curse them.

Although Thorbjorn had cause to hate all his previous in-laws, especially the thieving sea-rover Sweyn, he did not want them bringing an army against Harald. But to exile Sweyn's brother Gunnr just because Harald was peeved at his mother's choice of a new man, showed how young the boy was.

Thorbjorn sighed. There was little chance his godson would learn caution from his kidnap. Only maturity would teach that. But the more attacks Harald survived, the greater was the likelihood that he would hold the Jarldom until Rognvald returned from his pathetic, self-indulgent voyage and behaved in a responsible manner again.

Of course, that was not how others saw the pilgrimage. 'Worthy of the old heroes, a second Rognvald outdoing the first.'

Orkneymen liked a bold leader – until his intrepid spirit killed him. And there was always another jarl in waiting. Rognvald was *not* here and neither, at present, was Harald. But Erlend was.

Dropping anchor wherever he could sow dissent and make fabulous promises, the man who proclaimed himself rightful heir could not be ignored much longer. Even by Harald.

What if Erlend would make a better jarl than either Rognvald or Harald? Nobody questioned Erlend's claim, as the son of a previous jarl known as Smooth-tongue. An impeccable bloodline.

Who would join Erlend in an attack on Harald?

The usual answer came. The damned Asleifssons. Harald's spiteful decision to exile Gunnr had blown Sweyn towards Erlend like the weathervane he was. Wherever there was an opportunity for profit and prominence, that braggart would be shouting his great 'I am'.

I am the jarl-maker, I am the booty-taker, I bested Thorbjorn, the voice in Thorbjorn's head jibed.

He swore. Lost in unpleasant thoughts, he'd held the quill over the ledger and squeezed until ink had run down to the nib and blobbed onto the page, smearing the reason for the payment.

Instead of reading *Pro redemptione Haraldi Maddadson*, 'for the redemption of', the smear made the first two words look like *Pro redeceptione:* 'for the repeated deceit of' Harald Maddadson. As if some divine being had read his mind.

He crossed himself and shivered, then jumped at being addressed.

'My lord?' His steward began tentatively. 'What do you want done with the new thrall? The woman.'

'Why should I want anything done with her?' snapped Thorbjorn. 'Can't you see I'm busy.'

The steward stared at his feet, which stayed rooted to the spot. He persisted. 'You said to chain her in a stall, feed her and then you'd give further instructions. That was two weeks ago and we need to at least clean out the stall. T'aint good for the beasts.'

Thorbjorn winced at the thought of the foul conditions in the cow byre and struck the man for his stupidity. 'Where's your common sense! You could have moved her. Did I tell you to keep her like a pig? And you should have reminded me sooner.'

He'd completely forgotten about her and was no longer sure why he'd taken her in the first place. The rage that had torched Skarfr's longhouse had burned itself out and more important matters had claimed Thorbjorn's attention.

Scores had been settled in a warrior's way and Skarfr himself was out of reach – another young oaf, not so much older than Harald, punished in absentia. Matter closed. When Skarfr returned he would know who had done it and why, but there was no reason for others to speculate on either.

Nobody had reason to accuse Thorbjorn, nor any proof, but he wanted no thralls' gossip complicating his life. As if his life wasn't complicated enough!

'Take me to her,' he ordered.

The man blanched but obeyed.

As they walked down the well-trodden path between dwellings and stables, Thorbjorn considered his options. She belonged to him, by the signed word of Skarfr's dead master. He could kill her but that could lead to the very gossip he wanted to avoid. One look at her had ruled out other forms of enjoyment, and she would hardly look more attractive after her recent treatment.

She didn't.

Black hair streaked with grey hung lank and unkempt over her face, revealing glimpses of dull blue eyes and waxy skin, reminiscent of a dead fish. Her practical dun overdress hardly showed the stains of imprisonment and food slops but the stench made Thorbjorn recoil.

Keeping enough distance to protect his nose, Thorbjorn spoke loud and slowly, in simple words, so she might understand him, whatever her origins.

'I own you now.'

She shook her head furiously, a spark lighting in her eyes. She might even have been pretty once, years ago.

'Skarfr!' She spat the name at him as if it might unlock her chains.

He had already wasted too much time on this and must be clear and quick. 'No. Your owner was Botolf the skald, and he is dead. He gave you to me.'

'So, you say the old bastard who called himself Skarfr's godfather was my master, do you?' The woman flung the words at him. 'I think not. And burning a house down is a strange way to claim an inheritance, so it is. Where's Fergus? What have you done with him?'

Shocked as much by the torrent of words in intelligent Norn as by her impudence in speaking at all, Thorbjorn reached instinctively for his dagger but controlled himself. He wanted to stop gossip, not create more, and he had no intention of closing in on such a foul being, even to kill her. At least he could speak to her normally and be understood.

His words were clipped. 'The other thrall is dead.'

She gave an animal cry and dropped to her knees as if he *had* used his dagger on her.

He pressed the point. 'You are alone. If you obey orders and work hard, you will be well treated.'

She lifted her head, defiance rekindling in her eyes. 'You call this

—' Her chains clanked as she raised her hands and pointed at the filth-smeared stall. *'Well-treated?'*

No thrall had ever spoken to him like this.

'I call it a lesson,' he said. And turned his back on her.

'Clean her up.' The steward started at his lord's sudden attention 'Put an iron collar on her and send her with the two servants going on our merchant ship to Ness this afternoon. They can unchain her aboard ship and if she throws herself off, they'll pay with their lives.'

The perfect solution. His mainland estate could have three extra pairs of hands instead of two. Any gossip would be strangled at birth among his loyal retainers and until he could be sure she was of no use to him, the woman might as well work for her keep.

He flung his last words over his shoulder. 'If you run, you'll be hunted down for a slow death, an example to your fellows. Say *Thank you, master.*'

The woman murmured some words in a strange tongue and before he could react, added, 'That's 'Thank you master' in the Írish language. Ah, sure and it means more if I say it in my own tongue.'

Thorbjorn grunted but let it go. Thralls might look like humans, but they were as different from his kind as filth-loving pigs.

CHAPTER 25

BRIGID, PENTLANDSFJORD, ORKNEYJAR

When the iron collar was unlocked and removed, in silence, far out on a cold sea, Brigid bit her tongue to stop the words, 'Thank you,' from coming out. The rope binding her hands was cut and she scratched the itch that had been driving her crazy, until she drew blood. Fleas no doubt. There would be more itches until she had access to a fine comb, water, soap and clean bedding, and somebody to check her over. All she had now were two gaolers.

The woman who'd released her sat back down, crammed between an oarsman and a barrel of dried herrings, her back turned on Brigid, as Brigid's own back was to the second servant seated behind her.

As the blood rushed back into skin that had been pinched and patterned by restraints, so did the agony of loss pierce her numb spirit. She clenched her hands into fists and spread them wide, working the circulation, working the pain.

He is not dead. I would know.

That one could not be trusted, with his fine Írish looks, black hair and a darkness in his soul that showed in his blue eyes when he made his threats. Ach, she'd been threatened often enough but that one took pleasure in the imagining. She was glad she'd cursed him.

She savoured the words again. *Go bhfaighidh tú bás gan onóir. May you die without honour.*

Wherever Fergus might be, his eyes would show the good soul he had in him. So she'd seen him all those years ago, a boy among the raiders sacking their village.

He is not dead.

Would he understand her message? *Drom Reagh.* Their Írish home, to remind him of the settlement which had been destroyed. To remind him they had survived, to love and live together. 'Thralls,' the Orkneyjar lords named them but *they* were the slaves. In thrall to their own overlords, to their greed, to their endless killing.

The ship rolled in the swell and Brigid looked at the same heaving sea she'd crossed with Fergus, when they'd been taken from their home. So many years had passed. Years watching the boy, Skarfr, endure the spite of his godfather, the old skald. Years she and Fergus were worked to the bone by the old man, as miserly in spirit as with sustenance.

So, he'd willed his *thralls* to that one, had he! Not if Skarfr had anything to do with the matter. Ah, sure and she could work, and wait out the years for Skarfr's return. And Fergus would find her.

She fixed her gaze on the horizon, steady when all else heaved and dipped.

CHAPTER 26

SKARFR

*A traveller cannot bring
a better burden on the road
than plenty of wisdom.*

The Wanderer's *Hávamál*

Rognvald went to the village himself to fetch Hlif, leaving Skarfr to ensure that all the ships were ready to sail. Was there significance in the Jarl going to fetch his ward? Was he sending a message? What would the healer and the villagers think? What would they say?

Skarfr tried to reassure himself. Rognvald already knew the villagers believed Hlif to be Skarfr's wife and surely no healer would speak of her condition to the company leader.

But Pilot was with the Jarl. What if he explained that Rognvald was her guardian and what if the healer *did* reveal all she knew?

Checking the ships were seaworthy was a nominal task, a mere question to each captain, and Skarfr had time on his hands to envisage Rognvald's anger at such a betrayal of trust. He imagined every moment of his inevitable exile in this arid place.

Finally, the brush foliage parted and the Jarl appeared in the distance, accompanied by his men and the tiny figure Skarfr knew all too well. When they came near enough for him to read their smiles, Skarfr's tension eased. Nothing had changed.

He glanced at Hlif, who was still too thin but had some colour in her cheeks. She smelled of freshly washed linen, her gowns stain-free and her hair neatly coiffed in pristine white, all signs that she was taking care of herself again. Even though her eyes avoided his, he saw the pain her smiling mouth hid. Lacklustre unsmiling eyes, their shifting greys dulled.

Everything had changed.

'Skarfr will be glad you're back,' Rognvald told her with a smile. 'He can count ships on his fingers but not water barrels.'

Hlif responded in the same light tone. 'I only took to my bed to make sure I was appreciated.'

The falseness grated on Skarfr, so he was relieved when the banter ceased and Rognvald gave the order to launch the ships. His spirits always lifted when running a ship out to sea, then clambering in and taking an oar or the steerboard. But the best moment was when the unfurled sail caught the wind, filled like a woman's belly when she was with child.

He gripped the steerboard so tight his knuckles were white.

'Skarfr!' Pilot rebuked him. 'This is the calmest sea I've ever seen and your mind is still on storm watch.'

'Take a break, Skarfr,' ordered Rognvald, and he passed word down the ship for the new watch to begin.

Rocked by the gentle swell, his face caressed by the light breeze and salty spray, Skarfr dozed. Men with fishtails murmured in the water below, giving the ship safe passage and teaching a little child, newly come among them, how to turn somersaults on the seabed.

He was pulled back from the dreamworld by Pilot shaking him. 'This is the river estuary, Skarfr! We've reached the Ebro. *Our* river.'

Skarfr wondered whether he was really awake. How could the landscape be so different from the long sandy beach they'd left behind them? Mudflats stretched around them as far inland as they could see, either side of a wide channel that must be the River Ebro.

Wildfowl whistled and screeched, pecking and stabbing their paths across the silvery mud or wheeling in strange formations overhead.

'Roseate birds!' he exclaimed. Larger than swans and with round bodies as if they'd each swallowed a pillow. Not just one but dozens, hundreds, standing on one leg or flapping giant wings to show flashes of black feathers.

'Yes,' agreed Rognvald, staring. 'Roseate birds.'

'Can you catch some?' asked Hlif hopefully. She'd obviously compared them to swans too. And was thinking of them roasted.

Pilot shook his head. 'Too dangerous. Even if a couple of men took the rowboat, they'd not make it far across the mud without sinking to Hell. Nasty death, choking in mud.'

Hlif grimaced and Skarfr tried to lighten the tone.

'If it's a change from dried shark you're after, we still have one barrel of anchovies,' he said. 'You put one on Bishop William's ship and the storm didn't take it.'

Her face brightened a little. 'Good,' she said.

Yes, good, he thought. *One step at a time.*

'We'll reach the city of Tortosa soon enough,' said Pilot, 'just as the sun's past its highest. Then we'll get all the provisions you could ever want.'

Skarfr sighed. Sunshine again. He was never going to get the chance to try out his sunstone.

In a V formation like the birds above, the *Sun-chaser* led the other eight ships into the mouth of the great river. As they left the expanses of marsh and mud behind, the banks became more clearly defined, with lofty trees overhanging the river and shorter shrubs visible behind them.

The Ebro was so wide, the ships could have sailed side by side but for many other boats vying for space. Pilot steered them to the right bank and the other ships fell in behind. Light craft and cargo ships sped past them downstream, heading out to sea. Skarfr felt dizzy at the way they all avoided each other.

Rognvald observed, 'You spoke true. This must indeed be a major trade route.'

Pilot nodded at the boats passing on their left. 'They're headed for Barcelone. And the ones ahead of us can keep going on this river for three months, all the way to Zaragoza.'

His eyes gleamed as he spoke the name and Skarfr inferred that this Zaragoza-place was well worth the journey.

A heavily-laden cargo ship came perilously close to ramming them but, as if by magic, Pilot's instructions dovetailed into the actions of the other vessel, and both sailed smoothly on their courses.

'How do you know what the other ships will do?' asked Skarfr.

'There's rules on a busy river like this. Basically, keep to steerboard. And let them as has the wind to steerboard go first. And if you're going to collide, man the oars or sink!'

'But—' The many questions crowding Skarfr's head were forgotten as the tedium of passing trees and scrub was interrupted by the appearance of wooden jetties and mooring posts. The harbour was impressive enough but the city towering above it was magnificent, from the fortified citadel at the top and the grand cathedral below it, to the bustling community around the docks.

'Tortosa,' breathed Pilot.

'This is where we make our fortune,' declared Rognvald, but even his confidence seemed subdued at the sight of yet another Hispanic city that made Orphir look like a cluster of cave dwellings. His pride and joy, the magnificent new cathedral of St Magnus, looked little better than the yellow sandstone walls and arches of the houses here, winding up towards the castle.

The usual shifts were organised to guard the ships, under the leadership of Cup-bearer and Magnus Havardsson, then Rognvald and the other six captains took a cadre of men up the paved streets, marvelling as much at the drainage channel running down the middle as at the brickwork of what seemed to be ordinary dwellings by local standards.

They'd barely left the docks when a dark-skinned man in a turban and robes accosted them, joined by several of his fellows within an instant, all talking at once and laying hands on the newcomers.

Before Skarfr or Pilot could explain that these were muleteers offering rides up to the citadel, Black-hammer had shouted, 'Saracens!' A swarthy veteran of many voyages and no pilgrimages, Black-hammer had been hoping to contribute to the crusades against the Infidel and now saw his opportunity.

The rest of the company were enthusiastic in their support and, in the time it took to yell, 'Ambush!' the brawl was blocking the street, with the Jarl in the thick of it.

In his defence, Skarfr would say that he was trying to correct a misunderstanding and restore peace when he punched Jón Halt-foot on the nose, but in truth he'd been wanting to hit someone for days and it felt good.

'Hit him again!' shouted Hlif, weaving towards him and avoiding the flailing fists which mostly connected over her head.

She confronted Jón's accusatory stare with the brazen lie, 'I didn't mean you.' Instead of apologizing, she fished a clean rag out of the purse attached to her belt, beside her usual accessories. 'Staunch the blood with this. You're dripping.'

'Sorry,' Skarfr told Jón. 'Accident.'

Then he whirled around to deliver a jab to the belly of someone wearing white livery with a red cross on it, who'd just arrived on the scene, along with more of the city's watch than Rognvald's company could dispatch. Especially once they realised that these were actual peacekeepers – their hosts, in fact.

Such realisation did not come easily to men enjoying the crunch of fist against bone and the satisfaction of letting blood, which was every bit as good for the health as modern physicians believed.

Skarfr rapidly assessed the odds as a number of white-coated guards rushed into the fray and decided it was time to use his head for something other than butting. If shouting about the innocence of the 'Saracens' could stop the scrap, Pilot would have succeeded long since. Instead, his voice was hoarse as he redirected his explanations and changed language, to explain to the guards that Rognvald was a mighty prince from a foreign land, who had mistaken the muleteers' approach for an attack. Which was understandable, Pilot pointed out, as the Moors had been the enemy, the last time he'd been here.

Nobody listened to him.

Skarfr ducked under the halbard waved half-heartedly in his direction and rushed behind the guard, kicking him in the back of the knee as a bonus, a move that Thorbjorn had taught him. The guard crumpled and Skarfr was free to run away from the fighting to where the mules were tethered, watching the action with their ears back, and shifting hooves anxiously.

He sliced through their ropes and with whoops, whistles and whacks, he made the beasts run into the confusion of men. They brayed and stamped, swinging their baskets as they looked for an escape.

Instinctively, men held back. They would cheerfully jab superfluous people with any weapon to hand but working animals were worth more than they wanted to pay in recompense.

The Moors clearly shared the same priorities. They claimed their terrified beasts, taking them by the harness, clicking encouragement and helping the mules carve a way back to safety. Skarfr let them go past, then formed a solid barrier with his axe, discouraging any of his fellows who thought to continue their entertainment.

The guards were also taking their opportunity to rope their charges, until Rognvald's company capitulated, and the Jarl made it clear they would go quietly.

Finally, Pilot had a chance to be heard and he repeated his explanation, adding further eulogies to his introduction of the mighty foreign prince. Rognvald had a black eye, a ripped tunic and an air of total satisfaction. Undoubtedly an Orkneyjar Jarl.

Skarfr grinned, sheathed his axe, and held out his hands in surrender as he walked forward to join the somewhat battered company and took his place beside Rognvald and Hlif, as they were marched up to the citadel. Heads high, the men behaved as if their captors formed a guard of honour. After all, they'd been heading this way anyway.

In great indignation, Bishop William was speaking Frankish to the guard, who understood not one word and merely shoved him in the back.

'When I am received at your cathedral, there will be repercussions for this treatment of one of the Lord's anointed,' Bishop William declared loudly. His split hand and bruised face suggested that there had already been repercussions for his treatment and Skarfr knew the bishop could acquit himself with a warrior's skill in battle. And he had God on his side.

Lighter of heart than he'd been for days, Skarfr sensed Hlif beside him, taking three steps for his two. She held her skirts above the paving and avoided the occasional pile of equine dung but showed no sign of fainting or faint-heart. Just one of the company.

They marched through an entrance three times the height of a man and were brought to a halt in a courtyard. There was no time to admire the red stone walls and crenellated towers, the wooden beams under the ceilings of sheltered walkways, or the carvings. Their leaders were here to receive audience and judgement.

Whether they would have been brought as quickly to the rulers of Tortosa if they had not caused a public disturbance, was an interesting question. With Pilot as interpreter, Rognvald, Skarfr, Hlif and the six captains were ushered into the great chamber where the rulers of Tortosa received petitions and directed the business of the city. And sentenced criminals.

One of their escort led them to the front of the hall, facing the lords' dais, where three men sat in state. The rest of their guards lined up along one wall with others clad in the same livery, white with a red cross.

Other guards in the hall were dressed differently. The three banners hanging above the dais suggested three different factions and none portrayed the red cross on white background.

One banner showed four red vertical bars on a yellow background. The second was in quarters, and featured a yellow castle on red, and a lion on white. These corresponded with the colours of the guards' tabards. On the third banner, a knight was killing a dragon, on a red background. Skarfr could see no reason why this should be interpreted in a simple red cross on white, but this seemed to be the case. He wished he'd listened more carefully to Pilot's gossip about Tortosa politics.

He looked again at the three men who occupied the carved armchairs on the dais. One for each faction? Clean-shaven, about Rognvald's age, with hooded eyes and a serious expression, the man in the middle was probably the most important one but it was the man on his right to whom their captor spoke.

Motive was the mother of learning and Skarfr's Hispanic was improving in leaps and bounds. He was also becoming aware of how selective Pilot's translation was. Rognvald would not have responded well to the description of his company, had he comprehended it.

The leader of the guards told his superiors, 'We have heard of these northern barbarians, who leave destruction in their wake. Today they have attempted murder against our citizens. Were it not for the resourcefulness of the Genoese guards, they might have succeeded.'

Skarfr took full credit for the resourcefulness. *Mules*, he thought.

Then, *Genoese*.

So, Genoa was represented among the rulers here, as the Almerían trader had indicated. Sea-state to some, pirate-state to others, Genoa would not be too punctilious about how it benefited from trade with Rognvald, as long as it *did* benefit.

The leader of the Genoese guard presented his case. 'These invaders came on nine warships, moored without seeking permission, then attacked the Muslim muleteers who politely offered them mounts. Their leader is a man without honour, who was at the forefront of the assault.' Here he indicated Rognvald, who smiled, his purpled eye already closing up so he looked more like the ship's cat than a jarl. 'Hanging would be too good for them!'

Pilot translated smoothly, 'There was a disturbance of the peace, and we arrested these men, not realising their status as subjects of the King of Norðvegr, led by the Prince of Orkneyjar himself.' Pilot indicated Rognvald with the same gesture used by the Genoan guard and Rognvald bowed. 'I'm sure allowances can be made for a misunderstanding.'

The Genoese ruler replied to his guard, 'You have done well,' but he gave no judgement, merely glanced at the man in the middle.

The ruler on the other side, a man with pinched face and squeaky voice, said, 'The matter appears to have been dealt with and is trivial. Throw them in the dungeons and let's not waste any more time.'

He looked to the man in the middle, who was slow to speak but whose deep voice rang around the hall. The silence that reigned as he spoke showed respect. 'We must uphold the agreement with our Muslim citizens, or it is we who have no honour, but we must also show justice to these newcomers. So, we must hear more.'

The previous speaker pulled a sour face but merely said, 'Castile and Leon will accept whatever the Prince of Aragon decides.'

Aragon, noted Skarfr, dismissing the Castilian noble as irrelevant, clearly a lowly representative of southern Hispania.

'Genoa too accepts Aragon's judgement, my lord Raimon.'

Pilot summed up for Rognvald. 'The Prince of Aragon, also Count of Barcelona, Raimon Berenguer IV, will pronounce sentence.'

The Jarl frowned but he understood lineage and had more sense than to challenge such a man. At least until after he'd given a judgement.

Aragon ordered Pilot, 'Be brief. Recount what occurred.'

The tale of the Saracens' provocation had grown during the march up to the citadel and been well-rehearsed. Pilot also included the fact that only two years earlier, the three rulers had themselves laid siege to this city, on holy crusade against the very Muslims they now protected. How were men from the far north to ascertain who were friends and who were enemies, in such changing times?'

Aragon let his head rest on one hand, deep in thought. Then he said, 'But *you* knew.'

Pilot's face went white. He stammered, 'Yes, I-I tried to tell them, to stop them.'

Suddenly Aragon's hawk gaze turned to Skarfr. 'I think you

understand our speech.' He didn't wait for assent. 'Did you know these men were no Saracen enemies?'

Skarfr nodded.

'And what did you do to protect them?'

Thumped my shipmates would not do as an answer so Skarfr said, 'I set their mules on them.'

A ripple of laughter went around the hall and was quickly stifled. Aragon tried to hide a smile behind his hand.

'And was this rather original technique effective?' he asked.

'I believe so,' said Skarfr.

There was a long pause and Aragon's expression resumed the gravity that seemed natural.

'I have reached a judgement,' he declared.

CHAPTER 27

SKARFR

*Men become friends
when they can share
their minds with one another.*

The Wanderer's Hávamál

'Before I pronounce that sentence, please answer one more question. Where are you going after Tortosa?'

Aragon's request was a thinly veiled order, but Skarfr thought 'Please' was promising. He opened his mouth to answer that they planned to sail up the Ebro and acquire as much booty as they could, but Pilot frowned at him and cut him off.

'Narbonne,' Pilot said firmly. 'My Lord Rognvald wished to see the wonders of Tortosa, so we made this detour.'

A twitch of Aragon's mouth suggested scepticism but he didn't probe further.

Pilot translated for Rognvald but the gist had been clear enough and the Jarl was already nodding approval, saying, 'Narbonne'.

Skarfr broke into a sweat that had nothing to do with the heat as he realised how close he'd come to landing them in prison or worse. Telling the ruler of all the lands along the Ebro that Rognvald's company intended to raid and plunder the river settlements would not have been his finest moment.

Then Aragon delivered his verdict. 'Our Muslim citizens must receive compensation for an unprovoked assault on them. I set this at ten gold dinars, unless anyone was killed or maimed.' He looked at the Genoese guard, who shook his head.

Rognvald winced when the fine was translated.

Aragon went on, 'I accept that there was a misunderstanding caused by the ignorance of our visitors. I do not accept the plea that government here changed so recently that our Muslim citizens could have been mistaken for enemies merely because that was once the case here. We claimed this citadel two years ago, as Pilot well knows, but I doubt very much whether Prince Rognvald knows any of this history or even knew the name Tortosa before coming here. The ignorance of those accused makes the plea illogical.'

He fixed Pilot with an unblinking stare. 'You, however, know Tortosa and its history. You knew the muleteers were our citizens going about their business. You did not prepare these foreigners properly.'

Skarfr thought this grossly unfair as Pilot *had* bored them to tears with names and politics, to which none of them had listened. However, Pilot said nothing in his defence, merely bowed his head in acceptance of the accusation and waited, his clenched fists the only sign of tension.

'So,' decreed Aragon, 'Pilot will leave this company, which he has failed. He will pay the compensation of ten dinars.'

An exclamation escaped Pilot. There was no way he had so much coin. Skarfr wondered whether even Rognvald had, or what could be offered instead. Would his sunstone pay Pilot's debt?

'The company will be our guests for two days,' Aragon went on, 'during which time we can profit from each other's conversation. You will have the freedom of Tortosa and you will behave in a civilised manner, showing respect for all our citizens. This includes the Muslims and Jews. You should stay away from their separate communities on the other side of the Carrer de la Cortadura and in the walled dockyard further north.

What are Jews? wondered Skarfr. Clearly this group of people was a significant and respected community here, as were the Muslim Saracens. This status was strange enough in a Christian city but rendered even more bizarre by the fact that only two years ago Tortosa had been a Muslim city. How could they all live in peace now? It was even more of a miracle than Rognvald and Jón Halt-foot being friends.

In his experience, Christians were zealous in their approach to converting 'heretics' and it was easier to fit into their prayers and services than to speak out for a different faith. Especially when that faith allowed the worship of many gods. What was one more god – or one more saint? Even the Christians added new saints to their pantheon and Skarfr was happy to let St Magnus intercede for him and Hlif with the White Christ. If only he didn't have to wait until Jórsalaheim. He sighed, fingered his hammer pendant and concentrated on what Aragon was saying.

'Pilot will be our translator while you are in Tortosa and will then accompany me when I sail for Zaragoza to join the Queen in the Summer Palace. For three months' navigation up the Ebro, I shall pay Pilot the sum of ten dinars.'

Pilot couldn't wipe the grin from his face as he translated for Rognvald, who asked, 'What shall we do for a pilot?'

Aragon had thought of this too. 'I know a suitable man, who will convey both you and your message directly to my dearest ally – with due respect to those present.' He nodded at Genoa and Castile. 'Ermengarda of Narbonne keeps a most civilised court and you will not need a translator. Your man here,' he nodded at Skarfr, 'knows our language well enough. And I hear from our Bishop that your prelate speaks Frankish fluently, as well as Latin.'

He addressed Skarfr directly, 'I don't suppose you care for poetry or music?'

Skarfr's answer was so enthusiastic that Aragon invited Rognvald to join him at table that evening and, with Pilot's aid, to prepare better for Narbonne than they had for Tortosa.

The Genoan and Castilian representatives gave grudging approval of Aragon's judgement, impatient to move on to more important matters. Then Rognvald's company was hustled out of the hall by the same guards who'd marched them in, who did not appreciate being told to escort the noble visitors to the guest sleeping-quarters.

Given their liberty (within the restrictions of 'civilised behaviour') each man indulged his own proclivities. Skarfr and Jón Halt-foot accompanied the Jarl, Hlif and Bishop William to the cathedral, where the word 'pilgrims' ensured peaceful and private accommodation for Hlif and the Bishop. No doubt the latter would enjoy a lengthy conversation with the Bishop of Tortosa regarding the treatment of visiting prelates and the difficulties of funding and staffing a large religious community.

Refreshed in soul, Rognvald sought his next priority and when all three men were waist deep in the steaming water of the baths, he waxed lyrical about the cathedral interior and how St Magnus Cathedral would be just as fine when it was finished.

As Skarfr's muscles relaxed, his thoughts drifted back to other baths, to other companions. He remembered the time when, as a boy, he'd shared the baths with Fergus and realised that even thralls had friends and enjoyed gossip. He'd not thought of Fergus as a thrall for so many years, the thought came as a shock.

With a pang of guilt, he realised that he'd not officially freed Fergus and Brigid, as he'd promised to do. There had been so little time before the pilgrims set sail. He owed them so much and he'd forgotten to make good on his promise. Instead, he'd spent most of that time with Hlif. A man could always find time for what mattered most to him.

Still, he reassured his conscience, Fergus and Brigid were as good as free, running what was their farm in all but name, with a cosy longhouse for home. He had repaid them well for their kindness to a lonely boy and when he returned to Orkneyjar, he would confirm their status. A mere formality that could easily be put right and would make no difference to how they lived.

***

The next two days were an education in southern courtesy. Skarfr learned from Rognvald that Jews were heretics, but of a different kind from Muslims. There were such individuals in Norðvegr, merchants and doctors, living discreetly with their families in their own manner, but there were no communities such as this.

Truly, travel broadens the mind, thought Skarfr. And men worshipped many gods. He felt even more justified in his own beliefs. Far better to respect more gods than to call down the wrath of those slighted.

Fraternising with the rulers of Aragon was less eye-opening. Familiar with the formalities of the Norðvegr court, Rognvald and his men rose to the occasion, determined to correct Aragon's first impression of them.

At the high table in the great hall, Skarfr was treated to a variety of spiced vegetables whose names he had to ask, while he listened to as learned a debate as he'd heard since he visited the isle of monks with Thorbjorn.

Pilot worked hard, translating Aragon's ambitious plans for a judicial code, or Rognvald's vision of leadership. Both men drew on their faith in God for these principles of earthly conduct and their accord was so strong that the Jarl swore he would introduce Aragon's *Usatges* laws to the Thing Council when he returned to Orkneyjar. Aragon even promised to send Rognvald a bound copy of these laws, in Latin, when his project was complete.

Still murmuring 'aubergine' in the same reverent tones Hlif had used for anchovies, Skarfr found himself the centre of attention and had to decline further food and wine, so he could speak of poetry and music. Before he'd even begun to give examples of the three hundred and twenty-two well-known words suggesting swords, from *Yggr's fire* to *battle-serpent*, Skarfr sensed he was losing his audience and cut short his discourse.

'You will find a more discerning audience in Narbonne,' Aragon promised Skarfr. 'Ermengarda's court attracts the best troubadours in Occitania.'

Skarfr was careful to deflect the implied praise to his liege. 'Then Jarl Rognvald will shine, for his reputation as a skald is without equal in our country.'

Rognvald smiled at his skald, returned the compliment, and suavely directed the conversation to his true objective.

The nine ships left Tortosa to a send-off that included a fanfare and distribution of honey cakes among the spectators who were attracted by the sight of this colourful band of foreigners. Aragon himself was at the harbour to watch them leave, ostensibly from courtesy to the Prince of Orkneyjar but probably to verify that they headed *down* river. He repeated his warnings about the dangers on the high seas between Tortosa and Narbonne, from monsters to pirates, which added spice to the prospect, in Skarfr's eyes.

Rognvald was not displeased with his stay and the ships were laden with exotic produce such as olive oil and dried fruit. Ermengarda would pay Aragon handsomely for these goods in Narbonne's own trade items, and there was to be a suitable profit for the Orkneymen acting as merchants.

As oars were shipped and sails filled, the new pilot directed the steerboard. He was a quiet little man, but no doubt competent. Skarfr could see Pilot still waving from the docks and knew he would miss him. What adventures they would have had together sailing to Zaragoza. Adventures, riches and honour, a saga in the making. Pilot would have those adventures.

Skarfr indulged in a moment's envy, imagining what might have been, then tried to accept the fates' re-direction. Why had his cormorant been so insistent he follow Pilot's stories of the great trading river if the company was to be turned back so quickly? He would feel a fool when they met Eindridi again, who would surely mock his naivety and mock Rognvald for listening to him.

He glanced at the Jarl, who was watching the wind-tell and the sail, looking forwards, abstractedly fingering his pathfinder brooch.

He dropped his hands when he caught Skarfr looking at him and said, 'Did you know Aragon is nicknamed *El Sant*, the saint?'

Skarfr shook his head but was not surprised. Aragon's piety and ascetic nature had been as evident as his intelligence and hospitality.

'Some meetings change our lives,' Rognvald observed, a faraway look in his eyes. Noting Skarfr's attention to the pathfinder brooch, he clasped his hands and declared, 'I do not need this pagan symbol anymore. I have all the guidance I need now, from the Lord Jesus. This is just jewellery.'

A merchant ship gaining on them caught the Jarl's attention, sparing Skarfr any need to comment. Rognvald yelled instructions to the men midships, controlling the sail. He turned to the pilot and confirmed an adjustment as the wake from the merchant ship hit them with enough force to rock the *Sun-chaser*.

The pilot yelled something at the crew on the merchant ship, insulting their mothers, sisters and dogs, then all was calm again.

Skarfr pondered Rognvald's cryptic pronouncement. Maybe the visit to Tortosa had not been about him at all, although he had brought it about. Maybe the meeting between El Sant and the Jarl was destiny at work.

CHAPTER 28

SKARFR

Hail to a good host!
A guest has come inside,
where should he sit?

The Wanderer's Hávamál

Awe lessens each time an experience is repeated. Having been awed by Tortosa, Skarfr was impressed, but less so, by Narbonne. In contrast with the hilltop citadel rising above the great Ebro river, Narbonne was a seaport, a walled city behind a great harbour. Instead of looming high above the ships as they arrived, like Tortosa's citadel, Narbonne's castle buildings and cathedral tower peeped above the fortified walls, suggesting their hidden treasures rather than flaunting them.

However, the harbour lived up to its reputation as mercantile heaven, a place where east and west met, traded and each parted the richer. Amid the usual bustle of loading and unloading, counting and weighing, Rognvald's company found empty berths, tied up the ships, and agreed on shore parties and ship watches.

Although clothes and appearances suggested a variety of

nationalities manning the vessels and labouring in the harbour, none were turbanned. Perhaps it was as well that the Orkneymen's new tolerance of Moorish citizens was not put to the test, but Skarfr would have preferred dark-skinned muleteers to the smug faces there to greet them on the quayside. He gritted his teeth.

'Eindridi! Guthorm!' Rognvald greeted his fellow-captains affably. Presumably, they had been alerted to the arrival of the Jarl's ships.

'We wondered whether the storm had taken you.' Eindridi's words were harmless enough and coming from another man would have shown concern. 'We've been here for weeks!'

He grinned and his eyes challenged Skarfr. 'I suppose you wasted your time following tales of a river flowing with gold.'

Rognvald had warned him that there must be no settling of grievances in Narbonne, to bring dishonour on the company, so Skarfr endured the dig and the sneer.

Eindridi's gaze flicked down to Skarfr's chest and his eyes narrowed. It was a change of expression so fleeting that Skarfr would have thought he had imagined it if he had not been fully aware that the pouch was in full view. Eindridi should have no idea of its contents, nor have such avidity in his eyes.

'No time was wasted,' Rognvald replied calmly, refusing to rise to the bait. 'We must present ourselves in a proper manner to the Lady Ermengarda; we have gifts for her from the ruler of Tortosa.'

Eindridi blinked, the only sign of his surprise. He'd no doubt hoped to show his superior local knowledge but he recovered quickly.

'I'll take you to her,' he said, as if the Viscomtesse of Narbonne was his best friend.

Skarfr had no option but to follow that swaggering figure, along with Rognvald, Hlif, Pilot and the captains. From the harbour, they passed through the nearest gate in the city wall, then along the meandering streets to what seemed to be the outer wall. Once through that, they discovered that a river cut the city in two, with one bridge linking the two halves. A gate led through another wall to the part of Narbonne where Ermengarda's palace was situated. There, Eindridi sent a pageboy ahead with a message.

As if Rognvald couldn't have done so himself! thought Skarfr.

Pilot had taught him enough of Occitan, the sister-tongue to Hispanic spoken in Narbonne, for him to communicate clearly, albeit with mistakes. He suspected many of the captains had also picked up enough not to be hoodwinked. As had Rognvald. And the crew would always work out a combination of foreign vocabulary and gestures to ensure that shore leave met their needs. If Eindridi thought he'd be at an advantage, now he had a smattering of Occitan, he'd be disappointed.

They all understood the reply. Ermengarda would receive them in her antechamber and the boy would lead them there. The determined thuds of their boots echoed on the flagstones as they marched along stone corridors, past niches and windows. They passed knights in effeminate gauzy tunics, wearing hose instead of manly breeches, and ladies in a rainbow of silky gowns. All turned to stare at the Orkneymen.

Clearly, they were a novelty here, even more so than in Tortosa. They stared back and the Narbonnais politely dropped their gazes, returned to their conversations and dalliances, or whatever lords and ladies entertained themselves with in such a place.

'Is there a hole in the back of my gown?' asked Hlif. 'They're looking at me as if I have a cat sitting on my head!'

Skarfr smiled. 'If you did, you'd fit in better.' He tipped his head towards a lady whose high headdress was an eccentric confection of fur and fabric. Her hair was in two coiled plaits like rams' horns and the combination did indeed make her look as if an animal were perched on her head.

Hlif laughed, another noise that echoed oddly and earned disapproving looks.

So be it, thought Skarfr. *Let Óðinn punish those who lack hospitality. Ermengarda is undoubtedly an ugly virago swathed in silk, sneering down her pinched nose at those whose customs differ from hers.*

He was right about the silk, which was blue.

The ruler of Narbonne was looking out of the window and turned when she heard them, before the boy made his introduction. The sunlight made a halo of her golden hair, shining through the jewelled net gathered at the nape of her neck, drawing attention to the smooth line of her throat. The drape of the blue silk gown was graceful over her slim arms and body. What Hlif would probably call high-waisted in style, the bodice emphasised small curves in a graceful manner. Taller than Hlif, she wore stillness like her own skin, poised and regal.

Skarfr wondered whether this could really be the ruler of Narbonne, so young, so beautiful. As a boy, he'd mistaken Sweyn and Inge for two golden gods when they'd jumped off a longship, dazzling in the sunshine. But Ermengarda truly was the goddess Rán visiting Midgard. Her blue robe enhanced the cool grey of her eyes as she weighed up her visitors and then spoke.

'Estela, you may return to the ladies now and I will not forget your kindness to Beatriz.'

Skarfr blinked, realising that there was another person in the room, in the shadows, back towards him. Her hair was as black as Ermengarda's was golden, flowing to her waist in a maiden's unbound freedom. Younger than Ermengarda. She had a lute tucked under her arm.

'It is a pleasure to teach someone with such talent,' Estela replied.

'By strange coincidence, that's exactly what my lord Dragonetz says. You may leave me now.'

Ermengarda's tone was ironic and made her seem much older than the girl. But when Skarfr saw Estela's face, he realised that she was more mature than he'd thought, on the cusp of womanhood. Her eyes made brief contact with his and the red silk of her dress brushed against him, as she made her way out of the chamber. Topaz irises. Tawny rings like gold fire. Her face was flushed, perhaps in response to Ermengarda's last remarks. Then she was gone.

Hlif coughed, bringing him back to his senses and an awareness that Eindridi was juggling for the position Estela had vacated, in front of Ermengarda.

Subtlety and courtly manners were all very well but Skarfr could leave those to Rognvald. He elbowed three men out of the way, including Eindridi, who was taken unawares and stumbled, swearing.

Not a courteous act in front of the gracious lady of Narbonne, thought Skarfr, hiding a smile as he bowed low.

'My lady, I speak on behalf of the illustrious Prince of Orkneyjar, leader of our gallant company of pilgrims.' Skarfr gestured to Rognvald, who bowed. He continued quickly so Eindridi could not interrupt him. 'We come to your renowned court fresh from Tortosa, where we were received with honour by the Prince of Aragon, who recommends us to you. He assigned a pilot to us, who can serve as translator.'

Pilot took his cue and bowed but Skarfr wasn't giving up the speaker's role yet. 'Our ships hold Aragon's gifts to you, to which the Lady Hlif holds the inventory. She is in charge of all supplies and trade from our vessels.' He couldn't help a note of pride creeping into his voice as he presented Hlif, who curtseyed.

Ermengarda took her hand and raised her, smiling. 'You will find I too know how to read and write inventories. The people call me the shopkeeper of Narbonne behind my back, but without trade and accounts, our coffers would be empty and their pleas for justice would go unheard. We will talk later.'

She hesitated, still holding Hlif's hand. 'Perhaps you would like a cooler gown for our hot climate?'

What delicacy in offering Hlif something more fashionable to wear. Skarfr could see Hlif was tempted but she merely thanked Ermengarda, at the same time as Rognvald spoke.

'No,' he said, frowning. 'That would not be appropriate for my ward.'

Ermengarda dropped Hlif's hand and addressed Rognvald. 'My Lord Rognvald, you and your ward, and all your party, are welcome in Narbonne. I am certain we will have much to speak of.'

The Jarl took her hand, kissed it and began to recite poetry.

Skarfr thought he'd leave Pilot to translate the glowing compliments. Or even Eindridi. He wanted no part of what could only end badly. For better or worse, the unthinkable had happened. Rognvald had fallen in love.

CHAPTER 29

SKARFR

*I felt like I was rich
when I met another traveller –
people's joy is in other people.*

The Wanderer's Hávamál

The surveillance of Narbonne's harbour by city guards was so efficient that only a few men were needed guarding the ships. After a day and night on board, they had ample time to explore the city, and their watch came around again a week later. The nine captains also did ship duty in rotating shifts, and Skarfr was charged with making random visits to report on any problems.

He had forgotten what a man *did* when he was not constantly watching sail and sea, fretting about the weather and the course they were on, worrying constantly about the woman he must ignore.

Presumably, his restlessness showed, as the Jarl told him, 'Check the ships then look around the city. Be young, for the love of God!'

He was almost disappointed that there were no problems with the ships. Everyone and everything was 'fine'. One-eye hissed at him, as if to prove all was normal.

Seagulls emitted their raucous cries and swooped down for

scraps of food. A gang of cormorants sat on mooring posts, still as statues. One turned her head towards him.

Go and play! she told him. Then, as if at some signal, all the cormorants took flight. They wheeled and settled on the surface of the water, in between the bobbing ships. They splashed each other, ducked and dived, squabbled over fish. Played.

Skarfr walked back to the gate in the city walls and strolled aimlessly through cobbled alleys. The old paving in one street was composed of huge stones, rounded and smoothed, like the backs of giant tortoises. What people had been capable of building a street like this, so straight and so solid?

Alone, with nowhere he had to go and nothing he had to do, he looked around him, at the stone buildings leaning on and towards each other, at the workshops and people inside them. Already, he recognised some of the streets and named them by the elements which had drawn his attention. Cobbler Street, Cats Alley, and the Jewish Quarter.

Tortosa had taught him to see different communities in various parts of a city and now, although he saw no Muslims, he did find streets where men wore dark robes, and spoke in a language he did not know. A few sported long beards and sidelocks, unlike any hairstyle he'd seen before. The Jews gave him curious looks but he felt no hostility, although he did have the feeling someone was following him.

He looked sharply behind him. Seeing nothing unusual, he shrugged. He was still jittery after all he'd been through. Rognvald and the cormorant were right. He needed to play.

Skarfr soaked up the atmosphere. He passed an open doorway and heard a girl singing something plaintive and haunting. He might not understand the words but the sound spoke to him.

He did indeed need to play. How long had it been since he'd played his pipe? He'd oiled it carefully, protected it from salt water and sun, and kept it safely in his pack, but an instrument could languish from neglect, just like a person.

Reaching an open place where streets crossed, he found a well and some large flat-topped stones, convenient seats. He accepted their silent invitation and delved into his pack. He rooted around, ignoring his lucky bird-bone, his pouch of silver and gold bits, his spare tunic and the comb Hlif had given him, until he found the oiled cloth parcel. He unwrapped the wooden pipe that had accompanied him as a boy and now as a man.

The first notes broke, ugly, but then he found his breathing, that sweet spot between control and expression. He shut his eyes and replicated the song he'd heard, feeling the melody reach out to imaginary listeners.

When he finished and opened his eyes, the listeners were real. Four ragged boys were sitting cross-legged before him, attentive and eyes sparkling. They waited.

Skarfr would not disappoint his audience. He launched into the traditional tunes of Orkneyjar, pouring his memories into the lilt and melancholy. Vast grey skies and a little orphan wanting to be the hero of the sagas beaten into him.

His audience grew, parents joining their children and clapping the rhythm to his jollier tunes. Reluctantly, Skarfr finished his impromptu performance, stood and bowed, opened his arms wide to thank his audience.

He had no idea what words they spoke in that strange tongue, as they reclaimed their children, returned to their business, but their reverences to him said, 'Thank you,' clearly enough.

One man stayed behind, not of the Jewish community, to judge by his brightly patched tabard and hose. His face was clean-shaven, adding to the impression that it hovered between male and female, fine-boned and mobile.

'Come here tomorrow, when the sun is so high,' he said, pointing up at the orb in the west, 'and I will make music with you. I play guimbarde.'

Skarfr had no idea what manner of instrument this might be, but his curiosity brought him back the next day to discover it was a sort of droning whistle made of bamboo. The guimbarde player placed it in his mouth, made a humming noise, and twanged the part which extruded, to create sounds ranging from a bee's hum to the thunder of distant horses' hooves.

Once again, an audience gathered but this time the mood was joyous and the guimbarde set people's feet tapping until they could resist no longer and the men lined up to dance in a way Skarfr had never seen before, moving as one in a pattern that grew ever faster. The women giggled as they watched, especially when a man fixed his attention on one of them. Like birds, thought Skarfr, dancing for their mates.

After several such meetings, the guimbarde player told Skarfr he must travel onwards with his group, but he would not forget their music-making and wished Skarfr to remember him. Bemused, Skarfr accepted the guimbarde handed to him, too valuable a gift for him to know how to properly respond.

He could not offer his pipe in exchange as that would be discourteous, negate the other's generosity by giving payment.

'I will make a name-tune for you,' he stammered, 'and I will play it wherever I voyage. But you must tell me your name, so I can tell my listeners what the tune is called and who inspired it.'

'Guimbarde,' said the musician with a teasing smile, and they parted, ships that passed.

When Rognvald told Skarfr that there was to be a tournament of song and he would recite one of his poems for Ermengarda, in front of the lady herself, Skarfr was less taken aback than he had been by the Jarl's spontaneous composition at their reception. He hid his misgivings when Rognvald asked for help in preparing a speech and, with input from Pilot, they worked together until they'd both mastered not just the words, but their delivery.

Rognvald seemed to be deeper in love every day they stayed in Narbonne and Skarfr could only try to present the Jarl in the best possible light and remain in the shadows himself. Like the beautiful girl with the lute. He wondered idly whether she would perform during this evening of song.

CHAPTER 30

SKARFR

Don't hold on to the mead-horn,
but drink your fair share.
Say something useful or stay quiet.

The Wanderer's Hávamál

Thanks to Hlif working her housekeeper's magic behind the scenes, and to the help of a Narbonne washerwoman, Rognvald's men wore well-laundered tunics and breeches for the evening's entertainment in the great hall.

The Jarl himself was resplendent in a fine wool cloak with braided edges, fastened with the pathfinder brooch. When the trumpet sleeves of his cloak fell back, gold and silver arm-rings were revealed. He'd even hung a gold chain around his neck, with a huge hammer-head pendant hanging below it. For this evening's tournament of song, he didn't seem to mind pagan symbols as long as they were gold. His brown hair gleamed almost red in the torchlight, as did his beard, still more suited for sailing than for court. Even his head appeared to be circled in gold. He looked like a man who'd raided a dwarven hall for his accoutrements.

Hlif wore her favourite turquoise soapstone beads in a triple row over her pinafore top. This was the only accessory she'd brought to dress up her practical travelling clothes.

Neat, and sensibly dressed, she faded into the background amidst the bright silks of Ermengarda's courtiers but to Skarfr no woman there was more beautiful, in body or spirit. He doubted whether any other woman in that hall could voyage for months on a dragon ship without complaint, never mind organise all provisions and trade, cooking, and apportion rations fairly. Not even Ermengarda.

From their table along one wall, Skarfr observed the golden Viscomtesse and her guests at the high table. Guest of Honour was clearly the Queen of France, Aliénor of Aquitaine, whose visit was the talk of the chateau. The two women rivalled Rognvald and each other in their glittering jewellery, as befitted their status and the occasion. Ermengarda wore a gold net over her hair, sparkling with what looked to be diamonds. Aliénor's coronet was studded with emeralds, as were her bracelets and her wide embroidered belt.

The Queen's Commander, Dragonetz, was also there, his brooding expression suddenly lighting up with mischief, in a change of humour that reminded Skarfr of Thorbjorn's mercurial moods. Dragonetz had a reputation as a warrior too but, tonight, it was likely to be his equally renowned talents as a troubadour that were called upon.

The beautiful girl, Estela, was there too, and seemed to be attached to the Queen's contingent. She'd entered the hall after most of the guests were at table, her lute tucked under her arm. She looked as if she were hobbling slightly as she went, between Lord Dragonetz and a turbaned Moor, the first Skarfr had seen in Narbonne. Skarfr's first thought was that the Moor was the girl's servant, for she seemed to lean heavily on him. However, he took his place at the back of the hall, where he exchanged some words with the men there who wore the padded leather jerkins of guards. Not a servant's behaviour. And the girl sat beside the Moor while Dragonetz continued to the high table.

When serving-boys entered the hall with platters of extravagant dishes, the food claimed all Skarfr's attention. He wondered whether he would ever again be excited by smoked haddock and bannocks after eating fluffy wheat bread, and meat or fish he barely recognised beneath the mouth-watering flavours of cinnamon and orange sauces.

After food and spiced wine had relaxed the audience, Ermengarda signalled to a drummer-boy, who beat a dramatic roll to commence proceedings. Most of Rognvald's men had drunk rather more than was wise so their stamping was enthusiastic and noisy.

When she could be heard, Ermengarda announced, 'In honour of our visitors,' she looked towards Rognvald's table, 'I declare a Torneig of Song.'

The Norðmen saw it as only polite to respond with more stamping and banging.

Skarfr could have hidden under the table. Not since he was a boy had he been so humiliated by drunkenness in a great hall – and then it had been his own inebriation. But even Rognvald could not control men so far in their cups. At least the Jarl himself was sober, as was Hlif, who flashed Skarfr a look of sympathy.

'To the winner I offer this prize.' Ermengarda clapped her hands above her head and a servant ran to her, knelt and held out a tasselled cushion on which something rested. Once more the Viscomtesse raised her arms but this time to display a sword belt and scabbard.

'In the most supple leather from al-Andalus, tooled in designs of the south and with my pledge that the finest leather-worker in Narbonne will add the blazon of whoever wins.'

Skarfr felt a pang of regret that he could not compete for such a prize. The scabbard alone was worth more than he could ever earn. But this was Rognvald's night to shine.

To add to Skarfr's pain, Aliénor offered a suit of chainmail as prize, so heavy she could hardly lift it to show it off.

But Rognvald was not to be outdone in generosity. He heaved himself to his feet, to the accompaniment of enough fists hammering on the table, and boots stamping under it, to confirm the solidity of the palace foundations.

'And I,' he said, doing his best with the strange tongue, 'offer this!'

In one swift movement, he pulled the large golden clasp from his own tunic.

'I can translate for you,' Skarfr offered one last time, under cover of the men's loud support.

Rognvald shook his head, took the brooch to Ermengarda and dropped it on the table in front of her, as if he were offering his own soul.

Skarfr's breath caught at the brave, foolish stubbornness of his liege; at the brave, foolish stubbornness of love itself. What if Ermengarda ridiculed the man she surely saw as a barbaric foreigner? He could see it was so in the expressions of guests around the hall, less schooled in courtesy than Narbonne's ruler.

She held up the brooch as if she recognised how precious it was.

'This is a luck rune,' the Jarl explained, 'That was mine from boyhood.'

Ermengarda made her voice carry. 'You do us too much honour, my lord. Such a prize carries a piece of your heart with it. Choose again, please.'

And everyone in the hall heard his reply, deep and strong. The words Skarfr had rehearsed with him.

'I leave all of my heart a willing prisoner in this hall, my Lady Ermengarda, whether I give away a trinket or not. Narbonne keeps me stronger captive than a man chained inside Cubby Roo's Castle, where the walls are as thick as a boat is wide.'

There was a heartbeat pause and then he roared, 'Let the Torneig begin!'

Skarfr thumped his hand to his chest for Rognvald to see how proud he was. What these 'sophisticates' thought didn't matter a rat's arse. His liege lord had been braver and more eloquent than any of them would ever understand. Only he, Skarfr, knew what courage it had taken Rognvald to speak his heart, in public, in a language he hardly knew.

Amid the stomping and banging, Ermengarda acknowledged

Rognvald's words with a graceful bend of her slim neck, and gave the official signal to begin.

A man in drab clothing, introduced as Macabru, sang a miserable song that went down well with the audience. He reminded Skarfr of Bishop William ranting about heathen ways.

Skarfr was once again translating for Rognvald, but the subtleties of Occitan poetry were as lost on him as on the Jarl, and he even felt a bit of stomping and table-bashing would enliven the proceedings.

The evening picked up when the young lutenist, Estela, performed, her voice as sweet as her beauty was a treat for the eyes. The melody lingered after she'd finished and took a bow, and even though he understood only half the words, Skarfr felt moved by the music.

'She will be a true musician,' was Rognvald's judgement.

He agreed, mentally rehearsing what he might say about Rognvald's poem for Ermengarda, hoping he could convey the brilliance of skaldic verse. And it would be brilliant, no less so because Rognvald had not yet composed the poem. He would rely as usual on the inspiration of the moment and his own skill in spontaneous versifying.

'Are you sure you don't want to perform too?' Rognvald asked him once more.

Skarfr shook his head. He *was* tempted but his duty was clear. Rognvald must shine at his brightest in front of his fair Ermengarda, without any competition. Skarfr's status as Rognvald's best skald was hard-earned and he knew his own worth. He also knew when to step back.

'I *will* be performing,' he told Rognvald. 'I will need my skills to do justice to your composition in their language and to teach the Narbonnais the beauties of skaldcraft.'

Rognvald gave an ambiguous 'Humph.'

His audience in the Bourg came to Skarfr's mind, how they'd loved his pipe music. 'I can always play a tune for them.' His pipe was in his pack with the guimbarde, underneath the table.

The Jarl showed none of the nerves Skarfr felt, his pulse skittish as he realised this was their turn. Rognvald stood up again, and Skarfr with him, speaking for his lord.

'My Lord Rognvald, Prince and renowned troubadour of Orkneyjar, wishes to offer a poem to the Lady Ermengarda, in our language, which I will translate for you afterwards.'

All eyes turned towards them. Rognvald pushed away the stool on which the previous performers had sat, plucking their lutes, and he took up a skald's stance, his gaze ranging the hall, demanding attention. He used his hands and his voice to convey the emotion, to emphasise the alliteration and rhyming of verses so good that Skarfr shook his head in admiration.

> *Vísts, at frá berr flestu*
> *Fróða meldrs at góðu*
> *vel skúfaðra vífa*
> *vǫxtr þinn, konan svinna.*
> *Skorð lætr hár á herðar*
> *haukvallar sér falla*
> *— átgjǫrnum rauðk erni*
> *ilka – gult sem silki.*

The verses carried on with a virtuoso play on Ermengarda's name, linked to the ships in the harbour and their reliance on the rule of the beautiful ruler of Narbonne. Every word formed a love poem for Ermengarda, to whom Rognvald looked, his heart in his eyes, as he finished and bowed.

Then it was Skarfr's turn to convey the beauty of the skaldic verse to an audience who understood none of the words, let alone the play on them, or the clever images. He would have to explain everything, as if he were training an orphaned seven-year-old to be a skald.

'My prince has asked me to explain some of his skald in your language,' he began, and immediately knew 'skald' was the wrong word. He struggled on, hoping not to make too many more mistakes.

'It is our way to make pictures with kennings so that *skorð haukvallar,* the 'pillar of the hawk-plain,' means 'sleeve'. We paint pictures and make names with sounds so that listening to our poetry is part of making the meaning. My Prince would like you to know that the *Ern* in the poem is an eagle and *ogeroa* means 'lets down her hair' so you should hear these two words together in *átgjǫrnum rauðk erni,* as we would do.'

He bowed towards 'ERMenGARda' to make his meaning clear. 'And when my Prince uses the word *ogeroa* we hear also *geroa* and *geroi,* the last word meaning the ships propped up round the shore, perhaps propped up by this same name we hear in the music of the line.'

This time it was the Prince himself who bowed to Ermengarda and she acknowledged his poetic tribute and practical hope with a serene smile and nod.

Skarfr sensed he was losing his audience and desperately tried to convey how clever the double meanings were, how great the compliment being paid to Ermengarda. Then he could recite the whole poem in a literal translation with some hope of them understanding how lucky they were to hear such a poem.

Ermengarda's mouth smiled as he spoke but her eyes were flitting elsewhere.

When he was still in full spate, someone at the back started clapping with mad enthusiasm, and then, as is often the way, the whole audience joined in and he admitted defeat.

Stopping his discourse mid-sentence, he bowed and gestured to Rognvald, who responded graciously to the applause and seemed content with both his performance and the response. Skarfr hoped the Jarl understood none of the comments being made, 'boring' being the least insulting.

A wise man sounds foolish when he speaks another's tongue, Skarfr thought bitterly. *'But who is the more foolish? The man who speaks only one tongue or the man who speaks four but makes mistakes in three of them?'*

'They do not have our level of skill,' he told Rognvald, 'and I hadn't finished!'

Rognvald put a hand on his back, said, 'Leave it at that, Skarfr. Play them a tune instead.'

Let them think Orkneymen boorish! He would play something childish that they understood.

He retrieved the guimbarde from his pack and played clopping hooves and clapping rhythms for the Narbonnais, as if they were small children. His lip curled at the enthusiastic applause but he bowed and smiled. Skaldic verses recited here were pearls before swine.

'You can't expect our level of sophistication in foreign courts,' Rognvald chid him gently. 'El Sant was the exception, not the rule, and I doubt whether even he would have understood our poetry. Enjoy their singing for what it is, not for what it isn't.'

Thus admonished, Skarfr settled back on his bench to observe Lord Dragonetz with Estela, who was apparently his student.

What was it that Ermengarda had said? Estela was referring to some young woman she taught, saying it was a pleasure to teach someone with such talent and Ermengarda had replied, 'That's exactly what Dragonetz says.'

Something in her tone had suggested undercurrents. Skarfr wondered whether Dragonetz was more than a tutor to the lute player, whether the romantic songs favoured by Ermengarda's court were drawn from life or were fantasies. Whether Rognvald had been infected by this notion of romantic love or whether he truly had feelings for Ermengarda. Skarfr glanced at Hlif. Feelings, not fancies.

Whatever their feelings for each other, the Queen's Commander and his student provided excellent entertainment, she playing lute and he playing the audience, who were crying by the final notes – with laughter.

Dragonetz won the tournament, a popular choice, and Ermengarda awarded him two of the three prizes. Rognvald added his praise to theirs but spoke in the man's ear and received assent.

'Lord Dragonetz is a worthy winner,' he declared, 'But with his permission I am awarding my prize to his student, for the pleasure she has given us.'

He held up the great gold brooch with its many pathways and waited until Estela approached him, her topaz eyes shining, her face flushed.

'Wherever you go, you will never be lost,' he told her. 'When you seek direction, the Pathfinder rune will answer you. Óðinn and Thórr will recognise you from now on.'

She stammered her thanks, glanced back towards Dragonetz and accepted her prize with a mix of grace and disbelief.

'I thought you had lost faith in the old gods,' Skarfr couldn't resist saying.

'For me, but not for others,' Rognvald said, without taking offence. 'My thanks for all you have done this evening.' He removed the heavy gold chain from his neck, opened the link to which the hammer-head was attached and gave it to Skarfr.

Another gift to weigh on his conscience.

'Sire, it is too much,' murmured Skarfr, 'but I thank you.'

'Yes, it probably is too much,' agreed Rognvald, 'so serve me well.'

Skarfr watched Estela head for the group surrounding Macabru, no doubt to talk poetry with such an expert, however miserable. Lord Dragonetz was himself talking to female admirers. But the way they ignored each other was something he recognised. He could feel the same invisible bond between them as between him and Hlif. He hoped the gods would give them a future together.

'She's very tall, isn't she,' Hlif commented, following his gaze towards Estela.

'Too tall,' he judged, hiding a smile.

CHAPTER 31

SKARFR

When you recognise evil,
call it evil,
and give your enemies no peace.

The Wanderer's Hávamál

When Rognvald told him to accompany Hlif on a trading mission, Skarfr thought it was too good to be true. The usual twinge of conscience asked, *Does he know?*

Even more suspect was the fact that Rognvald had challenged the Queen's Commander to some Norð-style contests of physical skill, and this was the day they would compete. Surely the Jarl would have wanted his saga-maker there to witness his prowess? Unless Rognvald thought Skarfr might instead see him fail. Even if Dragonetz' reputation was exaggerated, he had surely earned the nickname *los Pros* (the brave) given to him during the Crusades.

Another explanation was that Rognvald no longer trusted Skarfr. Whatever the reason, he accepted the duty and found himself riding out of Narbonne, with two of Ermengarda's men as guides, and a companion whose missionary zeal about salt made her so voluble his input was hardly needed.

'I can't believe we have permission to go to the salt fields! Ermengarda's given me a letter with her order of salt as well as the quantities we are to take for ourselves. You have no idea how valuable this is, Skarfr. I've negotiated enough to make us all wealthy when we return home.'

'What if it gets wet?' Skarfr was so relieved to hear her sounding so bubbly, so normal, that he was prepared to discuss salt for as long as she wanted.

She chewed her lip, thinking. 'If the containers aren't waterproof. They must be covered,' she concluded.

Her mount was the gentlest of palfreys but there was no elegance to Hlif's riding skills and she bounced along, apparently unconcerned by what bruises she might have later. When he spent time with the King's Hird in Norðvegr, Skarfr had refined his childhood experience of riding on a bad-tempered pony. Months of training with this elite group had included how to do battle from horseback. As Skarfr's horse was little friskier than Hlif's he doubted whether his training would be needed, but it would at least protect him from any of the stiffness she would undoubtedly feel.

A couple of hours' rambling across marshes and out to the seashore west of Narbonne was an easy morning's work, made even easier by their conversation. Neither of the guards spoke Norn so their privacy was guaranteed for the first time since they'd been in the healer's shelter. Of which they did not speak.

'I didn't expect the Jarl to give away his pathfinder brooch, or his gold hammer,' said Skarfr, knowing that Hlif would understand all that was expressed in such an act. Rejection of the old gods, rejection of their influence on his destiny. Acts of great generosity. Legacies to him and to the musician, Estela.

'It was generous,' was Hlif's view. 'But also part of some change in Rognvald since he talked with El Sant. I think he is preparing his soul in some way for Jórsalaheim, as part of this pilgrimage. It's not just a saga any longer.'

That was Skarfr's thought too. 'He seeks out Bishop William

more, takes the sacrament and makes confession at every opportunity.'

'Yes. And he has forbidden me to read the runes,' Hlif told Skarfr.

Only then did he realise that the rune pouch was missing from her belt, where the usual weights, scissors and scrip were still clipped in place. No doubt Ermengarda's instructions were folded in the scrip, along with some small coins.

Skarfr hesitated, knowing how strongly Hlif reacted against being told what to do, then he forged ahead. 'Maybe it is for the best. Rognvald was always so bad-tempered afterwards, hating himself for going back to the old gods. The White Christ wants no rivals.'

This was the tricky bit. 'And you are not yourself either, afterwards. The reading takes something from you.'

She took so long to reply, he thought he would get a tirade but all she said quietly was, 'The visions come anyway, even without the runes. They told me that was my one chance of having a baby.'

This was the moment he'd been waiting for; the moment he should give the long speech he'd prepared to reassure her. Instead, he spoke from his heart. 'If this is your fate, it is mine too and we face this road together, whatever it brings.'

She studied the road ahead as if she could see their future in the haunches of the two guards' horses or on the marshes, where rose-feathered birds swirled their black under-wings in squabbles and flight.

'The sea took him,' she told him. 'Aegir will offer something in return. It will be your choice, whether to accept such a difficult gift.'

He remembered her making this strange prophecy before, in the healer's house, but what comment could he make about a future he could not see? He did not press the subject and the sight of water-fields, rectangular and salmon-tinted with salt, drew Hlif's attention back to her trading mission.

The guards halted beside a man who was lowering a wooden sluice gate between two of these water-fields. One was empty, a crust of white crystals lying across its bed. The other was so rosy Skarfr thought this must be how the strange local birds acquired such a colour. By dipping in the rosy water. He wondered whether he too would come out roseate if he swam in the salty pool. He'd heard of the white and black lakes in Írland, which would turn sheep from white to black or a grey-haired woman to a raven-haired beauty, depending on which lake they chose. But he'd never heard of a rose-hued lake and this marvel deserved a line in the Rognvald's saga.

Long-legged stork-kin, roseate as their fish-soup

The man introduced himself as Saltmaster. He checked the gate was firmly in place, then had a brief exchange with the guards.

He turned to Skarfr. 'The guards say my lady Ermengarda sent you with instructions for me?'

Skarfr gestured to Hlif, who pulled the folded parchment out of her scrip, showed the seal to the saltmaster and let him see the numbers. He nodded, pointed to a large wooden building and set off towards it.

Once the horses were tethered outside, Skarfr followed Hlif into what seemed to be a counting-house, with weighing scales on a table, and sacks of varying sizes on the floor, some empty and others showing white or grey contents.

The haggling began, an act of courtesy in trading rather than a serious negotiation, as Lady Ermengarda's message was clear regarding her agreement with Hlif. Skarfr was refining verse that linked rose-feathered birds to the goddess Freyja, when he realised that Hlif was picking her weights back off the table, attaching them back on her belt.

'Saltmaster has to send to the storage cabin for some sacks,' she told Skarfr, glowing with success.

After speaking rapidly to the guards, Saltmaster said, 'I'll take the men with me and they can bring back a cart with the extra sacks. But you wait here. The storage place is secret and heavily guarded. We will be very quick and nobody will bother you here. Everyone knows the main stocks are elsewhere and this is out of anyone's way if he is travelling."

Skarfr nodded understanding and the three men left, taking two of the horses with them.

'And,' Hlif continued, 'we've added four small sacks of *fleur de sel* to the large sacks of coarse sea salt Ermengarda promised us. We turned up at just the right time!'

'And a small sack of *fleur de sel* is a good thing?' hazarded Skarfr. He had his back to the door, which had been left open by the saltmaster to let the light in.

'The best!' She beamed. 'They're those white crystals we saw. Ermengarda says they balance the humours, especially for those prone to an excessively sanguine temperament, and they give unequalled succulence to any fish or meat. Rognvald will be in heaven.'

'Not unless he fasts afterwards and prays for his sins of gluttony to be forgiven.'

'That's just spit in the wind.' She dismissed Rognvald's Christian piety. 'Nothing stops him enjoying well-cooked food. Especially if the salt is a present from *Ermengarda.*' She made lovesick eyes at him and he laughed.

In a flash, the expression in her eyes changed to horror, and she pushed Skarfr to one side.

'Thieves!' she yelled and pulled her scissors from her belt.

Skarfr whirled around to face the assailants.

Two of them.

Hlif was already jabbing at one of the men with open scissor-blades, which glanced off a leather jerkin but scored blood on the bare arm. A mere distraction, but one that bought time for Skarfr. He drew his dagger and followed up on Hlif's scratch with an angled cut under the arm, where the leather seam was vulnerable.

A curse confirmed the deeper hit. And also confirmed who Skarfr's opponent was.

There was no time to wonder what Horse-snipper was doing here.

Skarfr was grateful to Hlif for stepping back out of his way and he hurled himself at the bleeding attacker, crushing him in a clinch. Then he used his superior strength to push Eindridi's man back into the doorway with full force, smashing him into his partner. The two men lost their balance and fell in an awkward heap outside the building.

Looking down on them from the doorway, swinging his axe with menace in case they thought to try again, Skarfr yelled, 'I'm counting to ten then I cut off the nearest body part! One, two...'

Stumbling to their feet, the men took the hint, unhitched their horses, and ran with them. They kept looking behind them until they felt safe to mount and ride off. Without the advantage of surprise, they had no chance against Skarfr and they knew it.

Once they had vanished over the horizon, he turned and went back into the counting-house. Hlif was standing with her back to the far wall, watching the door, scissors in one hand and her wand in the other. He would not like to be at the receiving end of either weapon.

He enclosed her scissor-hand in his and felt it tremble.

'It's all right,' he said gently. 'They've gone. I'd rather you put those away.'

She gave a faltering smile. 'Now you know what I can do with them, you might be more interested when I talk about salt.'

'A man can never learn too much about salt,' he told her.

'They were from our company, weren't they? The man who killed Pilot and escaped? With a new partner.'

She'd come to the same conclusion he had. 'They were going to steal your sunstone.'

Her indignation was already overcoming her fear. 'And they didn't care if they killed you to get it. In fact they probably intended to kill you. And me too.'

Skarfr nodded. 'Eindridi's men. They'd have given him the sunstone. Our murder would be a mystery, discovered when the guards returned, put down to robbers. It would be Ermengarda's problem and she'd probably pay Rognvald something in recompense. Eindridi would have been very pleased with himself.'

'Everyone knew where we were going,' she said ruefully. 'I've been talking about it for days. Why didn't you kill them?'

Skarfr flexed his muscles to ease them. He was starting to stiffen a little now his blood was cooling. 'That would have embarrassed Rognvald, killings within his company while in Ermengarda's realm.'

'Besides,' he grinned, 'I intend to accuse them and Eindridi and, with sufficient encouragement, they'll confess all. Rognvald will have no choice but to mete out justice and rid our voyage of these murderers. If Eindridi is not stopped, he'll cost Rognvald the pilgrimage, maybe even his life.'

Betrayal, he thought. *Rognvald is right to fear betrayal.*

By the time Saltmaster returned with the guards and a cart full of salt sacks, Skarfr and Hlif had recovered their equilibrium and were keen to return to the ships. However, courtesy required that they eat the bread and cheese offered, drink a glass of watered wine, and doze on a bench till the hottest part of the day was over.

When they made their triumphant return to the docks and unloaded their portion of the salt, they found the *Sun-chaser's* crew too excited about the day's games to have any interest in their outing.

Skarfr tolerated the accounts of Rognvald's prowess against Dragonetz in throwing a spear, in wrestling and in swimming. He put up with a blow-by-blow account of the Narbonne knight's skills in the contests, lesser of course than the Jarl's. Skarfr wondered what version of the day's events was being told in Ermengarda's court and who *had* actually won the contest overall. His loyalty said Rognvald was the winner but Dragonetz' reputation gave reason for doubt.

His patience ended when Mouthy started to tell him all about scoring with a stick and a ball in an impromptu game of *Knattleikr*, and who'd smacked whom in dispute over an own goal.

'Enough!' he said. 'I need to speak with Rognvald. Where is he?'

'The *Crest-cleaver* with Eindridi,' was the answer.

His heart sank and Hlif glanced at him, a query.

'Mouthy will help you store the salt,' Skarfr told her, as if that's what she was asking. 'I have a serious matter to raise with the Jarl and if Eindridi is there, so much the better.'

She nodded. So, he would make the accusation in public.

Men within earshot looked at him, curious, then returned to their gossip about the games.

After a short walk along the quayside, Skarfr found Rognvald as predicted, on the *Crest-cleaver,* in what seemed to be a serious discussion with Eindridi.

Skarfr did not hesitate. 'My lord,' he burst into the conversation and both men looked annoyed at his rudeness. 'Two of Lord Eindridi's crew members followed us to the salt fields. When I was alone with Hlif—'

Did Rognvald's expression harden and Eindridi show amusement? Skarfr rushed on, '—these men tried to kill us and were no doubt sent to steal this.'

He pulled the pouch out into view, so Rognvald could see it. He looked around the deck but couldn't see Horse-snipper or the other attacker, so he challenged Eindridi directly, 'Send for Horse-snipper. He'll say who the other man is, and who sent them.'

He stared hard at Eindridi, who looked even more amused. He would lose that smile soon enough.

'And,' he added, 'Horse-snipper has a wound under his arm where I stabbed him in self-defence.' He turned to Rognvald. 'My Lady Hlif is a witness.'

The Jarl showed no surprise, merely ordered Eindridi, 'Tell him.'

'What a frightening experience.' Eindridi oozed sympathy. 'Two against one and you fought them off, defending Lady Hlif in fine style. I am mortified that two of my crew behaved in such a manner, but we did not choose all the men on our ships.' Here, he glanced at Rognvald, making him culpable for any misdemeanors Eindridi's men had committed.

He went on, 'You have explained the mystery I was telling the Jarl about. You see, those two men have disappeared. Completely.'

He returned Skarfr's angry gaze with that same smile, mockery in his eyes, and suddenly Skarfr *knew.*

Eindridi had indeed been mortified – that the men had failed – and he'd 'rewarded' them. They had disappeared. Completely. No witnesses.

Rognvald said, 'Lord Eindridi has asked me to rearrange the crews a little or he will be three men short.'

The effrontery of Eindridi pleading for replacements left Skarfr speechless.

The Jarl commented further, 'I suggested we wait and see whether the men return, but your news suggests Eindridi was right. They have gone, and will no doubt find low company like themselves. We will speak of them no more.'

He changed the subject, effectively blocking Skarfr from protesting. 'We sail in two days. Make ready.'

Later, on their own ship, Skarfr tried to reopen discussion, explain what he knew to be true, but Rognvald had made up his mind.

'Let it go, Skarfr. Eindridi is in amenable humour and is useful to us. We must all learn to be tolerant of those whose traits are not ones we appreciate. You especially.'

This was so unfair that Skarfr had trouble holding his tongue. After all, Rognvald had placed Skarfr with Eindridi so he could get to know how horrible the man was. Inwardly, Skarfr took the name of all the gods in vain and cursed Rognvald for his compromises and changes of direction. The White Christ had much to answer for. No good Norðman would accept Eindridi's goading, regardless of the crimes Skarfr knew he'd committed. Skarfr certainly would not.

CHAPTER 32

INGE, STRJÓNSEY, ORKNEYJAR

'Burned Skarfr's house to the ground and took Brigid?' She repeated Fergus' words, not because she didn't believe them, but because she did. 'I'm sorry. I'm so, so sorry. But I don't know what I can do.'

The sun hid behind clouds and Inge shivered, heedless of the rosy sunset as she listened to the man's halting story. They were standing in the porch, which no longer seemed a sanctuary. Nowhere was safe from Thorbjorn.

His face drawn and harrowed, illness engraved on grief, the thrall was the shadow of the hale peasant who'd rowed her across the Pentlandsfjord to her family home. Away from certain death at her husband's hands.

Her voice shook. 'If he thought I cared, he'd do even worse things. And—' she broke off, couldn't say such cruel words. He said them for her.

'And she might not be alive.' He licked dry lips. 'But if she is, then I will find her. She saved my life once, when I was young, and now I must save hers. That's what she meant by naming our village in Írland. That all would be well, only this time I'm the one who must think and act.'

Noises came from inside the house. Finn must be wondering why she was outside so long, with some servant. She turned towards the door, half wanting to help, half not wanting to get involved.

'He won't recognise me,' Fergus said, urgently. 'A man like that can't tell one thrall from another. I can find out if she's there, or if she's been there – and if not, I must wait for the master's return.'

'That will be years!'

'Aye. Then I must find work where nobody will fuss or poke his nose in my business.'

The conversation inside the house was growing louder and Inge realised with horror that her husband and his guest were coming to the door.

For one mad moment, she wondered where they could hide. Then she steadied herself, found a smile for Finn as he came outside with Shoe-awl, as the cobbler was known.

'This is Fergus,' she told her husband, 'a labourer from the family estate in Ness. Sweyn sent him with news that my brothers have gone roving to Írland, to take Gunnr's mind off his exile.'

Fergus' eyes widened but he didn't contradict her, and she rushed on, too deep into the lie to stop now. The gods might know where her brothers were but she didn't have a clue. As if Sweyn would ever send a message to his sister that didn't demand food and lodging for twenty men or more! But Finn was a good man and thought others were like him. He would believe her.

'He's a good worker who's been ill,' she gabbled, 'so if you're willing, perhaps we can—' She faltered. Husbands did not like wives hiring their men.

Finn's smile was wide, warm and honest. All she was not. 'We can always use a good worker. Can you herd sheep?'

'Aye,' said Fergus. 'And look after cows too.' He winced as if a spasm of pain hit him.

'I see you need a bit of recovery time,' Finn observed. 'Shoe-awl, take Fergus with you down to Fleece-fast and let him know he now has a man who will share the load, once he's recovered from illness and voyaging. And tell him I'll make good the provisions if he can find a bench there for Fergus.'

Finn's request was as good as an order.

'Thank you, Sire,' said Fergus. 'And my lady. I will be no trouble to you.'

Too late, thought Inge. Not telling Finn the truth about Thorbjorn was for the best but now she had lied to her husband for the first time, and it felt so wrong her stomach heaved. Did she imagine a question in Finn's eyes? Was she always going to imagine a question in his eyes from now on?

The sun finally dipped below the sea, chased by one of the wolf brothers. Inge believed it was Hati, and she knew exactly how Sol felt with 'the one who hates' nipping at her heels.

CHAPTER 33

ERLEND, ORKNEYJAR

When he was growing up, Erlend's insistence on playing *Poisoned Tunic Murder* had cost him all his friends. As he came to realise, the other boys were scared stiff of calling down the gods' punishment for acting out such a tragedy. Boys should never pretend to be women, least of all the two evil sisters who embroidered poison into a tunic that would kill the wearer instantly.

Worse still, all the characters, murderers and victims, were members of Erlend's family. The evil sisters, Frakork the Witch and her sister Helga, were Erlend's great-aunt and his grandmother. And they'd intended the hair shirt to kill Helga's stepson, Paul, known as Paul the Silent.

The boy who played Paul considered himself lucky because he knew he would survive and enjoy ruling Orkneyjar, even if he didn't get any lines to speak. Paul would strut and look smug while his more popular half-brother, Harald Smooth-tongue, admired the beautiful tunic.

The other boys had their lines to speak, and the drama always unfolded in the same way.

'It's not for you,' shouted Frakork the Witch, in a voice that cracked from falsetto to a man's.

Then Harald, always played by his son Erlend, grew jealous and angry. He grabbed the tunic (Erlend's Sunday best for church-going) and put it on. At which point he writhed, as if a thousand needles pricked him. Sometimes, he even managed to froth at the mouth, while the other boys huddled together, no longer acting.

If he had stopped there, the drama might have been forgotten in a slingshot contest, but Erlend lived the story more intensely each time. His father's murder in an ironic twist of fate. His family's story.

Before he died as Harald, he would go for 'Paul' like a mad dog, thrashing, biting, punching and screaming repeatedly, 'It should have been you!'

When he'd been pulled off 'Paul,' Erlend would sit in a huddle, closed in on himself, head hidden in his folded arms, while the other boys inspected the damage to the unlucky Paul.

Erlend's grandmother, his father's murderer, never caught them acting her story, which was just as well. What she might have done would have made a new story. *Poisoned Boys' Murders.*

Soon, word spread round the community and no boys went near the strange youth Erlend had become. His mother was a pale presence in the house where his grandmother ruled, watching over her son's son like a gaoler.

When he was fifteen, she finally sent him away to a foster-father in Skotland to train as the jarl's son and heir he should have been. He learned self-control from his foster-father's dour example, and, now he could no longer act out *Poisoned Tunic Murder,* its events lost their immediacy.

He still asked questions about his family history, unsatisfied with what he'd been told. He could never have asked his mother. Or, perish the thought, his grandmother.

His godfather Anakol told him the story was a fabrication but when Erlend prodded him for the truth, his evasions covered Harald's death like a misty shroud, hiding the corpse beneath. The dead person was always there and every man had the spirit of his ancestors inside him. What form did that spirit take in Erlend?

He knew he looked like his father, with a narrow face and long nose like a land wight in an old tale, but with his grandmother's green eyes. Murderous green eyes. His inheritance was evident in his body and he had no choice but to accept both legacies: the Jarldom of Orkneyjar and the capacity to kill for what he wanted, by any means. He also had witchcraft in his blood.

His grandmother had wanted Paul dead, but it was the witch who'd supplied the means and Erlend was fascinated by her. He interrogated Anakol at every opportunity but the answers only piqued his curiosity.

'Well yes,' said godfather Anakol, 'Your great-aunt Frakork is a witch, but that doesn't mean she's bad... And yes, she gave the orders and watched while her enemy's house was burned down, with him in it, but that she was within her rights...'

Then, five years later, the sea-rover Sweyn set fire to *her* house with her inside, in tit-for-tat revenge for his father's murder. You would have to be an anchorite in a cell not to hear Frakork described as 'the witch Frakork,' an official title now she was dead, burned alive by Sweyn.

Erlend understood from this that even his powerful, murderous aunt was mortal. And that, far from Sweyn being sympathetic to Erlend because Frakork had murdered both their fathers, he was an enemy, The feud between families applied to Erlend too, which was most unfair given that Erlend had once cheered Sweyn on. Years before he murdered Frakork, Sweyn had made Uncle Paul disappear. Erlend had hoped he would be 'the Silent' forever.

'It should have been you that died, *Uncle* Paul,' he said when he heard the news, and he smashed his hand into a wall.

The one certainty about Sweyn was that his own interests came first, and the sea-rover lived by a simple code. Frakork had murdered his father, therefore all Frakork's family were his enemies. Erlend wished he could be loyal to his family in such a straightforward way and seek vengeance against Sweyn. But how could he feel outraged that the murderous witch had been murdered in her turn? Surely, that was the gods' justice.

Such a train of thought led to the unthinkable, that what was just for Frakork was just for her sister. Erlend balked at the idea of his grandmother dying in such a way, told himself the poison had been Frakork's doing, that his grandmother's sentence of losing her son was punishment enough. He knew he was lying to himself but still he presented excuses.

Sweyn would never understand such complex feelings, so it was safer to consider him an enemy. That way Erlend would make no mistakes as he recruited men and found allies. Under Anakol's guidance, he had grown into a man thought by others to be good company, with no visible trace of his strange childhood. He had learned from playing *Poison Tunic Murder* how to lose friends, and in subsequent years he had perfected the art of keeping them.

Someone who probably *would* understand Erlend's ambivalence towards his family was Frakork's grandson, Thorbjorn. Erlend had toyed with the idea of approaching his distant cousin and winning his support, but the man was advisor and foster-father to Jarl Harald. Thorbjorn ruled Orkneyjar in all but name, through his loyalty to Harald. Before Rognvald left on pilgrimage, Thorbjorn was known as Rognvald's man, so he was already in a strong position with the two Jarls in power. Why would he want to rock the boat?

The answer was clear enough. Because Rognvald was not there and Erlend was. The bigger a threat Erlend became to Harald, the more likely Thorbjorn would be to support him. Orkneyjar needed a second jarl, one who was present, not one gallivanting across oceans on a pilgrimage.

Accompanied by his crew of thirty, Erlend left his ship anchored in the haven of Kirkjuvágr, beside merchant knarrs and small boats. They strode past the building site of the new red stone cathedral, the north-east corner of which already two stories high. Jarl Rognvald's attempt to buy popularity.

Erlend snorted. Where was Jarl Rognvald now? Following his selfish piety instead of looking after his jarldom. He wasn't worthy of Orkneyjar.

Pushing through the market-day crowds and stalls, Erlend made his way to an alehouse in Kirkjuvágr, ready to buy drinks and listen sympathetically to complaints about taxes and the weather. He would hesitate, then confide that the King of Skotland had named him rightful Jarl of Orkneyjar. He would not mention that the king was nine years old. He would make expansive gestures and impossible promises. He would pay for many cups of ale.

Erlend did not lose friends anymore. He made them with ease and Orkneyjar would be his.

CHAPTER 34

THORBJORN, ORKNEYJAR

Thorbjorn wished he could have held back longer from ransoming Harald, but he hid his impatience and extracted details about the kidnap from his sullen foster-son. He looked down the long scrubby slope of sand and marram grass to the seven beached ships. One was upside down, swarming with men at work repairing it. The sound of hammers came faintly on the breeze and was more pleasing to Thorbjorn's ears than his foster-son's whine.

'I've told you already. I took an oath of allegiance to Norðvegr and King Gillisson said I'd be released as soon as the three gold coins were paid.' He shrugged. 'And here I am. Can I go now?'

Why were you so stupid as to be caught? Aloud, Thorbjorn asked, 'Why did the king need your oath?'

'How should I know? Maybe he intends going to war and wants me to go too, bring Orkneyjar armies and ships.' Harald's eyes brightened. 'We should prepare the men.'

'Wonderful idea!' Thorbjorn's voice grew louder as he lost control. 'You might be interested in the rota so you can find them. You'll find one group in the training yard, others repairing ships on the beach.'

He pointed to the men who were now on one side of the hull,

turning it right-side up, their work done. Harald's eyes followed the gesture without interest.

Thorbjorn's patience snapped. 'And a hundred and fifty men are on the five ships scouring coastal waters for Erlend's army.' He shouted the last words inches from Harald's face. 'To find out what the fuck he's up to!'

Harald stepped back, not noticeably daunted, which was a point in his favour, and silent at least, which was another point.

'By all the gods, Harald, you're twenty-four, not four! You should have your own sources of information by now. While you were being entertained by the King of Norðvegr, Erlend has declared himself Jarl and has brought an army to our shores to claim his share.'

'Well, I didn't know, did I! It's *your* job to tell me things. *You're* the advisor. You should have told me straightaway instead of obsessing about what Norðvegr is after.'

Thorbjorn shook his head in amazement. 'The two things might be linked. Norðvegr might be ensuring you stay loyal to him and to Rognvald, his choice of jarl, whether Rognvald is here or not. Malcolm of Skotland has backed Erlend's claim.'

'But Skotland supports my claim!' Harald was indignant at such treachery. 'And Malcolm's just a little boy.'

'So were you when Skotland supported *your* claim to be Jarl. And you've now given an oath of fealty to Norðvegr.'

'So,' Thorbjorn could see the wheels turning as Harald exercised his flabby mind and slowly put the puzzle together. 'Norðvegr has me in place while Skotland gets Erlend. Rognvald has always been Norðvegr's man – after all, he was born there – so if he doesn't come back, there's still an Orkneyjar jarl loyal first to Norðvegr – me, since I gave the King my oath.'

'Yes,' Thorbjorn agreed. 'Orkneyjar belongs to Norðvegr but shares borders with Skotland on the mainland. They look at each other with jealous eyes and we must keep them both sweet. And now your oath of allegiance to Norðvegr is a smack in the face for Skotland, which put you forward as jarl in the first place.'

'That's not fair!' objected Harald. 'I was kidnapped and forced to give my oath!'

Thorbjorn felt he deserved sainthood for holding back his opinions on that subject. Instead, he prompted, 'And if Rognvald does come back?'

'There will be three Jarls.' Harald frowned. 'That won't do. Erlend would never have become jarl in the first place if Rognvald was here. Together we'd smash him in days. So, if Rognvald returns, Erlend will turn tail and hide in Skotland.'

'Then there would be two Norðvegr-jarls,' pointed out Thorbjorn, 'and Skotland would not be happy at all. Your oath to the King of Norðvegr has changed the balance.'

Harald shrugged. 'Let's kill Erlend then.'

'Tempting as that is, he's made himself popular in Orkneyjar and he does have Skotland's backing, which was enough to get you made jarl. Not all Orkneymen want Norðvegr going unchallenged.'

'You worry too much, Thorbjorn. If we can't kill him, we can let him take Rognvald's place for now and have Ness. That will keep everyone happy.'

'Except your friend, the King of Norðvegr.'

'Then we'll tell Erlend he has to win approval from 'my friend' the King of Norðvegr. That gets rid of him for a year and when he comes back, he can have Ness *and* Rognvald's half of Orkneyjar for all I care.'

'It might gain us time,' Thorbjorn reflected. 'We'll need to meet with him, somewhere safe.'

Harald picked up his leather jerkin. 'Maybe we can fight him first,' he said. 'I'm off to the training ground. Are you coming?'

Thorbjorn grunted assent. The excuse of 'training' would give him opportunities to pin Harald to the packed earth often enough to ease his frustration without doing considerable damage to his liege lord.

Doing damage, however, was exactly what Thorbjorn needed. He was tired of behaving with an old man's restraint. Harald's excitement at the prospect of war might be childish but Thorbjorn too felt the thrum in the blood at the prospect. Almost a year without raiding. Torching one longhouse and taking a thrall had been small satisfaction compared with torching a village.

He almost wished for another clash with Sweyn, so he could best a worthy opponent and hone his men against sharper steel. He was tired of fighting with blunted weapons, tired of being careful.

While his thoughts rode mad stallions, his feet trod the habitual path to his own house. He'd had enough of Harald for one day and would dine alone. He walked past men and women following their own set paths to their own homes and day's end boredom, as alike as clods of earth, and as stupid. He was better, different. His skin tingled with the presentiment of adventure.

Perhaps he should have kept the thrall. The defiance in her eyes was a challenge he should have met. Men like him weren't meant for expedience, for giving advice to jarls. They were meant for action.

The rush of blood was compulsive now and when a pretty girl in a sage green overdress crossed his path and accidentally jostled him, he squeezed one of her breasts through the fine wool.

'My Lord Thorbjorn,' she teased, her eyes wide in mock-surprise.

What was the name? Girls were always impressed when a nobleman remembered their names. She wore yellow ribbons in hair as brown as hazelnuts, long and loose. He liked the idea of 'loose'. And was far from deterred by the youth and maiden's status conveyed by her unbound hair. And she had pert breasts.

'Hilda.' The gods were with him, and he'd remembered, though anyone less like the battler suggested by her name could not be imagined. Sweet, silly and available. He'd probably noticed her before and recorded the details for future use. The blacksmith's daughter, so neither noble enough to litigate nor common enough to pass on disease. Just right.

'You look irresistible,' he told her. And she did. He didn't have to lie, nor was his smile feigned. His eyes would convey his response to her body, his anticipation. He touched her hair gently, watched her shiver at the touch.

'Yellow ribbons suit you.' He drew back his hand and felt the way her body leaned towards him, seeking the contact. 'Forgive me. I presume.'

'I like it.' She smiled back and the banter became barter.

Thorbjorn whispered in her ear, she nodded, turned on her heel and walked out of the village, towards the empty grassland and distant standing stones, towards the ancient tomb, the trysting shelter he'd mentioned.

He waited a few minutes for discretion's sake, then followed.

In the gloaming, that endless summer twilight on the islands, Thorbjorn watched the girl lurch across the greensward, heading back to the village. As he'd promised whatever-her-name-was, he hadn't killed her and she would make it home. Unless some ruffians actually stumbled across her and made the story he'd given her come true.

The only witness to his presence was one of the ancient standing-stones, far across the grassland, the sun long set behind its brooding silhouette. He turned back to the entrance tunnel behind him, stooped to walk its length into the stone chamber and peered into the darkness.

Since Rognvald's men had etched their names and pilgrims' crosses on the walls, cruder additions showed the use to which the shelter had been put.

Thorny fucked. Helgi carved.

Or the more subtle *Many a fair woman has stooped here,* with its punning reference to the low entrance tunnel.

Thorbjorn felt no urge to add his mark to the walls. He'd carved it on the girl.

The frenzy had passed through him and left only melancholy. Was man no more than this? This was the true legacy of

Orkneymen, not sagas but a record on the walls of names and who'd fucked here.

Despite himself, Thorbjorn reached out to a stone column on his right, traced the outline of the dragon he knew was there. Long fingers, which stroked hair so gently, followed the exquisite lines Skarfr had carved. Rognvald and his men spoke of the dragon's creation as if Óðinn had touched the boy while they sheltered from the blizzard. As if Óðinn had carved with Skarfr's hand, spewed poetry through his mouth.

Skarfr. A numbskull barely able to stutter when Thorbjorn took the boy under his wing! If Thorbjorn hadn't mentored him, trained him in mental discipline as warrior and thinker, Skarfr would know nothing, be nothing.

But the Norns who decreed a man's fate had not even invited Thorbjorn to witness the birth of the stone dragon. He'd been writing accounts in ledgers while Rognvald and his men chased adventures in the snow. As if Skarfr was meant for sagas, and his own doom was to be advisor to idiots.

If only Harald had a tenth of Skarfr's genius, what sparks they could light. Not a torched longhouse but a blaze of twin souls, finding heaven and hell in roving and reading, as they had when sailing together. Or among the monks on Papey Meiri.

Thorbjorn had witnessed Skarfr's reverence when he'd first seen illustrated manuscripts. His wonder at the illustration Thorbjorn made for him, the cormorant. The first time was precious, could never be replicated. Although he'd been back to Papey Meiri many times, with other companions, Thorbjorn had never created anything as inspired as the cormorant page.

The boy he'd created, and grown tired of, had no right to forget the debt he owed. No right to become someone special, someone who made Harald and Erlend look like the clods they were. Someone whose name carried resonance.

Thorbjorn could take an axe to the dragon, cut his name-rune *thorn* across the fire-breathing maw, write 'Thorbjorn carved this,' kill the beast. Be like the ignorant thugs who'd carved their names and crude messages on the walls. He could do it. But he would never kill the beast inside him. And he would never be like other men. He would always have that refinement they lacked, understand the dragon-carver as they never would.

Abruptly, he withdrew his hand, severed his contact with the little carved dragon.

Women always came between us. Women.

He scrunched up the yellow ribbons, now spotted with blood, and cleaned his dagger with them. A couple of hours until she was home, which would give her time to reflect on the story he'd given her to tell. To realise nobody would believe her if she told the truth, or if they did, nobody would be naive enough to challenge the word of the Jarl's advisor. There were advantages in his status.

No doubt women would pass on their tittle tattle. Some already knew enough to avoid him but there were always new hunting-grounds further afield, always young girls.

Tonight, he was tired of them and the ghosts in this once-hallowed stone barrow were spooking him. He needed a cosy hearth and adulation. He would go to the farm nearby, bestow his patronage on them and enjoy the hospitality of the old couple there. He felt benevolent.

CHAPTER 35

SKARFR

*One word chased another word
flowing from my mouth
One deed chased another deed
flowing from my hands.*

The Wanderer's Hávamál

The ship rose and dipped as gently as Ermengarda's palfreys. Before nightfall, they passed the marshy coastline and found a long stretch of sand, where they could beach all fifteen ships in tranquillity.

Around the cookfires, enjoying freshly caught fish with watered wine, the Orkneymen relaxed. Wine of such quality needed no honey and Skarfr wondered whether Hlif could arrange a permanent trading deal to improve stocks on Orkneyjar.

He stayed close to Rognvald, and Eindridi avoided them both, so there was no sour taste in the atmosphere either. The Jarl seemed more like his old self and turned his melancholy over leaving Ermengarda into a skaldic challenge, which he launched with plaintive verses on the theme that he would never forget her.

Skarfr wondered cynically whether the sentiment was more

poetic than deep. Maybe the romantic poses in some Occitan poetry, the unattainable lady and the pining lover, had found their way into Rognvald's compositions.

Never had Skarfr heard the word 'love' used so often as in Narbonne, with nuances that had never crossed his mind before. Why on earth would a man fix his heart on a married woman and consider all this silliness as more refined than sharing a bed with his wife? Even worse, the troubadours wasted their poetic talent on double meanings about sneaked trysts and swiving, rather than heroic deeds. Such a waste.

Even Rognvald had been affected by these ways, so unsuited to a warrior. He spoke regretfully of how he'd proposed marriage when Ermengarda sat on his lap, how she'd generously turned him down, so he could fulfil his destiny and reach Jórsalaheim.

Hmm, thought Skarfr, considering this poetic licence and remembering the careful politeness Ermengarda had exhibited to her foreign visitors. Her courtiers had barely disguised their contempt. Except for Lord Dragonetz, who had competed with Rognvald as an equal, and displayed only respect. However, even he had disappointed as a troubadour. His performance had been embarrassing to Skarfr although it had clearly pleased the court audience. Maybe, with a better education, Dragonetz could have been a *drengr*. Thorbjorn could have made him one.

Armód followed Rognvald in turn, and in theme, mourning the loss of such a fair lady.

Gods! They are all infected with the Occitan languishing disease! Skarfr wondered if their poetry would ever recover from the visit to Narbonne.

Then Oddi followed suit, with many compliments to the lady of Narbonne, wishing her a sunny life.

This image stuck in Skarfr's mind, fair Ermengarda in golden sunrays.

'Skarfr?' Rognvald turned to him, expecting a verse, and his best skald could not refuse. He stood, claiming attention.

Half in fun, half for the pleasure of the poetry itself, Skarfr pictured Ermengarda, remembered El Sant's words about her and recited,

Saint's friend, she reigns as sister-sun
Her beams warm the word-wine
drunk in her hall.
Her beams warm the word-wine
shared on golden strands
by steel-wielders who drew fire
from her fair flame and–

Skarfr drew his axe and held it high so it glinted in the setting sun and pointed to the small crescent, newly visible in the sky.

sent it to her brother moon.

'That's your best yet,' Rognvald told him, his own face beaming like Ermengarda-sun. '*Word-wine* is well found. I think we will be missed in Narbonne!'

Maybe, thought Skarfr. *If so, it will be among the children in a certain square in the Bourg.*

It felt good to perform as a skald again, and in front of an audience who knew that mead was Óðinn's gift and meant poetry. Explanation was death to verse, he decided, and he pitied those who did not speak his language.

As the days passed, Rognvald's verses for Ermengarda changed in tenor from wistful to motivational. Not languishing but fired up to do great deeds worthy of such a lady, and of her sacrifice in letting him go. The mood in his crew lifted accordingly as men scented adventure coming their way on the sea breezes. They had not used their weapons in months and they oiled them carefully, hopeful that the next landfall would exercise their blades.

Skarfr had taken over the navigation after leaving El Sant's pilot in Narbonne but there was little honour in this while merely following the *Crest-cleaver's* lead, as instructed by the Jarl. When Eindridi's ship headed for a long sandy bay, all seemed promising for another pleasant – if boring – evening around the cookfires.

There was a sense of inevitability about what happened next, despite Eindridi's assurances that the lord of the stronghold visible on the hill was friendly.

As the ships were drawn up along the sands, a very unfriendly band of fifty or so men charged out of the trees fringing the beach, hurling stones and insults, then ducking back under cover.

'By God, we'll teach these peasants better manners! Eindridi, watch the ships with your men. The rest of you follow me!' roared Rognvald, drawing his sword and rushing at their attackers.

The Norðmen did not need telling twice. Brandishing every weapon they possessed and shouting loud enough to wake the dead, they dashed off in pursuit, sending a black cloud of crows scattering heavenwards, and forest creatures diving for their lairs and burrows. The human inhabitants clearly made the same decision and retreated up the slope as fast as they could run through the trees.

When Skarfr broke through into a clearing, he was just in time to see the last residents scrambling through the castle door, which slammed behind them. A few arrows hailed down from the battlements and as ever more Norðmen broke through the woods, they stayed with Skarfr, well out of range.

Panting, Rognvald arrived, with Jón Halt-foot, Mouthy, and Erling, one of the captains, not far behind him.

'We won't take it in an hour,' Skarfr observed.

Rognvald's expression was fierce and he raised his voice to carry. 'But we *will* take it, however long is needed. And all the booty we can carry!'

The cheer was more terrifying than the previous shouts; Skarfr would not have liked to be inside the castle, listening. This was the outlet the men needed after months of restraint.

Rognvald blew his horn to signal a return to the beach and once there, he gave his captains their orders.

Although watches were set, sleep was disturbed only by anticipation of the coming siege.

At first light, Eindridi and his party, the captains and men of the six ships, headed into the forest. Their aim was to find a way around at a low level, so they could attack the castle from the north.

Leaving a small band to guard the ships, Rognvald and the rest of the men would form an impenetrable barrier on the south side of the castle, killing anyone who tried to leave. And then the second part of the Jarl's plan would be enacted. Armed with axes and torches they lit from the cookfires, the men climbed the hill and set up camp.

The formal request for surrender was met with the expected flight of arrows and no appearance of the lord within, so Rognvald gave his next command.

The men began to cut down trees.

The tricky part was getting stacks of wood close enough to the castle walls to serve their purpose, without losing men to the archers within. But they had time on their side. They could maintain the siege for weeks if need be, getting food and water from the ships as needed. Each day, the inhabitants of the castle would weaken as food and water rations ran out. The true enemy of those under siege was the knowledge of how they must die.

Skarfr studied the castle walls, noting that the stones were almost certainly held together with lime. This gave him an idea for a quicker end. And perhaps a kinder one. That would depend on the lord inside the castle.

CHAPTER 36

SKARFR

Don't praise the sword until after the fight.

The Wanderer's Hávamál

Skarfr waited for a southerly wind then had two piles of branches stacked high, out of range of any missiles sent from the castle wall.

'But they're too far away to do any damage,' objected Jón Halt-foot.

Rognvald looked at Skarfr, waited for elucidation.

'We use the smoke for cover,' explained Skarfr, 'and light fires ever nearer the castle. The more smoke, the more cover we have. And with the wind blowing towards the castle, we can pile on earth and pour water on these first fires as we get nearer the walls.'

Rognvald nodded and ordered, 'Light the fires!'

The green wood did not take easily but a torch thrust into the centre of each stack burned strongly enough to start both fires, which then gave off thick, noxious smoke. The wind performed its role admirably, blowing the smoke in billows as far as the castle walls.

Coughing and choking, the men on the battlements threw down

burning pitch and brimstone, but, as they had no view of their targets, all that did was to add fuel to the fires the Norðmen laid, closer and closer to the walls.

'Thanks be to Thórr,' murmured Skarfr as he watched the fires burn through the lime binding the stone. The moment a section of wall crumbled, he led the men through and into the inner courtyard.

Then he unleashed the dragon.

Blade and blood were all that mattered for long enough to subdue the half-hearted defence, but a misstep still meant death. Skarfr let instinct guide his steps and his whirling axe, as he made his way through to the tower, seeking the castle's lord. He dispatched one opponent and quickly found himself in a circle clear of other challengers. Their reluctance to come within reach of his blade was evident.

He blinked to clear his eyes, which were still streaming thanks to what was left of the smoke. Men outside the walls must have followed their instructions to put out the fires after they'd served their purpose. Drifts of smoke could be seen heading northwards to where Eindridi and his men waited to capture any fleeing castle-dwellers, especially the lord.

Cup-bearer Roaldsson paused briefly, obviously on the same mission. 'Have you seen the lord?'

'No, I'm still looking,' Skarfr called back.

'If you tidy things up here, I'll take men north, squeeze any who've escaped between us and Eindridi. He won't get away.' Cup-bearer didn't wait for assent but charged off again, heading into the smoke.

Skarfr looked around him to see whether his help was needed, but the defenders seemed to have demonstrated their only skills when they ran out of the woods and threw stones on the beach. The Norðmen out-matched them in every way.

But not without paying a price.

'Mouthy!' yelled Skarfr, too far away to stop a stealthy knife in his shipmate's back. The old warrior had been too focused on the man fighting him to see the foe sneaking up behind him.

He staggered, gave one last swing of his axe, which finished the smiling defendant. Then he twisted around to face the second man, but he was running away, out of Skarfr's reach, shouting 'I surrender!'

Mouthy crumpled to the ground on his side as Skarfr reached him. The opponent was no longer a threat, his smile gone and his eyes blank as his hands flopped over his bleeding stomach.

Skarfr could see the knife deep in Mouthy's back. The man must have been petrified, to leave such a valuable weapon. Pulling it out meant his friend's death but so did leaving it there. He crouched beside his companion and put a hand on the old man's heart, felt it weakening.

'You are a true *drengr*,' Skarfr told Mouthy. 'This day's work brings you much honour in the tale that shall be told.'

Mouthy smiled through the blood bubbling up, his hands clutching his axe.

'Now,' he gasped. 'I'm ready.'

Skarfr grabbed the hilt of the knife and jerked it upwards, feeling the body's resistance and loosening, in that moment of intimacy between victim and weapon-wielder. But this time, his own heart was breaking as Mouthy's stopped. Blood gushed and his friend's spirit flew from his mouth in one last breath.

Skarfr looked up, searching the sky for what must surely follow. Mouthy had earned such a tribute from the otherworld. Black wings flapped overhead.

'Crrk,' the cormorant insisted, circling, on her divine errand. Then she flew away over the castle, squawking once to Skarfr as she took a warrior's soul to Valhalla.

'We'll meet again,' Skarfr told Mouthy, 'when the end comes.' He looked at the human shell, so small and shrunken that he wondered at the spirit which had kept the old man alive so long.

He stood, looked around once more but nobody wanted to be killed. Everywhere, defenders were on their knees, throwing down their weapons.

All too quickly for many of them, Rognvald's horn called the men back to reason, to the search for the lord and his loot. Skarfr shrugged. If the lord or any of the men had escaped over the north-side battlements, Eindridi would have them.

He had to speak with Rognvald, tell him how Mouthy had died. He found the Jarl leaning over a fallen Norðman, pressing a cloth against his neck. Rognvald acknowledged Skarfr's approach with a grunt and told the wounded man, 'You're in luck. Skarfr pisses honey so that'll heal in no time.'

Erling groaned, whether in pain or at the thought of the treatment, Skarfr couldn't tell, but Rognvald gave him no option. The Jarl moved the cloth so Skarfr could urinate on the wound, which he did with as much accuracy as he could muster. Being asked to do so was both practical and a compliment, as the treatment was known to be most effective when the fluid came from a true warrior, but nobody enjoyed the procedure.

Rognvald then wrapped the cloth around Erling's neck and tied it as a scarf. 'Flesh wound,' he said. 'You'll be fine.'

Jón Halt-foot had joined them in time to see Erling stagger to his feet, head bent to one side to protect the injury.

'Crick-neck!' he crowed, with his usual tact. 'Erling Crick-neck!'

With a smile as wry as his neck, Erling accepted his new nickname and winked at Skarfr. 'Could be worse,' he said.

There was time to think of many possible nicknames drawn from Erling's recent experience but he stopped that train of thought by adding, 'Could be Erling Halt-foot.'

Jón was first to laugh and to say nobody had been braver in the battle for the castle than Erling Crick-neck – unless it was Skarfr.

Increasingly embarrassed by accounts of his exploits, Skarfr interrupted yet another description of his skill with an axe, to tell Rognvald, 'Sire, we have lost Mouthy. His is the story we should be telling.'

Instantly, the banter stopped.

'How?' Rognvald asked.

'Bravely!' Skarfr replied. 'A warrior to the end. He won his fight but a second man stabbed him in the back. He died with his axe in his hand.'

'And a prayer to God on his lips?' Rognvald queried.

Skarfr knew the importance of the Christian death ritual for Rognvald, and he nodded. Mouthy had certainly been praying to *a* god as he died.

'Have no fears for Mouthy's soul,' Rognvald reassured him. 'The Pope blessed our pilgrimage and any who die during the voyage, even if unshriven, have earned their place in heaven.'

Skarfr thought that Mouthy could choose his own afterlife, having earned two.

'He was brave and loyal,' he said, already missing the cheeky quips and fortitude of his companion. *That* was how to grow old, if growing old was a man's fate. He hoped he would not live long enough to find out.

'Brave *and* loyal,' repeated Rognvald, meeting Skarfr's eyes for a long moment, searching for something. 'With nothing on his conscience. To die in a state of such grace is not given to every man.' His gaze moved to Bishop William administering last rites to a dying man, his portable altar box open on the bloodstained ground.

'It seems we have lost one of Cup-bearer's men too,' Rognvald said. 'May they rest in peace.'

Brave and loyal. With nothing on his conscience.

Bile rose in Skarfr's throat. The dragon had left him and he ached from fighting, ached worse from this double talk that he was probably imagining every time he spoke with Rognvald. This was not honourable and he could not continue this pretence. Hlif was wrong about how Rognvald would react to the truth about them; their only crime had been secrecy. That could be remedied.

Before he could speak and clear his conscience, Cup-bearer Roaldsson rushed towards them, spilling his news before he was near enough for the first words to be heard.

'There's nobody north of the castle. We went into the smoke as far as we dared but found nobody. Have you got the lord?'

'No.' Skarfr couldn't understand what he was being told. How could the lord not be in the castle and not be out of it either? 'I'll go with you,' he told Cup-bearer. 'The smoke will be dying down and we'll keep going till we find them. The lord must be out there.'

As must Eindridi, he thought but didn't say. Maybe Eindridi was giving chase, had been duped in some way. Maybe.

CHAPTER 37

SKARFR

*It is better not to pray at all
than to pray for too much.*

The Wanderer's Hávamál

Skarfr and Cup-bearer dashed around the castle walls, where the fires were little more than embers now, to the north side, which was still a little smoky. Visibility would have been clear but for smoke ahead of them, in the forest.

The men charged off towards the grey billows but were soon choking and came to a halt.

Skarfr grabbed Cup-bearer's arm. 'You were right,' he panted. 'Not a man to be seen and we can't go further, but this is all wrong. We're heading *towards* the fires. The forest is on fire.'

Cup-bearer sounded his horn, signalling the retreat. There was no urgency now.

'But who could have set the forest on fire?' he asked, then light dawned. 'Eindridi,' he answered his own question.

Skarfr nodded.

'Maybe he was trying to trap the lord and his men between the fires and the castle, where we were waiting,' Cup-bearer suggested, being positive.

'Then where are they?' asked Skarfr.

Cup-bearer's dirt-streaked face settled into grim lines and with sombre expressions the two men took their findings back to Rognvald.

'The lord has gone,' Skarfr told the Jarl. 'Under cover of smoke. Someone started a forest fire.'

The Jarl looked towards the trees where the erstwhile opponents were all chopping and digging, making a fire break to stop gusts blowing the flames towards the castle. The last sparks were being stamped down or covered in earth. Neither the Norðmen nor the castle residents wanted to get caught between two blazing walls. Fire was a treacherous servant.

'Eindridi?' asked Rognvald, without emotion.

Also treacherous. 'Is nowhere to be found. And we are missing many men, members of his crew and others too.' It would not do to point the finger without proof, so Skarfr added, 'Perhaps they have gone back to the ships for some reason. Eindridi might even now have the lord a prisoner aboard the *Crest-cleaver*.'

Rognvald had come to his own conclusions and ignored this suggestion.

'No doubt, the 'friendly' lord paid him well and they're long gone, having set fire to the forest to cover their escape. I seem to be short of men I can trust.' His eyes met Skarfr's, kept contact longer than was comfortable.

He knows. Shame formed a leaden ball in Skarfr's gut.

Rognvald clasped his arm and promised, 'I shall give you more than an arm-ring before this trip is done. You merit much. Ask me for your heart's desire.'

The words were out before Skarfr could stop himself. 'I would marry Lady Hlif.'

The Jarl seemed to age and sadden, like a man returned from a stay with the dark elves, who can never settle again in the world of men. When he finally spoke, every word dropped another stone in Skarfr's gut.

'This is something I told you was impossible, for her sake and for yours. The curse of her father's deed dooms your marriage, dooms your line and yet, like a saga hero, you wish for the one thing that will destroy you both.'

Skarfr called on his dragon's courage and his cormorant's arrow-straight dive after a fish. He knelt but lifted his head and spoke firmly. 'Sire, perhaps you are mistaken, but if not, then this doom is one we must face together, Hlif and I. This is meant to be. I ask your permission and hope for your blessing.'

'You speak for the lady.' Rognvald's tone was deceptively bland but Skarfr knew him well enough to catch the hint of menace.

There was no way back. No way to laugh off his suit as a joke, best forgotten. 'I do speak for the lady,' he said.

Rognvald expelled a long breath. 'I have been waiting months for you to tell me this, Skarfr.' His self-control wavered, his voice sharp with disgust. 'To tell me that you have courted my ward behind my back, broken your oath of loyalty to me, betrayed me. Hlif is a mere woman.' He made a gesture of dismissal. 'Incapable of reason and all too capable of deceit and wilful disobedience.'

Skarfr tried to speak in Hlif's defence but Rognvald cut him off. 'No. You have had your say. Now I will have mine.'

In the background men were taking a break from their labours, the fires tamped down. Small altercations broke out as the Norðmen entered the castle once more, this time with clear intent to plunder. Abandoned by their lord, weary, the few men who'd tried to stand in their way made only token objection.

As if they too wore a disguise of smoke, Rognvald and Skarfr were left undisturbed; the wait for the Jarl's words was an eternity.

'This is my doom,' began Rognvald. 'For your courage and skills, you merit a reward not a punishment but you are adamant that you shall have Hlif, so I give you this choice. Renounce her—'

Skarfr shook his head. *No going back.*

Rognvald ignored the movement and made his offer. 'Renounce

her and you shall remain at my side, rich and honoured, on our journey, in Jórsalaheim, and in Orkneyjar when we return. Your father died for a jarl, and your name will be one to make him proud.'

For a heartbeat, Skarfr could see himself, honoured. Fulfilling his destiny, the stuff of sagas. But he had made another oath, bound their two hands fast with twine, joined forever through the hollow of Óðinn's standing stone on an Orkneyjar moor.

'And Hlif?' he asked, steeling his heart. If Hlif would be better off without him, then he must make the sacrifice.

Rognvald made that same gesture of dismissal. 'You will complete this pilgrimage on separate ships. On our return she will go to a convent in Ness, where she can practise her housekeeping skills to her heart's content. She would be well cared for.'

She might like that, thought Skarfr. She might forget him. Maybe what they shared was a fleeting joy that would become a warm memory.

He swallowed, 'I will let her choose and abide by her decision.'

'I think not.' Rognvald's eyes had no softness in them. 'You said you spoke for the lady so you shall know what it is to make a hard choice, to decide what's best for someone under your protection. You shall hear the other choice and give me your answer now, for both of you.

'You may marry with my permission but not my blessing.'

Skarfr's heart leaped. Happiness was possible. He was no more frightened of Hlif's curse than she was. They would defy the unfair legacy that burdened her. He started to thank Rognvald but was once more cut off.

'Payment must be taken,' the Jarl told him.

The words of the rune-reading rang ominous in the grey twilight.

'If you don't give her up,' warned the Jarl, implacable, 'your name will be a byword for treachery, you will be called *niðingr*, an oath-breaker.'

Skarfr flinched.

'For breaking your oath to me, you can never return to Orkneyjar but must live in exile.'

Skarfr's head churned. They could marry! But – in exile. 'Where shall we live?' he blurted out.

'Why should I care?' asked Rognvald. 'But in view of your service to the jarldom, we won't leave you here. I am no Eindridi.'

Should Skarfr feel grateful? Surrender to some foreign ruler never meant a welcome by the fireside. He pictured his own hearth, Brigid and Fergus telling stories of Írland, tucking him in a blanket when he fell asleep in the warmth. Home-longing flooded him.

But Rognvald had not relented. 'We'll take you to the next place where people offer hospitality and we'll leave you there. Both of you.'

Skarfr's mouth was dry. He had no fear of death but these two futures both appalled him. How could he put either of these dooms on Hlif? How could he tell her he had chosen without speaking to her, after blurting out his hope of marrying her? He had brought this on them. Exactly what she'd said would happen if he tried to sway Rognvald.

He could *not* speak for Hlif. That was the solution! 'I will not choose,' he told his liege, who regarded such defiance without blinking.

'Then you both forfeit your lives,' decreed Rognvald.

'You would not!' shouted Skarfr, drawing men's eyes towards them, distracted for an instant from their piles of loot.

'I would,' Rognvald replied, grave and calm. 'I am the Jarl and the Thing will approve of me punishing those who betray me.' He shrugged. 'When I inform them.'

When he returned to Orkneyjar. Without Skarfr and without Hlif.

When Skarfr most needed divine intervention, a sign, there was nothing. No rune-reading, no pathfinder brooch, no cormorant. Words jumbled together in his mind. *You will make sagas. There is a price to pay. Honour is all.*

As if reading his thoughts, Rognvald said, 'Your father gave his life for his jarl without hesitation. Would you throw away the honour he earned?' If he'd stopped there, Skarfr might have weakened.

But the Jarl turned the knife. 'What you feel for Hlif is nothing. The natural stirrings of manhood, nothing more. You will forget her. I will find you a wife worthy of you and we will put this moment behind us. What do you say?'

Skarfr glanced down, saw how tightly his hands gripped the shaft of his axe, how the muscles stood out on his forearms. The dragon rippled. A reminder of all he shared with Hlif in this world and beyond. A sign.

He stood, swung the axe up in a smooth curve and sheathed it behind his back, noting with satisfaction that Rognvald blinked instinctively.

'I gave my oath to Hlif,' he said.

Speaking the words cut through the knot in his guts and he knew this was the right, the honourable thing to do. Let other men be the judge of his actions – and of Rognvald's. 'I shall keep that oath.'

'Then you have chosen between us. As you did when you broke your oath of loyalty to me.' The Jarl was bitter, all the wine-sweetness turned to vinegar between them. 'You shall travel with Cup-bearer. I want both of you out of my sight. Go, tell Hilf her doom.'

Skarfr knew better than to speak again. His brief elation had gone up in smoke and the facts lay heavy as cold pottage in his belly. Sailing with Cup-bearer added insult to injury. Exile. Some unknown place. Never to go home. Her curse. His dishonour. So many dead dreams. And he must tell Hlif all of this in the same breath as saying they could marry.

CHAPTER 38

INGE, STRJÓNSEY, ORKNEYJAR

This time Finn's tone was grim when he came back from the boats on the shore and joined Inge at her loom in the porch. His mind was not on kisses. 'There's been word from Orphir. The messenger set sail as soon as the tide turned, to go to Hjaltland and recruit men from all the islands. The time has come, as we thought. Jarl Harald has summoned us against Erlend. I'm taking the longship and thirty men. That leaves enough here to protect the village, just in case—' His eyes didn't meet Inge's but they both knew what could happen.

'Erlend's not interested in Strjónsey. We'll be fine,' she told him. She reached up to stroke his cheek. 'It's you I'm worried about.'

'I'll be fine too.' He imprisoned her hand, rubbed his bristly beard against it.

'Ouch! It's like stroking a hedgehog!' She exaggerated her pain, enjoying their little ritual, increasingly confident in playful words. She who'd used words as a weapon and drawn blood, would never take for granted the joy of lightly teasing a man, of tenderness and restraint. However, she knew the darkness of her first marriage had tainted her, left some savagery within that could be unleashed into a laceration of words, reducing manhood to jelly. She knew this because she had done it. And she swore she would never do so again.

'It's a show of strength to force an agreement,' Finn was telling her. 'Harald and all our ships will make Erlend realise what he would face if he takes his claim to outright war, and Thorbjorn will do the clever talking so it doesn't come to that.'

Inge's stomach clenched as always when she heard the name but she no longer showed any outward sign.

'Thank the gods, Sweyn and Gunnr are well out of it.' she said. 'Their rancour against both Erlend and Harald might sway them in either direction. And there is no love lost between Sweyn and Thorbjorn.'

Finn gave her a sharp look but she maintained the neutral expression of one discussing distant politics. Whatever he might have said was lost as his attention was diverted to a handful of men heading up the path towards them.

'My lord, I've told the men to ready themselves,' said Shoe-awl. 'They'll be at the ship for tide-turn tomorrow, as you ordered. The usual crew, but the carpenter is ill with gout and the tanner is showing his age, so with your leave I've replaced them with the baker's boy and the new thrall. He's been begging to come with us and says he's handy on board a ship. What do you say?'

Looking far cleaner and healthier than when he'd first arrived on Strjónsey, Fergus' eyes were fixed on Inge, pleading, and she knew why. If he sailed to Orphir, where Thorbjorn lived, he might hear news of Brigid.

Finn hesitated. 'I know nothing of the man.' He wanted no weak links on board.

'He's a worker, I'll say that,' said Fleece-faster and heads nodded in agreement.

'He's my lady's thrall, not mine,' Finn said. 'So I'll let you be the judge, Inge.'

She too hesitated. What did she know about this man, who was not her thrall? Would she trust him with her husband's life just because he once saved hers? He had merely been following Skarfr's orders.

And he had risked his life on Skarfr's orders, shown loyalty.

However, if he picked up Brigid's scent, what loyalty would he show Finn?

'He is a good man,' she declared, 'and would prove useful to you.' She stared at Fergus, willing him to understand that she was ordering him to be so. 'And loyal,' she emphasised, 'whatever transpires.'

Fergus met her eyes. 'I understand, my lady,' he said.

But he gave no promises and Inge had deep misgivings as she left the band of men talking, while she went indoors to oversee preparations for the evening meal.

CHAPTER 39

FERGUS, ORKNEYJAR

As their ship neared Orphir, Fergus saw more and more striped sails converging on their destination, like the pack of sea wolves Skarfr called them in his poems. Far too many to beach them all, and the newcomers lay at anchor, men ferried ashore by the small boats dropped down from their host ships or sent out from the shore.

Fergus had never seen such a gathering and his heart thumped, knowing only too well the terror that two or three such sails could instil in the lookout and the villagers who watched the sea-raiders approaching. But this time, he was among them, and he timed his breathing to the steady rhythm of his oars to calm his heart.

He knew that the finer manoeuvres among so many ships were best done with sail furled and oarsmen working hard to negotiate passage between their neighbours' hulls. They yelled a bluff greeting or a curse, whichever seemed more appropriate as they found their station and dropped anchor.

Take me with you, he willed Finn, as a few men were selected to go ashore in the small rowboat that drew up alongside. He had to get to Thorbjorn's house. He'd jump ship that night and swim if he had to, whatever price he paid for deserting. They'd have to catch him first.

Finn looked at him, unsure, then nodded. 'And you, the new man,

Fergus. Nobody knows you, so keep your head down and use your ears among the servants and traders. Anyone who's been to market in Kirkjuvágr recently might have some news about how much support Erlend has. And how many ships. Ask around while we're at the Jarl's *Bu*. Find us there tomorrow morning.'

The gods were with him. The moment the rowboat reached the shallows for the men to jump out, Fergus sloped off on his own, his pack on his back containing all he needed to eat, and to sleep rough for a night. He merged with others like him, anonymous in coarse brown tunics and woollen breeches, carrying their axes and daggers, farm-fresh faces sombre with the prospect of battle. There would be many a man seeking hospitality with beasts in byres while their lords slept on the benches in the Jarl's *Bu*. And a mug of ale in a peasant's house would be a boon.

Fergus followed a man who'd mentioned just such a house and he was soon supping ale and eating a morsel of bannock from his pack. Thank God for Orkneyjar hospitality, even if it co-existed with their enthusiasm for murdering each other in their own houses.

He did as his lord had bidden him and listened, hearing many questions but no answers regarding Erlend's forces and Jarl Harald's plans. He *did* hear of those lords who were absent, with their entourages, and who should have been in Orphir by now.

Sweyn and Gunnr were excused, but much missed, and Harald was blamed for their absence. If Gunnr was exiled, he could hardly be here to support the Jarl, could he? And Sweyn was his own man, off raiding somewhere. However, other missing lords were suspected of being much closer, their ships among those in Kirkjuvágr harbour with Erlend. He'd made good promises, had Erlend.

Somewhere in the flow of facts, suggestions and ribaldry, Fergus slipped in his questions about Lord Thorbjorn. He'd have a houseful tonight and all the servants would be at the Jarl's *Bu*? He'd surely reward well for extra help. And Fergus couldn't deny an extra penny would be useful.

The men were keen to show off their superior knowledge of Orphir to this country bumpkin with a strange accent.

'Thorbjorn will be at the *Bu* tonight,' said one. 'He wouldn't miss such a gathering! You can always call at his house, ask his man there, or one of the women servants, if help is needed. I doubt you'll be lucky though.'

Another said, 'My lord is above such domestic matters and has no woman of his own to run his house since he divorced that barren bitch.'

As the conversation turned to anecdotes damning womankind, Fergus quietly sought directions to Thorbjorn's house and made his escape.

Within hours, he had discovered that Thorbjorn was short of women servants, having recently sent three to his estate in Ness. But no men were required, thank you, and my lord was not one to host strangers, so Fergus had best find himself a bench elsewhere.

Laying his pack down as a pillow in the straw of an empty sheepfold, where he was not the only one to seek a night's shelter, Fergus wondered what to do. Not where he should go but how to get there. And for the first time since Brigid was taken, he was kept awake by hope, not by fear.

※

Summer rain was just as wet as winter's and, without losing his grip on the rope he was letting out, Fergus shook his head like a dog to get the drips out of his eyes. He glanced behind him at the solid bulk of their captain but his expression was not reassuring.

If he'd gone on the run in Orphir, Fergus would have been on a ship heading in the opposite direction, not to the Isle of Egilsey for some ill-omened meeting between Harald and Erlend, but to Ness and Thorbjorn's estate there, where he was sure he'd find Brigid. But he'd thought to do so honestly.

Instead of deserting, he'd approached Finn and told him that word had reached Fergus in Orphir of a farming problem at the Lambaburg estate, and Lady Inge would wish him to return there. His insides had squirmed beneath that honest lord's grave study, but

Finn had obviously swallowed the lie. Unfortunately, he had different priorities from Fergus'.

'After we return from Egilsey,' was Finn's judgement. 'Then you may return to Lambaburg. And I'll pass on the message to Lady Inge.'

Now Fergus was wondering whether he *would* return from Egilsey. He should have run while he had the chance.

Finn's was one of the five ships heading for the Isle of Egilsey and none of his men were happy at the prospect. All knew what had been agreed with Erlend, after he realised how many ships had come at Harald's summons. He'd decided to talk, somewhere neutral.

Five ships apiece, and each of the two leaders would take five men in a rowboat to the island and talk terms. To reach Egilsey, there was no need for their ships to cross each other's paths and risk tensions exploding into battle. Erlend would sail his ships from Kirkjuvágr, counter-sunwise, and Harald would take the natural sunwise route from Orphir, which was longer.

But it was not the possibility of Erlend setting up an ambush that troubled Finn's men. It was the island itself, Egilsey. Fergus saw more of them crossing themselves at mention of the place than touched their amulets, but whatever god's protection they sought, their unease rippled like the waves in an ill wind.

'Privilege to be chosen, my arse,' muttered one of Fergus' shipmates, pulling up his oilcloth hood.

'Are you going soft, Knob-nose? You look like my grandma in that thing!' came the cheerful insult.

'What manner of place is Egilsey?' asked Fergus, knowing his accent would explain his ignorance.

'One you don't want to go to,' said Knob-nose, his nickname not totally accounted for by the shape of that appendage.

The man teasing Knob-nose took pity on Fergus. 'It's where Jarl Magnus was martyred, became a saint.'

'Then it's a holy place?' Fergus was confused.

'It's a place where two Jarls took five ships apiece and only one came back alive,' said Knob-nose drily. 'I wonder which of them chose Egilsey, Harald or Erlend, and what the other one thinks of it.'

'My money's on Thorbjorn,' suggested a sailor whose bald head was faring better in the rain than those with long locks plastered to their faces. He added with approval, 'Devious bastard.'

There was general agreement and nothing more was said on the matter.

Fergus watched the scrap of cloth fluttering on the mast and wondered which way the wind would blow him. His choice felt increasingly doomed, but he could not have left Finn before this fateful meeting, and could not have betrayed Inge. Apart from how wrong such a return for their kindness would be, until Skarfr returned, they were his only hope of survival. When he found Brigid, he would need their help. *If* he survived.

'Fergus!' Finn's call cut into his thoughts, and he left his post amidships to stumble back to his captain by the steerboard.

'I want you to have forewarning,' said Finn, his face serious. 'I am to be one of the party going ashore with Jarl Harald and Lord Thorbjorn, and I want you with me.'

Not a clever idea. 'But I'm just a thrall,' protested Fergus.

'That's why. The Jarl wanted me because he trusts me, and Lord Thorbjorn was specific that I must bring a low-born vassal who can handle himself well in a tight corner.'

Fergus' heart raced. Thorbjorn must have seen him, recognised him, despite him being so careful. And if he *hadn't* recognised him already, then he surely would when they were together in such a small group. But there was no way of refusing.

'Yes, my lord.'

Fergus swayed and rolled along the ship, back to his post, where his shipmates already knew what Finn had asked.

'Don't envy you,' commented Knob-nose.

For a moment, Fergus thought the man knew who he was, that everyone on ship knew, then his common sense asserted itself. Knob-nose must be referring to the danger of the meeting itself, the risk of treachery. If Fergus stayed silent, Thorbjorn would never recognise him. As long as he didn't speak, didn't risk his Irish accent triggering a memory.

But Knob-nose didn't look like a man averse to a fight, so Fergus asked, 'Why?'

'The man who murdered Magnus. He was a cook, a nobody Jarl Hakon took with him. What was his name again, Baldie?'

'Hlifolf,' the other man replied. 'Cursed forever, he was. And his descendants, forever. He had a daughter, Hlif. Jarl Rognvald took her in to make sure she had no children.'

'Aye, I remember now,' Knob-nose followed his own train of thought. 'Cursed forever, that's how it goes. Who do you think will get the blame for Erlend's murder? The Jarl who orders it or the nobody who carries it out? Think on that, and on why Thorbjorn might want a nobody there.'

'Don't listen to Doom and Gloom.' Baldie was too hearty to be credible. 'Orkneyjar likes two jarls and two jarls it shall have.'

'Only if two jarls leave the island alive.' Knob-nose had the last word.

CHAPTER 40

ERLEND, EGILSEY, ORKNEYJAR

Erlend ran his tongue around his dry lips, watching Harald's rowboat approaching the cove, where he and his five men stood waiting, prepared. One man was holding a banner high, to show who they were and to indicate good faith. But good faith required two honest parties.

Why had Harald – or rather Thorbjorn – chosen this island? Purely to unsettle Erlend, who could not refuse without seeming weak? Or was there some tactical advantage? And why did Erlend's imagination insist on seeing himself as Magnus, betrayed and outnumbered, rather than as the successful executioner? As if he didn't have enough stories in his head of bane and doom.

To settle his nerves, Erlend enumerated the ways in which they were ready. They were all wearing well-padded gambesons, and carrying daggers and axes. Their position on the rocks above the beach meant that they could assess the garb and mood of the newcomers. If Harald wore mail or a helm, or if his approach were belligerent, Erlend's boat was in the next cove and he could make good his escape with one of his men, while Harald and his men were slowed down by the sand. The other four men were expendable.

Harald's boat was now near enough for him to see the dip and splash of oars but not to verify that only six men were on board.

One of Erlend's expendables muttered, 'We could easily have hidden two or three men behind the rocks, made sure of the advantage – or made things even if they break the terms.'

'I told you,' Erlend replied sharply, 'No man shall say I won the jarldom by breaking an oath. This shall be done fairly and set the tone for the years to come, when I shall rule these islands.'

He ignored the surly, 'If you live,' uttered under the man's breath and counted heads as the boat drew ever nearer.

One. Two. Three. Four. Five. Six. And no helms.

His pulse steadied and he stood tall. He was the rightful Jarl of Orkneyjar, more so than the man, younger than him, who jumped out the boat and strode up the sand with a tall, dark-haired warrior beside him. They were so confident; they didn't even look behind them to check their four followers were close enough to assist if need be.

Harald was even uglier than Erlend had been told, unmistakable with his low forehead and bulging eyes. Beside him, Thorbjorn looked even more like a saga hero, his grin mischievous and his joy in action palpable.

Neither of them was slowed down by the sand, thought Erlend ruefully. They gave the impression they could break into a run and hound him for hours if they chose, dogs chasing a doomed deer.

His men shifted, uneasy as the newcomers approached. Erlend spoke first to show he *was* a warrior, and a cunning one. No Magnus fated for sainthood.

'My Lord Harald and my Lord Thorbjorn,' he acknowledged. 'I've long waited for this meeting.' He was pleased at his respectful but dominant tone, at taking control.

Thorbjorn flicked black hair out his eyes, startling one of Erlend's men into reaching for his sword hilt.

The Jarl's advisor laughed, held his hands wide and open, to show no weapons. 'Surely only a few hours, Lord Erlend,' he joked. 'And we are the tide's servants or we would have been standing where you are now.'

Was this mockery? A threat? The rock on which Erlend stood

shifted like sand beneath his feet. Would he die here? He forced himself to open his own hands equally wide in a no-weapons gesture, to smile. But he knew his own smile lacked the spontaneity and charm of the one opposing him.

Harald spoke. 'Enough, Thorbjorn. We'll be here all day if you make dances with words that nobody else understands. We need plain speaking.'

Thorbjorn sketched a mocking bow. 'Then we shall have it.'

'Yes, plain speaking.' Erlend's words came out as a plea.

This was not going how he had planned but he recovered enough to revert to his prepared speech. 'I claim what is mine, half of these islands and half of Ness, by right of my father Jarl Harold Hakonsson—'

'Smooth-tongue,' Thorbjorn supplied helpfully.

'Known as Smooth-tongue,' Erlend added, riled. 'And by decree of King Malcolm—'

This time Harald laughed, and Thorbjorn interjected, '—who's nine years old.'

'Who's King of Skotland and who has *good* advisors.' Erlend wished Thorbjorn in hell. He proceeded doggedly, 'And many stout Orkneymen support my claim, which we can back up with force of arms, if need be. I do not wish such bloodshed, hence this meeting.'

It wasn't perfect but it could have gone worse, so he paused.

'Tell him, Thorbjorn,' ordered Harald.

Suddenly, Thorbjorn's impish manner vanished, and the advisor was all business. 'We acknowledge your claim and your support, and would also prefer an agreement to bloodshed. Orkneyjar has only one jarl at present and our tradition allows for two. Therefore, Jarl Harald will bestow on you those parts of Orkneyjar ruled by Jarl Rognvald and one half of Ness, and will accept joint rule.'

Erlend nodded. This was too easy. Where was the catch?

'On condition that—' Thorbjorn continued.

Ah. Here it comes.

'—you gain the consent of the King of Norðvegr, our liege lord, for Jarl Harald has no right to appoint a jarl. If you gain such approval, then we will call a Thing and confirm you as jarl.'

Erlend's thoughts raced while he played for time. 'That sounds reasonable but... how will I get Norðvegr's consent?' Would Norðvegr endorse him at all, given that Rognvald was a Norðman born and bred and had been chosen by a previous King of Norðvegr?

Thorbjorn was succinct. 'Go there. And plead your cause as eloquently as you have here.' That irritating quirk of the mouth was back.

'But that will take—'

'Months,' agreed Thorbjorn. 'And you can return to your lands after the winter. With no bloodshed.'

Fuck. Erlend had been the one played for time. But he had no option. It was everything he could have hoped for. Eventually. And he could be patient.

'I accept. If I gain Norðvegr's approval, and you support my claim before the Thing, we will draw up allocation of our lands as you say.' He stepped forward to shake hands with Harald and seal the agreement.

The two men flanking him automatically stepped forward with him, bringing one of them as close to Thorbjorn as Erlend was to Harald.

The two leaders clasped hands and swore their oath loudly, on the blood of the White Christ and on Thórr's hammer.

At the same moment, one of Erlend's men dropped to his knees, blood gurgling from his slit throat, eyes wide in shock, and then glazed as life left him.

'Jesus, Mary and all the saints save us!' gasped one of Harald's men in a foreign accent. Clearly a peasant from his clothing, he was green-faced and retching, which earned a long, contemptuous stare from Thorbjorn. Who held his arms wide again in that gesture of truce, then wiped and sheathed his dagger. He'd been so fast, Erlend hadn't seen the weapon drawn. Neither, presumably, had Erlend's men.

The moment hung like a thundercloud, uncertain whether to spit rain, flash lightning or move with the wind to another region of sky.

Erlend could draw his sword and let the fighting begin. But what of his oath? There had been no breach of the agreement. He swallowed. One expendable was dead, and he had the right to be offended, to demand manbot. But to jeopardise his jarldom for one killing?

While he hesitated, Thorbjorn spoke. 'Let all Orkneymen know the price of betraying their jarl. We take our dues, *Jarl Erlend* and you would be wise to encourage loyalty to a ruler, rather than foment treason. We too claim what is our right, and this man,' he nudged the dead man with his boot and the corpse tumbled onto its face. 'This man was a traitor to his jarl. He represents all such traitors. We forgo our right to make further examples as a sign of goodwill to the new jarl.'

Harald spat on the ground. 'We have an agreement, Jarl Erlend. God speed and grant fair wind for Norðvegr.'

Without one backward look, Harald and his men turned and marched back to their boat, launched it and soon became black specks bobbing on the sea.

Should he have stabbed Harald in the back, wondered Erlend. Or Thorbjorn?

'Bury him,' he ordered.

'What will you do, my lord?' asked the expendable who still lived. Such was the will of the Norns.

'Set sail for Norðvegr.' And find a warrior who was a match for Thorbjorn.

CHAPTER 41

FERGUS, ORKNEYJAR

'That man is my thrall,' Thorbjorn told Finn as they walked back to the rowboat, heedless of the spilled blood and humiliated jarl they left behind them. 'I don't know how you came by him but there's no harm done if you return him now.'

Finn's answer was slow in coming, and Fergus had difficulty controlling a desperate urge to piss. He'd seen recognition dawn in Thorbjorn's eyes when he'd forgotten himself and called out, and he'd known what would follow, but he was trapped on a small island with nowhere to run. He kept walking, eyes down, as if by not looking at the lords he could turn their attention away from him. The group reached the boat that would take them back to the ships.

'You are mistaken, my lord.' Finn's calm rebuttal was a smack in the face for Thorbjorn, whose sharp indrawn breath boded ill. 'He is my thrall, a nobody I would not wish on you, so clumsy he is. They all look the same, these thralls, so I can understand the mistake.'

Another pause marked Thorbjorn's indecision.

'God's breath, Thorbjorn. You were outstanding! You shall have your pick of the armoury and silver too.' Harald gave Thorbjorn a hearty clap on the back, apparently unaware of any undercurrents and brimming with triumph. 'You showed him all right!' He mimed a killing slice with a blade, and Thorbjorn winced at his liege's gauche enthusiasm.

Harald jumped into the boat and Thorbjorn followed him, stern and silent.

Moving from sheer force of habit, Fergus ran the boat down to the sea with the other men, and jumped in when it was afloat. He took an oar and rowed for his life, eyes fixed on the diminishing shore. He could feel Thorbjorn's stare drilling into his back as the welcome sounds of the ship grew louder.

When they were close enough to board, Finn placed himself as if by accident between Thorbjorn and Fergus, told the thrall curtly, 'Hurry up, you useless man. The tide will turn before we get away.'

Fergus' feet touched the boards of Finn's ship and he let out the breath he'd been holding. He placed as many thwarts as possible between him and the rowboat below.

'Dolt,' Finn flung the insult after him, then told Thorbjorn, 'If I respected you less, my lord, you could have him.'

Finn swung aboard and moved to his position by the steerboard. As he passed Fergus, he said quietly, 'I think you'd do well to attend that family emergency in Ness sooner rather than later, on the first ship you can catch.'

Trembling and white, Fergus just nodded. What new trouble had he brought on this man and his lady? Thorbjorn was not the forgiving kind.

CHAPTER 42

BRIGID, NESS

B rigid had tried to make herself useful without treading on any toes, but she was still an outsider and the only thrall.

At first, she merely carried out her orders: brought the moss to dry for kindling, scrubbed vegetables, swept the floor and spoke only when addressed. She was all eyes and ears, noting how relaxed the household was under the steward's management, with the lord away. How the atmosphere tensed when Thorbjorn was mentioned. Or when his mother was having one of her good days and hobbled around, leaning on her stick, inspecting and interfering. Life was easier when the old lady sat by the fire, lost and drooling, or lay in her bed behind the curtain, too weary to rise.

Impossible to believe that this husk of womanhood had mothered such a firebrand and yet, there were days when Brigid could feel old age stalking her too, working her to the bone. Maybe she too would be a crone before Fergus found her. She reckoned the years in her head. Why, she must be thirty-nine, too old for the manual labour expected of her as the last-come, least-valued in this domestic community.

By observing what was needed and where, she went beyond her orders, smoothed the day-to-day running of the community and was paid in the occasional 'thank you' and smile. She even risked patching up a child who'd scraped his knee, tumbling with the pack of little ones who ran like scavenging dogs around the settlement. Their older brothers were at work learning the trades of fishing and trapping, sailing and boat-mending while their sisters fetched ground meal from the mill, or swilled out the crone's soil-pail into the midden.

Fetching and carrying all day. Their backs will pay for it, thought Brigid, as she massaged her own. The stiffness would ease during the day but surely she had not ached like this a few months ago. Maybe her imprisonment had left traces, or maybe the humid airs of this region affected her. She sighed. Knowing the cause would not change the problem.

At night, she stretched out on a thin mattress in the small house, little more than a hut, that she shared with the two women who'd come on the ship with her. She'd known worse for comfort and was not complaining.

The walls were mostly turf with some stones mixed in, held upright by wooden posts driven into the ground. The thatched roof kept out the rain but added to the permanent smell of damp. Lighting a small fire on the stones that served as hearth merely added smoke to the atmosphere, and the servants were in the habit of warming themselves in the lord's big stone house. Under the high arched roof beams, the hearth was big enough to host a crackling fire, with a stewpot hung above it.

However, being with two other women in their own little house felt safe. There was a space in a solid wooden kist for her belongings but she didn't need it. She was wearing all she possessed. At night she folded her overdress beside her and placed her shoes neatly beside them. They were well-worn but good leather and serviceable, a reminder of better times.

The women might not like her but they shared what they had. She'd even been given a vast wool shawl, which served as blanket, pillow and cloak as the summer nights grew autumnal.

The shawl's big blue and green checks made her think of the skies and fields of Skarfr's home, *her* home with Fergus, and she would wrap herself as tight in its comfort as a swaddled baby. She tried to show how much she appreciated such a gift but Ellisif, the woman who gave it to her, turned her head, walked away from such unwanted effusion. Like a bellwether with her sheep, where Ellisif led, the others followed. In her mind, Brigid named the woman so: Ellisif Bellwether.

Maybe Brigid should tend to the animals, so she had some contact with other living beings, but that had always been Fergus' work. They had been together so many years, she had forgotten the rhythm of pulling on a goat's teats or walking sheep to new pasture without losing stragglers. So many years together.

He will find me!

She might not be skilled with animals but she knew how to make the most of their produce. She'd been sole housekeeper and cook, first for Botolf and the boy Skarfr, then as her own mistress. If she baked some bannocks, made curd and cheese, dried fish, then the people she lived with might open up to her. She must bide her time.

Just when Brigid thought she was making progress, the sideways looks began again. Her back ached so, she began each day tired and ended it exhausted, and the knowledge that she was unwanted weighed her down even more. When the underlying hostility came to a head, or at least action of some kind, Brigid was almost relieved.

The question seemed innocent enough, but not the way all eyes turned on Brigid and all work stopped, as if there had been an announcement that a maiden must be chosen to placate the monster. And Brigid was to be the dragon bait.

Ah, sure, and I'm getting fanciful from being alone in strange land, she chid herself.

'Who will go foraging with me today?' asked Wulfhild, a young woman who looked as wild as her *Wolf-fighter* name suggested, her hair an unbound thicket of hazel curls around a square, weathered face. Brown eyes, sharp and restless, and muddy ankles above bare feet completed the feral impression.

Yet she had her place in the household in a way that Brigid did not. Wulfhild was welcomed each day when she returned with basket full of moss, herbs and berries, and wished well when she left each morning, the wicker basket empty on her arm. But she always went alone, wherever it was she went.

'Brigid will go,' stated Ellisif Bellwether. Eyes flicked towards Brigid and away again. Some nodded. All seemed to understand something that Brigid did not. The hairs on her neck rose with the intuition that she faced some terrible danger.

'I don't know what to do,' she stammered. 'Maybe someone else would be better...'

Ellisif Bellwether didn't even look at her but turned, brought down a wicker panier from a shelf above the sleep benches and passed it to Brigid, who tucked her arm through the handle, from force of habit. Wulfhild was walking towards the door, the matter concluded.

'Go,' ordered Ellisif Bellwether.

Brigid went, trying to shake off the sense of foreboding.

―――

Wulfhild set a fierce pace and Brigid was puffing in the attempt to keep up with her, resigned to a view of the younger woman's back. They passed the last hut in the settlement, then the peat-diggers cutting their grid into the edge of the vast bogland, and kept walking, presumably to reach some mysterious destination.

Vast silvery skies were reflected in a thousand pools, puddles and rivulets. Water did not run in the natural twists of burns or brooks familiar to Brigid, but rather in criss-crossing straight lines, like the grids of cut peat. Or it gathered in black holes.

The shallow slope disguised any flow, but the dragonflies and hoverflies seemed not to mind whether the water was stagnant or running. A blanket of purples and reds proved on closer inspection to be mosses and heather in bloom.

Until she misstepped, Brigid hadn't realised how closely she'd been following in Wulfhild's footsteps, walking blithely from one clump of grass to another. But when one foot slipped into a puddle and was sucked down, sinking ever deeper into black mud, she cried out, flailing her arms to keep her balance. Lopsided and leaning like a capsized ship, it took all her strength to prevent her whole body following the errant foot. And still it sought bottom, found nothing but watery slime.

Untroubled, Wulfhild turned and backtracked at a leisurely pace, steadied Brigid so she could pull her foot out of the ooze sucking at her calf. With a reluctant squelch, the mire returned her leg but kept its tithe for passage.

'My shoe!' Brigid's lower leg was caked in wet mud and she was as barefoot as Wulfhild, who shrugged.

'Pass me the other 'un,' she told Brigid.

Too shocked to wonder why, with some vague notion that Wulfhild knew these marshes so well she could maybe hook one shoe with another like an angler catching a pike with a minnow, Brigid took off her precious shoe and passed it over.

Wulfhild threw it into the black pool to join its mate, still holding Brigid's arm with the other hand.

'No!' Brigid's involuntary shriek and jerk broke her out of her passivity but she wasn't stupid enough to try to rescue her shoes.

'Why?' she asked Wulfhild, fighting her tears.

Her companion watched the smooth surface of the pool, which shimmered in a mockery of serene clouds.

'One shoe's no use,' she replied. 'Give it to the spirits and pray.'

Brigid didn't have to ask what to pray for. She looked around her with growing horror. She was miles from any fellow humans with a madwoman, in a place that was trying to kill her.

'A warning, that was,' said Wulfhild, 'So you listen and learn. And look carefully.'

Brigid swallowed hard but she had no choice. She nodded.

'Never step in water. You can't tell what's underneath.' Wulfhild admonished, 'but you might see a line of rushes beside a run of water. You can walk on them, follow them downstream.'

Then she snapped, 'Are you listening?'

Miserably, Brigid nodded again. But there was no sign of any rushes around them and she was never going to remember so many details.

Wulfhild picked up a handful of the bright ruby-red moss nearby and squeezed it. Water gushed out. 'Never step on this, whatever the colour. Some's so green it hurts your eyes. It lives on water and water lives in it. Won't hold you.'

The living moss looked quite different from the dried stuff Brigid used to start fires. She had more respect now for whoever had collected it.

Wulfhild pointed to fine-lined brown patches of what looked like shiny earth. 'Not safe.'

Keen to show that she was not totally ignorant, Brigid said, 'Rosemary,' and reached down to pick some young sprigs of the herb. Only to have her hand slapped away from the blue-green leaves.

'Poison. Don't touch,' Wulfhild cautioned. 'The marsh plays tricks on you but that one's easy to spot. No rosemary grows on the bog.'

Her gaze fixed on something further away. Brigid looked in the same direction but could see nothing.

'Come, the berries are over there,' said Wulfhild. 'Tread anywhere there's grass or shrubs or heathers. They need land under 'em. Dried peat will hold you but it's so soft it's scary. Best not unless you really need to.'

Her heart pumping madly, Brigid followed Wulfhild carefully, noting the plants on each firm foothold, avoiding the sprawling moss and innocent little puddles or runnels.

Walking was stop-start. Find a safe step; move, stop, check.

Sure enough, they reached low-growing shrubs covered in golden berries.

'Cloudberries,' Wulfhild told her. And they did look like clouds, clumped together in sunset colours. 'They grow on land so you're safe around them. Pick as many as you can find and then fill your basket with heather. Ellisif dries the heather-tops for tea, says it's good for coughs and such.'

Tentatively at first, Brigid began picking the berries. She couldn't resist tasting a handful and enjoyed the sweet moisture as they burst against her tongue. With curds of goat milk they would be such a treat.

After they'd picked the first bushes, the women moved further apart to reach new treasures. Brigid felt more confident as she realised Wulfhild was right. Where the low-growing shrubs grew, the footing was sure. They kept moving further apart to reach more berries and Brigid stopped checking where Wulfhild was.

Until she glanced across and realised the younger woman had gone. She was alone, with bog stretching out for miles in every direction. Could Wulfhild have gone so far as to be out of sight in the time Brigid had been distracted? Or was she hiding in some dip or trench? Whatever the case, Brigid knew she'd been brought out here to die.

CHAPTER 43

BRIGID, NESS

Grey skies and bogland swam into a featureless spin as Brigid looked around her. No sun to guide her and one section of marsh looked the same as another in endless repetition.

Which way had they come? She had no idea which direction Wulfhild had taken when she disappeared, but Brigid was sure the other woman had not been taken by the mud. As she knew she would be unless she stayed still, waited for someone to find her. Which she knew would not happen. As surely as she knew Wulfhild was heading for home, Brigid knew her abandonment had been deliberate. And if she stayed still, night would catch her, as would its creatures. She shuddered.

Tales of ballybogs filled her head, those mud fairies that slobbered and slimed their way through peatlands. She stared at a black pool and could see their mud-brown heads rising up, neckless above ball-round bodies. Their ears were pricked like hounds on a scent and their noses were so long they hung below their bottom lips. Their open mouths sucked and gobbled like the bog itself, mocking, as they led her astray, protecting their domain.

She shook herself. No ballybogs were needed to lead her astray. Sure, and she could go astray all by herself without help from ugly beasties. And as for the mischievous shape-shifting *Púca*, who was also well-known to frequent the peat bogs, why he was welcome to appear in whatever guise he chose. There was no being on this godforsaken heath she'd trust, so what did one more monster matter?

Spending the night here was out of the question with so many dangers, both real and fancied, so she must start walking. She prayed to her name-saint Brigid and to the old goddess Bríd to guide her steps.

All Wulfhild's instructions filled her mind in a panic-stricken jumble. *Poison, don't touch, don't walk on this, do walk on that... was heather safe or did it sink?*

Be calm, she told herself. *One barefoot step at a time.*

But in which direction?

She looked around her more attentively and realised that the snowcloud shrubs formed a linear mass, that she had been picking them from right to left, never crossing through them to the other side. Just as Wulfhild had been picking from left to right. She pictured the moment they'd seen the snowcloud berries ahead of them, like a path crossing their own. So, she should turn her back on the berry shrubs to head for home. And from then on, she must find patterns in the landscape to keep to that direction even if her feet must zigzag to find their paths. She adjusted her panier on her arm and took her first step onto a tussock.

If only her back didn't ache so. And now, her front was sore too, as if in sympathy. The fullness and tenderness in her breasts was like that when her monthly flowers came and yet this was not her time. In fact, she had not been so visited for two or three months. Or was it four? She'd lost track and had been grateful. She couldn't have imagined what to do with *that* extra problem in the conditions Thorbjorn had kept her in.

Oh. Surely not at her age. Brigid nearly lost her footing as she realised why she ached. Then she felt a fierce joy, a new responsibility. She would survive this bog and hold her head up in front of those murderous drabs, sly as snakes and slippery as eels. She would remember every word of Wulfhild's lessons and put them into practice. If she wondered *why* Wulfhild had been quite so diligent in her teaching, pondering that question could wait.

Instead, she regarded the plants around her, knowing her life depended on identifying each one. No longer anonymous marshes, the bogland teemed with varied life as she discovered its features in every safe step.

When she saw a line of rushes, she had to summon all her patience to walk slowly towards them, step by careful step. One little detour around an inviting expanse of lethal moss and then she reached the firm bed where the rushes grew beside a stream.

The slope was so slight, she had to test the water with one hand to see where the resistance formed, but – thank God! – there *was* a slope. She headed downstream. The rushes might not take her all the way, but she was going home, with a full basket. And then she'd show them all.

※

Brigid's legs were shaking as she walked into the settlement but she intended to keep going until she reached the big house, so she could plonk her basket on a trestle table as an act of defiance. She gritted her teeth and ignored the pain from cuts and scratches. She'd known worse. And her aching back was now a source of pride.

But when she reached her own hut, she knew she'd reached her limits, and the temptation to stop and rest *for just a few minutes* was just too much for her. She blinked as she walked through the door into the dim rushlight. *Rushes,* she thought, feeling dizzy. She should have picked some and added them to her basket.

Then someone was wrapping her wool blanket around her, holding her, saying in a warm tone, 'I knew you would do it. Sit down, let me take your panier, rest your feet.'

Brigid clung to the panier. Nobody was going to take it from her and pretend *they* had collected such treasure.

'It's all right, Brigid. You're safe now,' the voice soothed, surely the saint herself, or the goddess. Human Brigid cared little which it was, as long as she brought comfort. 'You've done well. The others will be here soon. Wulfhild was waiting and saw you coming. She told me first and she's gone to fetch them.

As her eyes adjusted, Brigid could see the speaker. Neither saint nor goddess but Ellisif Bellwether, truly named. And didn't Bríd have such an animal for familiar? Perhaps Brigid had died after all or was now in a delusion as dangerous as the bog.

As she sat on the chest, speechless, the hut filled with women, each of whom came to Brigid and hugged her. Wulfhild curtseyed instead, a gesture not of mockery but respect. More rushlights were lit.

'I told them you would do it, and you did. The gods have spoken,' Wulfhild said, her eyes reflecting multiple glowing wicks.

Too dazed to speak, Brigid allowed someone to put her feet in a bucket, to bathe her feet and legs. Warm water and hands soothed her, sent comforting waves rippling up through her belly. It made no sense, such kindness after trying to kill her.

Dry-mouthed, she spoke the question aloud. 'You sent me out to die. Why?'

Ellisif took her hands gently, said, 'We will have time to speak of this fully but never in the big house. That's why we've come to you here.'

'Out on the bog, you needed me,' said Wulfhild, 'and you learned. Now you need never fear what is out there.'

Brigid wasn't so sure about that. She would prefer never to go near the bog again. But she listened.

'The master, Thorbjorn, has dangerous moods,' said Ellisif, picking her way through words as carefully as Brigid had negotiated moss and black pools. 'We must trust each other completely to survive them. And he will be back here in a month or so, as is his habit. For the hunting. We warn each other, we cover for each other and,' she looked towards Wulfhild, who nodded, 'there is a bothy out on the bog where a person can hide until the black humours have passed. Not of the bog, you understand, though it has black humours too. But of the master's. And we can hide a pretty girl in the bothy, if we need to, for her protection.'

'I will show it to you,' said Wulfhild. 'You are one of us now.'

'Just the women?' queried Brigid.

Ellisif looked at her steadily. 'I think you know why.'

Brigid's thoughts skidded sideways like a foot sucked into mud. 'And Wulfhild? She is young, she is pretty. Does she hide in the bothy when Thorbjorn returns?'

'It is too late for me,' whispered Wulfhild. 'And now he has moved on. So I help others.'

'Dear God!' Brigid began to cry, a luxury she could only now afford. 'I'm with child,' she sobbed, and the joy of it mingled with the terror of it, as all the women shared in both.

CHAPTER 44

INGE, STRJÓNSEY, ORKNEYJAR

Inge had watched the ships returning; now her impatience got the better of her. She ran part-way down the path to greet Finn but her smile faded and her arms fell back to her sides when she saw his set expression, the anger in how he marched. Her fists clenched instinctively, readied for self-defence, but she told herself to wait, to listen to what he had to say, to soothe him.

'I've been so worried for you, waiting,' she began, then wondered whether that implied she thought him weak. She had never considered the effect of her words on other men except to hope they stung, and she was unsure of how to be a good wife. She did so want to be one, to this kind, brave, loving man.

She licked her lips, continued, 'But I was sure you would win.'

Had he, she wondered? 'Did Erlend cause problems?'

'Your thrall caused the only problems.' Finn's harsh tone was a slap in the face and his words made no sense.

'Fergus?' she queried, bemused.

'Aye, Fergus, your thrall from your family estate, from years gone by, or had you forgotten all that?'

His sarcastic tone drew blood and she knew her flushed cheeks gave her away. She bit back the angry retort prompted by guilt, and tried to keep her voice calm. 'What has happened to make you speak so?'

'*Your* Lord Thorbjorn recognised his thrall and wanted him back.'

Inge snapped. 'He is not *my* Lord Thorbjorn and Fergus is not his thrall.' Old habits got the better of her and she jibed, 'And no doubt you bent over backwards for *your* Lord Thorbjorn and told him, "Whatever you want, my lord, of course my lord, have my lady's thrall and welcome."'

The instant the words were out, she regretted them, but it was too late. Finn's face shuttered, his usual warmth closed within, unreachable.

And his words cut her to the core. 'Your faith in me matches your reputation as a wife.' He took a deep breath, steadied himself. 'I told him he had mistaken my thrall for his and he did not pursue the matter.'

Finn stopped walking, gripped Inge by the arms and stared into her eyes. She stood very still and held his gaze, refusing to be intimidated.

'He will though, some time. Your husband,' Inge flinched, and Finn corrected himself without showing any remorse, 'your former husband is a man who bears grudges. You lied to me about this thrall, and I do not want to be drawn into some spite match between you and Thorbjorn.'

Finn released her suddenly and she felt abandoned by him. His strength, his support withdrawn. Because of Thorbjorn. Would she never be free of the man she'd been made to marry? She wished him dead. She should poison him, stab him, set dogs on him. But would killing him free her? Or merely tie her to him forever?

'Fergus has gone to Ness,' Finn informed her, cold as the sea. 'He said to tell you he had family business there.'

She opened her mouth to tell him the truth, all of it, about Skarfr and Fergus and her escape. About what Thorbjorn had done to her. All of it. To hell with the consequences. She could not bear Finn's coldness, the unfairness of it.

He held up a hand to stop her. 'Not one word. I will hear no more of this thrall, whether truth or more lies. When Thorbjorn makes his claim, I will decide how to answer it. You see, Lady Wife,' he loosed each word like shot from a sling, 'I am not afraid of Thorbjorn.'

She dared not speak in case she made matters worse. Could they be worse? And she watched him walk away, his broad back filling the entrance before he disappeared into their house. His house.

Their first argument and no doubt their first night apart. All her fault and yet, not in the way it seemed to Finn. If only she could tell him of the debt she was repaying, but his parting words chilled her to the marrow.

He *should* be afraid of Thorbjorn. And she must do nothing more to bring the two men into conflict. This rift between Finn and her was summer lightning, a flash and over. She could win back the only husband she would ever want. She had to.

CHAPTER 45

SKARFR

He finds,
when he is among the bold,
that no one is bravest of them all.

The Wanderer's Hávamál

Before Skarfr took his place on Cup-bearer's ship, he had to endure Rognvald's words to Hlif, passing sentence. The Jarl's icy judgement was far worse than any outburst of rage could have been.

'I took you in, a murderer's daughter. I nurtured you and gave you the chance to earn respect as my housekeeper. To earn honour. For your own good, I told you that you could never marry. You went behind my back and behaved as if you belonged to this man.'

On a normal day, Hlif might have disputed the word 'belong' but today was not a normal day and her face was screwed up in the effort not to cry. Speaking in her own defence was not possible and Skarfr knew he could only make things worse if he spoke for her – again.

'I disown you from this day on,' Rognvald decreed. 'You will marry this man and be his responsibility, no longer my ward. You will be a wife. A married woman cannot be a housekeeper. Even the old gods deny their powers to a married woman.'

Hlif flinched at each blow but there was no pity in Rognvald's voice when he said, 'Throw away your wand and rune-dice because they are useless to a wife and mother. No völva was ever married.'

Only now did Skarfr realise all that Hlif was losing, but it was too late to change his mind, to let her continue being the Hlif he knew and loved, a free spirit.

'Seek forgiveness from God,' Rognvald concluded. 'You shall have none from me.'

He turned his back on them both, acted as if they were invisible, and went about the business of readying the ships to sail.

When Jón Halt-foot approached Hlif, Skarfr was coiled, ready to spring on him at the first insult, whatever the consequences.

'Shit only stinks when it comes out.' Jón spat on the ground then glared at Skarfr, who controlled himself with difficulty, out of respect for Hlif's hand on his arm.

Then Jón's tone softened. 'Nobody manages a ship's provisions as well as you do and I'm sorry you're paying for this man's cunning ways.' He shook his head. 'Women aren't safe on ships,' he concluded.

Instead of a heated rebuttal of the insult to Skarfr, and explanation of a woman's capacity to look after herself, thank you very much, Hlif said, 'Thank you, Jón,' and her eyes grew suspiciously wet.

'If that had been me, you'd have told me where to go,' Skarfr pointed out to Hlif, under cover of the pre-departure bustle all around them.

'He meant well,' she said simply.

'I always mean well!' He was indignant. 'But you lecture me anyway.'

She looked at him from sad grey eyes. 'I expect better from you than from the others.'

There was no understanding women.

'What on earth will we do with One-eye?' she asked.

Before Skarfr could give one of the answers which came first to mind, someone yelled his name.

'Skarfr!' Cup-bearer was calling him to the ship and he didn't want these to be the last words between them until the next shore – their last shore.

'*Elskan min*,' he said to her. 'Sweetheart. It will be all right.'

Her smile was as sad as her eyes. 'Yes.'

'Skarfr!' Cup-bearer's tone brooked no delay.

Hlif boarded Rognvald's ship and Skarfr joined Cup-bearer.

His disgrace surrounded him like a bad smell. Men looked away from him and left him out of their banter.

Even Cup-bearer told him curtly, 'You might as well be useful until you leave the ship. Take the steerboard and check we follow the Jarl's course.'

Then he cold-shouldered Skarfr, setting an example for the crew.

Leave the ship. Skarfr remembered Eindridi casting him off. He'd had Pilot and Mouthy with him, he'd been full of righteous indignation and looking forward to adventures. Now, he felt shame and apprehension. How would he provide for Hlif, in exile, with no lord and no home? Sudden longing for his house in Orkneyjar flooded him. He would never see that home again.

Wallowing in self-pity and remorse, he went through the motions required to keep the ship on course. The horizon was unchanging, tedious as the blue sky and turquoise sea. If he remembered El Sant's warnings about sea monsters and pirates, he dismissed them as tales for children. Barely a fish broke water in the even ripples that were disturbed briefly by the ships, and then smoothed instantly after they passed. Always the same. This was a half-life, without comrades, without Hlif and without prospects.

He should be feeling more optimistic as this was what he wanted, wasn't it? He and Hlif would be together. But all pleasure leeched from that thought because of what she was losing. Their life together would always be poisoned by the knowledge of its price. He remembered Hlif's rune-reading for Rognvald. To change your destiny was possible but there was always a price to pay.

Exile, no home, no lord – and no honour for either of them. What would Hlif be without her visions? Without the respect men gave her as housekeeper? A mere wife. The word, the thought which had pleased them both so much, turned to ashes by the price they paid.

Even his cormorant had forsaken him. Days passed, each made heavier than the one before by Skarfr's brooding. He began to wish they'd reach the place of his exile, get it over with.

What changed was the weather. Rain led to banks of fog forming and Rognvald signalled to drop anchor for the night. Skarfr would have offered to try out the sunstone the next day but wounded pride kept him silent.

He was on watch as day dawned, a slight brightening. The fog had cleared enough for him to see two islets, obstacles to avoid rather than places to land. Rognvald's orders were shouted across the water: time to set sail again, away from the islets.

Taking a last look back at the nearer land, grey and forbidding, Skarfr realised that something was strange about it. When a swirl of fog lifted for a moment, he saw this was not land at all but a massive warship, rising three times as high as the *Sun-chaser* and twice the length, its sides bulging outwards.

A dromond! He had never seen one before, but he'd heard enough sailors' tales and he knew who sailed them. Aragon's warning about pirates in these seas no longer seemed a fantasy and wounded pride must be set aside.

'Saracens! A dromond!' He yelled the warning up the ship to their horn boy, who sounded the alert. The message went from ship to ship but Rognvald was furthest away, and his instructions would take time to arrive.

Skarfr had nothing to lose. This was his chance to win honour and either die fighting or find favour with Rognvald again. By the time Cup-bearer had roused himself from sleep and ascertained what was happening, the ship was steering towards the Moorish dromond.

Its crew must have heard the horns and shouting, as they hung fine clothes and rich fabrics over the bulwarks, taunting the Norðmen with promise of treasures aboard – and a fight waiting.

Cup-bearer's men needed no such motivation and, despite their coldness to Skarfr, they accepted his leadership when action was in sight. Cup-bearer was too keen on being first in the fray to argue about where the orders came from. He merely pointed out to Skarfr, 'They'll hurl more than insults at us – how will we survive brimstone and burning pitch?'

'If we go in close, it'll miss us!' Skarfr told him, his lethargy dissipating with the fog and his battle dragon roused.

Rognvald had manoeuvred the *Sun-chaser* around and caught up with Cup-bearer's ship. In battle, differences were put aside; the Jarl listened to Skarfr's plan and gave the go-ahead. Sails down, the two ships were rowed alongside the great dromond until they bumped against her, the prow of the *Sun-chaser* next to the stern of its sister-ship. The dromond's sheer wooden side blocked the light and, as Skarfr had predicted, the overhang did protect the longships from the fiery barrage that rained down from above.

So far, so good, but there was no way of boarding a deck which was two levels above Rognvald's ships. One level above was the lower oar deck, which had only oar-holes and no entry from outside.

Skarfr looked up, seeking a way to climb up. If only a man could get up there and pull his fellows after him. A rope?

The only protrusion on the wooden face was an anchor, upside-down, with a fluke hooked into the bulwark.

Maybe, thought Skarfr. Distraction would be required.

Quickly he explained his plan to Cup-bearer, who nodded, then he sent the message to Rognvald. The Jarl clambered forward to the prow in order to give his orders directly to the men in the other ship.

'The plan is good,' he told Cup-bearer, as if Skarfr were not there.

Differences between men were not always forgotten in battle, Skarfr realised, his heart sinking.

Rognvald was changing the plan. 'But your men can shoot the arrows from a distance. I have a man brave enough to attempt to reach the anchor. I don't need yours.'

Skarfr' hopes of redemption dropped to the seabed.

Cup-bearer was already instructing the rowers on the larboard side to steer the ship away from the dromond and back out to sea. Shouts and whoops came from the Saracens as they saw the ship fleeing. And stopped when Cup-bearer's archers let fly their arrows.

Skarfr watched Rognvald's men hacking out wooden panels with their axes, under cover of the hail of arrows. He watched one of Rognvald's crew boldly climbing to the anchor, letting it down to bring up a second man, and a third.

Then they set to work with axes at the higher level they'd reached. Once the warship was breached, horns were blown on and four ships jostled to get close enough for the men to go through the holes and overrun the dromond. With them, they took spears, useful as grappling-hooks as well as whatever weapons came to hand.

Although his moment of glory had been stolen from him, Skarfr took his chance of honour in battle. His dragon roared. He laid about him as if he could kill his own fate with every blow and left a swathe of dead and dying in his wake as he sought the leader, just as he had at the castle – but this time, no Eindridi would cheat him of his prize.

Men forming a circle around some hidden man, caught his attention and he carved a way towards them. He saw Crick-neck take a blow and fight on. Crick-neck was not Mouthy and needed no help. Nor did the comrades Skarfr passed so he left them to deal with their own opponents.

A warship this size carried as many men in one vessel as in their nine ships, so numbers were even, but if, as Skarfr suspected from the rich fabrics, there were more merchants than warriors on the dromond, the odds were in favour of Rognvald's men.

Skarfr was all dragon. He charged at the circle of men in robes and turbans, swinging his axe. Fierce and unstoppable, his momentum took him straight to the man at the centre of the circle. A man dressed in gold-embroidered robes. A man who was unarmed and stood awaiting his destiny.

Skarfr held back from harming him, as much because of the

man's calm stillness as his lack of a weapon. As reason and self-control returned, he added a fortune in ransom to his motives for keeping the leader alive. And he was Skarfr's capture – if Skarfr could take the man from his guards, who *were* armed.

Prepared to succeed or die, Skarfr grabbed the Saracen leader and used him as a shield to push through his men, backwards. The unexpected direction gave Skarfr crucial moments before his exposed back might receive the expected dagger.

When he was stopped by a blunt force, he thought that he'd met his end, but a familiar voice said, 'You need fear nobody behind you.'

Rognvald's solid body protecting his back allowed Skarfr to stand still, hold onto his prisoner and merely wave his axe at any Saracen who thought to come within reach. Skarfr's hopes rose again as the Jarl and he were partners in the battle dance that was closer than any courtly one. He *would* earn forgiveness.

A large party of Norðmen converged on the Jarl, and soon the victory was apparent to the captured Saracen leader, who shouted something to the men still standing. They dropped their weapons and huddled together, some near to their leader.

Rognvald nodded. 'Take these to my ship,' he said. 'We'll see what they're worth.'

'I took the leader,' Skarfr blurted out, his blood still pounding from the fight, all he wanted to say scrambled in his head and none of the words coming out. *For you. I took him for you. So you'd forgive me.*

Rognvald looked at him coldly. 'So you did. Then he can travel with you. And if he's worth coin, you shall have your share.'

Matter concluded, he yelled his orders to the men. 'Kill the rest, find any treasure, then burn the ship.'

'I'll take these men to the ship,' Cup-bearer told Skarfr. 'You oversee the search and make sure none of our men are left here when the dromond's set on fire.'

This was all the respect Skarfr was going to get, so he swallowed his bile and began searching for treasure. Until he was distracted by a glimpse of a brown woollen skirt.

CHAPTER 46

SKARFR

*I know only one thing
that never dies:
the reputation of one who's died.*

The Wanderer's Hávamál

'Hlif!' yelled Skarfr, pushing past the bloody scenes as the Jarl's orders were carried out with enthusiasm. Rognvald's men moved aside for Skarfr and resumed their activities as if the brief interruption had never happened.

What in the gods' names was she doing here and how had she reached midships on the top deck, unscathed? Even though the Saracens were no longer a threat, the Norðmen would not be slow to slice first and ask questions later. Why had she put herself in harm's way? She knew better than to cause additional problems when men were fighting. For once, Jón was right – this was definitely no place for a woman.

He called her again but she did not turn. As they did for him, men made way then closed the space after she'd passed, so Skarfr's view of her was intermittent, often blocked by the bigger bodies of the men.

He reached the main mast, knowing he should have caught up with her by then, but she was nowhere to be seen.

Still calling her name fruitlessly, he looked along the top deck of the dromond, its construction so different from Rognvald's ships. Everything in twos. Two masts and two triangular sails, two small wooden castles – now hacked and splintered, but they must previously have offered protection at night or in poor weather. There were even two steerboards. If all oars were manned there must have been sixty oarsmen on the top deck alone. That's when he realised. *The top deck.*

She must have gone down to the lower deck where the second tier of oars was located. He quickly found the hatch, and went down the ladder, two rungs at a time, into the darkness.

What little light there was came through the empty oar-holes.

'Hlif, stay back!' Skarfr called so as to be sure he wouldn't hit her by mistake. He seized one of the stowed oars to replace his lost spear and swung it around him until his eyes adapted enough to see that the only other person on this deck was sitting on a bench, well out of reach of his flailing oar.

'You can put that down,' she told him. 'There's only us here.'

'You shouldn't be here!' His worry was churning into anger at what might have happened but her next words cut him off.

'I don't mean just you and me.' She spoke in Occitan to someone hidden under one of the benches, someone small. 'You can come out now.'

Whether he understood the words or just the situation, a little boy emerged, holding One-eye.

Hlif pointed to herself and to the cat, just to be clear about the matter, and said '*My* cat.'

Then she held out her arms to take the monster, who immediately began purring. She draped him over one shoulder, a floppy, furry shawl, and she took the boy's hand.

'One-eye jumped ship, ran through the hole in the dromond,' she explained, 'so I had to follow him.'

Of course she did.

She continued, 'I found him on the top deck, so scared I couldn't catch him. I chased him along the deck then he came back down here. I heard him meowing under this bench and found the boy. Then you arrived. Making a lot of noise and terrifying all three of us. He was just settling too!'

Whether Hlif meant the boy or the damned cat, Skarfr had no idea. He moved a step towards them, aching to take her in his arms, but the cat hissed and the boy cowered.

'It's all right,' Skarfr said, 'I won't harm you.' He made his tone gentle but he could not change how he looked. 'What are we going to do with him?'

'I'll take him and One-eye back to the *Sun-chaser*. Rognvald won't hurt a child.' Her voice wobbled a bit. The child she'd been when Rognvald took her in as foster-child was still part of her. The child Rognvald had cursed twice over.

'No, he won't.' There was no time for all that Skarfr wanted to say to her so he trusted that she knew. They would soon have all the time in the world to talk. 'Maybe the child can be ransomed, returned to his people.'

She nodded. 'I'll suggest that.' She started to walk, pulling the boy with her. He didn't put up a fight so Skarfr assumed they would follow him if he climbed back up to the top deck.

Once there, he led them along its blood-slicked planks, attracting curious looks but nothing more. Rognvald's men were fully occupied, turning over bodies and turning out packs, grabbing valuables and fine fabrics, holding them above the befouled deck.

Hlif retched behind him, then asked, 'How can you bear this? So much killing?'

Skarfr paused, turned to answer her. 'I unleash the dragon.' He shrugged. 'This is a man's way of life and a man's way to die. We sent these men to their heaven.'

'Rognvald and all good Christians would say they sent the heathens to hell.' Hlif's tone was bitter.

Walking on, Skarfr told her, 'A woman should not see such things.'

'A woman does not look away from blood!' she snapped. 'Or from the truth of things.'

Skarfr reached the ropes that had been tied to the bulwarks through the oarholes. Some men were already swarming down them back to the ships, but Skarfr carried on until he reached the anchor, where Jón and Oddi were lowering those who had been wounded in the battle, one at a time.

'Help me lower them!' he said to Oddi.

Then he helped Hlif onto the upside-down anchor, where she sat and took the child on her lap. One arm held him tight, and she reached up with the other, laid a reassuring hand against the cat wrapped around her neck. The unlikely combination was then lowered by the three men.

Skarfr's heart was in his throat as he watched them bump their way down onto the *Sun chaser*. He knew all was well when Hlif yelled, 'Raise the anchor!' and an indignant yowl showed that One-eye was now pretending he had not been scared for one moment.

He took his turn down a rope and scrambled along the *Sun-chaser* until he could climb over the sides to join Cup-bearer and the hostages. As soon as all the crew were aboard, the order to row was given. Only the Jarl's ship remained, waiting for the fire-starters to shin down the one rope left in place. The others were being neatly coiled as the ships pulled away and a plume of smoke rose from the dromond.

A small sound escaped the Saracen leader as he watched his ship go up in flames but his face was impassive. The men with him did not have the same control.

As the blaze consumed the whole ship and the dromond sank, still shooting sparks, a fiery wake trailed golden across the water. As if a fortune in gold coin had melted and slipped into the sea.

Then the Saracen's impassivity faltered and tears streaked the grime on his weary face.

'You fools,' he said in perfect Occitan. 'You couldn't even find the treasure. And now nobody shall profit.' Then he clammed up and wouldn't say another word.

In contrast, Rognvald and the skalds on his ship, were garrulous, composing poem after poem on the defeat of the dromond. Skarfr endured the verses that were shouted across the water.

He had been there during the storm of swords, painting the dromond red. With gritted teeth, he had witnessed Audun Rodi 'scaling the black sides of the heathen ship' and now Rognvald's verse vaunted Audun Rodi as the hero of the victory, first to embark on the ship.

No mention of Skarfr in all these poems. The Jarl's one-time finest skald composed his own verses in his head and they used more words for 'black' than all the poems recited aloud. 'Black' was not reserved for description of the dromond and dead enemies. Black and bitter stormclouds hung over his head while others saw only blue skies.

The cormorant had lied at Skarfr's birth. He would not make sagas. He would neither sing them nor be sung about.

CHAPTER 47

THORBJORN, ORPHIR, ORKNEYJAR

Thorbjorn wrote the figures in his ledger, accounting for the bondsmen's extra payments levied to pay for Rognvald's cathedral, which was sucking coin faster than each layer of red and yellow sandstone bricks rose. The people might be happy to have the relics of their own Saint Magnus house in a shrine worthy of him, but the bones were the only residents to have a roof over their head, after fourteen years' building work.

Rognvald had taken the credit and the Bishop's blessing when St Magnus' remains were moved from the old church to their ornate shrine, in what would undoubtedly be a magnificent cathedral in hundreds of years' time. Then the Jarl and the Bishop had set sail as pilgrims, leaving Thorbjorn Klerk with a financial headache and a never-ending building project.

The finest workmen from Dunholm might know all about buttresses and dressing stone but, as far as Thorbjorn was concerned, they were leeches drawing blood from the Jarl's coffers. So he told himself, as he dipped his quill and balanced the numbers in neat script.

And yet there was something fine about such a legacy. As fine as the books in the monastery at Papey Meiri. What had Brother Kristian said, the scribe who copied the holy works and illuminated the margins, another foreigner from Dunholm? 'A cathedral is a hymn that touches the skies and sings of God's glory, to touch the darkest heart.'

Small wonder that the White Christ was gaining followers while the old gods were forsaken, when Christians devoted their lives to a building that even their sons' sons would never see finished. When they cared nothing that their names would be forgotten because their places in heaven were guaranteed. Without honour and without sagas. And yet.

Thorbjorn blotted his work carefully. There was satisfaction in neat script, in records that would last beyond a clerk's death. Such writing could reach into the future, say more than runes carved on a tomb wall, tell bigger stories. He was clerk *and* warrior.

He would have it all. Honour, a name never forgotten. His death would be as big a blaze of glory as his life, his funeral pyre visible from Hjaltland to Ness, such a hero he would be. He sometimes wondered about heaven, but what sort of death could it be that gave time for shriving? Not the warrior's death that would be his. With a place in Valhalla. His sons would wail and daub their faces with ash, knowing they could never live up to such a father. And the women–

But why did he have no sons?

'Thorbjorn?' Harald's sudden appearance startled him but luckily the pen was once more in its holder, his writing complete.

He gathered his straying thoughts. He *would* have sons. This awkward, disappointing, *ugly* man he'd fostered since childhood would not be the only boy he raised. The gods could not possess such a cruel sense of humour.

'Do you think Gillisson will endorse Erlend? If not, there will be war. Should we prepare for war? Rognvald won't be pleased – if he comes back. When will that be – if he doesn't die? Gods protect him,' Harald added in automatic piety, the least he could manage for the man who had also been a foster-father to him.

Rognvald had no sons either. And if Harald was the result of their joint upbringing, maybe the world was better without offspring from either of them, thought Thorbjorn with a sudden dip into dark brooding. Harald would not wail or improve his face with ashes for a foster-father's death.

The small hairs rose on Thorbjorn's neck and his nose itched with premonition. Would Harald throw *him* to the wolves one day?

He answered the stream of questions. 'Norðvegr will back Erlend to avoid conflict with us or Skotland. Rognvald will be away for years and yes, gods protect him.' Thorbjorn allowed his words an edge of irony as a comment on Harald's lack of feeling but it went unnoticed.

The Jarl looked down his nose at his advisor. 'You said 'us'. I am the Jarl. You mean Norðvegr would not want conflict with me.'

'Exactly so,' Thorbjorn replied smoothly, wishing he could take a belt to the man as he occasionally had to the boy. 'And I will command your army if he is foolish enough to challenge us.'

'Oh, yes.' Harald's sensitive pride deflated.

Thorbjorn said. 'We should always prepare for war.'

Harald's eyes lit up, as always, at the prospect of action. No bad thing. 'I've watched them, the lords, these last few months. Finn's a good man to have with us,' he said.

Bile filled Thorbjorn's mouth. 'Maybe. But he is untrustworthy. He stole a thrall from me and lied about it.'

'Not still harping on about that, are you? Take it to the Thing in the spring and get reparation, so you can forget about it. We're too busy now. The ships are ready to leave for Ness so we get there before the season begins. I want you to choose new hunting dogs with me and finish their training. You do want to go, don't you.'

'Yes,' said Thorbjorn. 'I am ready to go hunting.' He had unfinished business on his estate in Ness. Finn could wait until spring.

CHAPTER 48

FERGUS, NESS

Fergus told the ship's captain that he was returning to his master's estate. After some negotiation, and another coin, the captain agreed to make an extra stop. He would land close to Inge's family home in Lambaburg before continuing to Wick.

The destination gave Fergus' story the ring of truth, if some Orkneyjar noble ever checked. Also, he wished to speak to the honest steward before walking south.

Careful to give the impression that this was the only money he carried, Fergus produced two coins and handed them over, then took his place as a passenger, praying that the departure was speedy. There was no reason to think Thorbjorn would seek him here rather than on Strjónsey but his thumping heart would not heed reason.

He scanned the harbour for any signs of armed men looking purposeful. So many! But each time he watched two or three together, they headed for a different ship, checked on its loading, or joked with crew members. They were not looking for him.

Even if Thorbjorn divined where Fergus would go, he would be busy with state matters after the meeting with Erlend. With any luck, Harald would keep his advisor close to him in Orphir.

Huddled in his jacket against the wind and spitting rain, Fergus wondered what he had done to draw down the wrath of the

Norðmen's gods. His own God would not punish him for that one good deed, saving a woman's life. Nor for the brief time he and Brigid had been happy, managing Skarfr's farm. After all they had been through, surely they had earned some respite from a thrall's life. Fergus believed in the justice of the afterlife, but he was not dead yet and life was relentlessly cruel.

Please God, he prayed. *Let her be there. If she is well, I can endure anything.*

He cast out of his mind all thoughts and memories but Brigid. Her quick lies when the raiders came to their village; her housewifery that made a sweet-smelling home of the drear and dirty dwelling they were sold into; her comfort to the boy he'd been, that became the love of man and wife. And so they were, man and wife.

As if to cheer him, the fickle sunshine appeared from behind a blanket of slate-grey rain-clouds, and sent its rays across his face, a warm caress. Fergus let the peace of sky and sea fill him, trusting once more that all would be well. He heard the words in Brigid's soft brogue. *All will be well.*

The captain kept his word and hove to within sight of the tower that rose high above sheer cliffs, but before the coast became rocky. Fergus waded ashore, then paused on dry land to don his boots again and get his bearings. The captain was right not to get too close to the rocks below the old broch that was now Lambaburg keep. Wild waves smashed against the rocks and swirled back, only to ride into the turbulence again.

The legend of how Sweyn and his steward let themselves down from the tower, scrambling down the rocks and diving into the foaming sea was even harder to believe when a man was looking at the forbidding descent. And the even more forbidding ascent. Approaching Lambaburg by climbing the cliffs was suicide, and, despite his earlier despair, Fergus did not want to die.

He walked up the slowest, safest path from the landing point, making a wide detour so as to approach the keep from the green plain dotted with outbuildings and cottages. He passed the stables where he'd lain in fever.

He wanted to be clearly visible, not risk the only welcome an unannounced stranger was likely to get: an arrow in the head. The last time he had been here, he'd been too delirious to take in his surroundings and had not realised how bleak and impregnable the keep was. If he could bring Brigid here, they would be safe as Inge's thralls – or was that, Finn's?

He had no idea how these humiliating laws worked but he knew that thralls were considered to be possessions. Botolf had bought him and Brigid, but Skarfr had become their master when he'd come of age and inherited his dead parents' longhouse.

Had Skarfr legally become their master, he wondered? What if Thorbjorn's claim to own them was justified? If only Botolf's letter had never been sent. If only Skarfr had freed them as he'd intended.

The confusion would be sorted out when Skarfr returned but that was years away. If he and Brigid could hide somewhere safe until then, under Inge and Finn's protection, all would be well.

'What's your business?' shouted a guard from a small window high in the keep ahead of Fergus, who walked across the narrow swathe of well-trodden ground that formed an entry bridge. On either side of this bridge was a sheer drop down to rocks below.

'Lady Inge sent me from Strjónsey,' called back Fergus. 'I have messages for the steward.'

'Pass, then,' yelled the guard.

From another window, a stone flew towards Fergus, who ducked instinctively and nearly lost his footing. His head swam as he looked down at the rocks below, heard the sea gnashing its white teeth. For a moment he thought the sea was yelling his name, then he realised the two guards were shouting at each other.

'I've told you, Arse-for-brains, that's not funny. One day someone will go over the edge and you'll have some explaining to do, as to why an important message went missing.'

'He's not important,' the other guard called back. 'Look at 'im! And it *was* funny! Did you see the way he skipped? Like he was dancing on hot ashes.'

Fergus smartly crossed the remaining distance to safe and solid ground inside the keep, rushing through the tunnel flanked by more arrow-slits where no doubt there were more guards with a dubious sense of humour.

Once inside the inner keep, he remembered the layout of the circular accommodation, and sought the quarters where he would most likely find the steward.

When he'd explained his predicament, the steward weighed him up, asked, 'You are in truth bound to Lady Inge?'

A thrall's word counted for nothing but Fergus gave it anyway, hoping his face looked honest. Whatever led to the judgement, the steward nodded.

'If you come back, it shall be here for you. If you don't come back, what do you want me to do?'

Fergus had thought of that. 'If a person comes and asks you for Skarfr's purse, then they speak for me and may have it.'

He fished inside his doublet, drew out his treasure, and opened the drawstring. He took out a silver ring and hung it around his neck, hiding it underneath his tunic. Then he retrieved two coins and gave one to the steward, who took it reluctantly.

'Yes,' Fergus insisted. 'You should have it. You were good to me and are being good to me now.' The other coin he tied into the folded waistband of his breeches.

Then he sought directions to Lord Thorbjorn's estate, pretending he had a message for him from Lord Finn.

'And don't be tempted to cut inland. Keep to the coast, for though it's longer, and more up and down, it's less dangerous than the bogland.' A thought struck the steward. 'But Lord Thorbjorn's not yet come to Ness for his autumn stay. You could wait here till we have word he and Jarl Harald are come. You could even travel down with Lord Thorbjorn.'

Fergus shook his head, trying not to show his terror. 'I'd best go now while the weather's good. If I put my feet under the table here, I won't want to go at all. There will be a man I can leave my message with, so there will. If not, I can wait there till Lord Thorbjorn arrives.'

The steward did not look convinced. 'As you will. Take a pack with you. Three days should do it if you're as strong a walker as you look.'

It took five days. Fergus lost count of how many times he told hostile locals that he had a message from Lord Finn for Lord Thorbjorn and watched their hackles flatten into simple distrust of strangers. Such distrust did not preclude accepting an offer of labour in exchange for a meal and clean straw, or even a mattress for the night.

Gossip from Orkneyjar was even better currency than chopping wood, and so Fergus always left his hosts better informed about their two jarls – or their three jarls, if you still counted Rognvald.

He was uneasy about leaving such a public trail of his journey, but he could not avoid habitation without risking the wilderness he'd been warned against. Neither could he disguise the accent which marked him as a thrall, so he chose the lesser of two evils. Being apprehended as an escaped thrall would end his quest, and probably end him too, so he must be openly on a message for his master.

He never grew used to the feeling that some demon was just over his shoulder, and he developed the nervous habit of looking back to check. This made little sense when he was heading into the demon's lair, but sense did not calm his twitches. Pray God, Thorbjorn did not return early to Ness and reach his estate before Fergus did.

The last set of directions pointed his way up a valley, a couple of miles from the sea. He slowed down when he saw the first cottages and knew he'd reached journey's end. What if he was wrong about Brigid being here? What if he was too late?

He forced himself to close the last steps between him and the answers he feared as much as hoped. There was no way to prepare for the news he dreaded, so he must take whatever came, like a man.

The inevitably suspicious residents had formed a semicircle across the path to what was clearly the main residence, a house bigger than the one Thorbjorn had burned down. Fergus had a sudden urge to torch this one, behave as *they* did, the Norðmen, with their never-ending feuds and murders; but thralls could not indulge in such behaviour.

'What do you want?' asked an older woman, arms akimbo, blocking his path. The men with her wielded shovels, hammers, an axe: whatever had been to hand when word of the stranger reached them.

'I have a message for Lord Thorbjorn,' stammered Fergus, suddenly aware how thin his excuse sounded now he had finally reached his supposed destination.

'From Lord Finn,' he added, making it worse if any of them knew that only the despised Inge linked Finn and Thorbjorn. And of course, they would know!

'Well then, you've wasted the walk,' mocked the woman. 'Lord Thorbjorn's not home yet though he should be on his way in a week or two, or even sooner if you're lucky.'

Her tone said she'd seen through him.

'I have all the latest news from Orkneyjar,' he proffered desperately, his Írish accent stronger than ever. If he could just have a look around, see if Brigid were there. Otherwise, he'd have to ask outright, and he had a feeling the shovels and hammers might come into use. 'Maybe you could find a mug of ale for a man, and I'll tell you all I know…'

The silence held its own threat and Fergus waited, hardly breathing. Then he jumped as the woman yelled, 'Brigid, come on out!'

And then she was there, ducking out of a doorway, running towards him.

'It's some cloth-head looking for you, to judge by his accent, for it's the same as your own way of murdering our tongue.'

Brigid pushed past the woman and threw herself at him. All he could do was to open his arms and fold her against him.

'*Mo chroí*,' he murmured, taking in the scent of her hair, shutting his eyes to stop tears falling. 'Sweetheart.'

'Tell him!' ordered the woman.

Brigid gently loosened his arms, stepped out of his embrace. The men slipped away, back to work, but the woman stood as if on guard.

Fergus looked at his wife. Despite signs of fatigue in the lines around her eyes and face, she looked well. There was a glow about her, a bloom he did not recognise. She was neatly dressed and groomed, and obviously well fed, rounder than he remembered. He'd been expecting what exactly? A starving prisoner, ill-treated? Was he *disappointed*, for God's sake?

'What?' he asked her, wondering for the first time whether she needed rescuing at all.

'I'm with child,' she said, her face lighting up.

He took an involuntary step backwards and her smile faded, uncertain.

Though his stomach clenched, he owed her everything and he would not renege on his duty.

'That changes nothing between us,' he told her. 'I will raise him as my own.'

At that she laughed. 'Oh, my dear eejit,' she said. 'That one never touched me in such a way. I'm too old and ugly for him. This is *your* baba.'

When she came into his arms this time, there was no barrier between them and he wished time would stop, let them stay like this until they took root and turned into trees, forever entwined.

Apparently, Ellisif thought otherwise, although the twinkle in her eyes belied her waspish tone. 'Take the man to your cottage, Brigid, and you can do your celebrating somewhere you don't embarrass the rest of us. Then we need to talk.'

Fergus had not realised how ominous the word 'talk' was. Ellisif did not mince words.

'And you can't keep that ring,' she concluded, her sharp eyes on the silver ring with its blue stone, in its rightful place on Brigid's finger.

'But I can take Brigid away with me, back to Lambaburg,' he objected, wondering why he had to explain himself at all to this woman. She was not their mother.

Brigid placed a hand on his. 'We need to listen,' she said quietly, the stars gone from her eyes and resignation taking their place. She took the ring off, gave it back to Fergus.

'Keep it safe for me, until I can wear it again,' she told him.

With rising panic, Fergus listened, wanting to put his hands over his ears, keep his dreams.

'We can pretend you were never here and the master need know nothing. But we can't hide Brigid's absence. He sent her here for a reason, and if she's gone, first he will kill the two women he sent with her.'

'No!' Fergus did not want to believe what he knew was true.

Inexorably, Ellisif went on. 'Then he will track Brigid, with men and dogs. He will find her, even if you have a head start. And he has papers showing he owns you. The steward at Lambaburg dare not defy Lord Thorbjorn. He will hand you both over. You don't seem to understand that you are thralls.' Her exasperation at Fergus' naivety showed.

There was a pause. He was not so naive. His imagination skipped over what Thorbjorn would do.

Ellisif remained matter-of-fact. 'And who knows how far behind you he is. Maybe he's on his way right now. All we know is that it is the season for his arrival, so every day you stay, you add to the risk for both of you.'

'But I can't leave Brigid with... him.'

Brigid's hand tightened around his. 'You can and you must, for the child's sake. That one wants me to stay alive, some kind of torment for Skarfr, so until Skarfr returns, I am safe.'

She must have seen his horror as she amended quickly, 'Safe enough, anyway. As safe as I was in Botolf's house. And I have good companions here.'

'I can't,' repeated Fergus.

At that moment, the doorway darkened and a man rushed in.

Fergus jumped to his feet, drew this dagger, but it was only one of the hammer-wielders.

'He's coming,' the man gasped. 'The master sent word ahead to make all ready for him.'

The women rose to their feet, white.

'There is no more time,' said Ellisif. 'Get Wulfhild. She must take him to the bothy and away by the bog.'

'You must,' said Brigid, 'for my sake and the baby's. We will see each other again, if you go now. But not until Skarfr returns. Then you must come for us quickly. Tell Inge. She will understand.'

Fergus found himself organised and provisioned for the journey so quickly he had no time to argue further. He knew there must be some other solution but could think of none, alone as he was. Thrall as he was. *That* was the deciding factor. He was an object, with no rights and no family.

He felt his heart rip in two when he left Brigid, as if they really were two trees grown together and destroyed by the separation. She stood tall and proud, her hand smoothing her belly, reminding him.

'Wulfhild will see you safe,' she said. 'Till we meet again.'

'Till we meet again,' he replied, fearing the words' echoes. *In this life*, he vowed. *In this life.*

CHAPTER 49

THORBJORN, NESS

Thorbjorn had left Harald with three new dogs to test in the northern forests. Their various merits had been represented by the fewterer who kept the kennels and who'd trained the young hounds from puppyhood to one-year-olds. Any of the three would make good all-rounders against deer but in a boar hunt, the huge brown mastiff would have the advantage.

And only Harald could work on bonding with *his* dog so the final choice would be instinctive. To give Harald his due, he had both the patience and the skill to bring out the best in a dog. No doubt the two deer-hounds would be called True-nose and Flop-ears like Harald's last two dogs. The boy was practical but lacked imagination.

Thorbjorn was astute in selection and experienced in training but lacked patience and had no desire for doglike devotion, from hound or woman. True-fuck and Long-face, he told himself, enjoying a joke he could not share.

Hound or woman, he preferred to use them and leave them, in kennels or minding someone else's hearth. Enjoy the hunt and leave the daily responsibility to those better suited to menial tasks.

And now he was free of Harald for a few weeks. Free of advising jarls, free of scribing figures, free to cause havoc on his own estate, and to follow his own whims.

He walked from the shore up to the coastal village which marked his way up the valley and home. Striding easily, to the rhythm of such pleasant thoughts, he reviewed all that needed to be made secure.

His men carried his ship behind him and once it was upside-down in its winter berth by his house, they could set to the annual caulking and repairwork. He'd noticed a couple of loose planks and some frayed lines. The carpenter and the ropemaker would have some work to do.

The procession of a lord and his longship past their cottages did not go unnoticed by the villagers, who called out friendly greeting. Thorbjorn responded in kind. As if he didn't know they hid their prettiest daughters from him. He would always find them, when he was in the mood.

So he smiled and exchanged pleasantries, remembered names (not the daughters') and was rewarded by the peasants' bashful pride at such an important man knowing who they were. He was charming, tolerant.

One man even blocked his path, said, 'If you need any building repairs out on the estate, my lord, me and my son are ready and willing.'

'I'll let you know,' replied Thorbjorn, exuding affability and good humour.

Emboldened, the man asked, 'Did Finn's man find you then?'

Thorbjorn snapped, 'Finn's man?' but he knew straightaway. He barely listened to the stuttered explanation.

'Not yet but he *will* find me,' he replied between gritted teeth. And his stride quickened, heedless of the pain caused to the men carrying the ship, labouring to keep up. Portage was a discipline requiring pace and teamwork.

But Thorbjorn had no interest in portage. He could scent prey.

His servants and bondsmen were assembled to greet their lord when Thorbjorn reached his estate. His pulse settled when he saw the thrall among the women, which answered one question to his satisfaction. She was going nowhere.

He put his other question to the group as a whole. 'I heard there was a man looking for me. Finn's man. Has he been here?'

Without any hesitation, his housekeeper told him, 'Aye, there was a man with a funny accent sniffing around. After her, I think.' She jerked her head towards the thrall, who looked panic-stricken.

'I told the stable-boy to send him on his way. With dogs.' Her smile showed why she was Thorbjorn's favourite servant. What was her name again? E-something. Ellen? Ellie? Ellisif, that was it. One of the few people he trusted and the only one here who'd known him from boyhood. Like a mother to him, he thought, smiling inwardly, knowing the reputation of mothers and, more particularly, grandmothers in his family.

'They chased him onto the bog so I don't think you'll have trouble from him again,' Ellisif said with satisfaction.

That was irritating. They should have held the man here for him to deal with. But they knew no better and had thought to please their master. The woman was still here – that was all that mattered.

Thorbjorn felt the urge to get a horse, chase after the man, finish him off in person, but he knew the bog well. A horse could go no more quickly than a man, even if the equine senses were more certain in picking a route. He was tired and the matter was taken care of. Let the bog do its work.

The thrall started to weep.

'Control yourself, woman!' the housekeeper snapped. 'I'm sorry, my lord. Until this unwanted visitor came, she's been fitting in nicely, doing more than her share of the work. She'll snap out of it – won't you?'

'Yes, I'll do what you want me to,' stuttered the thrall.

A tall girl, barefoot and wild-looking, with unkempt hair and dirt-streaked face, patted the thrall on the back, whispered something in her ear and the woman seemed to brighten a little.

'Wulfhild, you're late to greet the master,' the housekeeper admonished her and the girl hung her head.

'No sense in her,' Ellisif told Thorbjorn, who was getting bored with this trivial exchange.

'There's two things you should know, my lord, before I draw a bath for you and you can shake off the travel weariness,' the housekeeper said briskly. 'The abbot has called and left you a book. Philosophy, he said it was. And he hopes you'll go to the abbey to talk about it.' Her disapproval of such an item was evident but Thorbjorn felt the day improving in leaps and bounds. Intellectual stimulation was definitely needed.

'And the second?' he queried.

'The thrall is with child.'

Thorbjorn looked at the topic of conversation with new interest. She cried harder but she looked healthy enough for all the tears. Much better than when he'd last seen her. And rounder. This changed things. Skarfr was so sentimental about family.

'If the baby's a girl, we'll keep her,' he told Ellisif. 'I'd like my bath now. You can all get back to work.'

CHAPTER 50

ERLEND, NORÐVEGR

Erlend had learned that being the King of Norðvegr's guest required patience. But he had the winter in which to gain the endorsement he needed, and a city to explore. When freezing fog and snowstorms kept him indoors, he had worthy opponents at tafl, such as the lean youth sitting opposite him.

'Your move,' his adversary told Erlend.

He studied his two knights, although he already knew the board by heart and the impetuous attack by his young guard had changed nothing. The choice remained the same. Each knight was in a position to attack and pin two enemies but there would be a cost. And what was he prepared to sacrifice?

If only he had such a knight supporting him as Jarl. He saw again the flash of a blade, a man dropping to the ground. A *drengr's* laugh. Thorbjorn Klerk. Unfortunately, Harald's advisor was loyal to his godson and could be neither bought nor corrupted. The alehouse of Kirkjuvágr said so. And so did Erlend's foster-father Anakol, who might be no warrior but who understood politics.

And that same alehouse also asserted that only one warrior was a match for Thorbjorn, had even bested him more than once in cunning, though never tested in a fight, one on one. Sweyn Asleifsson, the man who'd set fire to the witch Frakork in her home.

The man who'd kidnapped Uncle Paul and made him disappear. The man who'd set Rognvald on the throne of Orkneyjar. The Jarl-maker.

Erlend contemplated the hereditary enmity between his family and Sweyn. Was there really nobody else of equal stature? He knew the answer.

But even if *he* could set aside old scores, what would make Sweyn see a future at Erlend's side? Would he be prepared to stand against Rognvald, if the old Jarl should return to find his jarldom taken? Would Sweyn stand against Harald – and Thorbjorn – should the resident Jarl fall out with the new one?

Perhaps he was over-thinking. Rognvald was not here and would probably die at sea or in foreign lands. If he did return, he would be old and his time would be over. Norðvegr's support for Erlend would make that clear to all Orkneymen. He dismissed the pilgrim ex-jarl as irrelevant.

Which left Harald, who might become a problem one day. After all, Uncle Paul had ruled happily on his own, despite the old saying, *One jarl rules for himself but two jarls must heed their people.* And if Erlend had Sweyn on his side, he would never meet his uncle's fate.

When he considered things in that light, Sweyn would be paying a blood debt in supporting Erlend. But he doubted the sea-rover would see it that way. He must be motivated on his own behalf by renown, vengeance or plunder – preferably all three.

Renown. Sweyn would enjoy any opportunity to show himself as superior to Thorbjorn. The two men posed a challenge to each other just by existing and had always been uneasy allies, kept on a leash by Rognvald. And now they were unleashed. That was a good start.

Vengeance. Sweyn already resented Harald for exiling Gunnr. Erlend must widen that rift, remind Harald of his mother's flagrant disrespect, ensure that Harald showed no forgiveness to her lover. Spite would do the rest.

Plunder. Ideally, plunder that offended Harald, which meant Sweyn taking booty that belonged to the Jarl. Erlend stroked his beard.

Like himself, Harald would be off the islands for the winter, but he'd be in Ness. Before the Jarl returned to Orkneyjar, the tribute ships from Hjaltland would set sail to bring their riches to him on his Ness estate.

What if a certain sea-rover intercepted those ships and helped himself to their cargo? As a reminder to his liege not to offend such a powerful lord? Word could be sent to Sweyn that such a venture was possible and prestigious. What a fool Harald would look, and Sweyn's saga would contain one more heroic tale.

Anakol could set up a meeting in Orkneyjar. The new Jarl Erlend would meet with Sweyn to propose an alliance, with his support against any reprisals from Harald and Thorbjorn. Before Sweyn's raid if possible but afterwards would also have advantages. Either way, Erlend would win.

He reached down to the table and made his move.

It was only a little sacrifice, really, to reconcile with an erstwhile enemy rather than pursue a quarrel. And his knight would be without peer.

CHAPTER 51

SKARFR

*Better to be alive,
no matter what, than dead –
only the living enjoy anything.*

The Wanderer's Hávamál

Another cove and another cookfire.
But this cove had been chosen by the Saracen leader, who'd suddenly found his voice. He knew the people who lived in the settlement inland and they would be welcomed back, so Rognvald sent one of the Saracens with Jón Halt-foot and a band of men, to negotiate a ransom. Skarfr was not among them.

When the party returned, they were accompanied by double their number, all robed turban-wearers.

Once more the cry, 'Saracens!' went up from the Norðmen but Rognvald's horn insisted they wait, as did the expressions on their comrades' faces as they neared the camp.

Jón Halt-foot came forward, without any apparent signs of injury, and the captain from the dromond stood beside him, much more cheerful at the sight of the Saracens.

'There's a town inland but it's under Moorish rule.' Jón shook his head at his own folly. 'They have done us no harm – yet. They wish to speak to the dromond captain. And if they are not treated well, thousands will descend on this camp and kill us all. We are being watched and the town awaits the message that all is well. As you might guess, there will be no ransom.'

Rognvald sighed and Skarfr was almost pleased to see the Jarl frustrated. He himself cared nothing for the ransom, which would bring him no honour if there were no saga of how he earned it. And in exile, he would have no saga.

The Saracen leader spoke quickly in that liquid tongue Skarfr now recognised as Arabic, although he could only understand the odd word, such as *Allah.*

The Moors bowed to each other and nobody drew weapons, which Skarfr took to be good signs.

Rognvald asked the dromond captain, 'What is your agreement with these people?'

The hostage ignored him and spoke to Skarfr instead. 'These are my people. You have spared my life and treated me well on your little ship, so I spare yours. You may eat here, then go on your way, with no hindrance. You and all your fellows.'

There was no need for Skarfr to translate the perfect Occitan for the Jarl, so he didn't. The Saracen leader's public respect for him was a salve to the wound of the Jarl's treatment of him, and petty spite was his only recourse.

Rognvald, however, was not a spiteful man. He bowed to the hostage and said, 'You are a free man and may leave in all honour. Though there is enmity between our peoples, your men fought bravely and your warship was a fine prize. Our victory is all the greater because of this.'

Whatever the other man's opinion of the victory, he did not reply, but gestured to his men to follow him.

'Wait!' yelled Hlif, holding up her skirt with one hand and running along the pebbles. With her other hand, she towed a reluctant boy.

Skarfr had completely forgotten about the child and was seeing him for the first time outside the confusion of battle. He must be about six or seven years old, black-haired and black-eyed, wearing a beige cotton tunic over loose breeches. Just old enough to learn the ropes on a ship and to be useful: climbing the rigging, blowing the horn or cleaning the bilges.

If that was indeed his life, he did not seem keen to return to it. He turned on Hlif, kicking and biting, a human version of One-eye in a foul mood.

'Ouch!' Hlif dropped his hand as a kick hit home but, before the boy could run, Skarfr scooped him up and dangled him by the waist in mid-air. Hands and bare feet lashed out, as ineffective as the curses he shouted.

The Saracen leader regarded the scene, showing nothing of his feelings or what his relationship to the boy might be.

'You can keep him,' he said, turning his back. The Saracens walked away, robes catching the breeze, until they melted like ghosts into the hazy distance.

The boy had calmed somewhat when he realised he wasn't being sent away, but Skarfr saw no harm in letting him dangle a while longer. How terrified of the Saracen captain the child must be, to prefer Skarfr.

He remembered a different boy on a beach, a boy who wanted to sail a-viking and who'd been mocked, rejected and reviled by his hero, Sweyn. A boy who was then rescued by Rognvald and trained as a warrior. His heart softened a little and he set the child down on the pebbles.

'I don't want a heathen boy,' said Rognvald. 'Leave him here.'

'No! I'll look after him,' Hlif cried.

Her instinct to protect the child, to *mother* him, put an arrow through Skarfr's heart.

A cormorant flew overhead, her 'Crk, crrk, crrk' a sign. But of what? Was she remembering another child, a baby left on a beach to die? The human baby she'd fostered.

'*We'll* look after him.' The words were out of his mouth before he had thought of the consequences of defying the Jarl – again. Rognvald's face turned puce.

For one terrible moment, Skarfr thought the Jarl was going to leave all three of them here in Saracen land. A death sentence.

Then Rognvald said, 'I don't want him on my ship. All three of you can travel with Cup-bearer until we reach Sicilia.'

Skarfr and Hlif exchanged glances, understanding what would happen when they reached Sicilia. And now they were three.

The only cheerful person as they took the ships out to sea was a small boy, who sang in his own language. No doubt a saga of Moorish courage, thought Skarfr sardonically. And then wondered what kind of place Sicilia might be.

Any navigator could locate a port as important as that of Sicilia's main city, Palermo. The regular to and fro of merchant ships made it easy to hail them, find one heading towards Palermo rather than away, and to follow it into the huge natural inlet that was Cala harbour.

All around the horseshoe shape formed where sea met land, berths and mooring posts were spaced along the wooden supports, with stone steps leading to the walkways above.

As Skarfr manoeuvred the ship to its place beside the *Sun-chaser*, he saw a no-nonsense tower on his right, guarding the entrance to the city, guards visible on the battlements and in front of the doorway.

Moorish fortifications. Not just the tower, but the harbour itself, and the buildings glimpsed behind the walls showed the skills of these master architects. Infidels they might be, but Skarfr could only marvel at yet more examples of their construction that were both solid and beautiful.

The infidels themselves were present in shocking numbers, standing out in their strange garb, walking around the docks as if they still owned the place. Yet all knew that this had been a Christian kingdom for decades.

Despite the temptation, the Norðmen *had* learned their lesson in Tortosa, and nobody shouted, 'Saracens!'

The captains went ashore, received their orders from Rognvald and passed on a summary to their men. Skarfr was irked at being relegated to the status of mere deckhand, receiving second-hand bits of information, but knew he would soon be even less than that. Rognvald's saga would be leaving Sicily without his best skald.

'Skarfr! Hlif!' Bishop William summoned them.

He rarely spoke to either of them and his expression was as sour as if a bird had shat on his portable altar. Skarfr even looked up, hoping to see such a bird. But the sky was empty.

'The Jarl wishes me to marry you, so that you are united in the sight of God.'

'Now?' asked Skarfr, bemused.

'Here?' asked Hlif.

'Now and here, on the ship,' confirmed the bishop. 'And as quickly as possible. We have much to do before sailing again.'

Hlif insisted on putting on her string of beads for the occasion, despite the bishop's impatience. With no other ceremony, the deed was done. Around them, the crew were bailing out the bilges and oiling weapons, cheerful at the prospect of going ashore.

Nobody paid them any attention. Rognvald was nowhere to be seen, making it clear that this was an entry in the accounts book, settling debts, not forgiveness.

They took mass from the consecrated altar and were blessed with as little grace as Bishop William could muster. *Man and wife.* How they had dreamed of this day.

Hlif's eyes swam with unshed tears, and he took her hand.

'*Elskan min*, sweetheart,' he whispered to her, 'we have been man and wife in the gods' eyes since the day we made our hands fast through Óðinn's stone beside the lake.'

She blinked and smiled for him.

'Get your packs and the child. We're going through the tower gate with Rognvald,' Bishop William told them, putting his altar away.

Skarfr and Hlif shouldered their packs, all their possessions in the world, which suddenly seemed stupidly inadequate.

'Sea-born,' Hlif called to the boy, using the name she had given him. She looked at Skarfr almost apologetically. 'Bishop William will kill him if he stays here.' He was mystified for a moment, then realised she did not mean the boy.

She picked up One-eye and lodged him in his accustomed place, his head pillowed against her pack and legs dangling down her bodice. Predictably, he hissed at Skarfr.

It seemed there would be four in their new family, not three.

CHAPTER 52

SKARFR, SICILIA

*Now the words of the One-eyed
Are heard in Óðinn's hall
For the benefit of humans...*

The Wanderer's Hávamál

When he received the visitors in the throne room, King Roger II of Sicilia was wearing ceremonial robes, a crown and a puzzled frown. He was much shorter than Skarfr but exuded confidence in his own status, something Skarfr envied.

The impression of intelligence in his black eyes was confirmed when he replied to Rognvald's requests, which included employment of one unwanted Orkneyman. 'Our brother of Aragon must have thought highly of you, if he offered you his precious *Usatges*. He is usually concerned that the value of the book's cover will be wasted on the recipient, never mind the contents.'

King Roger sucked his neatly-trimmed beard in silence, then declared, 'You are welcome in my city for the time it takes you to reprovision. I need hardly tell you that your men must respect our customs and our citizens – all of them, regardless of their clothes.'

Rognvald bowed his head and Skarfr looked down at the

Moorish tiles. Nobody walking through the city could be blind to the mix of Christians, Muslims and Jews going about their business. Skarfr did not give a rat's arse about any of them. He did wonder how the only Orkneyman in the city would be treated.

The King came to the point. 'What are this man's skills?'

It was like being a lame horse for sale in a market.

Before Rognvald could reply, Hlif spoke up. 'He has trained as a warrior with the Hird of the King of Norðvegr and proved himself in battle many times. His ingenious plans have won impossible victories and he is always in the thick of the fighting, leading men by his example.'

She glanced at Rognvald, defying him to contradict her. He did not and she added to her accolades, 'He is a peerless skald and his poetry has moved audiences in the halls of kings.'

Skarfr squirmed with embarrassment. He had played praise singer to Rognvald many times but had never imagined how it would feel to be the subject of one. This description of him was more of an exaggeration than any he'd ever composed. He opened his mouth to say so but the King spoke first.

Of course, King Roger had noticed the horse had a limp. He addressed Rognvald: 'If he is such a paragon, why are you leaving him here?'

Whatever the rift between them, the Jarl gave a man his due. 'He is all that,' he said. 'But he can't be trusted.'

Hlif flared up. 'My lord King, this is calumny! Skarfr's only crime was to want me for a wife, and we are both of an age to make such a decision.'

The King had not missed any detail. 'Such a decision is made by the lady's male guardian. And by the man's liege lord. Did you ask the Jarl's permission?'

'No, but—' began Hlif.

The King sliced the air with his hand. 'Enough!' he said sharply. 'You must learn a woman's place. A *wife's* place.' He sent a sympathetic look towards Rognvald, then spoke to Skarfr.

'You, tell me what you can bring to my court. I have warriors and poets, and much more than that. They speak Latin, Frankish, Occitan, Arabic, Hebrew and many more languages – but not yours, so there will be no interest in your poetry. Why should I give you a place when you have betrayed your lord's trust?'

Skarfr's heart thumped. In all his gloom about the prospect of living in exile, he'd never considered that he might not be wanted. What else did he have to offer? He could play the pipe well. How childish that would sound, from him, a man who had never been a child. And what a childhood he had come through, waiting cruel years for his inheritance. He longed now for his house, its cosy hearth, the solicitude of Brigid and Fergus.

But his inheritance was lost to him. He had nothing but his pipe, his guimbarde and a bone fragment in his pack, and—

The legacy Pilot had left him.

He pulled the pouch out from under his tunic and said, 'My lord King, I am also a navigator, thanks to the pilots who have joined our ship during this voyage of adventure. The first one gave me a sunstone.' He drew the clear crystal out into the window light, turned it so it seemed to concentrate rays of sunshine and throw them out again. 'And the second one taught me how to use it, with other tools of navigation. I can find the sun and sail a ship when clouds are in the sky.

The King's eyes lit up. 'Can he do this?' he asked Rognvald.

'Yes,' the Jarl replied, concluding the deal on the lame horse.

Skarfr thought he probably *could* do what he'd claimed. It was a pity he hadn't had the opportunity to practise.

'This becomes interesting.' King Roger's enthusiasm was clear. 'Yes, I'll take him. He could be extremely useful when we take up arms against Manuel Komnenos again.'

Manuel Komnenos, the Emperor? Living in Mikligard? The city Eindridi had praised, the city where he'd been in the Vangarian guard. Sicilia intended to take up arms against the Byzantine Empire? What a saga that would be!

Skarfr realised what Roger meant at the same time as Hlif named the legendary place.

'Mikligard,' she breathed.

The King rushed on. 'You will spend time with my map-maker, find out which routes he needs further information about and, with your sunstone,' his eyes gleamed, 'you can sail where he tells you.'

Skarfr had no time to ask what a map was.

King Roger clapped his hands, told a pageboy, 'Send for Muhammed al-Idrisi. I want him to meet someone.'

Then he told Rognvald, 'You may leave this couple with me. If the navigator earns his keep, they will have no complaints.'

Rognvald nodded. The page in the accounts book totalled and balanced. Judgement given. 'May he give you good service. I must return to the ships now. We've taken longer than anticipated to get here and I want to reach Jórsalaheim before winter.'

He turned to Skarfr and said, 'Our time together is ended.'

He left so quickly that Skarfr had no time to speak, even if he could have found the words. *This should not have been the ending*, he thought.

CHAPTER 53

SKARFR, SICILIA

It is much better
that one alone should know this,
which is the last of the spells.

The Wanderer's Hávamál

Their quarters were eminently suitable for a family of three and a cat. From their top storey window, Hlif and Skarfr could see the harbour; from it, they watched nine longships leave without them.

Hlif rigged up curtains, one to give her privacy with Skarfr at night and one over the window to keep the room warm, now winter nights were drawing in. She discovered where to get the best bread and fish, as well as where she could gossip with other women at the communal laundry. Skarfr stopped thinking of it as gossip when she explained to him who was important in Roger's court and who wasn't, and why. She was interested in Skarfr *becoming* one of those who were important.

Despite Hlif's care and efficiency in running their home and looking after the child, Skarfr felt homesick most days. He found comfort in Hlif's arms but could not forget what he had cost her. As with the almond milk used for cooking in Sicilia, there was a bitter taste beneath the sweetness of their lives.

He was trying hard to make the best of everything but he even missed their dreamwalking. He would never tell her so but, without it, he felt they were so... ordinary. He could not forget loving her as a saga hero loves a völva, not just as a navigator loves his wife. He *did* love her but this was not how he'd imagined their life together.

And then there was the boy. Maybe he'd been right to doubt his capacity to be a father. He never saw the boy as his and was always too busy to see much of him.

Even One-eye emphasised what a failure Skarfr was. He strutted around the alleys, picked fights and increased the caterwauling at night with the verve of a much younger tom. Hlif reckoned most of this year's kittens in Palermo would be black with white moustaches.

Skarfr worked harder, to distract himself from the sense of loss he felt at home. His best moments were spent with Muhammad al-Idrisi, in the map-maker's workshop. Prior to their meeting, Skarfr had only seen travel routes drawn in sand or charcoal. He'd been impressed by an Orkneyman's carving, a wooden profile that showed how to approach one of the trickier islands from the sea. When the coastline matched the carved cliffs and rocks, that was the moment to turn for a hidden cove. But he'd never seen anything as precise or as detailed as al-Idrisi's maps.

Surrounded by parchment and inks, the two men turned Skarfr's mental picture of a shoreline, of rocks, of islands, into lines and squiggles. The interior lands on these maps were as magical to Skarfr as the dream world, and he wanted to explore the little triangles al-Idrisi said were mountains. He wanted to sail on one of the tiny ships bouncing on the blue map-seas. Never since Thorbjorn penned and illuminated the cormorant had Skarfr seen such beautiful work.

When Al-Idrisi drew what he called 'planispheres', and made the world's circle around his map, using a tool with twin points, Skarfr felt blessed by the gods. He watched al-Idrisi write, 'In the year of our lord 1150: Palermo: Sicilia: By the Grace of God Roger II Rex Siciliae', followed by the King's full honorific, and the hairs on the back of his neck stood up. Surely, these maps were a gift to the future and he, Skarfr, was witness to their making. More than that, he was contributing to them. The feeling he would make sagas returned, briefly.

Then he would go home and go through the motions, feigning happiness.

Until the eve of the Midwinter Solstice, when everything changed. He and Hlif sat on the rocks by the harbour, watching the sun go down together, while Sea-born did handstands on the jetty and made the fishermen and traders laugh.

'Do you remember midwinter in the tomb?' Hlif asked him.

He remembered. The two of them in the otherworld, touched by fire and a dragon, while Rognvald and his men carved their runes, oblivious to the magic around them. Skarfr's world had flamed red and gold as the dragon spoke to him, spoke *through* him while Hlif stood over him, arms spread out like drying wings. And he had carved the dragon on the wall of that ancient tomb, defying forces so old the very air crumbled around him.

The dragon on the wall, whose image rippled now on his arm. Four prancing legs, clawed feet and a proudly arched neck. One huge, slanted eye in the profile of a head looking back over its right shoulder. Tongue lolling as the mouth breathed fire. Scallops on back, neck and head to make scales.

The gigantic dragon in the tomb, its foul breath as deadly as the flames from its maw, testing Skarfr with its riddling words, marking him as prey until his brave cormorant dived into the scaled dragon. Skarfr had carved that eternal conflict and eternal union in stone while Hlif watched over him, her wand raised. She'd tamed the flames with charcoal and art of her own, seared the tattoo onto his arm, seen him for who he was, in this world and beyond the veil. She'd been there when his poetry was set free, when a different kind of fire announced the turning of the year.

'When the sun set and the rays shone onto us through the tunnel,' he murmured. He didn't have to say more as they could read each other's eyes, see the sunlight in them once more.

'Sea-born,' called Hlif, her eyes never losing contact with Skarfr's as she traced the lines of the dragon on his arm. Its tail flickered. 'Time to go home now.'

When they were in bed that night, mellow with wine, and satiated with lovemaking, Hlif whispered, 'Think of me before you fall asleep. Meet me there, in the tomb...'

They fell asleep in each other's arms and woke in the dream world, with no barriers between them.

She said, 'Rognvald was wrong. His words have no power over my visions but I believed him. *That* was what took my visions.'

He felt the burden of guilt lift. 'I know they matter to you,' he said.

'Freyja's gift to me is something no man can take away and I pray to her now we have left the Jarl, not to Óðinn. Her message is for you too.'

With the voice of prophecy, she told him, 'Rognvald was wrong about you too. He thought he could exile you because you are still a child to him.

'But he has never been able to keep Sweyn Asleifsson in exile. He has never been able to control Thorbjorn Klerk. He cannot keep a hero in exile and what you do for King Roger of Sicilia will make the Jarl of Orkneyjar rue the day he lost you. If Orkneyjar is still your heart-home, when that day comes, you will go there and be welcome. You are a man now, a *drengr*, master of your own destiny.'

His heart sang. What if she was right? What if he *was* making a saga and Sicilia was part of it, not an abandonment at all? They would sail against Mikligard in the spring and what a fine saga that would be.

If he served King Roger well, he *could* dictate his own terms to Rognvald and return home. He could complete the pilgrimage, sail to Jórsalaheim, catch up with Rognvald and demand a proper hearing. He could catch up with Eindridi too. That snake's double-dealing merited a punishment worse than exile. Pilot's murder would be avenged.

He could demand that his case be heard by the Thing in Orkneyjar. He could prove his loyalty to the Jarl *and* to the Jarl's ward. No man could argue that he'd been disrespectful of Hlif. In fact, there was a compelling argument against the doom Rognvald had placed upon her, a doom that he, Skarfr, had changed. Like a hero in a saga, he had lifted the curse upon her, and she was now happily married. A wife. The word tasted sweet again. He had been a fool, hag-ridden and victim of night fears.

Hlif was a wife *and* a mother. He acknowledged the truth he'd been avoiding. He was a father and he must choose what kind he would be.

Full of a renewed sense of purpose, he said, 'I shall take Sea-born to training tomorrow. It is time he learned to be a warrior.'

Only quiet breathing answered him.

The morning would come soon enough to start the life that would earn him his place in Orkneyjar once more. He and Hlif had paid the price for changing their destiny. They had the gods-given right to live their choice. They would see their longhouse again, be served by Fergus and Brigid, admire whatever new cow and other livestock were on the farm. They would tell stories around their own hearth of the adventures they had had, here, in Sicilia, and wherever they voyaged next. On their way home.

The veil between worlds was so thin tonight that, behind closed eyelids, he could see the dragon he'd carved, pulsing on the tomb wall. Alive again.

And as he too slipped into dreamless sleep, Skarfr heard a swish of black wings and a cormorant cawing.

EPILOGUE

INGE, STRJÓNSEY

'I understood that you were hurt,' began Finn, unable to look at her.

Inge's heart leaped. He knew.

He carried on slowly, as if each word were an iron trap with killer teeth. 'It can't have been easy to be put aside by your husband, rejected and thrown out of your home.'

She stared at him, stammered, 'That's not—' but he cut her short with a gesture.

'Let me speak. This is hard enough.' He swallowed hard. She saw the convulsion of his throat below the prickly beard. *Kissing a hedgehog.* Her eyes prickled and she blinked back the tears. She had not needed her 'I will not cry' face for so long that she struggled to wear it. She'd always known the Norns would steal this from her, this second marriage. This first and forever love.

'I thought over time you would forget him, even though he is twice the man I am. Twice the warrior and ten times as clever.' He smiled wryly. 'Better looking too and he won't have a belly on him like I will.'

Then he did look at her and the pain in his eyes knifed through her. 'But time has passed and still you flinch when his name is mentioned and blanch on sight of him. When you speak to him, you are a stranger to me, so distant. You still love him and I don't know what more I can do to make you my wife, not his.'

He reached out to touch her but his hand clenched into a fist, dropped to his side. 'What can I do, Inge, to cut through this knot and free us?'

'Nothing,' she whispered. 'Nothing.'

She saw the hurt in his eyes, felt him draw on his strength to walk away, to leave her. It was for the best. Telling him the truth would not free the two of them but unleash demons.

Fare thee well.

Her hands would not be still and she clutched at her bodice, wringing the wool fabric heedlessly, catching the twin rows of blush-hued glass and bone beads that she'd worn to look her best for him. His wedding gift to her.

She cried out when the string broke and the beads scattered on the ground, as they had on her wedding day. She would never gather them up this time, alone, and a storm of sobs shook her as she crouched to pick up the little spheres of lost happiness. Her 'I will not cry' face shattered like broken glass into all the tears she'd never shed.

When Finn turned back to comfort her, took her in his arms, she felt weak as a kitten, boneless.

'They're only beads,' he told her. 'I don't understand. I will buy you new ones.'

She could not keep lying.

'He didn't send me away. I left him,' she said quietly. 'I escaped. Before he could murder me. Skarfr and his man Fergus rowed me to Ness, and I owe them my life.'

She wiped her runny nose against his sleeve so she could finish and be done with it. 'Thorbjorn forced me before our wedding. Outside the Jarl's *Bu*, against a wall. Some men saw us and pretended they hadn't. While the feast celebrating our *alliance* went on in the hall, people drinking and enjoying themselves. I hated him. I despised him.'

There was no gain in holding back. 'He spread the word around that he'd repudiated me, was divorcing me, so as to save face. And I prefer that to be what people think, so he leaves me alone. So he leaves *us* alone.'

Then she told the hardest truth, the one she didn't want to believe. 'I am terrified of him.'

Finn still held her as if she were a piece of fragile pottery but something had changed.

When a man learned of a woman's violation by her previous husband, he either dismissed it as a domestic matter or his blood turned murderous black. Inge knew which spirit moved Finn, without needing to look at his set jaw or clenched fists.

May the gods protect him. For she could not. Not against Thorbjorn.

AUTHOR'S NOTE

This series began with a fateful trip to Orkney and my interest in the Viking prince who stopped off at Narbonne on his pilgrimage to Jerusalem. Jarl Rognvald makes a larger-than-life appearance in my novel *Song at Dawn,* Book 1 of *The Troubadours* series, where he is a foreigner amid southern sophistication, and in *Among Sea Wolves* I had the fun of revisiting Narbonne from the Vikings' point of view. Now, the flamboyant Occitan courtiers are the foreigners and the Vikings make allowances for their ignorance.

Not so much fun was the realisation that I'd painted myself into a corner with the timeline in *Song at Dawn.* Rognvald's fleet has to reach Narbonne in the summer of 1150, having left Orkney in the spring, in *The Ring Breaker.* The journey is possible in that timeline but not including raids in Galicia for months and a castle siege at Christmas, as recorded in the *Orkneyinga Saga.* I found this annoying as I do try to keep to known historical events.

However, the *Orkneyinga Saga* was written in the 13th century as a work of literature drawing on stories about events a hundred years earlier, which had been passed down orally, so it is even less trustworthy than most histories. The more I plotted the pilgrims' voyage, the more I realised the *Orkneyinga Saga* version was impossible. I wondered briefly whether my Vikings could have crossed northern Spain by two great rivers but my Spanish-dwelling writer friend Jane Harlond confirmed that we couldn't do it. Not even with portage, or rollers, or all the clever methods Vikings travelled miles between waterfalls on Russian rivers. None of it worked to climb watershed mountains and reach the small stream that is the source of the River Ebro, then climb down (carrying the ships) until the Ebro was broad enough to sail.

Back to the drawing-board. What *did* happen? There is no way Rognvald would have sailed to Narbonne, then sailed the whole route *back* along the eastern and southern coast of what is now Spain, through the Straits of Gibraltar, up the western coast of Spain to Galicia for months of raiding and siege of a castle. And then done this a third time to head for Jerusalem!

This realisation freed me to move the siege of the castle in place and date, and to skip some raiding. I worked on a 'give or take a year or two' margin of accuracy regarding the change in king of Scotland. I Otherwise, I think dates tally with historians' estimates, in so far as medieval historians agree at all.

My practical research for *Among Sea Wolves* included navigating my way around the garden with a small crystal of Icelandic spar, the most probable candidate for the sunstone mentioned in *Hrafn's Saga* and some monastic inventories. I experimented with casting and reading a set of tiger's eye rune-stones, to put myself in Hlif's shoes as a Viking seer – for storytelling purposes only. I sympathise with the medieval academics who stress that runes are letters, not magical spells, and who struggle with the misappropriation of Viking culture by modern groups ranging from Wiccans to neo-Nazis.

Sailing from Orkney to Sicily was quite a challenge, both geographically and in handling a dragon ship. I looked up shipping charts and tides, watched yachting videos and did 3D mock-ups with pencils to represent the ship, the coastline, the wind and the tide. I don't think I could even sail pooh sticks downriver so was very relieved when my sailing chapters passed muster with two advisors who do know their rigging.

I very much enjoyed writing the song contest from *Song at Dawn*

AUTHOR'S NOTE

from the Viking viewpoint. I've taken huge liberties with the poetry I've included from the *Orkneyinga Saga* because I find literal translations so weighed down with allusions that pages of explanation are needed and the beauty is lost. Apart from the music of the language and use of alliteration, Norse poetry is full of clever puzzles and 'aha' moments – for a Viking audience. We don't have the same frames of reference to instantly understand allusions within allusions but the more Norse poetry I read in translation, the more I enjoy it. If you want a scholarly translation that still captures the feel of the original poetry, do read Ian Crockatt's superb work.

Poetry is at the heart of this series and it was a privilege to be granted permission to use Dr Jackson Crawford's translation of The Wanderer's for chapter headings. This 13th century written collection of older verses, giving advice on how to live a good Norse life, seemed the perfect way to introduce events in Skarfr's life.

Hlif's background was inspired by the suggestion that she might be Hlifolf's daughter, in Michael P. Barnes' *The Runic Inscriptions of Maeshowe*, Orkney, an in-depth work analysing each message. Barnes gives alternative readings and draws few conclusions, and the *Orkneyinga Saga* is contradictory and does not match the messages in the runic inscriptions. All the runic messages I've mentioned in the Maeshowe scenes in *The Ring Breaker* and *Among Sea Wolves* are on the walls in the burial chamber, including anonymous ones that I ascribed to Rognvald, although he is not named in any of the runes. My feeling is that he could have been there; a man so powerful and confident would not need to sign his work.

I've worked out a timeline for the runes. *Among Sea Wolves* takes place many months after the break-in so the famously rude graffiti about the burial chamber being used as a trysting-place would have been carved during this period, not during the initial break-in.

Here's my detective work from Book 1 *The Ring Breaker*.

Four events are recorded in the runes, which have not been dated exactly, beyond 'mid 12th century'. This is the order I've taken them in.

Hokon alone carried treasure from this mound.

AUTHOR'S NOTE

Some time before the pilgrims broke into the mound, others were there and took treasure away. There would surely have been grave goods but these could have been stolen hundreds of years earlier and the tomb sealed, as it appears to be when the pilgrims 'broke in'. So I take the naming of Hokon in the runes to be a joke.

The Jerusalem-farers broke Orkhaugr. Hlif, the Earl's housekeeper, carved.

I take this as a fact, indicating that Rognvald's band broke into and discovered the burial chamber, not Jarl Harald. According to the *Orkneyinga Saga*, Jarl Harald spent Yuletide in Orkhaugr, where two of his men went mad, and there is some confusion about whether it was Rognvald or Harald who broke into Maeshowe. Archaeologists agree that there was a break-in through the roof and I prefer the idea that at least some of the pilgrim graffiti dates from before their voyage.

Many a woman has stooped to come here.

This jibe relies on the pun 'stooped' as the tunnel entrance has no headroom so physical stooping is required. And the more vulgar messages make clear the other way in which women stooped. The burial chamber became a meeting-place for sexual encounters. This must have happened *after* the initial discovery, over time. So it makes sense to me that Harald sheltering in Maeshowe was the fourth event, at a time when the place was entered by the tunnel and known as a shelter.

I've ascribed the dragon-carving to one of Rognvald's men during the first break-in but there could well have been further visits by the pilgrims when they came back from Jerusalem and carved some more messages and crosses, and maybe a dragon. Or Lion of St Mark. Or griffon with sea eagle. But Skarfr and I know what the carving is, truly.

I hope that my research has created a journey into the past that you enjoyed as much as I did. May we travel such dangerous roads together again soon!

ACKNOWLEDGMENTS

Many thanks to:

my editor Lorna Fergusson of Fictionfire Literary Consultancy;
Babs, Jane and Kristin for your invaluable critiques and support;
The Sanctuary writers' group for providing exactly that and for all your expertise;
Dr Jackson Crawford for sharing his expertise in Old Norse and, with Hackett Publishing Company, for permission to quote his translation of *The Wanderer's Hávamál* in chapter headings;
Ryerson and Paul for being my specialists on boats, sailing and rowing – all mistakes are mine, not yours;
Lexie Conyngham for a list of starter research books;
Patricia Long, Orkney guide, for sharing her knowledge and love of Orkney;
Lesley Geekie for being my woman at the scene;
Fran Hollinrake, Custodian/Visitor Services Officer, St Magnus Cathedral for information on the history of the building and on masons' marks;
Staff of Historic Monuments, Scotland and of Maeshowe Visitor's Centre for information and support;

Midwinter Dragon map © Jean Gill, created using Inkarnate.com and a base map of Orkney from Ordnance Survey Open Data with inset derived from File:Scotland location map.svg by NordNordWest, created by Wikipedia User Nilfanion;
and Jessica Bell Cover Design for the amazing covers for all my books.

SELECTED REFERENCE WORKS

Selected reference works

Extracts *from The Wanderer's Hávamál* translated and edited with Old Norse Text by Jackson Crawford. Copyright © 2019 Hackett Publishing Company, Inc

The Orkneyinga Saga – Project Gutenberg (Public Domain)
The Saga of King Heidrek the Wise – Project Gutenberg (Public Domain)
The King's Mirror – Project Gutenberg (Public Domain)
The Saga of Grettir the Strong (Penguin Classics)
Michael P. Barnes – *The Runic Inscriptions of Maeshowe, Orkney*
Neil Price – *Children of Ash and Elm*
Ian Crockatt – *Crimsoning the Eagle's Claw*. The poetry of Rögnvaldr
Ian Crockatt – *The Song Weigher*. The poetry of Egill Skallagrimsson
Jamina Ramirez – *Femina*
Jóhanna Katrín Friðriksdóttir – *The Women of the Viking World* (Bloomsbury)
Judith Jesch – *Women in the Viking Age*
Grace Tierney – *Words the Vikings Gave Us*

Fiction

Erik Linklater – *The Ultimate Viking*
A.D. Howden Smith – *Swain's Saga*

Historical Articles

Judith Jesch – 'The Nine Skills of Earl Rögnvaldr of Orkney'

Judith Jesch – 'Earl Rögnvaldr of Orkney, a Poet of the Viking Diaspora'
Lucy Collings, R. Farrell and I. Morrison – 'Earl Rögnvald's Shipwreck' (Viking Society for Northern Research)
Debbie Potts – 'An Introduction to Skaldic Poetry'
Brenda Prehal – 'Freyja's Cats: Perspectives on Recent Viking Age Finds in North Iceland'
R. W. Reid – 'Remains of Saint Magnus and Saint Rognvald, Entombed in Saint Magnus Cathedral, Kirkwall, Orkney' (Oxford University Press)
Albert Thomson – 'Masons' Marks in St Magnus Cathedral' (An Orkney Miscellany 1954)

Online

www.vikingeskibsmuseet.dk especially the articles, logs, diaries and videos about the voyage of the reproduction longship *Sea Stallion* from Denmark to Dublin, via Orkney.
https://skaldic.org/ The Skaldic Project, especially the compilation of indexed kennings

Nidavellnir Nalbinding on Facebook and YouTube, for information and practical demonstrations of this pre-knitting technique, and for the expertise on Viking textiles of Emma 'Bruni' Boast, a Viking-Age Archaeologist and Nalbinding Specialist based in York, UK. Member of the Guild of Mastercraftsmen UK.

ABOUT THE AUTHOR

I'm a Welsh writer and photographer living in the south of France with two scruffy dogs, a beehive named 'Endeavour', a Nikon D750 and a man. I taught English in Wales for many years and my claim to fame is that I was the first woman to be a secondary headteacher in Carmarthenshire. I'm mother or stepmother to five children so life has been pretty hectic.

I've published all kinds of books, both with traditional publishers and self-published. You'll find everything under my name from prize-winning poetry and novels, military history, translated books on dog training, to a cookery book on goat cheese. My work with top dog-trainer Michel Hasbrouck has taken me deep into the world of dogs with problems, and inspired one of my novels. With Scottish parents, an English birthplace and French residence, I can usually support the winning team on most sporting occasions.

www.jeangill.com

- facebook.com/writerjeangill
- x.com/writerjeangill
- instagram.com/writerjeangill
- goodreads.com/JeanGill

Join Jean Gill's Special Readers' Group

for private news, views and offers, with an exclusive ebook copy of

How White is My Valley

as a welcome gift.

Sign up at *jeangill.com*

The follow-up to her memoir *How Blue is My Valley* about moving to France from rainy Wales, tells the true story of how Jean

- nearly became a certified dog trainer.
- should have been certified and became a beekeeper.
- developed from keen photographer to hold her first exhibition.
- held 12th century Damascene steel.
- looks for adventure in whatever comes her way.

HUNTING THE SUN

The adventures of Hlif and Skarfr continue in *Hunting the Sun: Book 3 of The Midwinter Dragon, coming in 2025*

Discover the Troubadours, Dragonetz and Estela, in *Song at Dawn, Book 1* of the award-winning *Troubadours Quartet*

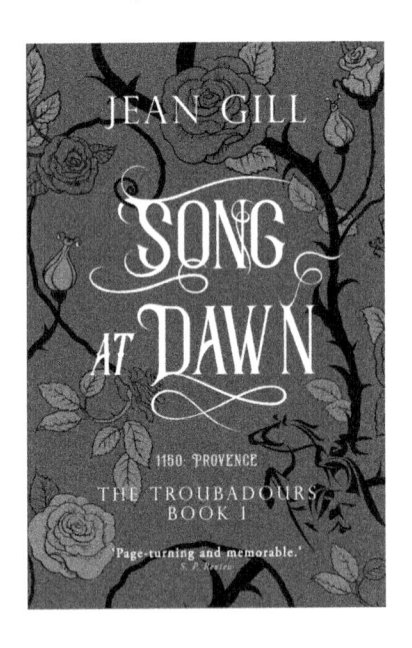

Printed in Great Britain
by Amazon